"A compassionate and ruthless debut, *To Die Is Different Than Supposed* demonstrates the infinite ways families can be haunted and how hurts can slide forward and back in time. Butterworth offers tragedy and hope through the Gable siblings, providing a fascinating exploration of how they wrap their personalities around the adults who love them and fail them—and how they rescue and reclaim themselves."

—E.A. Petricone, Shirley Jackson Award–winning author of *We, the Girls Who Did Not Make It*

"*To Die Is Different Than Supposed* relates the arduous passage of a family from the depths of disintegration and rancor to the seemingly impossible aggregation of their souls. Told with raw honesty, Butterworth reveals multiple layers of disappointment, broken dreams, and promises. She peeks into hearts full of hurt, into the secrets that have torn the family apart. Butterworth is a testament to Tolstoy's dictum, 'All happy families are alike; each unhappy family is unhappy in its own way.' But there are rings of fire and the redemption that comes from traversing them. Upon the death of the patriarch, when all the masks have fallen, in front of a mythical funeral pyre, a triumphant bond of love is forged going forward into the future. This is an impressive debut novel to be cherished."

—Jorge Armenteros, author of
The Curvature of an Absence

"*To Die Is Different Than Supposed* is a deeply moving and suspenseful story that centers around the death of James Gable, a celebrated, all-American contemporary poet, who was in equal measures loved and feared, hated and admired by his emotionally struggling family, a vulnerable and engaging crew that includes his current (and second) wife, an ex-wife, and six children, one of the latter deceased. Gable's children grapple, often alone and at odds with each other, with the legacy of their neglectful, complicated, and self-absorbed father. My favorite character was Jackson, the eldest son and the most rebellious and tortured of the family members, but he also sets an impressive example with his tough and independent spirit. I addictively followed the trajectory of Jackson's thoughts and emotions as he witnesses a horrific tragedy and then, the fracturing of his family. Although each character has in his or her own way been damaged by the destructive words and actions of the deceased patriarch, all—even if only in spirit, with Lex—will survive him in this heartbreaking and tender story about family and loss."

—Margaret Chen, author of *Suburban
Gothic* and *Three Terrible Tales*

To Die *is* Different *than* Supposed

A NOVEL

ALISSA BUTTERWORTH

RIVER GROVE
BOOKS

Published by River Grove Books
Austin, TX
www.rivergrovebooks.com

Distributed by River Grove Books

Design and composition by Greenleaf Book Group
Cover design by Greenleaf Book Group
Cover image: © stock.adobe.com/benjaminlion; stock.adobe.com/
Rafinade; stock.adobe.com/alona_s; stock.adobe.com/Stephen

Publisher's Cataloging-in-Publication data is available.

Print ISBN: 978-1-63299-990-0

eBook ISBN: 978-1-63299-991-7

First Edition

To my family: first, found, forever.

O I perceive after all so many uttering tongues,

And I perceive they do not come from the roofs
of mouths for nothing.

I wish I could translate the hints about the dead
young men and women,

And the hints about old men and mothers, and
the offspring taken soon out of their laps.

What do you think has become of the young and
old men?

And what do you think has become of the
women and children?

They are alive and well somewhere,

The smallest sprout shows there is really no death,

And if ever there was it led forward life, and does
not wait at the end to arrest it,

And ceas'd the moment life appear'd.

All goes onward and outward, nothing collapses,

And to die is different from what any one
supposed, and luckier.

—Walt Whitman, Song of Myself, 6

CHAPTER ONE

Ella

MONDAY 3:30 A.M.

Tonight I see the ghost again. I'm not expecting him. I never do.

I dream that I'm awake, sitting up in bed, tied up in sheets and the duvet. My dream mouth cottony dry. I try to get the spit moving again, working my tongue against the top of my palate. My back pressed against the headboard, pulling my blankets up under my chin.

Something moves around my bedroom. There are muffled sounds, strange variations in the darkness that I strain my eyes to see. There's a soft whooshing going back and forth near the door—I'm hit with that dank wall of air you're met with when you're standing waiting on a subway platform and the train blazes by. It smells that way, too, of the underside of earth, tunnels long closed, thick and humid and uncomfortably warm, falling over my face like a damp towel.

This should scare me, but it doesn't.

The ghost takes a moment to form himself fully, which he lets me know he only ever does on my account.

"I wouldn't, otherwise," he says. "But if I didn't, I'd scare you so bad you'd die." His voice sounds like chirping birds.

I look for him, his now-familiar shape settling into itself as it has since I was little. I sense out a head, a set of shoulders narrow and sloped, arms hanging down, blurring into the curtain of shadow that might pass for a lower body. Two dark velvety wings arch out nobly from the ghost's back.

"You *know* I'm here," he says dejectedly. "Why do you always doubt it at first?"

I lean back into the headboard, the dream. Shrug my shoulders in the direction of him, a half apology for my disbelief.

"Well, anyway," he says. He's drawn himself together finely from the shadows he's made of, so well I compliment him on his work.

"Thanks," he says, hugging his arms around himself in a way that feels distantly familiar, like I've seen someone from another life do the same thing.

I've been sleeping in the middle of the bed; when I reach my hand out for the nightstand that's positioned on my right side, it's not quite there. On it is a lamp, two flashlights, and my cell phone, which also has a flashlight app if I wanted to use it—I don't like to be caught unprepared in the dark. No clock in my room, though. I don't like knowing how few hours are left until work in the morning. My hand gropes for a moment, fluttering like a nervous bird. It meets nothing but air.

"You need the lights?" he asks, voice falling. Hurt, almost.

I shrug again, not letting his dismay affect me.

"I'll give you dark," he suddenly booms, his words shaking my bed like the room's caught in an earthquake. His body loses form;

he shoots as tall as the ceiling, arching his back, throwing his arms and wings out, becoming the blackest black he can muster. He eats all the light in the room.

He's trying to scare me, but he's been doing this since I was seven—I know his tricks.

"It's a shame," I say, taking a deep breath. "You looked so solid and tidy until—"

The ghost lets out a howl that raises the hairs on the back of my neck, but I don't let on. The room is clammy and close; my ribs feel like they fit too tightly, like my heart will jackhammer its way right through.

"If you keep being nasty," I say louder, trying to not let him hear the involuntary hitch in my throat. "I'll just wake up."

He doesn't really scare me, but my body reacts to his smoke and mirrors anyway. He told me once that's normal, that people and ghosts aren't supposed to be in the same space. But he'd figured out a way around it. Then he'd smiled, his teeth a little crooked.

He laughs hollowly, lets his eyes flare up a brilliant blue, striking against the darkness he's cut from.

"How do you know," he whisper-shouts right in my ear, "that you're not awake already?"

I shrug.

He doesn't consider that this is a problem I've already thought about—each encounter between us, for him, seems somehow a reintroduction.

But I remember his tendencies and his inclinations, what makes him shout or go silent. I know I'm asleep, that whatever he says is mostly bluster.

Though he's never said it, he's not capable of hurting me. That he wouldn't ever want to.

We're in a stalemate, him bluffing and huge, me nonchalant on my bed with my arms tucked across my chest, playing comfortable and easy.

I close my eyes, pretend that I'm asleep.

"You can't be asleep when you're already sleeping," he whines. I peek an eye open to see that he's coming back into himself, shadow compressing shadow until he's much the same as I've always known him—a solid form, dark as ink, with faintly burning blue eyes and wings that he tucks pertly against his back. He's about five feet tall when he's not throwing himself against the walls to scare me.

"Of course you're right," I say, patting the bed next to me, inviting him to come sit. He won't do it—the closest he'll get is perching on the foot of the bed, his legs hanging off the edge. Sometimes he kicks them back and forth as we talk, like a kid on a chair that's too tall for him.

"You should be afraid, El."

I push my bottom lip out. Even though the room is dark, he perceives the slight.

"You should be," he tries again. "You really should."

"Why?"

"Something's coming. And it's big." He pauses for a moment, unsure in his words. "It's big, and it will hurt you."

I don't speak.

"Say you understand," he whispers urgently. "That you'll be careful. And that you'll watch."

"What?"

"Please. Doors've opened on their own, I don't know why. It's never happened like this before. Something's on its way," he tells me, his shadow body taut and shimmering. He's anxious, fluttery. I've never seen him act this way before. For the first time in his presence, I feel afraid.

Not of him—but for him, for both of us. This talk of doors—he mentions them sometimes, but I never understand it.

"What's coming is going to change everything," he says.

I nod. "I'll be careful. Don't worry about me."

His blue eyes dim for a breath as he considers what I've said.

Finally, he relaxes. He stretches his wings out, one after the other, and resettles them in a more comfortable position.

He's discharged his message and is ready to move on to more palatable talk.

"Where's Owen?" he asks, mischief tied up in his question. And maybe a bit of concern. My ghost's never liked Owen much.

He should be happy—Owen's been gone a year now.

"Don't you know? Isn't that something you're kept up to date on?"

"Yeah," he says, his eyes flaring brighter, blowtorch blue. "But I guess I just wanted to make you say it."

We talk, him laughing when I tell him the story of how my pants fell as I ran for the door of a restaurant on a rainy night.

"Oh, I saw that!" he exclaims, sounding as much like a little boy as like a supernatural being, this bottom-rung ghost or angel, whatever he is.

He's funny, he's mercurial, and he loves to talk about action movies and sports and the lives of my three grown-up brothers. He talks like he knows them, and in many ways, he does. He's been coming to me in my sleep for as long as I can remember, nearly, and has asked about the boys from the first.

"Has anybody gotten fat?" he asks, swinging his legs.

"Since when?"

"Since ever."

"Well, sure. But they got taller too."

This fascinates him, the idea that these boys he's only ever heard about in my stories have become more than boys, are now grown men who live across the country. And that they rarely call each other or visit, far as I know.

"How can you watch me but not them?" I ask. "How do you know about Owen—"

"And your pants!"

"And my pants. But not the boys?"

His eyes dim. "I can't see everything," he says. "I only can go through some doors. Not all of them are open yet. And when you go through one, you forget some of what you knew before you did it."

"Doors? What can you see?"

"You, mostly," he answers, ignoring my question about the doors. "And dumb stuff. Like I can look out into outer space, if I want to. See stars no one living's ever seen before."

"That sounds amazing."

"Stars are just stars," he says simply, his eyes flaring up to blue again. "I like people better. Your people I like best."

"How do I know you're real?" I ask, a question I try to avoid but often return to during our talks.

"How do I know that *you're* real?" he says, teasing.

I sigh, slide down the headboard so I'm lying on my back. My feet are down near his bottom, where he's seated on the bed. I want to know, suddenly, what would happen if I kicked my foot out at him. Would it knock him off the bed, or would it go right through him?

"Don't try it," he says crossly. "I don't like being kicked any more than you do."

"How do you know what I was thinking?"

"I can be in your head. How dumb are you?"

"So you're just in my head, then."

"Now you sound like that stupid doctor," he answers, frustrated.

I remember the doctor, a thin man with a receding hairline who had posters of kids in wheelchairs giving thumbs-up hanging on his office walls. We had to go see him, my brothers and I, for a while after the accident. Jackson and I kept seeing him after the other two got to quit. I don't know what Jack ever talked about, but the doctor was interested in my dreams about the ghost who had started coming to see me.

"I didn't like him either," I say. "And I won't kick you."

"Better not. Or I'll throw you straight to hell. You'll burn up and then be brought back just so you can burn up again."

"You wouldn't."

"I would."

"I don't believe you."

"Well," he says, "I guess I wouldn't. Because you're interesting. And I take care of you."

"Is there hell, anyway? Like a real one?"

"You know I can't talk about that," he says seriously, enunciating each word like I won't understand him otherwise. "I only see what I see."

"I know," I say. "I'm sorry I asked you."

"It's okay. Tell me about what Remy does for a job again."

I lie on my back, and he perches there on the end of the bed. We talk.

He wants to know everything, from how awful my job as a substitute teacher is to stories he's heard for years and often asks me to repeat. Like what happened on one summer day many years ago when the boys went fishing and Adrian fell in the creek, what we all got for Christmas the year I was five, what it was like when my parents first brought Remy home from the hospital.

"The stories are realer than anything," he says. "Like things that happened to me."

"Thanks," I say. "I guess I tell a good story."

"I guess," he says, sadly. "It's blueing out."

I look to the window—he's right. Dawn's approach always signals the end of the dream, when I wake up in the real world and the ghost goes back to my imagination or heaven or wherever it is he spends his time.

"Please remember what I told you," he says urgently, even as the light coming in begins to fall on the floor just below his swinging shadow feet. "Please be ready."

"Okay," I say, not sure what he's talking about but wanting to be certain he's all right. This is how these nights always end now that I've gotten older: me feeling a terrible maternal weight toward the ghost—hoping he'll be okay, that he'll find his way to where he's headed. When I was young, the nights often finished with him reassuring me. I shut my eyes against his leaving, so I don't have to see him as he breaks apart. He told me to do this the first night he came; I haven't disobeyed him once. It'd be a terrible sight, his little boy form burning away like fog on a summer morning. It would be too much to stand.

"Why do you come to visit me?" I ask, the same parting words I've always said.

"I come because you're afraid of the dark," he says faintly and from far away, like he's on the other end of a tin-can telephone. "And because you always left a copper."

"Will you come again?"

And there is no answer from him; I don't expect there to be.

The real blueing dawn comes in through the gap in my curtains and wakes me soon enough. When it does, all trace of him is gone. Except, for the first time in my life, I'm left afraid after our parting.

You never know which moments are prophetic and which mean nothing. No way to tell what is imperative, a warning, and what is someone's dog barking in the dark or the wind picking up the way it does in March. A rattled windowpane can be so many things—a portent or a cold front coming through.

So many nights my ghost's come and left as quiet as a whisper, nothing but a sense of comfort and company in me when I wake.

This morning there is the warning and the fear in his voice when he gave it.

CHAPTER TWO

Jackson

AUGUST 1995

"If I died," Ella asked, "how much would you miss me?"

Our father paused. The sharp edges of her words cut him. He maybe tasted blood. Her question was shocking. We didn't talk about dying in our house, not outright, not even then.

In that pause destruction formed. The humid air of the August night rolled in through the open windows of the bedroom, collided with the secrets he carried. The secrets I carried. He took a deep breath.

In the space of an inhalation, our world could have been remade. His breath was wide as oceans, a vast eternity that shot out in all directions with the potential of what could have been.

It's strange to think about. How he could have changed things. It could have been righted, even then. If he'd been honest, just once.

Most nights I return to this moment in memory, just before falling asleep. Look at it from every angle. As if it makes any difference.

On this night, who were they? Ella was seven but old for her age, having seen things she wouldn't recover from. Tallish, dark tangled curls that matted at the back of her skull, wearing one of my old T-shirts as a nightie. Prone to crying jags, nail biting, chewing on the edges of her sleeve—that summer, we all were.

And our father, a small-town poet of growing renown, was still youngish, nearing forty, same dark hair as his girl; eventual father to six, one of whom wasn't born yet, one of whom had already died.

His eyesight was beginning to fail, and he couldn't bench-press as much as he used to. He sang in a thin, tremulous tenor we heard only in church, though he barely ever attended.

He could be kind. He had a wood-paneled study that children weren't allowed to go in. He could be a good father. He carried a linen handkerchief in his pocket, would mop his brow with it on hot days. He listened to old Johnny Cash songs on a cassette player that hissed between tracks. Had an uneasy relationship with his own dad.

He could swing a child high into the air, carry you on his shoulders for days. He was awful with his hands, couldn't fix a car or an air conditioner or a bookshelf. He'd rub Vicks on your chest if you had a cough. He always smelled of sage.

He liked his beer on the warm side, his steak nearly raw. He took great delight in signing our family Christmas cards "Happy Holidays from the House of the Seven Gables" during the few years we were all there together.

We were the Gables, four sons and a daughter. A mother and a father, a remodeled farmhouse next to a slow-moving creek—based on that alone, we had every right to an idyllic childhood. We had each other.

That was all behind us, though. The unthinkable had happened, first when our house caught fire, then when our brother Lex died, over and over until we were the Gables no longer.

"How much?" she asked again. Her still babyish voice astoundingly clear.

Eternity imploded, drawing back into itself until the fate of everything hung on what our father would say.

He cleared his throat. Tried to avoid the terrible responsibility of having a voice.

He could have begun to put us back together. Not returned us to our former glory—nobody can undo dying—but given us the semblance of a future in which we were still a family.

But instead, he was about to commit a sin that would lead to murder, though he wouldn't ever really think of it that way. In time, he'd kill each of his children—some of us lived through it, others didn't.

We died by bicycle, by a breakfast gone bad, a fist, a broken promise, a rowboat, letters no one else was supposed to see.

But we didn't know most of this yet.

I stood outside the bedroom, listening to her shift, him sigh. I watched them through the half-open door.

I was thirteen, oldest son, convalescent skinny from surgeries and bed rest. Headaches. Heavy cast on my left arm. Hair grown long—haircuts weren't the first thing on anyone's mind. Shirtless because fabric against my healing incisions hurt.

I tried to summon ghosts, begged to be haunted. I was dizzy with secrets not my own.

I hated my bedroom. They'd left the second bed in there; its emptiness ate at me. Nobody knew what to do with it.

Every night, I loitered in the hall. It felt safer, like maybe I'd find my missing brother there. The hall still smelled like new paint and renovation. The light bulb was burned out. No one knew, most likely, that I eavesdropped.

"I would miss you the most," our father finally answered. The atmosphere dropped around them. Thunder rolled.

"Now it's bedtime. Go to sleep."

He lay in bed next to her. He smoothed her hair around her ear with his hand, the way he'd done since she was a tiny baby. He did this every evening.

Sweat curled down my back. I bit my tongue, tasted our shared blood.

The rest of us, that night, were a portrait of a family at the end of its rope—fragile Adrian, age nine, reading under his covers with a flashlight. Bear, our black-muzzled mutt, running in her dreams on the living room floor. Little Remy, still kindergarten chubby and snoring across the bedroom he shared with Ella, our sister. Ella herself, tentative and sweaty, having asked our father a question that would reverberate forever.

In the hall, I knew his terrible secret but not what to do with it, so I stayed quiet. This was my great sin, one I'd commit a thousand times over. Knowing the story, but not who to tell it to. It eroded me, left me a shell of a boy with nothing inside but the secret, howling like a crazy wind.

There are so many moments where maybe I could have changed things, spoken aloud, saved someone. Myself. Been better than my father was.

This scene in the hall bothers me especially—sticks me, a splinter even after so long. So I return to it. I try to hear what the pause says as much as what the words do.

Come stand beside me. Be witness to this silent crime.

"I have another question," Ella said in a small voice. She sounded scared.

"Just one?" he whispered.

"Yeah, I think."

"Okay," he said. "What?"

She took a breath, leaned against him hard, burying her face in his chest. "If I died, would you look for me? Would you come?"

Our father didn't answer.

Ella sounded restless. Real panic rose in her—I heard it in her voice. Felt it, too. She was asking for all of us, not just herself.

"I would want you to look. Because I would miss you," she said miserably.

"I would miss you too," he answered. "I would miss you very, very much."

Even now, he could have stopped himself. He could have gone silent, simply held her. That would have been enough.

He put his head down next to hers on her pillow.

"I would look for you always." He smoothed her hair again.

"Yeah?"

"Yes. I would look for you, and I couldn't be happy until I was with you again."

There was his crime: his irredeemable lie. Because he would leave, and soon. He'd find happiness again, some form of it. He wouldn't come looking for what he'd lost, which in this case were his children.

I want to be the boy in the hall again. Even the acute pain of that summer can't keep me away. I'd like to step into that bedroom, tell everyone what I know.

To ask my family to forgive me for allowing him his lies. And I'd like to write a good ending to this story, the one that handsome family deserved, what that nice old house promised.

But we're not yet at the end.

CHAPTER THREE

Adrian

MONDAY 5:00 P.M.

"He was supposed to be here today," Calvin says, sliding into the back of my car. He's still in his soccer jersey, gold and navy checks blazing across his chest. His athletic pants swish as he moves. The front seat next to me is a pile of textbooks, tests, and other grading I've been ignoring but need to get to.

"Nice to know you're happy to see me," I say.

"Shut up," he says. "You know what I meant."

I do know, but we don't talk about it. His knees hit me in the back through my seat as he scoots across; the only open place for him is in the middle of the back seat, and he complains good-naturedly about not having enough room for his legs.

"You put the seat back like you're eight feet tall," he says, then turns from side to side, where Rett's and Adam's empty booster and car seats are strapped in tightly.

"No little guys?" he asks, putting his seat belt on while I check the side mirror before pulling out into the street.

"Nah, Liv's got them. We'll see them at your house."

Cal nods. In the rearview mirror I catch a glance of his face—cheeks a plummy purple, a gift his fair coloring gives him every time he runs around for more than ten minutes. It'll take a half hour for the exertion flare to die down. His finely drawn chin, still boyish, almost prettily set against his short, upturned nose. He's not very big for fourteen. Blue eyes clear as an April sky, lashes sandy and long. Hair wild and standing on end, dark with sweat.

"How was practice?" I ask, looking back to the road.

"Fine, I guess. I played sweeper."

"Bet you're tired."

"Not really," he says, but he tries to stifle to a huge yawn. "That doesn't mean I'm tired," he says quickly. "I just wasn't breathing deep enough."

I laugh, and he tells me about the upcoming game his indoor team is playing next week, how he's nervous since he's just been made captain and is afraid he won't get the coin toss right. I wonder how you can't get a coin toss right. He tells how during his lunch period, a kid in his class threw up next to the trash can instead of in it, and then two girls threw up in response.

"And you know exactly who it was who set off the puke chain, too," he says. I can hear the smile in his voice.

I smile myself and mentally go through kids I had as sixth graders two years ago. "So it's a guy," I say.

"Yup. Keep guessing."

"And he's prone to puking at the slightest provocation."

"Keep going."

"And when he does, he can't make it to the proper receptacle."

"So far you're only saying stuff I already told you."

"Was he in one of my classes?"

"Yeah. He was in Sixth Accelerated, but the other section from mine."

I play awhile longer, suggesting names of candidates, but the fun of the game seems to be waning.

"Where is he today?" Cal says abruptly, cutting me off in midsentence.

"The vomit king?"

"Don't be an asshole," he says mildly.

I nod, catch his eye in the rearview mirror. He looks away quickly, averting his eyes out the window.

"I don't know," I say. "He called me this afternoon and asked if I could give you a ride."

For a few minutes neither of us speaks; my attention is occupied with driving through the mess of cars on the streets downtown. We're heading to Cal's house, where he lives with Dad and Emily—Liv's meeting us there with our boys for a family dinner.

"He was supposed to come watch today," Cal says quietly.

"I'm sorry."

"That's why I played sweeper. I asked the coach specially to play it. So he could see me."

"It's probably a work thing," I say, hoping he knows I'm not trying to cover. I'm angry at Dad because he didn't give me a reason when he asked me to pick my brother up.

Just get him, he had said, and I'll see you both at home tonight.

"Doesn't matter," Cal answers. "It's always a work thing or a something else thing."

Though it has been raining all day, the sky's really unleashing on us now. I can't see very well even though I have the headlights up and the wipers going at full throttle. Finally, we reach the outskirts of Sawtell, where the older houses and stately homes of the professors who work at Larson College cluster.

"Tell me more about your day," I say, hoping to draw Cal out again. He's a good kid, sweet and silly most of the time—but when he's unhappy, he brings the very atmosphere down around him. I can't help thinking that the rain's timely assault might have something to do with his disappointment.

He doesn't answer, and soon enough we're pulling up in front of the house. Liv's car is already there, parked in the spot I would have put my own car. She's got the bigger, better vehicle, a Chevy SUV that can comfortably carry both boys, all their attendant junk, and still have room to lay the back seat fully down.

We park on the street instead but manage to land our feet in the same giant puddle as we get out. I pull my jacket up over my head and run for the house. Cal books it, his backpack and sports duffel banging against his back and each other.

The house is an original craftsman, dating to the earlier part of the last century. Our father and Emily put a lot of time and money into the place; it's finally, almost twenty-odd years later, starting to pay off. Before that, one part or another of the house was always undergoing some minor (or occasionally major) construction project. Even I helped when I first moved here to Washington. I rehabbed my own bedroom with only Vincent's aid.

We don't talk about when I moved west; I prefer it that way. I was just Cal's age then, fourteen, having trouble in school and at home. There was an incident in the boys' bathroom at school and an ambulance ride to the ER, and the next week I was on my way to stay indefinitely at my dad's house. My mom wanted me to come home to Pennsylvania eventually, but it didn't work out that way.

It turned out Dad was too busy to get me settled, so Vincent did so for him—at the time, he was a grad student of my father's. Just another young man dazzled by James Gable's poetry, hoping to glean some of that magic. Dad knew Vincent was hard up for money, so he hired him on the side to come babysit his crazy son.

Vincent's been gone seven years now, though I've taken Liv and Rett to see him in Arizona on his little ranchero, as he calls it. He's never met Adam, though we hope to get the kids out to see him again sometime soon.

The week after he learned that he had MS, Vincent and his wife moved to the desert outside Phoenix. They already had a little house there they visited in winter.

If it was good enough for Doc Holliday, Vincent had said, it's good enough for me.

But Doc Holliday went west to recover from tuberculosis, I had told him. And it didn't help him. And you'd be going east.

Ah, Ade, he had said. My consummate historian. If I only have a few good years left, I want to spend them in the sun.

When Vincent left, I lost the closest thing I had to a brother out here.

"Open the door, open the door!" Cal's shouting, banging on it with both fists.

I stand next to him, my hands jammed in my pockets, and wait. A figure comes, blurred by the bubbled glass in the window of the door, and then it opens. Emily's there, and as Cal shoves his way through, she catches him by the shoulder and plants a kiss on his cheek. He shakes her off and drops his bags just inside the door.

I follow, and after accepting Emily's kiss, I nearly trip on them. As he's gone through, Cal's stripped off his wet clothing. I see the trail he's left behind: sneakers, jersey, one sock and then the other, and finally a pair of track pants balled up at the end of the hall.

Emily smiles after him. She really loves his mess, the debris he throws off as he thunders through the world.

Cal shouts hello to Liv, then I catch Rett's happy squeal as Cal comes upon him. I don't hear anything out of Adam, but he hasn't been feeling well lately.

"I'm on the phone!" a gruff voice bellows. "Stop your noise, Calvin!"

Emily takes my jacket in the hall, hangs it up on the hook that it's always belonged to.

"I wish he'd speak a little kinder," she says, her smile apologizing for my father as it so often does.

I shrug and smile back; she follows me into the kitchen. Just off it, Liv sits on the couch. Adam's lying prone in her lap. His eyes are half-shut, rolling a little under the lids. He's asleep, and I don't want to disturb him.

"He okay?" I ask Liv, settling down on the couch next to her without jostling Adam too much.

"He's running a fever again," she says. "But he's finally sleeping, so that's something."

I nod, place my hand as softly as I can on his brow. He shifts a little on Liv's lap, his lips moving in a sucking motion. His perfect bow of a mouth. His smart white teeth in their clean row just behind it. He's two now, but still so much our baby. He feels a little warm, but he's also clammy.

"Doctor tomorrow?" I ask.

She adjusts him on her lap so she can stretch her leg out. He's heavy as a bag of cement. "You know I can't take off until later in the week."

I put my arm around her and try not to worry too much about Adam.

On the other side of the kitchen, Calvin comes back through the door that leads out to the garage. The washer and dryer are out there, and Cal's assembled himself a new outfit from the basket of clean clothes he must have found there.

It drives Emily nuts when he does that; it drove her nuts when I used to do it too, growing up. But she doesn't scold him, not with company here.

Rett sees me, and a huge grin breaks across his face, so large his jaw looks like it might unhinge. He is my brother Jack incarnate, dark curls and eyes that change hue based on what color he's wearing and his mercurial moods.

Rett's in a jam—too many of his favorite people are in one room, and he isn't sure whose side to trot to next. He loves Cal like nobody's business, and I'd like to think I'm a close second in his heart. Of course he melts for Emmy, as he calls Emily, and his papa is still shouting on the phone to someone.

I wave to him. He hedges his bets, sticking close to Cal.

The boys go together to a large table that's pushed up against the back wall of the kitchen. This is where Cal does his homework, where I used to do mine. Vincent and I made it together on a neighbor's band saw and with other tools the guy let us borrow.

Cal gets another chair from the dining table and sets it next to his. He helps Rett onto it, gives him a piece of paper and a pencil. Cal opens his own backpack, which Emily has rescued from the hall and brought there for him. He pulls out a binder, opens it, and looks at a page inside. A textbook comes out next, and soon he's working over some assignment, his blond head bent forward with the effort. Rett's dark one bends just as intently next to him, where he might be practicing his letters or pretending to do complicated math.

Emily sits on an easy chair across from us, and we fall into the kind of unremarkable conversation that all families have. She gets up from time to time to check on the thick vegetable soup she's been cooking all afternoon in the slow cooker and to put some crescent rolls from a can into the oven.

Eventually, we hear my father get off the phone. He's been wandering around the entire downstairs on a cordless extension and comes to put the phone back in its cradle on Cal's table.

He leans forward to see what the boys are working on. His hand idly strokes the back of Cal's neck. The remarkable thing is that Cal lets him do it, even leans into it some. Like a good dog who loves his master. Rett would shake me off if I tried to touch him that way. He's all kinetic energy these days, though he does cuddle up with us at night just before he goes to sleep.

My father gives both boys a final pat on the head and comes over to where the rest of us are sitting. He's wearing a pair of jeans he must have bought when I was in high school. They're frayed at the bottoms where he's walked on them, and his bare, hairy toes stick out. He's got on a rust-colored fleece that zips halfway up his chest, with an old used-to-be-white T-shirt underneath. His glasses hang on a cord around his neck, and his graying head needs a shave and a haircut—typical for him, all of it.

He settles himself in another chair and joins the conversation.

I don't say what I'm thinking—I'm angry with him for missing Cal's practice when he said he'd be there. He wasn't at work, wasn't holding extra office hours, and wasn't even in his study composing or revising some new poem. He was stalking around the house in his bare feet, talking on the phone and yelling at anybody nearby who got too loud for him to hear whoever he was talking to.

So many little ways a father can let you down. I try hard to avoid them, but some nights I can't sleep, thinking about some small thing that I said or did that day that might have hurt one of my sons. Because I have no way of knowing what they'll use to weave the stories of their lives, which action of mine will be saving or damning, what they'll take with them from the way I was and what they'll leave behind.

A man as young and a father as good as I am shouldn't worry about his legacy, Liv says.

But doesn't she worry about hers? I ask. Of course not, she says with a laugh. Boys always love their mothers.

Dad leans back in his chair, his feet pulled up crossed-legged under him. I hate when he sits like that; he looks like the girls I teach, the way they perch in their desks like they're ready to braid each other's hair and tell secrets. I don't mind when the girls do it, but in my father, it comes across as affected, something less than honest.

"I spoke to your brother on the phone," he says in my direction.

"Oh?"

"He's coming along fine with his latest piece. But they've moved his deadline up a day or two and he's having a hard time convincing anyone that he . . ."

He keeps talking, but it's hard to focus. So he talked to Remy then, not Jack.

"You should have been there at the dinner they gave for him, Adrian," he's saying. "He read aloud part of 'Drowning in Dry Dock' and did a very nice job with it."

I nod, disinterested. Several months ago, Remy was nominated for (but did not win) a prestigious prize (the Frederick Kelley Award for Freelance Journalistic Excellence, as my father can recite backward and forward) for an article he wrote for a fledgling magazine. There was a dinner at a swanky hotel in Manhattan that all the parents went to.

Remy said he could get tickets for Liv and me if we wanted to come, too. But with the boys and Cal, someone had to stay home. We couldn't miss work, either; between my fifth and sixth graders and Liv's second graders, it wasn't possible.

I don't want to sit and chat about Remy's accomplishments any more than I want to about Jack's failures; though if I was asked my opinion and thought it was wanted, I'd say that neither Jack nor Remy are so far to either extreme. We rarely talk about Ella, even less about my mother, living alone now in the old farmhouse in Harrington, Pennsylvania, and all the ghosts she must keep there.

"Where were you today?" I ask, which seems to surprise him. I don't know if he's surprised at what I said or that I spoke at all.

He uncrosses one leg and places it on the floor, but the other is still tucked under him. It makes me angry to see him sitting like that, his bare foot brushing the ground as he taps his toes on the hardwood floor.

"What do you mean, son?" he says, feigning innocence and confusion. He's bullshitting me, though.

"You were supposed to watch him play. If I knew that, I'd have gone in and done it. But you didn't tell me. Why didn't you at least—"

A buzzer in the kitchen goes off, and Emily says, "Dinner's ready!" She gets up to take the rolls out before they burn.

"Oh, that," he says. "I emailed your brother a few days ago."

I look at him, at his hair too long over his ears, the lenses of his glasses smudged and dirty and bifocal.

"And?"

"Well, I heard back, and he said he'd be calling this afternoon. I wanted to be home to catch him."

"He couldn't call you later?" I ask, trying to keep my voice even, cordial.

"That's not possible," he says, shaking his head like he's amused with me, like he knows something I don't and he's about to school me in it. "Obviously it isn't."

Liv puts her hand on my knee and squeezes, trying to reset me. I don't want to blow a gasket at him, but it's hard to manage when he's so patronizing and unapologetic.

"He's got to be up early," he continues. "And besides, Cal doesn't care."

But he does care. He won't say it and neither will I, but everyone sitting here knows it.

"Well, Dad, I think it's time to eat," Liv says. "Help me get Adam settled?"

He pulls himself up to standing and moves the few steps to the couch, closing the distance between us in no time. The furniture here is all brown, comfortably beaten leather. His chair maintains the imprint of his body though he's no longer in it.

He leans forward as I lean back, trying to avoid him as he gathers Adam in his arms. As he does so, his arm brushes my forehead. The small dark hairs on it look the same as always; they tickle when they meet my skin.

Liv slides away from me and stands. The two of them put Adam back on the couch, tuck a blanket around him up to his waist. He hasn't woken, my father took him up so gently. Emily brings the older boys to the dining table, gets them settled. I wait a moment by the couch, regarding Adam with an anxious constriction in my chest. He's sleeping hard. But I'm still concerned about the fever, his paleness.

Rett was anemic when he was younger, though; I wouldn't be surprised if Adam is too. Adam, who we called Addie when he was first born—he's got my eyes, but Liv's strawberry blond hair.

We join them at the table, where my father sits at the head. A place he does not always deserve. A bowl of very good soup is passed to me. The kids chatter, the women talk, and I feel confused and angry about my father, my sick son. And Cal, coming out of the school gym, his shoulders hunched under his bags, looking for my father's car parked somewhere in the rain.

Dinner passes.

"Come out here," Dad says to me as Emily and Cal clear the dishes when we're through. Liv offers to help, but Rett bumps his head on the underside of the table and starts to cry. She attends to him, Adam still asleep.

I follow my father out to the garage.

He flips the switch by the door, and the dark void becomes an inhabited space. Along the walls there are bins and other well-organized hooks and grommets, hanging off of and in which are all manner of things—nails, twine, old sports equipment, a lawn croquet set.

Three bicycles lean against the far wall, one each for my dad, Emily, and Cal. They like to spend Saturdays when the weather is good biking in the hills around town. I used to go with them when I was younger, too. But I don't even own a bike now.

They don't park their cars inside, so the room feels more spacious than a garage otherwise might.

The washer and dryer are also out here, with a small table Emily uses to fold and organize the laundry. There's a basket half-filled with clean clothes sitting on it. There's also a few socks and a stray bra on the concrete floor next to the table; this is what Cal must have pawed through when he came out here in his boxers after I brought him home.

"Damn it, I ask him all the time to not mess up the laundry," Dad growls as he leans forward to pick up the dropped clothes. He throws them artlessly onto the table, not back in the basket.

"He needed something, I guess," I say in weak defense of Cal.

"He should go upstairs to his own room, as he's been told to do, and get something out of his drawers just like the rest of us."

"He was practically naked, though."

"That's his own problem. He's not supposed to do that either."

I watch him grumble, then I appraise the rest of the room.

In the middle of the garage, on a pair of sawhorses, is a thing of great beauty. It's a rowboat made of marine plywood that practically glows. Fifteen feet long, it dominates most of the garage and is positioned on a diagonal so you have room to move around it. The sides are slightly convex, with solid planks riding from tip to tail in single, graceful sweeps. The boat flares out smartly at the stern into an almost-heart.

Cal and Dad have been working on it for months. They bought a kit off the internet and have been using online videos to help them figure out how to construct it when the instructions fail them.

I run my hand along the side of the boat but stop when I feel splinters pricking up against my skin.

"Needs sanding down," my father says, standing on the other side of the boat, looking at me.

"It's a damn pretty job you've done," I say, admiring their work. I haven't seen their progress in a month or so, and they've come along well. "What will you call it?"

He nods. "It's called a Chester Yawl, or the design is. We'll call it whatever we want."

"Any thoughts on the name?"

"None yet." He runs his own hand down the gunwale.

"I'm sure you'll manage," I answer.

"A boy needs a boat," he says.

I nod but don't look at him, still wrapped up in the progress they've made on the Yawl.

"You had that canoe we bought when we moved into the house," he continues. "All you kids loved it."

"Where will you float it?"

"Well," he says, "There's the duck pond downtown, but it's hardly big enough. I figure we'll take it out to Grant Lake, when it's ready."

Grant Lake's a fifteen-minute ride down the highway. He's right, though—there's no suitable body of water closer.

"When do you figure you'll be done?"

"There's sanding, then some type of waterproofing, and God knows what else."

"Long job."

My dad says something, but I'm imagining what it'll be like to float the boat, whether it will ride high in the water or sink down some.

He clears his throat, tries again.

"I want you to finish the boat with him. So it's ready for the summer."

"No."

He looks at me, perplexed. "Why not?"

I wonder what he's getting at.

"I need you to finish the boat with Calvin," he says.

My mouth falls open a little. This is their project, one they've worked on for months, talked about for at least two years before they started it.

"I can't," I say forcefully. "Why would you ask me that?"

"Because." He shrugs. "It should be a brother thing."

"No," I say. I choose my next words carefully. A hot anger builds in my chest, but I don't let him see it. "No, it's a James-Calvin thing. A father-son thing."

"I can't keep on with him, doing it," he replies, running a hand through his hair.

"Why is that?"

He shrugs again, then rolls his shoulders back and squares them off to me. "I've been asked to teach at a conference," he says.

"And?"

"And I'm working on the new manuscript."

"That precludes the boat how?"

He looks at me like I'm stupid.

"You know how it is when I write."

I can only sigh. I do know. When he wrote, as I grew up, he'd vacate his normal life entirely. He'd be present in the house, but he wasn't really there. He'd rush to his study as soon as he could, shutting the door against his kids and his wife in pursuit of some poem he'd dreamed up.

"Son, you're good with projects. You made that table he works at with Vincent."

"I did," I say, feeling dangerous.

"So you'll finish the boat with Cal. And then, when it's done, I'll take him and you to Grant Lake. We'll launch her together."

I don't know what to say, so I spit out the first thing to come to mind.

"Rett's got T-ball."

"I hardly think," he says to me, smiling in his patronizing way, "that T-ball would get in the way of you spending time with your brother."

"I'd hardly think that work would get in the way of you spending time with your son," I snap.

"He knows my work matters, and what that means. You do too."

He's right—during the six weeks I spent upstairs fixing up my bedroom with Vincent, he was downstairs working on a collection of poetry. He was on sabbatical that term and could not waste any more time than he already had on settling me into my new home.

"Adam's sick," I say, trying again though I know I won't get anywhere with him now that he's copped his terrible smile.

"Someone's kid is always sick," he says. "Yours, mine, whoever's. Cal can't finish the boat himself, though."

"He's really sick," I confide quietly. I don't know why I say it, except that some part of me believes it. That this is no run-of-the-mill thing, that it won't be as simple as an antibiotic and a week home from day care. I say it, voice that deepest fear of this illness that I know is coming, that's already acting in him.

My father laughs at me. He's got a nasty, sneering look on his face, a coldness to his voice.

"You don't know what having a sick kid is. Not a really sick one, anyway." He's flippant as he says it, flicking the back of his left hand at me like I'm dismissed. "Not like you'd be able to handle it, if you did. We know how well you manage when things get even remotely difficult."

I look at him, hard, trying to recognize in him something that's familiar. Something of myself, maybe. But he's foreign and bitter looking. He's illuminated from above by the same light bulb that makes the boat look so pretty—but it only shows the bad side of my father. I see his devil's face, his bushy eyebrows, his jutting jaw.

I close my eyes, breathing in and out. I imagine Liv's hand on my knee, willing me to calm down and walk away. It's one thing to say I don't understand what it's like to have a child who's unwell—though I'm afraid I do. It's another entirely to suggest, though perhaps rightly so, that if Adam's illness is serious, I won't be able to handle it.

"I'm leaving," I say finally.

"You can't do that," he says simply, like that's the end of it.

He cannot imagine a world where his children don't bend to his will. He bends us till we break, until we snap.

"I said I'm leaving."

"But I was just asking you a simple favor."

"No, you weren't. Please tell Emily thank you for dinner."

"Adrian, stop being ridiculous. No one's done a thing to you."

"And tell Liv I'm walking home."

I move toward the front of the garage, so I can pull open the door. I reach down, take the handle, feel the muscles in my arm and shoulder contract as I throw it open from the bottom. "Ade," he says, "son, come back inside."

It's gotten dark out, but I know the way home. My car keys are inside in my jacket pocket, but I'm not going back for them. I can't look at Dad again tonight. It'll be a long walk, almost five miles, but it's better than abiding one more moment with him.

"I'll pick my car up tomorrow," I say.

I feel a wild joy at turning my back on him. Walking out into the rain, past his and Emily's cars.

"Ade, Ade, come in and let's—"

These are the last words I hear from him, as I go down the driveway; the rain drowns out his voice. The rain is cold on my skin, and in seconds, my shirt is plastered to my body, my trousers the same. I'm still wearing my good leather shoes, but I don't care. Damn the shoes, damn the whole wretched evening.

I'll have to talk to him about it tomorrow when I pick the car up. He'll understand me or he won't, but I'll tell him again that he needs to finish the project with Cal. Then I'll head home, and he'll head to his office at the college to get ready for his Tuesday evening class.

But morning comes and Adam's getting worse—his fever is higher, and he's so drowsy he won't open his eyes unless we practically pry them apart. During the bustle to get Rett ready for school, for me to call out of work, to make an appointment with the pediatrician, my sister calls to tell me she had the strangest dream. I say I can't talk right now. I'll call her later.

I do call her later. I have bad news.

But I don't pick up my car. And I never manage to speak to my father again.

CHAPTER FOUR

Jackson

TUESDAY 11:40 P.M.

A ringing phone that I don't answer. A voicemail a moment later, and that's all it takes to throw my father out of the world.

I sit at the table, head in my hands. Phone beside me on speaker—*To repeat this message, press 7.*

I listen again and again, so many times my thumb gets tired from tapping the touch screen. I hear him speaking—Remy, the good son. The lighthearted one, probably the best of us.

Light from a streetlamp shines thin, coming in through the sliding glass door that leads out to my sad excuse for a balcony. There's barely enough room for me to stand on it—when I do, I'm gifted a view of the parking lot below. There're never more than two or three cars there, one of which is mine. Nobody's beating down the doors to rent one of the vacancies next to or below me.

I don't like living here, but I have my reasons for staying. I'm here because this is where the job was—copywriting for a company that produces church bulletins and diner placemats, among other things nobody reads. I've got a one-bedroom apartment in a complex that was built in the late seventies and carries with it all the gracelessness of that era, just off the Mass Pike halfway between Boston and the Berkshires. I could pay for better, easily, with my settlement money from the accident—but the job I'm working is easy and no one really knows me. So that recommends the place despite itself.

On the message, Remy gives the facts. The when and where, as clinical as a death certificate.

It was a pulmonary embolism. A blood clot to the lung. In his garage, alone. Emily came home from shopping and found him. The ambulance was called. Things moved quickly after that. But nobody could help him, and he was declared dead in a side room at the county hospital.

If you are lucky enough to get help quickly, Remy's message says, the chances of survival aren't bad. He might have had symptoms for a few days, only nobody knew it.

He wasn't lucky, and so he died.

I should call my brother back. I should call my mother, my sister, someone. But there's no words for what I might need to say.

An hour goes by, and I find myself walking around the living room, picking things up and putting them down again. I'm not crying but wonder if I should be. I try to screw up my sadness, but nothing comes. I try to believe he died, to figure what that means for me, but I'm having trouble reckoning either one.

It feels strange, that my father went so easy. He'd always had a touch of the pugilist in him, was a fan of that Dylan Thomas poem about not going gently. I'd always thought he'd put up a fight. But when that final, big pain came, I guess he caved. But who wouldn't?

Yet I didn't. I could have died after the accident, maybe should have. Once, my heart stopped during an emergency procedure to drain fluid from my chest cavity.

I spent the better part of three years in and out of the hospital, reconstructive surgeries and range of motion procedures, MRIs and head scans for my terrible, unrelenting headaches, until I was old enough to say enough was enough. By the time I was seventeen, I'd decided I was through with treatments. I'd learn to live with what I had left, which wasn't much.

Maybe I'm judging him, a little, as I wander around trying to figure out how to mourn for someone I don't fully believe is dead.

My hands come across one of the few pictures I keep in the apartment. I don't like to have photographs around—but this one has always struck a strange note with me, from the moment I found it under my mother's bed when I was a kid. She let me keep it, and I've had it nearby ever since.

It's of my mother and father, before they had any children, maybe before they were married. My father's hand is on my mother's back. The top of her head just reaches his shoulder. They both wear the bland, muted colors you'd expect them to in a picture taken more than thirty-five years ago, him in a light-colored T-shirt and tan slacks, her wearing a sundress that falls below her knees; the only adornment is the bright red geranium my mother has tucked behind her left ear.

It surprises me, no matter how often I see it, how young they are, how unafraid. The light seems to shine so brightly, it must have been blinding. Washed out—like the sun itself hung a little closer to earth then. I never in my whole life saw my parents as they look in this old picture, strong and fit and wholly unremarkable.

Looking at them that way, I've always thought that what I see must be what God meant when he made us. People, I mean. It's easy to see how they thought they could be anything as long as they were together. They shared a kind of spark, a certain homegrown holiness that you don't see with your eyes as much as you just sense it. They're the best parts of a Rockwell painting, the warm drowsy feeling that's left in you after a hard day's physical work.

This is the way I imagine them when I want to think of them in happiness—just on the brink, their faces turned brightly toward all that's coming. There is no fear in them—why should there be? They're together at the beginning of all things.

My finger pets the figure of my father, much younger than I am now. I see his dark eyes, his hair cropped close to his head against the summer heat. He stands, feet apart, one hand on my mother, the other resting lightly on his hip.

He does not smile. He looks at me with cool assurance, though—comfortable in his own skin in a way I've never been. I envy the way he stands there, of his left arm that works as well as his right, of the softness around his eyes—he doesn't know yet all the ways the world will hurt him. I'm jealous that he learns of darkness so late, when he's already grown enough to know what to do with what fear leaves behind in you.

I know the angle of his face, the way it's turned up a little into the sun. I know his voice, his smell, and what he would have sounded like had he shouted out my name right then.

Looking at that man, caught in his early twenties, I begin to cry. This is my father, and today he died.

I take the picture in its frame and carry it with me. I go to the kitchen drawer, grab the only pair of scissors that I own. Clutching them to my chest, I take the few steps to the bathroom at a trot. Kick the door open with my foot, get the light switch with my elbow. Drop the picture and scissors in the sink.

Then, looking at the picture of my father's face and my own image in the mirror, I lean in close, taking up the scissors, wondering where I should make my first cut.

My mind feels wild; my hands move despite me. I take the scissors to my head. I slide them closed. A dark bit of hair falls away. It lands on the picture, curling on top of my mother's smiling face. I do it again. I slip and nick myself with the scissors just above my hairline. A little path of blood winds down my forehead. It tickles. I keep cutting.

My heart shudders and rolls over in my chest.

How do you cut hair? You even it off. You make it look tidy and square. Eventually my arm cramps so badly I have to stop. I've reached the limit of my mobility, can't do any more.

I rest my arm a minute, draping it on the counter by the sink. In the mirror, I see myself—a mess.

How do you tie up a life? You even it off. You make it feel tidy, try to save from it what you can.

I marvel at the machine my father was, how he failed. How I will fail. How we all will fail.

I take up the scissors again in my left hand, the bad one, try my best to raise it to the right side of my head. I slice and chop again, but I tire quickly.

I have to try to finish it, at least, but I can't manage. My arm hurts too much and the scissors have slipped again, so my ears both have little nicks in them. Dark hair and little drops of blood fleck the sink. I turn the water on to wash them away, but they won't go. The photograph is blocking the drain. Nothing can go down it. I pull the picture out quickly, try to dry it with my bath towel.

People used to rend their garments and rub ash in their hair when someone died, I remember. I grin despite myself—nobody can say that I did nothing when I heard the news.

I should have gone to a barber. I should go to a barber now. But what do I say?

Help me look like my dead father, please. Here he is, right there in the photograph. Doesn't he look brave? Don't I look brave, looking like him?

Calvin

Adrian got this shitty room for us. It's not even a chain hotel—just a dump off the highway outside of Harrington. This place smells like damp dogs and cigarettes even though the inside of the door has a no smoking sign on it.

Ade's flying in tomorrow with Rett. He was supposed to come today, too, but whatever's wrong with Adam is a bigger thing than they thought.

"I'm like the goddamn cruise director," he said as we sat quietly after hearing the second round of bad news, in my living room in Sawtell a few days ago. He'd been making phone calls all morning after Mark had left. "Scheduling excursions and arranging accommodations for the dead."

I honestly thought that things were as bad as they could be, with him dead and all, but we didn't really understand anything until Dad's lawyer friend came by with what I thought was Dad's will. It wasn't really a will, more like a list of instructions and final wishes. Mark is the lawyer friend.

Mark brought this paper over, and we all sat, Mom, me, Ade, and Liv. Mom didn't want me to be there. She thought it was inappropriate for me to listen. I sat on the couch and didn't move when she said to go. She didn't bother fighting me about it, though.

What we found out is that Dad owned a burial plot back in Pennsylvania, in a town called Lawrence. The plot's next to his own dad and the brother who died. Mom nodded, said she already knew that. What she didn't know, though, is that Dad intended to be buried there whenever his time came. Mom thought he'd sell it to Bea, or that my grandmother would be buried there instead.

Mark kept reading off the paper, but by then I wasn't listening anymore. Eventually he finished and finally left. Ade started to cry in an angry way, saying "the selfish bastard" over and over. Mom wandered out of the living room like a ghost and put the teakettle on the stove without filling it with water.

Then Liv was beside me. "Are you okay, Cal?" she said, turning my face toward her gently with her hands. I shrugged, sighed. Ade walked out of the room, still cursing, talking to himself about "how the hell do you move a body thousands of miles across the country?" and "who do you even call to do that for you?"

"Do you understand what—do you know what your dad's wishes mean? What he's asking for?" Liv asked.

"He wants to be buried there, not here at home," I said. It was simple. She nodded, still holding my face. Adam started to cry in the next room.

"How do you feel about that?" she asked. I felt so bad for her because she was trying hard to see how I was. But I could see her body pulling away. She needed to go check on Adam. He was where her bad news was, not me.

"I feel like the way I feel about it doesn't matter much," I said quietly.

"Well," she answered, biting her bottom lip, already turning her head away so she could try to figure what Adam needed, "I suppose you're right, really."

We're here now at the Dingy-Inn—not what it's really called but what it may as well be. Mom does the dead bolt on our hotel room door. She comes and sits down on the edge of my bed. I wait for her to say something, but she only looks at me sadly and frowns. Then, she gets up again. Crosses the room, rattles the door hard.

"Just checking that we're closed up tight," she says. She goes into the bathroom, and I hear the shower running. She has it very hot because steam comes out from under the door. I'm glad that she's in there. Since it happened, no one's just let me be. She keeps creeping up next to me, just gazing. It's like she died too, and I'm being haunted by her terribly confused ghost.

I don't have a family anymore. Not really. I don't belong here in Pennsylvania. My mother doesn't inhabit her body anymore, and Ade has his kids, my other brothers and sister barely know me, and for all that my life until today that was okay enough, but now it's a terrible aching feeling to know I'm alone.

I run my fingers along the blue notebook that I stole from Dad's desk just after he died, before anyone could stop me. It's under my pillow because it doesn't feel right to have it balled up with my extra underwear in my carry-on, even though the poems in it are garbage. It's his drafting notebook, where he played with ideas before he typed his words on the ancient desktop he insisted on using.

My father taught classes on American poetry from the late 1800s, and on writing poems, at Larson College—which has been rising steadily in the rankings for the last fifteen years, he'd tell anybody who'd listen. He's half-famous, at least to some people, for his poems. Won some national awards.

His old work was considered deep, relevant, and honest. That's what a review he had framed on the wall said, at least. I've never liked reading his poems because they're autobiographical and deal with the time in Dad's life before me. That never mattered much before now.

The poems used to be from before me, anyway. When I took his notebook, I realized that he'd broken a very serious promise he'd made to me a long time ago. I hate thinking about it, what I read, scratched in his familiar handwriting.

Mom steps out of the bathroom just a few minutes after she goes in, her clothes on, hair still dry. I catch a quick look at her, and there's a vacancy in her eyes that makes my skin crawl. She faces the room door and rattles it again, and then undoes and redoes the chain lock. She snaps the dead bolt open and shut five or six times. Then she just stands there, looking at it. Like she doesn't know what a door is.

I'm in my pjs already, lying on my stomach and watching a show about guys who rebuild cars. My dad was always talking about rebuilding things, but he never did it. Ade said he was surprised about the boat, that he figured Dad was about as good with his hands as a grandma would be.

"Your hair could use a cut," Mom says too loudly. I roll over. She's sitting on the edge of her bed.

"There's got to be a barber in town," she says. She's staring across the room at that big mirror hotel rooms always have. I look at it, too, see us. She's in her nightgown now, but she hasn't taken any of her makeup off. She's so tired, and the places beneath her eyes look purple and puffed. My face looks very pale, like I have the flu.

"Not one I'm going to," I say under my breath. I don't expect her to hear me, but she whips her head around so fast she startles me. But she doesn't speak. I try not to look at her, looking at me.

She has pretty eyes, very blue. I used to like looking at pictures of her from when she was young that she kept in a box in her closet. Dad had a box too, full of pictures of my brothers and sister. He never let me see those. I had to sneak looks when he was out.

Maybe she should go take one of the pills her doctor gave her to calm down, but I don't say it. It would be too mean. I saw she'd brought them, though. In the little bag that holds her makeup, sitting on the bathroom counter by the sink.

I push the volume way up on the remote and pay attention to the TV. I know that she's probably staring at me and wanting to speak, but I won't let her. The guy on the TV show redoes two old Chevys and the show ends. I finally roll over, but Mom's gone, already lying in her bed on her side, not facing me.

I can't tell if she's asleep. She might have taken her pills. Maybe I should get up and swallow a few myself, but I know she'll be angry if she catches me. So I don't.

We lie in our separate beds. I keep the television on so that I can't hear if she starts to cry. Light fills the room, blue, not yellow. I appreciate the TV Guide Channel now so much more. It tells you what's happening, always. You get the feeling it always will, even if there's no more TVs for people to see it on.

The beds have those foam blankets that you only find in hotels. I pull it up to my chin, then over my face, then kick it down to my waist and start over again. It's itchy against my skin and smells bad.

I look at the clock. It's just a little before eight, but it feels much, much later.

I'm dozing when Mom's phone goes off. It sings out an annoying short version of an Adele song. Mom got it as a free download from a little card they gave out at Starbucks.

She doesn't move and the phone keeps ringing.

Finally, I roll over, get up, and go rummaging in her purse for the phone. She lies there, her mouth slack and cheeks puffing slightly as she breathes. She almost looks dead herself.

I find the phone and go back to my bed. She's missed five calls. Three of which came in the last few minutes. I recognize the area code first, one from home.

"Mrs. Gable?" the guy says when I accept on his sixth attempt. "Mrs. Emily Gable? This is Roger Sherm, from Sherm Funer—"

"You want my mom," I say, trying to make my voice sound deeper. I don't know why I do it, except I feel like playing with the guy some. He's calling from the funeral home Ade used in Sawtell. I remember the name of the place.

"Who might I be speaking to?" he asks, his voice tinny.

"This is Calvin Gable," I say. "My mother can't talk. We're waiting for our plane." We're not waiting for the plane, obviously, but he doesn't know that. He coughs and clears his throat a little.

"I'm sorry for your loss, son," he says. "But it's imperative I speak to someone in your family. Regarding the obituary."

I hate when people who aren't my parents call me that. I'm not his son.

"Do you even know what time it is?" I say, trying to sound angry.

"It's not yet five o'clock, sir," Roger answers.

"Do you habitually barge in on grieving families?" I don't know where the words come from, but they make me smile.

"May I please speak to your mother?" he asks, trying to wrestle control of the conversation from me. I feel it coming through the line.

I look over at Mom, the way she's curled into herself like the plaster casts they made of the dead bodies in Pompeii. I saw those in real life—we took a trip to Italy when I was nine.

"She can't come to the phone," I say.

"Is there someone else I can speak to, Calvin? Your brother Adrian? I'm so sorry to bother you, but—"

"No, he's not here either."

"Ah," Roger Sherm says. Then he doesn't say anything. Like he's waiting for me to fix some problem for him.

"What do you need?" I finally say.

"You're sure there's no adult present, son, who could speak to me?"

"No, Roger," I say, "just me. What do you want?" I hope he feels a little kick in the gut when I call him by his first name.

He breathes in sharp, then speaks. "Well, Calvin, I had some questions about spellings—names, places. Whoever took them down here at my office doesn't have very good handwriting. We need to confirm information in order to run the official obituary for your father. Is that something you can help me with? I need to get the copy to the newspaper by eight o'clock tonight. I really am sorry to bother you, son."

"I suppose I could, though you need to understand what a real inconvenience this is." I hear rustling, figure Roger's getting ready with a pen and paper.

"You ready?" I ask. "I don't have all day. I got a flight to catch."

"Yes, Calvin, thank you," he answers. "Okay, let's see now. Can you confirm your father's full name, please?"

"Can't you look it up online?" I ask.

"We, um, we need confirmation from a family member, if possible. To avoid mistakes. Would you like me to wait and try your mother again later?"

"No, she won't be around," I said. "James Wesley Gable. Do you need me to spell Wesley?"

"That's not necessary, thank you. And then, if I could have you confirm, if you can, names and spellings of your siblings and other surviving family to the best of your knowledge?"

"I said I would, Roger," I answer. "Gable. Like stable. G-A-B-L-E."

"Very good. Do you happen to know the name of your father's first wife?"

"Um, Beatrice," I say. "He always called her Bea."

"And could you run through the children from that first marriage with me?"

"I guess, yeah." We'll have to sit together at the church, in the front row, I've been told, my older siblings and me and Mom. I don't know what to think about it, so I try not to.

"I have Jackson A. Gable," he says.

"Yeah," I answer. "Just go through them all, and I'll stop you if you screw up."

"Okay. I have Adrian C. Gable, Ella J. Gable, and Rory W. Gable."

"No," I answer. "Not Rory. It's R-E-M-Y." I heard him scratching something out on his paper through the phone.

"I have Adrian listed as married to Olivia Setter, correct?"

"I guess so. I don't know about Setter."

"That's fine, Calvin," Roger says. "That's just fine. I have two grandsons listed, Adam and—would you mind spelling out the other boy's name for me? I can't read it."

"E-V-E-R-E-T-T. It's got two *T*s. Don't screw it up."

"That's just why we're speaking," he says. I begin to get angry at Mom because she's the one who should be handling it. But she's passed out, and I know there's no waking her.

"And your mother is Emily, yourself C-A-L-V-I-N James, correct?"

"Yeah," I said. "Except just put 'J' for my middle name. I'm not 'Calvin James,' like the way 'Mary Anne' is or something. Just the letter like my brothers."

He pauses; I guess he's writing things down.

"Are we done now? I've got this flight . . ." I'm getting very sleepy and want to hang up.

"I'm sorry, sir, just one or two more items, I think." I smile. I just got the bastard to call me sir.

"Fine, then."

"Your father is survived by his own mother, as well as a brother, a sister, and several nieces. Could you please, if you can, confirm the names of these loved ones?"

"Anna," I say. "Granna's name is Anna. Uh, I don't know Cat's—that's my uncle—his real name. Cat's a nickname."

"We have him as Nathaniel."

"That's right," I answer, even though I honestly don't know if it's right or not. "There's Aunt Georgia, and my cousins are Raleigh and Marlowe but I have no idea how to spell those."

"That's fine. And finally, your father is predeceased by his own father, as well as a son. If you could please con—"

"My grandfather, his name was Conrad," I interrupt.

"Yes, that's what my notes show. And your brother?"

I don't know what to say, because I have three brothers, not four. I never count the dead one in with the others.

"Calvin? Are you still on the line?" Roger says.

"Yeah." I breathe, looking at my useless mother.

"I have here Lex—is that short for anything? Or is that the given name?"

"Alexander, it's short for." At least he asked a question I know the answer to.

"Thank you, Calvin. I appreciate your time," Roger says. "I hope you have a safe flight, and again, my deepest regrets. Your loss is ours." I hang up on him. I put the phone on the nightstand. I want to crawl into bed with Mom, but she's got her back to me and I don't want to disturb her. Besides, I'm too old for that.

Instead, I lie down, close my eyes, and listen to my mother snore. The TV is still on but muted. The flicking lights shift as the picture does. I can sort of see them through my eyelids. Sometimes I feel tears start to burn behind them, but I try to think of something else and hope I'll fall asleep soon.

Next thing I know, a line of soldiers come up in front me. Ten, twenty, forty of them.

I must be sleeping, I know, but it doesn't make them any less scary or surprising when they show.

They stand in a block, lines straight as arrows. They're young and fierce looking. None of them are clean—dirt's streaked on their faces, their clothes. A couple have snow lying on their shoulders.

They're from all the wars America's ever fought in—some are in tricorn hats or slouch caps like pictures from Gettysburg, and others are in those metal helmets with the webbing that you see on soldiers during World War II. They have pale cheeks, and the sharp bones in their faces stick out because they haven't had enough to eat.

I don't understand what's happening. I keep trying to back away from the group. But as I move, they move, too, closing a little more of the distance between us with each step. My heart's racing, and I'm afraid they can hear it, that maybe that's what keeps them coming toward me.

It's like they're playing a game, but I don't know the rules and am pretty sure they're dead.

They look raw and hungry. Some of them put their hands up to their open mouths like they're trying to eat the air. They maintain a sad row, some of them saying through their fingers that they're on a secret mission, and I tell them they don't make any sense.

But the words we're saying aren't real words, they're in my head and inside their heads too. Somehow, I understand them even though there's no sounds my ears can hear. That's the scariest part.

And then my father is with them, dressed in a dark-blue old-fashioned officer's uniform, like what they wear in the old Westerns. The soldiers perk up when he arrives, throwing their shoulders back.

Dad says it's time to get to work, they've been lazy since he's been away. He is their general, there to whip them into shape.

He leads the boys through drills, thumping a long staff up and down on the ground to keep time. The ones in the tricorn hats pull little flutes from their coats and play a tune that doesn't make any sound, but we all hear it anyway.

There's one with a drum, too, who rat-a-tats the beat they march to. The General shouts to them about poetry and how he's got a warm grave waiting for each of them if they're only willing to fight for his right to keep his youngest son, me, in chains.

I'm a traitor to their glorious cause, he tells them; if I'm not subdued soon, every son will think he has the right to question his father.

The boys come to grab me. I can hear them with my ears as well as in my head. Dad laughs and eggs them on.

I back away from their fingers, which have turned into those of skeletons, yelling for my mother, though I know she won't hear me and won't come. They nearly grab me, but at the last moment a dark shadow comes from above. It becomes a wall between us.

A voice says, "Don't you harm a hair on his head. And stay away from that old general. He is a selfish bastard through and through." Like what Ade said back home.

The solider boys mumble and turn away. Dad gestures wildly behind them, but I don't know what he wants them to do.

The shadow comes around me like a warm blanket. Friendly. I smell both summer and Christmas at once. I breathe and feel a little less alone.

"What are you?" I ask. But it doesn't answer.

"Little brother," it says instead, "that was a funny trick you played on the funeral man."

Remy

SATURDAY 11:30 P.M.

"Bring your things," Mom says. I follow her down the path of pavers to the front porch. "Just don't let the dog out."

The house looms in front of me, not entirely unfriendly but not comfortable either. Little electric candles burn in a few of the upstairs windows, but in the middle (Ade's old room), the windows are dark. It reminds me of a kid missing a tooth, a jack-o'-lantern grin.

The stories I could tell about this place—they'd drive you to laughter, could break your heart. Coming home like this, late at night on the eve of the funeral, breaks mine.

It's a rambling old farmhouse with a wide porch, four bedrooms, and a winding brown creek that runs slowly behind it, down beyond our old shed. There was a fire here when I was five; half the upstairs had to be torn out and replaced. The gathering at the house after my father's service tomorrow will be the second such event here. The first was twenty years ago, for my brother. I barely remember it.

I have my right hand on the railing as I go up the six steps to the porch. My mother reaches out and opens the front door.

I pause a moment and stand just outside the threshold. I breathe; I shudder; I go through the door.

I'm so tired my eyes hurt. It's been days since I've slept more than a couple of hours at a shot; I don't expect anything different tonight. I have to be up tomorrow morning by 6:30. I promised Ella I'd help her run errands for the party, which I don't like calling a party, but *gathering* sounds wrong too. There's no good word for what we're doing here, burying him; he wasn't even an old man. Last month, on his birthday, my father was fifty-seven years old.

The service starts at eleven. And that's where I will give the eulogy.

Once we're inside, door solidly closed behind us so that Mr. Darcy doesn't get out, I finally get a good look at my mother. She's wearing her old pajamas that one of us bought her.

"Late night for you, isn't it?" I ask. I didn't expect that she'd still be up, waiting for me. She goes to bed before ten these days, wakes up early to walk the dog, Mr. Darcy, who she got when I left for college. She still has the same job she's had since Dad left, working behind the counter at the pharmacy my grandfather, the Admiral, took over after he retired from the navy. The Admiral was my father's father—he made sure Mom had a job because of the "shameful" way Dad acted about the divorce. That, and the Admiral always liked my mother. It's hard not to.

I don't know where Mr. Darcy is right now; he's a stupid, awkwardly balanced German shepherd. Mr. Darcy isn't a bad dog; he's just not a good one. He's too excitable, too interested in people, too much one thing and not enough of another. My mother loves him dearly and says he keeps her young. She cooks him rice and scrambled eggs each night for dinner.

"You're here," she says. She can't help it, she's smiling a little, having me home. I don't get to Harrington often these days, traveling for some assignment or another. It's a strange thing that's happened since I was nominated for the Kelley award. Namely, nothing's happened at all. I hoped I'd be offered a permanent position at a smaller publication thanks to the publicity, but instead I've carried on the same as always—picking up freelance opportunities where I find them. The quality and frequency of the assignments have risen, but I still spend most of my time finishing one thing while scouting for another.

I know everybody expects big things from me, but I can already feel myself burning out on this wandering kind of life. I spend all my time writing assignments for other people so I can pay rent on an apartment I barely spend any time in. I was thinking, before last Tuesday, that I wanted to have a serious conversation with my father about getting out of the industry altogether.

I would like to quit the thing I'm good at, but this isn't something I'm allowed to do. He'd have told me I was crazy for thinking of it. He'd always hoped at least one of us would become a writer, like him. I've always been a little surprised it ended up being me. Jack's the one with the best stories.

"I am here," I say. "Why are you here? Downstairs, I mean."

"You look so tall, do you know that?" she says, not answering my question.

"I've been the same height since I was a senior in high school," I say. "Maybe I just look tall because you're particularly short tonight."

"How was your flight?" Sometimes talking to her is like holding two entirely different conversations at once.

"It was fine. Didn't get in until an hour later than it should have."

She nods, then comes and hugs me tightly. "Oh, my boy," she says. Her head is pressed tight against my chest; she's pinning herself to me hard as she can. "Oh, I'm glad you're home now."

I clear my throat, hug her with my free arm. After an even tighter squeeze, she releases me. I look at her in front of me: her gray hair, her nighttime glasses that went out of style years ago. (Why wear the nice ones at night when you're lying around watching TV? she always says. They just get bent if you do that). Looking at her makes me want to cry, so I turn my face away.

"I put you in Adrian's room," she says. "I know that's where you like to sleep when you're home."

"Please," I say softly. "Please, you can go to bed now."

"Have you heard from Jack?" she says.

She moves into the living room and sits down. "Here, come sit by me on the couch." She pats a spot next to her. I obey like a six-year-old. I'm grateful for the chance to get off my feet. I really am so tired. So close to breaking.

Sitting close, Mom's eyes are swollen and red rimmed, same as my own. Her hair is sticking up in some places, tamped down in others. She looks unkempt and yet the very image of home. How many nights I've spent sitting on this same couch next to her, watching television—waiting for Jack to come home.

She's up because she's keeping vigil for him. For Jack. But maybe for my dad too.

"He's supposed to come here tonight?" I ask, closing my eyes and leaning my head against the back of the couch.

"I'm not sure," she says. I feel her small, warm hand patting me on the knee.

"Did you call Ella or Ade to see if they heard from him?"

"No," she answers. "I just thought you might have."

I shake my head. "He'll be fine. He'll show up eventually, or he'll get a hotel room. Don't worry about it."

"I'm not worried," she says softly. "Not worried in the way you're thinking."

"Then what?"

"It's just," she starts, "it's just, I wish he didn't have to be alone tonight."

"How do you know he's alone?"

"Because," she answers, "you know as well as I do, if he's not with us, then he's alone." She's right—when has Jackson ever sought out the company of others voluntarily? He's always moved on a parallel path to the rest of the world. He can see what we're up to but never ventures across the deep divide he imposes on himself.

"Do you want me to take your car out and look for him?" I ask, not fully thinking it through; it's not like it was when Jack was young, still living here. There's no guarantee he's even in town. Yet I feel like we should go looking, calling his name in the night. To try to bring him home, if we can. To find him, even if he doesn't want to be found.

"No, I don't think so. He'll come when he comes. I just wish he'd—"

"Be different than he is," I finish, opening my eyes.

She smiles at me with her soft smile. My mother has many smiles. I don't know if all mothers do. Mine has a hard-looking one that happens when she laughs at a joke in public, a shy one that she flashes when someone shares their gossip, and a soft one that I've only ever seen her use in this house, looking at one of us.

I feel a great pity for her because she had a husband and has raised a son who did and does not want her kind of love—but that's what she gives. To not accept it is to commit a great crime against her. Against our family, against love itself. I'm angry at Jack for it, and for my father dying on a concrete floor thousands of miles from us, and for the way I thought that she'd stayed up just for me. But obviously it's Jack she's concerned over—you always worry most over the one who strays the furthest. She loves me, loves all of us, but it's Jack she keeps a weather eye out for tonight.

There's pity in me, too, for Jack—maybe even for my father. How hard is it to suffer under the terrible affliction of someone else's love? How very tired it must make you, to run from it every day of your life. How there must be no real respite, always afraid that it'll catch up with you.

"You are such a good man," she says, putting her head on my shoulder. She wraps her arms around my chest, snaking one behind my back, between me and the couch. "You are so good, and this is a terrible thing bringing you home."

I put my own arm around her, kiss her on the crown of her head. We're quiet like that for a long time, listening to the house and the night outside, waiting for Jack to come in, waiting for something neither of us can name.

CHAPTER SEVEN

Adrian

SUNDAY 2:17 A.M.

Everett and I have to catch a very late flight because I didn't want to leave Liv alone with Adam any longer than I had to. We won't get the chance to sleep before the service; we'll go straight from the airport to the church, practically.

After the Mass, after the burial, we'll all go back to my mother's house. I couldn't find a suitable venue last minute, over the phone, that would be both private and big enough for all of us. My mother offered her home, and I took her up on it. Not thinking what it meant, her hosting his funeral afterparty. How it might feel from her perspective.

I don't know what's wrong with Adam, exactly. Doctors are concerned; numbers are being tallied. The very nature of his blood and body are being qualified. I'm terrified of how they might come up wanting.

Liv's father is coming in from California, but he's driving and won't make it for another day, at least. Her sister is in

Argentina on vacation and couldn't be reached. The only one I could call was Vincent—who, right now, is crossing the country in the opposite direction we are. He'll sit by Liv in the hospital just the way I would if I could be there.

I've decided to bring Rett along to Pennsylvania because his mother can't be distracted by him. I've also brought him because he'll need closure. But really, I'm bringing him because I'm selfish and need to have some connection to home, even if it's through a small, unreliable boy who I can't quite trust knows how to behave in a church.

I have to go to the funeral because it doesn't feel right to ship my father to Harrington without some kind of escort. Rett and I will be his honor guard, though no one knows what we're doing but us. His body isn't even on our flight. He was shipped separately on a cargo plane a day ago, collected (as I was notified) by a representative of Graumel's Funeral Services on the Harrington side.

Rett doesn't understand that the body's been shipped apart from us. He told two different families while we were waiting in line at the security checkpoint that his papa will be on the same plane as we are. How nice, they said, until Rett let them know that Papa was dead in a box and would be riding right next to their luggage.

Luckily, both families went toward a different gate than we did.

Once on the plane, I give him the window seat, ask him to look out the window and tell me what he sees.

"Nothing, Dad," he says, over and over. "Just blue clouds." It's night, though, so I don't know what clouds he's talking about. It's black out the window, so dark you can't even see the wing of the plane except for the little lights along its edge. Eventually, he falls asleep.

I touch him, his face, his straight button nose just like his mother's. His cheeks, dimpled when he smiles, like my sister's did when she was little. I want to remember him like this always. Before he sees what we're headed toward, all of us.

He knows what will happen: the coffin, the church service, the burial, the gathering after it. Rett has been crying, on and off, for days. I've been learning how to say goodbye to my father since the day I was born. Everett, though, not so.

He brings in his suitcase a picture he drew for Papa. He wants to know if it would be okay if he left it.

"You know, Dad," he said when we were waiting at the gate to begin boarding, "in Papa's hand. So he could look at it if he wanted to."

"You can," I answered. "You can leave anything you'd like with him. That's a kind thing. You're gold."

A flash of concern passed over him. I took his hand in mine.

"Rett, what's wrong? Are you okay? Do you feel sick?" I said, looking into his eyes as if that would help me divine what was happening in his head.

"No, Daddy. No, I'm okay."

"What're you thinking, then?"

He took a breath and pulled his eyes away, looked down at his feet like what he wanted to say made him feel ashamed.

In that moment I wanted to pull him toward me, take away the thing that brought trouble skirting across his face. But you can't do that. No matter how much it might hurt him, you can't take the ache from your son—even though he is young, even though he's buried in it, no matter how much you love him, no matter how hard you wish you could.

So, I held his hand and watched him hurt.

"Dad," he said, "Daddy, I want to give the picture to Papa. Like I said."

"That's fine. Just like you said."

"But I don't want to touch him."

I remembered a funeral for a boy when I was young. How I loved him but I didn't want to touch his face. Because he had died, and even though I knew touching wouldn't hurt me, I was afraid.

"That's fine, Everett. That's okay." I paused, thinking that I didn't want to touch my father's body either, really.

"I'll do it for you. You can just stand back and watch. I'll put it in his hand."

Next to me, Rett wakes up.

"Dad," he says, "it's still dark out. Why am I awake when it's still dark out?"

"Sleep, son."

He does for a while, and he wakes again.

"Daddy, this time I dreamed."

"Mmm?" I mouth, unwilling to open my eyes. There must be a word that means tireder than tired. I just can't call it up. I'm working up a pounding headache.

"I dreamed there was a little boy, but bigger than me. He could fly."

Of course he can. We're on a damned plane, Rett.

"The boy was talking to Papa, and Papa said to say he wasn't happy with the way you were treating him. How it was very uncomfortable in the box."

"Ah, okay."

"The little boy said walls will fall now. Doors are opening."

"This boy sounds very chatty."

"He says he's been banging and banging but you and Jack won't let him in."

"Hmm."

"Dad, does he mean Uncle Jack?"

"Rett," I say, "please, please be quiet."

"The boy said you'd say that," he whispers. I open my eye a crack and look at him, his chin jutting out, a glum expression on his face.

I put my hand on his head, draw him close. But Rett pulls away, looks out his window. "I don't want to sleep anymore," he says.

"So don't. I don't care what you do." I don't mean to snap at him, but I can't help it.

I close my eyes again, wondering what kind of stress Rett must be under to be acting the way he is. I realize, with a creeping feeling, that I don't like his dream. I don't want him sleeping, either.

CHAPTER EIGHT

Calvin

LAST TUESDAY 4:55 P.M.

I had indoor soccer the day it happened. Dad was supposed to get me when practice was over. But he wasn't there. He's missed so much stuff lately, and even though I know that means he's working on new poems (which makes him happy), it still bothers me.

Bothered me, I need to say now. He is past and passed. I'm still trying to figure out how to talk about him.

I stood around outside for a while, playing on my phone and texting Dad and Mom and Ade and Liv, too, because I figured somebody's messages must have gotten crossed and they'd just all thought someone else would get me.

At least it wasn't raining like the day before. Ade's car was still parked outside my house that morning. Maybe he was just picking up his car, and then he'd be here to get me soon.

There were still a few kids there even a half hour after practice let out, but soon enough they were all picked up or walked off toward home and I was left alone. I started getting stressed.

I paced around my gym bag, which I'd thrown down on the ground, not sure what to do next. I couldn't walk home because we live across town.

Finally, I called my friend Jon, since nobody was answering. He picked up, said he'd give his older brother the heads up to come pick me up. I got home from practice late, probably around six. The brother dropped me off without waiting to see if I made it inside.

Ade's car was gone from the street in front of the house. There weren't any lights on inside, but I tried the front door without thinking too much about it. It was unlocked, but nobody was around. I called out to them, then made myself a snack and flipped on the TV. I was still in my workout stuff, but I didn't feel like changing. Mom doesn't like when I do that—she says I get the cushions sweaty, and they smell. She wasn't there, though, so I did what I wanted.

I watched TV for a while and then it was getting kind of late. When it got to be after seven o'clock and no one had come home yet, I didn't know what to do. I tried calling Dad's phone again.

Dad's phone rang and rang. After a while I realized that I was hearing it ringing from somewhere in the house. It sounded far away, even though Dad had horrible hearing, so he always had it turned up way louder than anyone else's phone would be.

I kept calling it so I could at least find where in the house he'd left it by mistake. I walked all around the upstairs and the downstairs, calling his phone with mine and listening for his ringtone.

Eventually I opened the garage door, thinking maybe he went out to work on the boat a little bit before he left for his meeting. I couldn't remember anybody saying he had a meeting, but that's what it must have been and just nobody told me or remembered to write a note.

I didn't know where Mom was either, but if she thought Dad was going to be home to have dinner with me, she might have gone out or maybe gone shopping for groceries. She might even be at the meeting with Dad because sometimes Larson has faculty meetings with parties after them—receptions, I mean.

A reception didn't explain why no one answered at Ade's. I was more frustrated than worried.

But when I tracked Dad's phone to the garage, when I saw our boat lying off its worktable, which is what we call the two sawhorses that it sits propped on, one at each end, ones we cut notches into so it cradles the boat perfectly, the bottom cushioned by soft old bath towels so the horses didn't scratch the bottom of the hull and wreck the sanding we'd do, and eventually the stain we wanted to put on it—when I saw the boat askew, the back half still leaning on the worktable but the front nose down on the concrete floor, I began to feel afraid.

I reached around the doorframe into the dark garage, flipped the light on so I could see better. The boat was definitely disturbed, and on the floor by the nose there was his phone, some sandpaper bits he probably was using earlier, and a dark spot on the concrete that I couldn't see well from where I was standing because the boat and its shadow blocked it.

The TV in the living room was still loud behind me. I could hear the news coming on. They were talking about the weather, someone local who'd been cured of a disease, a guy who'd been at the international space station for nine months already and who made YouTube videos to pass his time.

I didn't do anything for a few minutes, just had my phone in one hand and the other hanging at my side, listening to the news. I didn't want to walk over to look closer at the boat in case it was ruined. We'd worked so hard on it for so long.

I didn't want to know why his phone was lying there like that, or if he'd knocked the boat over, why he didn't just pick it back up to put it right again. Because the boat for him wasn't that heavy. I couldn't move it myself, but Dad could.

There was a smell in the garage, too. Like somebody'd thrown up, and the afternoon had gotten too hot and things started cooking. But also like a dirty bathroom someone had been sick in from the other end, and there was more to it, too. A thick, layered kind of smell that eventually made me shut the door tight and step back inside. It was a bloody smell, I remember thinking later, once I knew.

I shut the garage door and called all the phones again except Dad's. I didn't know what else I was supposed to do. I thought about the neighbors and who might know what was going on. I didn't want to have to ask anybody, especially the Walkers. But Mrs. Walker is my mom's closest friend in our neighborhood, and she'd be the one who might know if something was wrong, and what to do about it.

I didn't want to go to their house. Their daughter Ashley is a few years older than me, and we were friendly when we were little but now all she does is text her boyfriend.

But nobody answered their phones even though I knew Liv would be home with the little boys at that time of night, especially because Adam's been sick. And there was the boat, that mess on the concrete, the smell. It was getting past dark, too.

I put my shoes on, grabbed my coat. I left by the front door, cut across our yard, and went up to the Walkers' house. There were a bunch of lights on inside. As I went up their steps, their porch light flicked on, and suddenly I was lit up. I saw Ashley looking at me from the little window in the door. I watched her turn her face away. I figured she was telling her mom who was there and would open the door and let me in.

But she stepped back, and I was left standing there again, feeling stupid and wishing that I'd just stayed at home and waited for them to get back from the reception. Then there were footsteps and the doorknob turning, and there was Mrs. Walker with a dishtowel in her hand. She smiled at me and looked very relieved. That confused me.

"Oh-I-am-so-glad-to-see-you-Cal-I-was-hoping-she'd-send-you-over-to-let-us-know-what-was-going-on-how-is-your-daddy-doing?" she said in one long breath, so that by the end she had almost run out of steam. Her last few words were quiet and harder to hear.

"Hey, my mom's—"

"Come in here, it's cold out tonight," she said, reaching to pull me in by my shoulder. I stumbled a little bit over the step up into their house, but once I was inside and she'd closed the door behind us, I realized she was right and that it had gotten cold out. I was glad to be inside a house full of people.

"What did your mother say?" Mrs. Walker said, turning around to look at me closer. "I didn't want to call her and be a bother, especially after all the sirens going earlier."

"I don't know what she said. I haven't talked to her."

"She must have said some—wait, you haven't talked to her?" She looked confused.

"I got home and no one was there."

"Cal, I don't understand. You got home from where?"

I started to tell her about practice, but then realized I still didn't know where my parents were. "Mrs. Walker, what'd you say about my dad? And sirens?"

Mrs. Walker looked at me carefully, like she couldn't tell if I was telling the truth or not, and she didn't take her eyes off mine. She lowered her voice then, threw her dishtowel she was still holding on the ground behind her, and took me by both shoulders with her hands.

"You asked me about your father," she said, her voice measured and tense and quiet. "I thought your mom sent you over here. But that's not the case?"

I nodded again. Began to feel sick in my stomach. Something happened. Something happened and no one remembered to tell me. This was bad.

"Okay," Mrs. Walker said. "Can you tell me what's happening? It's okay for you to come here anytime, by the way, but can you tell me why you're here tonight?"

"Because no one is home." I sounded very young. She tightened her grip on my shoulders, kept looking at me steadily in the eye.

"No one is home now, or no one's been home at all?"

"At all. I got home and no one was there, and I called everybody."

"No one left you a note? Did you expect them to be home tonight, Calvin?"

"I guess there was a meeting they went to and no one left me a note to say it, but no one answered their phones. And Dad's phone is in the garage. And the lights were off. It got dark."

"All right. Did you call your brother?"

"Yeah, and Liv, and no one answered. Neither does Mom. I found his phone in the garage by the noise and our boat was on the ground, half of it was. Did something happ—I think something happened in my garage, maybe."

She held me at arm's length, then leaned in and kissed my forehead. I didn't know why she did it because she's never been that nice to me, but when she leaned back, I started to cry.

"Let's have you come in and eat something, okay? Do you like pizza, Cal? What do you like on it?"

"Just plain," I said. She put her arm around me and led me into the kitchen, where Ashley was sitting at the table with a pizza box in front of her. I rubbed at my eyes because I didn't want to be caught crying.

"Ash," Mrs. Walker said, "get Calvin a plate and sit with him while he eats, please."

"Fine," she said like she was annoyed, but she got me a plate and put two pieces of pizza on it.

"Is it too cold? Do you want me to heat for you?" Mrs. Walker asked.

"No," I said, even though it was.

"You both just sit here and finish your dinner. I'll go over to your house, Calvin, just to see what's up. Is that okay with you?"

"Yeah. I left the front door unlocked by accident, I think."

"All the better for me," she said. "Make sure you eat, please. Ash, pop it in the microwave for him. It's been sitting there for almost an hour."

Mrs. Walker left the kitchen. After the pizza was heated up, it was actually pretty good. I ate three pieces and then a cupcake. Ashley and I talked a little, but I don't remember about what. Mrs. Walker came back holding my mother's address book, which she must have gotten from our house. "It's okay, Cal. I tried your mother and father, and I peeked my head in the garage and saw his phone was there. I just left it for now. I didn't want to mess your boat up."

She came over and sat at the table with us, across from Ashley, next to me. She put the address book down.

"I know Adrian's number, but he didn't answer either. I'd like to call one of your other brothers or your sister, if that's okay. Can you find their numbers for me in here? I would have done it at your house, but I didn't bring my cell over and I cannot for the life of me read your mother's handwriting."

"Yeah," I said, paging through the book. "Your best bet is to call Ella, I guess. She's 484-672-3373. That's Jack's number there, but he doesn't really talk to us. And I don't know if Remy's still on a trip or not."

"Thank you. Just give me a moment to call—"

"But can you tell me what happened to my dad? What you know, at least?" She looked at me, her eyes gone soft.

"Earlier this afternoon, I was walking our dog, and I saw an ambulance in your driveway, sweetheart. Your mother was getting ready to follow it in the car."

"What? I don't—"

"She yelled to me across the lawn, it was hard to hear because there was a lot happening with the EMTs, but she shouted something was up with James, she'd come home and found him in the garage. They were going to the hospital, she was going to go in her car."

"The hospital?"

"I didn't get very close because the dog was going nuts, but I yelled back what about you, and she said something about basketball tonight and then the ambulance and the car were pulling out."

"Basketball ended two months ago," I whispered. "It's indoor soccer now. Mom knows that."

"I didn't know that, otherwise I'd have come over and gotten you right away. When you came over here tonight, I thought your mom sent you to tell me what happened, since I'd seen her earlier."

"Can I see my dad?"

"Let me call your sister, and let me call the hospital. Then I will take you wherever you want to go. I'm so sorry for the confusion. But we'll sort it out. Your dad is okay." She got up from the table. I could hear her speaking quietly in the other room. Ashley looked at me with sad eyes and asked if I wanted any more pizza. I shook my head and looked at my hands spread out on the table. I pushed them into it hard so they would stop shaking, but it didn't help.

Mrs. Walker came in again and looked to Ashley, saying that her dad was on his way home. Ashley nodded and as we both stood from the table Mrs. Walker handed me my jacket.

"What did they say?" I asked as Mrs. Walker and I went out into their garage, which looks a lot like ours. We got into her car. I climbed in the front seat and buckled my belt, and then she said, "Your dad is at the hospital but they won't tell me any more than that. We need to get down there. Your sister didn't answer."

Neither of us talked much on the drive downtown. The hospital looked like the sinking hulk of a ship, the way it rose up in the dark and was lit in an eerie way, mostly from the inside. Like the lights would keep burning forever, even after it had gone all the way beneath the water.

We parked near the main entrance for the emergency room because that's where Mrs. Walker figured they'd taken my dad. It can take forever to get seen in the ER, she said, and you aren't supposed to have your phone on in there. People used to say the cell signals would interfere with the medical machines, but that's not really the case—it's just that it's courteous to not be on your phone while people are sick and in pain nearby you. So, the fact that no one answered our calls was a good thing because it meant he was still waiting to be seen. Because they take the sickest people first, she said.

I stood at the entrance, my nose full of the garage smell and my heart pounding away in my chest like a machine gun. Mrs. Walker took my right hand in hers, smiled, and then we walked in together.

There was a nurse at the front desk inside. Mrs. Walker and I went up and she asked the nurse if James Gable had been admitted yet, or if they were still waiting to do so. This was his son, she said, pointing at me; she'd brought me in to see him.

The nurse asked us to wait a minute, and we stepped aside so someone else with an arm that looked badly broken could be taken back into the area where they decide how fast to treat you—triage, Mrs. Walker called it. After that guy was taken care of, the nurse pulled up something on the computer and waved to Mrs. Walker to come over and talk to her. By that time, I'd sat down and was holding a magazine, so I stayed put. I heard, though, that Mrs. Walker said he'd been brought in by ambulance this afternoon, yes, and his wife would have been with him, Emily Gable. Yes, she thought he was fifty-seven years old. Yes, another son, an adult, might also be with him by now. She thought maybe the patient had taken a fall in his garage earlier that day, so it might be a possible head or neck injury.

Then she said the word *seizure*. I leaned forward in my chair, dropping the magazine to the ground beside my feet. "Could it have been a seizure, maybe?" Mrs. Walker asked. "Could he be in some other area of the hospital because of something like that? The ICU even?"

The nurse looked at her screen and asked for another minute, which stretched into twenty as she called one person and then another, trying to find my dad. Mrs. Walker came back and stood beside me, and we just waited. There were only a few other people in the waiting room—one who was holding a plastic trash can and looked like she was ready to throw up.

Finally, the nurse put down the phone, looked at the screen again, and called us both over.

"James Gable was admitted this afternoon around two o'clock to the ICU on the fourth floor. The family is there now," the nurse told us.

"Not all the family," Mrs. Walker said. "How do we get up there?"

"How old is the boy?" the nurse asked, looking at me with tired eyes.

"I'm fourteen."

"I'm sorry, no one under eighteen is allowed on that floor after six p.m."

"Then he's eighteen," Mrs. Walker snapped.

"How do we get up there?"

"Nonfamily is also not allowed upstairs after six," the nurse said.

"I'm his goddamned aunt," Mrs. Walker said, "on his mother's side." The nurse gave us a long look, then said, "Last elevator at the end of this hall. Take it to floor four, then follow the corridor around until you get to the set of double doors. Tell the nurse who you're there for, he'll let you in."

"Thank you," Mrs. Walker said in a cold voice. She held my hand tightly, and we walked past the desk where the nurse sat and down the hall. She pushed the button on the elevator, and we stepped inside.

"Calvin, I don't know what things will be like upstairs," she said. "Your dad might be very sick. You need to be prepared for that, okay?" I just looked at her and tried to keep standing up straight.

The elevator dinged, and we were at the fourth floor. Mrs. Walker had her arm around me as we came up to the set of double doors the nurse downstairs told us about. There was a little intercom on the wall with a button, and we didn't know what to do at first. Finally, Mrs. Walker pushed it and brought her face next to it and said, "Hello?"

"Yes?" a voice said through the grill of the speaker. "Can I help you?"

"We're here to visit James Gable, the nurse down at emergency told us to come up? It's his son and his—his sister-in-law."

There was a pause, and then the voice said, "I'll buzz you in. Go to the end of the hall and make a right. That's where those rooms are."

"What rooms?" I whispered as the door buzzed open.

"Just the ones your dad's in," Mrs. Walker said, and she slipped her hand down to the small of my back. "Let's go say hello, huh?"

We walked into the ICU, which wasn't a long hallway but a circle where the rooms were spokes of a wheel with the nurse's station in the middle. All the rooms had curtains for doors, and they were open for the nurses to be able to see in. It was a scary kind of quiet in there, just the sounds of people sleeping and breathing or machines breathing for them, but everything else so quiet you could hear the thrum of the lights if you listened closely. I could see flickering shadows and colors in some of the little rooms, so I thought TVs might be on but with the sound off. *This isn't the part of the hospital where people go to get better*, I remember thinking. *It's where they go to see if they will die or not. There were other places for getting well.*

We walked almost the whole way around the circle, trying to not look into the rooms where people were very sick. At the far side, there was a hall we went down, and part of the way along it there was a small waiting room with some uncomfortable-looking chairs lined up around the sides of it. It was far enough from the main ICU area that you'd be comfortable speaking quietly to another person, at least. There was a TV mounted high on a wall, also on but with the sound muted, and there was a little table in the middle of the room that had some magazines on it. The carpet of the room was that blue you only ever see in buildings where a lot of people will wear it down quickly, like in a motel or school or hospital.

Beyond the little waiting room there were a few more rooms, with people in them I guessed. There wasn't any machine noise coming from the rooms, though, so I thought that this might be where they put people who were ready to go to another floor of the hospital but who didn't have a bed available yet at their destination.

We stopped in the waiting room with the blue carpet. Someone was sitting in there, slumped in one of the chairs, and I guess we thought the person might be able to tell us where to go to find my dad.

I realized quickly, though, that the guy in the chair in that little room with his feet kicked out in front of him, head down nearly to his chest, wearing jeans torn at the knee and an old Larson College sweatshirt, was my brother.

I knew him by his sneakers, by the way his hair stuck out messy on the top of his head like mine does. I knew him by the way his body hung there, nothing holding him up but the chair. I had seen him like that once before, when Liv's grandmother died a few years ago. I saw Adrian there in the waiting room slumped over like somebody'd died, and even then I didn't put it together.

Mrs. Walker and I just stood there, waiting for something to happen. But Ade didn't move right away, and when he did it was like he was underwater. He rolled his head up and looked at us both, then settled his eyes on me. He'd been crying, maybe still was: that maybe the only reason he wasn't heaving was because we'd interrupted him by coming in on his private sadness.

"Who brought you here, Cal?" he said, but his voice sounded muffled, like he had a terrible cold.

"I did," Mrs. Walker answered. "He had to call a friend to bring him home from soccer practice because no one was there to meet him. The house was in disarray. He came to my place, and I saw the ambulance leave earlier from the house, and so I brought him on down to see his—"

"What time is it?" Ade interrupted, looking more awake.

"It's like eight thirty by now," I said.

"What day is it?" he asked.

"Uh, Tuesday," I said. "Why?"

"She said you had practice until seven. Then you were going to sleep over at somebody's house. That we were supposed to let you sleep so you had one more good day under your belt." All in one movement he thrust himself up out of the chair and was on his feet, coming toward us.

"Who said? What?"

"Your mom. She said you were taken care of—"

"You're Adrian, right?" Mrs. Walker said. "We've met at your parents' house. I'm Jenny Walker. I live next door."

"Right," he said. "I remember you."

"Adrian," she said, "can you tell me what's happening here, please? I see you're under great stress, but it's okay, there was a mix-up, Calvin's here now and can see his dad, say goodnight, I'll take him home and have him stay at my house so you don't have to worry about him being alone, and in the morn—"

"He can't," Ade said, his voice suddenly thick with something I didn't understand.

"What can't he do?" Mrs. Walker asked.

"Stay here with him, please?" Ade asked Mrs. Walker, pushing past her and into the hall.

"Please don't let him follow me right now. Keep him here."

"Okay," she said. "Calvin, come with me. Sit down here now." She steered me into the waiting room, put me in a chair and herself in the one next to it. We both just sat there, holding hands, waiting to see what the hell was going on.

"Your son's here," we heard Ade say, to Mom I guessed. "He's here, he's terrified. You said he was taken care of. You said he wasn't going to go home."

"Ade, honey, keep your voice down please—" Liv said. So she was here too.

"What the fuck is me yelling going to do? Wake him up?!"

Mrs. Walker and I were barely breathing, trying to hear what was happening in the room just down the hall from us.

"You let that boy go home to an empty house with blood on the floor! We could have arranged to have someone get him! He could have been here, could have seen him!"

"He had basketball. He's at Nate's house now . . ." I heard Mom answer.

"Emily, he is in the waiting room with your neighbor. Calvin is here."

"No he isn't."

"He is. You think I'd lie?"

"If he is here, get him out. He can't see his dad this way."

"Why not? I saw my brother dead when I was nine. No one forgot to tell *me* it happened."

I closed my eyes. I didn't want to see what came next.

CHAPTER NINE

Jackson

SUNDAY 5:41 A.M.

March is a bad time of year to spend the night in your car. It's nearing 6:00 a.m., but the convenience store I parked in front of is still buttoned up against the night. There's no chance of me getting in to use the bathroom.

My legs are stiff from the long drive, nearly seven hours, down through the Pocono Mountains and then the Schuylkill Valley, old dying coal towns aglow against the thicker dark that comes from the mountains blurring out whatever light might fall from the sad excuse for a moon.

The air is cold. I see my breath. I stumble along behind a dumpster that's housed inside tall wooden fencing. Here's as good a place as any.

I stand pissing. I should have gotten a hotel room. I should have just gone home. My left arm aches terrible in this weather. I try to stretch it, rolling my shoulder in the socket to find the edges of the pain. Once I find it, knotted and sharp, I work on it for a while. Today my arm is all pain, needling and thick, so stiff that to try to move it makes my teeth grind. If I run my hand along my shoulder, I can feel the smooth, straight scar the orthopedic surgeon left me with puckered under my shirt.

I go back to the car, get inside. It's cold and smells bad—closed up and damp, like dirty laundry.

My stomach growls. But I don't want to go to my mother's house. I buckle my seat belt, and turn the opposite direction on the road. I'm heading out of town, not toward it. There's a certain relief in that.

I turn onto another smaller road. It's dark and windy, but around a sharp curve there's a small diner that seems to be open. I pull my car into the lot and am able to get a better look at the sign out front—Schumaker's Pancake Barn. Again, as good a place as any. I put the car in park, turn the engine off. Open the door.

I make my way across the lot, where there's only a few other cars, and go inside.

There's a little lobby, and along the far wall, there are hooks to hang your coat. There's a single dirty denim jacket there. I don't particularly want to hang my own coat next to it.

I take my coat off anyway and hang it over my left forearm, bent as far as it can go at the elbow. It's a trick I picked up a long time ago—hide the damage there with a piece of draped clothing so that maybe it's not the first thing people look at when they meet me. Without my coat, I'm still wearing a hooded sweatshirt and under it is my dress shirt, a tie already looped loose around my neck.

I open the inner door, let it swing closed behind me so it hits me in the back as I move into the dining room.

There's only one other guy there besides me, obviously the owner of the denim jacket that probably has never seen the inside of a washing machine. He's tucking into a big egg and pancake breakfast, playing with his cell phone as he shovels food in with one hand. He doesn't look up as I come in.

There's a girl in here too, the waitress. She seems a little younger than my sister. I imagine them, briefly, as friends: doing their hair together before a school dance, laughing and lowering their voices when someone walks past the bathroom door.

The waitress has on a black apron, blue jeans that look uncomfortably tight, and a plain white T-shirt. Even though she's young and her cheeks are apple full, she looks painfully tired. Her ashy brown hair's piled up messy on the top of her head, with long bits hanging down her back that she didn't catch with her elastic tie.

She smiles, says, "Anywhere you'd like." It takes me a minute to realize that she means I can sit wherever I want.

The restaurant is small, only one room with maybe fifteen tables arranged around it. I choose one off to the side, as far away from Denim Jacket as I can get. I'm close to where the door to the kitchen opens and closes, swinging on a hinge.

I bet this place gets crowded and the kitchen is crazy later in the morning, but right now, all I can see through the little head-height windows in the door are two guys in stained aprons moving around in back, probably getting ready for the breakfast rush. I watch them and am startled when the girl plops a menu down in front of me.

"Hey," she says too loudly, trying to catch my attention.

I look at her and am wholly caught up, for a moment, in her eyes. They are both impossibly young and impossibly old—a hazel color, clear but cold, with little lines at the edges and dark half-moons beneath them. Looking at her this way, I feel like I might be seeing her for who she really is, a girl too tired to be kind but trying hard to be so for the sake of her job.

"Specials are eggs Benedict, and I think we're still doing corned beef. Hang on—"

"We still doing corned beef?!" she yells, turning her head toward the kitchen door.

I stop her quickly, raising my hand like she's the teacher and I want her to call on me. "Just coffee and toast for now, please."

"Sure," she answers, not looking at me, moving through the kitchen door where she yells something I can't understand to the guys in back.

In a minute she brings over a coffee cup, puts it on the table. Goes back, gets the pot of coffee, pours it, and leaves. I look around the room at the folksy decorations, paintings of cows and barns and quilt squares in frames. This place looks like all the restaurants of my childhood mashed into one—we never ate out anywhere nice, just places that were cheap enough for my parents to feed four or five kids without breaking the bank.

I don't see the waitress come out of the kitchen, don't notice her until she's standing across from me.

"Where're you from?" she asks.

"Huh?"

"Where," she says again, "are you from?" She's chewing gum, grinding it between her teeth.

"Why do you want to know?" I realize as soon as I say it how defensive it sounds. I don't mean it to, exactly.

"Just curious, really," she answers, pushing her hair back from her face with the heel of her left hand.

"I'm just passing through," I say, cringing. I sound like I'm in an old Western. "I live in Ohio," I lie.

"Ah," she nods, looking a little sad. Bored, too. She wanted to talk some. "I'll get your toast soon as it's ready."

I nod back, wonder why the hell I said Ohio. I've never been to Ohio in my life. My stomach grumbles again. The waitress is still back in the kitchen, probably talking to the cooks about whatever was on TV last night.

I have a terrible urge to speak, to talk to someone else about why I'm in town. I want to say that it's Sunday and I've known my father's been gone since Tuesday. When I came down Route 61, I tried to call and tell him I was back in town again. I dialed the number without stopping to think that he would not be there to answer. When his voicemail picked up, I heard Calvin say, "This is James Gable. Leave a message, and I'll call you back."

My father said that a hometown was the place you could always go back to. But there's no place here for me. It was taken from me a long time ago, or it was never mine at all.

"Toast's up, Ohio," the waitress says, putting it down in front of me and walking away again before I can say thank you.

Sometimes my father'd read stories out loud about wicked stepmothers, sons who left home to wander for years, girls who disobeyed their fathers and were locked in tall towers with only the mice and the birds for company. The stories ended, always, with a kind of holy resolution, a righting of the natural order of things. Stepmothers grew kind, daughters escaped from their prisons, sons came home to great feasts despite the years they were missing.

No one questions such endings. But they should.

I look at my toast. It's dry and brittle, too dark in some places and not brown enough in others. I close my eyes a moment. I open them again, finding nothing gracious or kind in me for my father. I've looked and looked and come away empty. I want to believe he didn't want things to end like this—but this is just what he was after. A gathering in a town far from his family, held in a place that doesn't want him back but now has to graciously receive him, a final kick to the teeth for the people who loved him and spent their lives trying to give him his particular terrible brand of happiness. My father knew enough about hearts to understand just where you could break them without killing a person completely.

And I love him still, some part of me. The same part that wants me, more than anything, to drive down the side streets in town just to see whose house is still painted the same color. The same part that wants me to call up old friends and see if they'd like to go fish or play tag in the field by the public swimming pool.

I want it, and it's the depth of the wanting that scares me. That I have to guard against. Because in that longing there is hurt and damnation and pain beyond what can be safely handled. There is my father damaging us with his violence and with his leaving, and there is nothing to be done about it except to try to forget. And so I try.

Remember the good; if there is no good, remember nothing.

The waitress puts a napkin down next to me. She drops it by my right hand and scurries behind me. I sense she's watching me. I open my hand slowly, take the napkin. On it there is a phone number for a guy named Tim, an address for the Sacred Heart church downtown, and the words "Celebrate Recovery—12 noon."

I look across the dining room. Denim Jacket is gone now, and the sun has come up fully, streaming in the windows. I didn't realize how long I'd been sitting, just staring at my toast. No wonder she thinks something is wrong. I almost smile.

"Don't be offended, Ohio," she says quietly. I hear her rubber-soled shoes come up behind me. "Can I sit?"

I nod. She pulls out the seat next to me, not across. I try to say with my eyes that I'm not offended at her gesture, not in the least. I actually think her giving me a napkin with the address and time of a twelve-step meeting is sweet, in its way.

"You look rough, is all," she says in a breathy voice. "I don't know where you're coming from or headed to, but if you're in town for more than just breakfast, you should check that meeting out. It's really helped my brother. He's Tim. That's his cell number. He's one of the organizers."

"That meeting won't be going on today," I say. "And I'm not a drunk."

"Okay. I'm not assuming anything," she says quickly, "you just seem like you might—"

"Jackson," I say. "Don't call me Ohio. My name is Jackson." She looks at me uncertainly, biting her lip.

"Jackson," she says. "I like that. Suits you. And the meeting's always at noon on a Sunday, after the last Mass ends."

"Is it?"

"Sure it is." She smiles. "So you need directions to get to the church, or what?"

"I'm not from Ohio."

"Okay?"

"I live in Massachusetts, actually."

She's quiet, watching me.

"What makes you think I need to go to a recovery meeting?" I ask.

Her face turns the slightest red, and she looks around the room, away from me.

"It's okay, I just honestly would like to know."

"Well," she answers, "you look like hell. Like you slept in your car or something."

"That's because I did."

"I just thought somebody there might be able to help you out, that's all."

"Thank you," I say. "It helped your brother, huh?"

"It did," she says. "It really did. Tim was in a bad way, for a long time. He used to—he, well, it just helped him a lot."

"Sounds like it did."

"To get there, you're going to want to take this same road back toward town, Jackson, and then make a right—"

I don't say anything. She bites her lip again.

"Damn, you can't go that way. They're closing Main off today because of a funeral."

I nod.

"We're such a small town that they have to reroute traffic when there's a big funeral. Ever seen such a place?" she says, smiling.

I try to smile back but can't. I know whose funeral.

She keeps on trying to figure out the best way to direct me. I have to cut her off.

"What's your name?"

"Maria."

"Nice to meet you, Maria.

"Same, Jackson. So head down Phillips, I guess, and then—"

"Go right onto Maple, and then another right onto Church."

She looks at me for a second, not sure what to say next.

"You had a GPS app going this whole time?" she finally asks, annoyed.

"No, I grew up here."

"But you're from Massachusetts," she says defensively. I've confused her, and for it I feel terribly sorry.

"Now I am. But I grew up here. I was born in Harrington Community Hospital."

"Me too," she says.

"I guess you were, if you're from around here."

"Well," she says finally. "What brings you home, then, Jackson from Harrington?"

"A funeral." I look away.

"God, I'm so sorry," she says, "giving you the meeting info when you're here for—"

"It's okay. Don't worry. You were kind."

"Who died?" she asks, wringing her hands together so that her knuckles turn white.

"My dad."

"Your dad," she says slowly, like she's thinking about something she wishes she wasn't. "My dad died, too. When Tim and I were little."

"What happened?"

"Car accident." Maria looks around the room. I want to ask her what she's remembering, but I don't have any right to do so.

"Is he the writer or whatever, Gamble?" she says suddenly, her face full of recognition. "Your dad, I mean."

"Gable," I answer. "But, yeah. That's him. Was him."

"I saw it on the news a day or so ago," Maria says. "God, I'm sorry I didn't realize you're his—his kid. His son."

"He made the news, huh? He'd have liked that."

She sits back and looks at me, taking me in. My toast has long gone cold.

"You know that's a pretty big thing here, this funeral?"

I nod. I didn't really consider that part of things.

"There's going to be a lot of important people there. Your dad—he's kind of a big deal."

"I know."

"There's going to be cameras," she says. "Local news but some bigger, too, I bet."

I hadn't thought of that. This is a private grief for me, and I can't imagine the world wanting to take it in at my side. Maybe some locals, but beyond that?

"Can I ask you something that might embarrass you?" she says.

"All yours," I reply.

"Who the hell cut your hair?"

I don't say anything.

"Look," she says, "no offense, but you can't show up there looking like you do." She's right, but what I'm supposed to do about it at this late hour I have no idea. "Do you have better clothes with you? At least something that's not jeans?"

"Yeah, of course I do. I drove all night, though."

"Right," she says absently. Her mind is busy working on other things.

"I have a jacket, too," I add.

"Do you have anywhere to take a shower, clean up?"

I shake my head.

"Shit," she says. "Can you at least find somewhere to shave?"

"Do you have a bathroom here?"

She rolls her eyes. "It's your hair, though, too. It's like a three-year-old hacked at it." She sucks her bottom lip into her mouth, thinking, then shouts toward the kitchen, "Mitch, get out here, can you?"

He comes, wiping his hands on his apron and looks at her. He's younger than I thought he'd be, not much out of his teens. He looks pissed to be called from the kitchen.

"Watch the front for me, please? My friend's sort of messed up here." Mitch grumbles but assents.

"Stay here," Maria says. "Wait, no, go out to your car. Get your good clothes, and your razor if you have one. Meet me at the bathroom, just back there." She stands up, points with one finger to a door I didn't notice that's flat against the wall, close to the swinging kitchen doors.

I nod at her, leave the toast on the table and push my chair back. In a moment I'm outside, then rummaging in the trunk of my car for my overnight bag, my suit jacket and trousers, my good shoes. I hoist it up in my good arm and slam the trunk door down with my bad.

The morning's broken fully now; it's beautiful. The sun's clear and strong, the sky bright and heady. A few clouds strain against the blue of it, but nothing else mars the expanse. I stand there a moment, head tilted back, just looking. There are certain views, sometimes, that are a privilege to see—you're lucky to be there, alive, staring at them. That's what this sky is for a moment.

In another minute, my arm starts to hurt from the weird way I'm clutching the bag and clothes, so I break my gaze and head inside.

Mitch is sitting at my table now, eating my long-cold toast spread with butter and jelly. He looks at me smugly. I'll still have to pay for the food he's eating for me.

I go past him, to where the bathroom door is propped open with a mop bucket. I have a hard time navigating around it and nearly trip as I try to go in.

"Jesus," Maria says, "be careful."

"Sorry," I say, handing her what I've got in my arms. She makes quick work of shaking out the jacket and putting in on a wire hanger she's produced from somewhere in the diner. She hangs it on the back of the door, with my pants. Then she unzips my overnight bag and rummages through until she finds a zip-top bag with my toothbrush and other toiletries. At the bottom, she comes across my electric razor.

She steps out of the bathroom again, which is just a single room, with a door that locks.

In a second she's back, carrying a wooden chair from one of the tables out front.

"Sit here," she says, placing the chair in front of the sink. "Let me see what I can do with you."

I obey.

She undoes her apron. Reties it around my shoulders so I look like I'm wearing a giant bib. I try to not look at myself in the mirror, though I can't help stealing glances at Maria as she hovers behind me, running her hands along her own temples before laying them gently on my shoulders.

"You really do," she says, spidering her fingers across the top of my head, "look terrible." Her fingers're soft and fluttery on my scalp, like the wings of birds might feel.

"Don't tell anybody I'm doing this in here," she says. "I'm probably breaking about a million health codes."

Who would I tell? I sit quietly as she works, running the buzzer across my head again and again, trying to even out all the places I couldn't manage to get on my own.

"I did it a week ago, nearly," I say. Maria jumps slightly, startled by my voice. I've been silent so long it seems she might have forgotten I'm a person, not a mannequin head she's practicing her barbering on. She doesn't say anything, just keeps buzzing and clucking now and again as she goes. Eventually, she says, "Head back," and I comply like a little kid on the first day of school.

She comes around to my left side, runs the razor up and down the length of my neck, around my chin, across my jaw. It feels warm against my skin. She bites her lower lip again as she concentrates. She steps back, comes around to the other side, and gets my right.

Days of stubble litter the apron around my neck, and little bits of hair that she's buzzed fall to the floor around my feet. Some's stuck to her T-shirt, too, but I don't mention it.

"There you go," she says, holding the razor in one hand. She's gotten me everywhere except the upper lip, where a stiff, dark line of hair remains.

"I could give you the Hitler," Maria says to me, smiling. "Or one of those little mustaches old-time Hollywood men used to have."

"Clark Gable," I say. I watch us in the mirror. Maria's hair brushes my cheek as she moves the razor in a quick motion just on the right side, so I have a half mustache remaining on the left.

"This style, we'll call the Jack Gable," she says, motioning at me in the mirror with the buzzer. "Should we keep it?"

I shrug, sending more hair falling to the floor.

"If you weren't going to a funeral, I'd leave you like that." Maria finishes off the task and the final bits of mustache fall to the floor. She clicks the razor off and sets it on the side of the sink.

"I'm going to leave for a few minutes," she says. As she speaks, she unties her apron from my shoulders, shakes it out. A confetti of hair falls everywhere—the floor, the sink, into the toilet. "Wash your face, brush your teeth, and put your good clothes on. Just watch you don't get hair all over you."

Maria leaves, shuts the door quietly behind her. I'm left standing in the bathroom alone. I have a hard time maneuvering around the small space with the chair still there, but I do my best to get my clothes on without creating too much mess.

I wash my face, trying not to meet my own eyes in the mirror. When I do, I see how bloodshot they are, how sick I look. My hair, at least even now, is buzzed so close that I look like a penitential monk. I stand here for a minute, looking and then not looking at myself, until there's a knock on the door.

"Jackson," Maria says, her voice a little muffled, "are you ready?"

I turn the knob, pull the door in toward me.

"You look so much better now," she says. "I'm sorry, by the way, for the napkin thing again."

I tell her not to worry about it, but she still looks like she is, a little.

"It's just, the way you looked, if I'd known what you were home for, I'd have never said." She clears her throat, swallows, tries again. "You just didn't look like you were here for a funeral.

You looked like you'd never been to a funeral in your life before, the way you were dressed."

"I haven't been to one before."

"Are you serious? How old are you?" she says, mouth open a bit in surprise.

"I'm thirty-three."

"Wow," she says. "You've led a charmed life,"

I turn my face down, away from her.

"Oh God," she says softly. "I've said another shitty thing to you today. I'm so sorry."

"It's okay. It's not that people haven't died, it's just I didn't go to their services."

"Ah," she says, because there isn't much else she can say. "Well, let me do you up right for this one."

She asks me to bend backward a little so she can help me get into my jacket. I didn't realize how short she is, how girlish she seems.

"Why are you helping me?" I ask as she fiddles with my tie after the jacket's on. She bites her lip, considering.

"Because," she answers, "I always hoped that someone would help my brother if he needed it."

"Did they?"

"You'd have to ask him," she says. "But, yes, I think along the way, somebody must have. You know, when maybe I couldn't."

"I doubt my sister'd do that for some guy who looked like hell early in the morning."

"You have a sister?"

"A trio of brothers, too."

"That's nice, to have brothers and sisters." She pats me on the chest, smoothing the tie down. "You're all set. Just need to have some breakfast now. Are you close with them, your family?"

"Not really," I say. "With one of them, I was."

"What happened?"

"He died."

"Jesus. Third terrible thing I've said to you so far."

"Not terrible," I say. "You're honest."

We sit down together at the same table where Mitch ate my toast. I put my hand out, palm side up, just looking at it. A moment's hesitation, then Maria takes my hand in hers.

"What're you thinking about?" she asks.

"That you're probably going to be the only good part of today."

"Funny," she says, "I was thinking something similar."

We're quiet a while. No patrons come in. It feels like a blessing, in its way.

"What else are you thinking?" she says, still holding tightly to my hand.

"I'm thinking that if I met you somewhere else, on a different day, I'd want to tell you a story."

CHAPTER TEN

Ella

JULY 1994

This was our best day. The one I try to linger in, when I have nothing else.

"Ella," Dad said, "let's fly a kite."

A kite, finally. We were at the park. My brothers played a noisy game with a ball on the big grassy field. Dad and I stood apart from them, still in the parking lot.

Time and the lack of it were things Dad talked about a lot. I don't know where I'll find the time, he'd say, to take Jack for new shoes or to stop at the grocery store after the faculty meeting or to get Lex to the dentist by 3:30.

I tried not to bother him. I knew that time was something he wanted more of and didn't have, so I didn't ask him to spend much on me.

But this Saturday, he wanted to be mine.

"Let's fly a kite," he said again. He grabbed my hand tight.

I looked up, and he was handsome. So tall that his head was

halfway to the clouds. He had a half-grown beard and a red shirt that seemed to be his favorite, since he wore it so often. His eyes were kind. They were dark, like mine. His hair stuck up like bristles on a hairbrush. He leaned down toward me and brought his face against mine. As his head came down, he grew so big that he blocked out the sun.

His skin was warm, rough. I closed my eyes and felt him there, his head against mine. The world became very small around us. He grabbed me around the waist, swung me into the air. The dress I wore swung with me, got tangled up on his head, he threw me so high. Down I came again, him laughing.

"First," he said, "we have to make it. Do you know how to make a kite?" Of course I did. I wriggled away, excited.

"You cut the paper and then you paste it down around the wooden parts and then you tie the ribbon—" I sang, dancing.

"Is that so?" he said, smiling. "Then what?"

I twirled around, doing my best moves for him.

"Hey!" he yelled, "Watch out for cars."

I went faster, threw my arms out, and spun myself right into the ground.

Came down hard on one elbow. I rolled onto my back and looked at it, startled. Blood seeped from a scrape the size of a half-dollar. It hurt, but I didn't want to cry.

"Whoa, baby," he said, crouching down next to me. "Let me see your arm." I held it out to him, squinting my eyes because the sun was in them. He squinted his own eyes, holding me by the wrist as he looked at my elbow.

"Hurt much?" he asked.

I shook my head.

"If I had a scrape like that," he said in a whisper, leaning his head in to share the secret, "I'd be bawling my eyes out."

I couldn't imagine him crying at anything.

"Really I would," he said, nodding. "You'd be so embarrassed. You'd say, 'Oh man, my dad is such a wuss.' I'd cry so much, I'd be howling at the moon."

What he said was so surprising that I didn't notice him brushing dirt off my elbow with a balled-up tissue from his pocket and then clamping the makeshift bandage on there until the bleeding stopped.

"I'd be so loud they'd hear me in England," he continued as he cleaned me up, "they'd hear me in Russia, they'd hear me crying from Mars." I looked at him.

"I don't know where you learned to be so brave," he said. "Look at your arm, now. It's three-quarters healed, and you didn't shed a single tear!"

I nodded.

"Want to see how bloody?"

I nodded again; he handed me the tissue he'd blotted my cut with. It wasn't very gory, after all. But I still felt brave that I'd gotten scraped and didn't cry.

"Your brothers," he whispered, "would have cried like babies if they'd fallen like you did." He stood, righting me onto my feet as he moved. He brushed the seat of his jeans off with his hands, threw the tissue I'd handed back onto the pavement.

"Let's head to the car, kid," he said. "Go look in the back seat. But walk, don't run." He covered the distance to the car in what seemed like two giant steps.

I'd seen nothing special in the back on the drive over, but I ran over anyway.

"What—what—what're we looking for?"

He got to the car before me, reached into his pocket, and pulled out the keys. Opened the door with them, hit that little button on the driver's door that opens all the locks at once.

"Go look," he said, "in the back. Under the blanket."

I opened the back door on the right side and saw, in the wheel well, the blanket we always kept in the car for emergencies. I was so used to seeing it that I didn't notice it was lumpy today. Something was under it. I looked back up at him, his face smiling at me.

"Go on, move it. It's for you." I grabbed the edge of the blanket—plaid, with little tassels sewn along it. I pulled. Dad had turned his back, looking toward the field to see what the boys were doing.

Under the blanket there was a plastic bag with some junk inside it. I pulled it from the car. The contents spilled out on the ground by the tire. I stood by the open car door, looking at what was in the bag. It wasn't big, either, just a plastic grocery bag with the name of a local hardware store printed on it. I just about recognized the letters in the name.

Tipped out on the blacktop was a weird tube with a funny pointed top, and a little scraper thing that also came to a pointy tip. That was it. It must be the paste. For the wooden parts, like in the movie.

Dad was still looking at the boys, and said to me without looking, "What do you think, Ella-girl?" I didn't know what to say.

"Where's the stuff to make the tail?" I finally said. "It has to have a tail."

"Of course a kite has to have a tail—there's blue ribbon and also some pink, I think. You can pick," he said, still looking at the field.

But there was no ribbon. I peeked my head back into the car again, looked around. Had the colorful paper and the ribbon fallen out? Were they in the trunk?

"Daddy, give me the keys. I need the keys."

"Here," he said, as I pulled on his arm. He wasn't looking at me. "I swear to God, if Jack's teasing Lex again I'm going to—"

He took a few steps away from me, toward the field.

"Guys!" he shouted. "Do I need to come over there?!"

I took the keys, went to the back of the car, where I'd seen my parents put the key to open the trunk before.

The car key was heavy, with a plastic top and metal bottom where it slid into the lock. It was hard for me to turn it, but I managed and then put my hands against the trunk. Pushed as hard as I could. I dropped the key on the ground. I couldn't see into the trunk. I needed to, though, to find the ribbons I was supposed to choose between to make the tail.

Dad was nearly across the parking lot now; the boys were yelling at him and each other. I put one foot up on the bumper of the car so I could try to see my way into the trunk better. In doing so, my foot slipped and I went crashing down to the pavement.

I screamed.

Dad turned, ran back toward the car, covered the distance between us in no time flat. He grabbed me around the waist, saying are you okay, are you okay as he set me on my feet, smoothed my hair down and looked me over.

I couldn't breathe through my crying. I balled the hem of my dress up in my hands and held it tightly. The Mary Poppins kids didn't cry when they made their kite. I wailed so loud they'd hear me on whatever planets came after Mars.

"What on earth were you doing?" he said. His voice sounded confused and far away. "What's this junk on the ground?"

"I was getting the ribbon," I whimpered.

"The ribbon's in the back seat with the other stuff to make the kite. I already told you." He stood back from me. I couldn't meet his eye.

"No ribbon in the back, Dad."

"You just didn't look hard enough. And never go in the trunk of the car, you understand? You could get hurt. You could get stuck in there. And I wouldn't know where to find you."

I nodded but didn't look up. Something was wrong. I worried about the kite, but more about making him angry.

"Guys! Jesus Christ, what are you doing?!" he yelled again, toward the field. Jack shouted something back but I couldn't hear what he said.

I moved, quietly as I could, beside Dad. I reached out my hand and grabbed his open one. His other was pressed against his forehead, trying to shield his eyes from the sun.

"Are you very mad?" I asked in a small voice.

"No," he said, "just a little mad. And not at you. Let's get back to the kite, huh?" I nodded, tried to stop sniffling. He smiled and turned his back to the field again.

"What'd you do with the stuff for the kite?" he asked.

"I couldn't find the ribbons."

"No, I said to get it from the back seat."

"I tried to find it in the trunk, I told you already, Dad."

"Where's the bag from the car?"

"Right there on the ground."

"This here tipped out is what was in the car?"

"Yeah," I said, starting to cry again.

"Oh shit," he said. "Damn it—"

"Very mad?" I said quietly.

He looked back at the boys, then at me, weepy, looking at the toes of my sneakers. His face was red, frustrated. He looked sad.

"Not mad, not at you. I brought the wrong stuff, Ellie."

"Huh?"

"This is the wrong damn bag. This is the stuff to fix the caulking in the bathroom—"

"Where's my kite?"

He shook his head, knelt. He put his hand on the side of my face. Looked into my eyes.

"We don't have the right stuff to make it," he said.

"Where's my kite? You said we'd make a kite." I stepped away from him and swatted his hand from my face.

"I know I did, but I messed up and grabbed the wrong bag."

"You said we'd do a kite. You said."

"How am I supposed to make you a kite without—"

"You said."

"I know I did, I'm sorry—"

"But you said, you said that we'd—" My voice rose higher and higher, until I was yelling at him. "You said, you said!"

"Okay," he finally said. "Let's try again."

I wouldn't look at him.

"Very mad?" he asked.

I nodded my head furiously.

"All right. I know you want a movie kite. A Mary Poppins kite. Right?"

I did, but what I couldn't believe was that he remembered the movie part of it.

I didn't look at him still. But I was also fascinated by the fact that he remembered Mary Poppins.

"We can't make a movie kite today, right now. Because I forgot the supplies."

I nodded again.

"We'll do the next best, okay? And we'll do a movie kite on another day."

"What's next best?"

"We'll do a different kite. It's a real weird one, though. An experimental kite, in fact."

I didn't look in his eyes. He was moving around me now, had the hardware store bag in one hand and was rooting around in the trunk with his other hand.

"Hold this," he said. He handed me a ball of twine.

"I need something to cut that with."

"Utility knife?" I said, remembering the one we kept in the garage.

"Nope, that's not here either."

"How you'll cut it?"

"Teeth, I guess," he said, giving me a big shark smile. Then he took the twine from me, pulled a length of it out, and before I knew what he was doing, started sawing at a little spot with his teeth. The twine broke after a moment. He spat on the pavement.

"Why's it experimental, Dad?" I wasn't sure what that word meant. He was busy tying the twine to the handles of the plastic bag.

"Because I had to make it with my teeth."

I watched him, stopped crying. He handed me the end of the twine.

"Take this. When I say, you run that way, away from me."

"Why?"

"To see if we can make it fly. The bag acts like the paper part of the kite. You'll have to run really fast, though."

"Okay."

"Can you run really fast?"

"Yeah, you know I can."

"If it doesn't fly, we'll keep trying, okay?"

I nodded, twine in my hand.

"Now, run!"

I went as fast as I could, ground pounding under my Velcro sneakers, but nothing happened.

"It's okay!" he yelled. "Go again."

I did and then he ran with it, and for a while, twenty minutes maybe, the world was made for us. My plastic bag kite he made with his own teeth.

The boys drifted over eventually, cranky, wanting to go home. We wound the twine up and put the ball into the bag. Dad gave it to me to hold in my lap on the way home.

"In the car, guys," he said, and the boys piled in.

Before I did, though, he knelt and put his forehead against mine again. He smelled like sweat and dead grass.

"I'm sorry we couldn't get your kite to fly," he said. "Very mad?"

"Not mad," I answered.

We went home, and the twine kite went on my bookshelf. I don't remember if we made the movie kite in the end. But I had him, that one day. He asked if I was very mad, and I could say, for honest, that I wasn't.

CHAPTER ELEVEN

Remy

SUNDAY 11:37 A.M.

"I don't really know where to begin," I say.

The crowd waits on wooden pews. They sit unnaturally still. It feels like I'm looking out at benches of mannequins. I'm exhausted. I just need to get through the next few minutes.

The church is packed with people, some stuffed into the vestibule and even the social hall. They've brought in the speakers and small TV sets they use to broadcast the Mass out to those overflow areas on Christmas and Easter. He'd be happy to see he'd filled the place.

My family entered Sacred Heart through a side door so that we wouldn't have to deal with the press of the crowd, some of whom have cameras and even television equipment. The priest, Father Baxter, has made it clear that there will be no recording of any kind during the service.

I close my eyes to try to avoid looking at my father's casket. He's parallel to the altar, not ten feet away from where I now stand. The lid is closed, but I know what he looks like, lying there inside. There's a wreath on top of the box, white funeral lilies stinking up the sanctuary.

"Thank you for coming," I say, opening my eyes.

I reach into my jacket. Pull out the single page, soft from being carried in pockets for the last half decade, and unfold it carefully. My hands are sweating, and I don't want to smudge the pen, ruin the letters that run along the page in orderly rows. His handwriting was always so small, pinched, all capitals, imperative but apologetic, somehow, for the space it took up. Like it needed an excuse for itself. He fit twice the words in the same space another person would.

I smooth the page down, centering it carefully on the stand in front of me. This is where they normally put the Bible during church. I move the small microphone up some so it will catch my voice better. I clear my throat. I look out at the people, and I try again.

"This is a letter my father sent to me five years ago. I've carried it with me most days since then because it was like he was talking to me even when he wasn't. Even when I didn't read it, I knew it was there.

"I scanned it a long time ago, in case I ever lost the one he really wrote me, but I've always liked the real thing better. If you look at it, you can see the places where he pushed hardest with his pen.

"Anyway, I just want to read it to you. Because I think then you'll get why I keep it with me all the time, and why I can't think of anything else to say about him other than this.

"So here we go." I clear my throat, smooth the paper one more time, and begin to read.

> *Remy, Well, you have really done it this time, as I'm*
> *sure you've already realized. Your mother is incensed*

about not only you leaving Kings College but also your not returning home to Harrington and refusing to speak to her on the telephone. I had about fifteen messages from your mother on the old answering machine in my study today.

According to Bea, I'm to strongly encourage you to remediate the situation. She feels you might be able to take a leave of absence from Kings if you can get yourself in front of the appropriate dean pronto, etc. I'm also supposed to advise you that "you can't get anywhere without a college education" and that "you're perilously close to ruining your good prospects."

That being said, I don't give a damn if you go back to Kings or not. Your mother thinks you might be involved with a girl too seriously for a young man of your age and that's why you've left school. Frankly, I'd rather that be the case. At least you'd have some company.

I figured early on that you'd be staying at Jackson's, which is why I'm sending this out the long way through regular post. You may never get it, even. You may choose not to open it if it does arrive. But I wanted to give you the time it takes for me to sit down, pen in hand, and write it to you. I often find the coldness of electronic correspondence to be ineffectual.

So you've left school. It seems everyone has their opinion on it, too, except for you. Your mother is angry, your sister is concerned. Your brother Adrian has his own thoughts, which don't bear repeating. You probably feel like there's almost no one on your side. You're probably right.

If I'm not writing to tell you to go back to school, or to demand that you head home to face your mother, what am I doing? I'm not really sure, truth be told. I feel like there are a thousand things I should have let you know and talked to you about along the way, and any one of them might be the key to fixing this whole mess. I can't recall a goddamn one of them though. That's the way of things, isn't it? You push a thing off so long that you forget the substance of it, you only know that it was important and meant something big.

When you were a little boy, you were the sweetest thing. At night when we put you to sleep, you'd close your eyes right off and be out. You were such an easy-going guy. Your sister would fight bedtime like nothing I've ever seen. She'd ask question after question so I'd have to stand in her doorway for a good half hour just answering. The big boys would laugh and fight with each other in their bedroom, so I'd have to knock on the wall to get them to be quiet. Adrian used to have those night terrors that woke up the whole house with his screaming.

Do you know that I'm fifty-two this year? Fifty-two is an age that I never saw myself at. When I was young, I could imagine myself at twenty, thirty, forty even, and as a very old man with a walker. Never fifty-two though. It's amazing, Remy, how the little things a man used to take for granted start going off. What I mean is how aware I am lately of my knees. When you were a child, I never thought about them. They were there, they bent when I needed them to without complaint. They carried me through my days. Now I wake up some nights with them aching like you wouldn't believe. My back too. Don't take a thing for granted, son. You'll end up missing it before you realize it was even there.

Emily and I got a call from your little brother's teacher last week. She wanted to keep him after school for a few afternoons because he can't stop talking out of turn in class. Emily was very upset about the whole thing. She couldn't believe that Calvin, who is so respectful at home, would act like that. I think she was even embarrassed. She sat downstairs waiting for him at the kitchen table so she could discuss his behavior with him when he came inside from playing. I didn't take part in the conversation. I listened to them talking from my study, heard Calvin begin to cry and say he was sorry to his mother.

I couldn't help it, Remy, I started to laugh. Sometimes I worry about him, you know. Calvin's alone all the time, not like you and the others were, and I think that he might be growing too serious. So it was a relief in a way to hear about him getting in trouble at school. Some mornings when my body's feeling ragged, I think of Calvin at twenty, same as you are now. I'll be old then. I think about you too, of course, and of your brothers and your sister. You in particular.

You went from that sweet boy who fell asleep so easily to a nearly grown man faster that I thought you would. So where is all this leading to? I don't fully know. That's the trick of it, the biggest illusion of all: that your parents know where things are headed. I wonder if you ever thought we knew where we were leading you. I doubt it. What do you even recall of those times when we all lived together in that house? I used to wake up at night with you when you were a baby. I held you, sang you songs even. I don't expect you to remember, of course. I just want you to know it happened.

It might be that there is nothing I can tell you. After all, you have always been the most intuitive of your brothers. You get a sense of a thing before you can see the thing itself. You've always been that way, son, and I wish that you could figure out how to use it to your advantage.

Maybe that's what's happened with you now. Do you feel something coming down the pike toward you? Is that why you had to leave Kings? I wouldn't dare ask you to explain yourself because a person is entitled to his own private struggles and his own pains. If you ever find yourself needing help, of course, you call me.

This is all just an old man's guessing and grabbing at the air. What I wanted to say is that maybe you should come out here to Washington for a while if you need some time to sort out whatever it is that's in your head. We could put you up in Adrian's old room with no trouble at all. Calvin would surely like to have you around. So would Emily. Of course I would too.

The more I try to tell you, the clearer it is that I have almost nothing to say that you don't already know. You were born knowing, I think.

I hope I might hear from you some night soon on the telephone. Your Dad.

"And that's it. That's all I have of him, in the end."

The crowd, all the way to the back of the church, is looking at me. For a moment, I look back at them: smiles on some faces, encouraging me, tears sliding down cheeks. Kleenex balled up in fists, heads nodding slightly, dowdy dress clothes rumpled. Somebody toward the front is sniffling so loudly I can hear them where I stand. The whole church smells like wet wool, and something stale underneath it.

I still try to keep my eyes away from the casket.

"Why are you here?" I say too loudly into the microphone. "What brought you here today?" I surprise myself when my voice booms through the room. I thought I was done talking.

My sister and my brothers are in the front row, Emily clutching Cal's arm like they're standing on the bow of a ship that's about to go under, the ocean a horrifying truth that even in the last seconds seems impossibly far off. Ade slides Everett off his lap, leans forward in the pew. He looks troubled, knitting his eyebrows together and glancing over quickly at Ella, who meets his gaze. I have to look over Dad's box in order to see them, so I try to not do it.

"It's okay," I say, holding up my right hand like I'm about to give an oath. My sister sits back again. Ade leans back too, but he's watching me carefully. I smile broadly, an exaggerated stage grin projected to the very back of the room. I close my jack-o'-lantern mouth and drop my hand to the side of the lectern again, trying to look at ease. "I just—I wanted to say a few words more. Thank you."

Thing is, I don't have anything to say.

I wanted to read the letter, sit back down, and let the priest finish the Mass. I can't make any sense of my thoughts. I'm scared of the way they're coming out of my mouth without me having any idea of what they are beforehand. I'm along for the ride like everyone else in the church.

"I don't think that I'll ever read this thing again," I say running my left hand down the letter still propped in front of me. "My father's letter. The letter from my father." I nod toward the casket. Raise one hand like I'm giving him a toast, though I don't have a glass.

Some of the people in the middle pews shift in their seats.

"Relax, guys. I've always been the good kid. So, anyway. I've been reading," I say, "a lot of Stephen Crane lately. Have you been, maybe? Because it seems to be terribly fitting to me, somehow. Have you read him?"

The encouraging smiles are gone. I avoid looking at my family. Behind me, farther back on the altar, Father Baxter clears his throat. The altar servers, two little girls with their hair pulled back, probably swing their feet under their long red robes.

"I'd like to share something: 'So it came to pass that as he trudged from the place of blood and wrath his soul changed.' Isn't that horrifically apt? Doesn't that talk about all of us?

"I have left the field, Crane says, and will never be the same because of it. It's from *The Red Badge of Courage*, by the way. If you didn't know. But it sounds like Revelation, which is the scary part of the Bible. If you didn't know. You also wouldn't know, but I've got this weirdly specific memory, where the stuff that I read sticks up there in my mind and comes up from time to time.

"Which is why when I first came up here, I nearly began with, 'Friends, Romans, countrymen . . .'—that's Shakespeare, which you probably did know. Antony's speech for Caesar's funeral. 'The good is oft interred with their bones,' you've heard the rest."

I can only imagine the look on Father Baxter's face right now, or Ade's or Ella's.

"So, Stephen Crane's been on my recent reading list. Do you know why? Because my father suggested him, of all things. And I listened, of all things. Now that line, about the blood and the wrath and the terrible way those things change souls, that line's been ricocheting around in my head since last Tuesday."

"Ade! Sit back, please, buddy," I say forcefully because he's starting to get up. There're a few other people in the crowd who're motioning likewise, or looking at each other and questioning with their eyes what's happening.

"Is this how you felt when they sent you away, Ade? This crazy kind of reeling in your head? It might have been. Would you tell me? You might. Except we don't talk about that. So I won't talk about that." I take a deep breath and close my eyes.

"Sorry, sorry," I say, smiling again. My mouth feels funny and Novocain-distorted. I put both my hands out in a gesture that's meant to be inviting, but it looks the opposite. I also don't need to turn my head to know that the priest is shifting uncomfortably in his seat.

"Please forgive me," I try again. "I'm obviously having a hard time with this." Ade settles back halfway into his seat, but won't go any further. He looks at me, expectedly. Hopes I don't go on.

"Stephen Crane was a poet, too. Like my father. Did you know that? About Crane, I mean. He wrote a cycle called *The Black Riders*, which is some of the scariest stuff you'll ever come across.

"This is a long way of telling you why I won't read my father's letter again. Or of me telling myself. Probably more the second, I guess. Even though I love that letter, and really have carried it around with me like a lucky rabbit's foot or something, for years. That part was true. So this letter, I always felt like it showed me the real part of my dad, like a part he wouldn't show other people but he felt I needed to see.

"It's possible, too, that the letter is all him posturing, trying to sound good, hoping that someday I'd share the stupid thing with someone else and they'd comment on his keen mind, his compassionate handling of my terrible situation. Because we all know he did that, spoke to us as though he was recording some vital thought for the ages, rather than just talking.

"Have you ever read any Kerouac? He says, somewhere, that 'one day I'll find the right words, and they will be simple.' Or something like that. But my dad never thought simple words were the right ones. He loved words more than he loved people, I think.

"Crane's got this poem in *Black Riders*, and it doesn't have a title. Doesn't that give you a creepy feeling, when something doesn't have any name to it? Like a ghost. It haunts you all the more because you don't know who it is. The character of it.

"I thought the letter was the character and the measure of my father. But it wasn't. Because nothing is simple with the man, not ever.

"Crane's poem, the untitled one, is scary. Like, end of the world level terrifying. It's one I read recently, a few weeks ago. And it's been echoing around inside me since, howling and getting louder. I might get the words wrong, a little, so go ahead and look it up when you go home if you want. That would be okay. But let me try, let me just try really quick to see if I can share it with you now.

"'In the desert,' it starts, 'I saw a creature, naked' . . . there's another word here, but I don't recall it, anyway . . . 'I saw a creature, / who squatting upon' . . . or on, I don't remember, sorry . . . 'the ground, / held his heart in his hands / and ate of it. / I said, is it good, friend? / It is bitter—bitter, he answered. / But I like it / Because it is bitter / And because it is my heart.'

"Isn't that terrible to imagine? A man so reduced, he eats his own bitter heart and enjoys it because of the poison it carries. There's a point in it, somewhere, about learning to let go of things, I guess, before they consume you. Before you consume you.

"I don't think I understood until just now what it means to be selfish. The vanity of it, eating your own pain. Finding familiar comfort. It's horrible. I hate that my father was the one who wanted me to read it in the first place.

"I never wrote back to him, never answered this letter I read you. I don't know why I didn't, except that I think I sensed that if I did, I'd be giving up something vital about myself. See, he was already eating his own heart. He didn't need mine, too, but he wanted it. To twist and turn it into a thing of art, a poem, to lay claim to something that was never his to take.

"He probably thought that his words never reached me, or if they did, that they didn't matter. He was wrong about that. Most of the time, we're wrong about other people, what we think about them, what we think they think about us.

"But sometimes we're not wrong, either. Sometimes there's a sense you can get of the motives of others and how, even when they seem like the comfort you've wanted all your life, you know somehow that they come from the place of blood and wrath. That's where and what he was, my father. Good God, he was.

"He said I got a sense of a thing before I could see the thing itself. That I could smell blood on the wind before I found the carnage field. He said I didn't need to explain what had happened, why I left school, but that's what he really wanted. I finished school, by the way. The thing I got a sense of, maybe, was him. The badness he carried around inside him. The badness that he ate and tried to make me eat beside him. The badness that tore up our family and fueled his work and his fury.

"So I don't think I will read this letter again. Because I think I have exhausted all it'll ever give me. And I'm just, really, so very tired."

My eyes are clenched shut against tears, but they spill over anyway and land on the letter. I open them again and move in a sudden, quick motion. I grab the letter in both hands, tear it right down the middle.

I gasp at the violence that's gripped me, but I tear again and again until the page is nothing but confetti in my hands. When I'm through, I drop the pieces on the ground around my feet.

I put my head down on the lectern. The wooden stand is hard. I let it prop me up. People must be looking at me, but I don't care. I have just torn up my father on God's own altar, and I feel nothing but empty.

"Can somebody bring me my phone?" I whisper. The microphone picks it up even though my head's down. "I need my phone. I need to delete that letter from my cloud drive. I need my phone, please, can somebody grab my phone?"

I don't know how long I stand, muttering, but eventually someone's hand is on my back, and another hand is on my shoulder. I unclench my fists from the sides of the lectern and raise my head slowly. My sister is standing next to me—I didn't realize she'd come up on the altar. Ade is on my other side. They each put an arm around me. Ella slips her hand into the inside pocket in my jacket, and slides my phone out. It's been in my pocket the whole time, but she's taken it so I can't get to it now.

The people in the audience look at me, faces flushed and blanched and puffy. The priest must be rising to his feet behind us now, shaking his head in disapproval.

My brother and sister move together, pulling me gently backward, away from the lectern, then forward, down the three little steps of the altar. We have to walk around the casket, and I nearly trip on my own feet.

I lean heavily on them, and we do not turn back around and bow to the crucifix on the wall like you're supposed to in a Catholic church. We give Jesus and James both the cold shoulder and slide, a trinity, back into our pew.

CHAPTER TWELVE

Jackson

SUNDAY 12:30 P.M.

"I didn't think you'd be here," I say stupidly. I'm standing in the living room, having just shut the front door as quietly as possible behind me. Even though I didn't expect anybody to be here at the house, I felt like I had to sneak in. That's the sort of thing coming home does to me—makes me feel like I've done something wrong even though I couldn't tell you what.

My mother must have heard the door shut, even though I tried to be silent. She's come into the living room, too, but from the other direction. She'd been in the kitchen, it seems, when I came in.

We look at each other, not speaking or moving, trying to figure out what's going on. She's wearing a black long-sleeved dress, dark tights, no shoes. She doesn't have makeup on; her hair's standing on end like she didn't bother to fix it after she got out of bed this morning. It looks better than mine.

I'm still in my coat, having left my bag in my car. The knot Maria put in my tie's neat, snug against my neck. I feel the heat of the room on the exposed skin of my scalp. I look rangy, exhausted, ill. I saw myself in the mirror at the Pancake Barn, after all.

Mom and I are caught—neither of us is supposed to be here, when the funeral service is going on at the church. We're both expected elsewhere, and each must've thought we'd find the house empty.

What we should do next seems to be beyond either of us.

"Well," she finally says, "it's good to know you've made it safely."

I just nod, then look down at my shoes. The carpet here's been vacuumed recently but around the edges of the room are fine, wiry hairs that must be from the dog that Remy's told me Mom adores. I haven't been here in at least five years. I'm a little ashamed of myself for it.

She doesn't ask me how my drive was, or if I'd like to have something to eat. She stares at me with her mouth open, about to speak but considering her words. I wish she would talk, just to say something to relieve the awful pressure building in my chest.

"I slept in the car," I offer, hands jammed in my pockets. I don't want to look at her, but I flick my eyes up to meet hers and immediately turn away again. She's got a way of looking at me that drills right through, that's like looking directly at the sun in all its intensity.

"You look good for it," she replies, her voice dull. "You look better than a night spent that way." I don't answer, just let my head hang down so I don't have to look my mother in the eyes. I wonder what kind of night she's spent, hope she got some sleep.

A sharp pain flares up behind my eyebrows. It feels like something's banging on the inside of my skull with closed fists. I can't help but to reach up, grind the knuckles of my right hand along my eyes, trying to get it to stop. I clench my teeth and wait for it to pass, hoping that she doesn't notice. I swear my headaches are worse in this house.

"Remy told me you weren't having headaches anymore," she says. I peek open an eye to find her standing with her arms crossed, watching me.

"Are you serious?"

"Obviously I'm serious, Jack. You look like you're in pain. It concerns me."

"It concerns you," I repeat slowly. "I look like I'm in pain. What an observant reflection to make. You're the 'Mother of the Year.' Jesus Christ."

I truly don't want to fight. But she's here when she shouldn't be, and so am I—her presence makes me angry, makes me want to hurt her for being witness to my inability to be a good son. My absence would feel less potent if it wasn't juxtaposed against her own.

So I'll call up what I have to, to make her know she's not a good mother. The things we do to each other are terrible, but they're ours and so there's some kind of pleasure in them, however dark. However bitter and mean.

"That's unkind," she says.

"You're unkind," I reply, keeping my voice even. "And don't talk to Remy about me. He has no idea what he's talking about, anyway."

"I'm just repeating what he said. That your headaches weren't a problem anymore."

"Maybe I have a headache because it's cold out and I spent the night in the car. Maybe I have a headache because I've been dealing with some pretty terrible shit over the last week. Maybe all I wanted to do was come in and lie down and not be bothered about headaches. But then here you are." I shrug my coat off and let it fall to the ground at my feet.

"Jack, you should see a doctor if they're getting bad again—"

"Relax," I say, looking away. I want to stop seeing her, dressed as she is, concerned as she looks. It makes me feel like a boy again.

"I don't mean to be pushy, it's just you know that with your accident, well, you know you have to be careful," she tries again.

"I am careful."

"You might need an MRI. Would your insurance cover that?"

"Please, can we not talk about this? Not today." I'm trying to allow her a way out, to stop talking and leave me alone so I don't loose all the heat inside me on her.

"I'm sorry," she says softly. "I didn't mean to."

"It's fine. Just stop now."

But she stares at me, expectant.

"God, stop looking at me that way. Stop. If I'm still having headaches in a few weeks, I'll call the doctor. I'll get seen. Get off it. Even though I'm not having headaches, really."

An awkward silence follows as I stand in front of her, trying not to rub my eyes. My head still hurts, but that's the last thing she needs to know. She's waving a hand in front of her face, as though she can fan the tears back into her eyes. "I just worry," she says.

"I know. I'll do the MRI if they want it. Even though it won't find anything that can be fixed."

"But at least we'd know where we stand—"

"Jesus, Mom. You do realize that whatever an MRI might find inside my head would just be more residual damage from the accident, right? Nothing that anybody can help, especially so long out."

"I said we didn't need to keep talking about it—"

"But you couldn't let it go. Maybe you stopped talking about it with your words, but you stand there like a wounded animal, asking me about it with that pathetic look on your face. Damn it, please, just leave me alone? Just for a few minutes?"

She takes a shuddering breath. "You seem very tired," she says finally.

"Obviously I'm tired. You think it's an easy drive here? You think it was a good night I had?" I don't mean to sound as hateful as I do, but I can't help the flood of anger rolling through me. My cheeks flush. She takes a step back from me, like she knows I'm fixing for a fight.

Of course she knows I am. That's how we've spent the better part of the last two decades, facing off against each other in this very spot in the living room.

"You could have come home last night."

"But I didn't. Because I knew there'd be bullshit to deal with, you trying to get me to do something or trying to force your way in, or whatever it would be that you'd find to push me on, even though this is literally the worst time to—"

"I was only concerned that you weren't taking care of yourself!"

I laugh in her face. "No one," I say, "has taken care of me, but me, for years. You included. You said 'we'd know where we stand' about the MRI as though you'd be a part of it. Like this is a team thing. Like this is something you get to have a say in."

Her lower lip starts to quiver; I've taken things too far. But if I don't speak the murder in my heart, I'll explode.

"Don't bother with me! Understand this: I'm here today, that's it. Then I'm leaving again. It will be a long time until I come back. And you won't have any idea if I get the damn MRI or not. Because I don't want to tell you. And I don't need one in the first place. My biggest problem's always been my arm, if you even remember." The words hurt coming out.

"I spent last night waiting for *you* to come home, do you know that? What it's like to not have you call, not know what's happening with you? I don't understand where things went wrong between us, Jack. I truly don't. I've always done the best I could for you."

She's right, of course—she's done her best, but sometimes someone's best isn't enough. When Lex died, my father was the one who took responsibility for my recovery; Mom couldn't bear walking into the hospital after she lost him.

I feel angry because, since I was thirteen, I've protected her from what my father'd done, and she's had no idea. I feel despair because in order to do so, I've had to keep myself at arm's length. She doesn't know what it's cost me. And besides, she'd always loved my brother Lex a little more than me, I felt; when he died, he took her heart with him, and there sure as hell wasn't much left over for me.

I could just tell her, right now, about what Lex found that day, what caused the fire in our house, what maybe led to him dying. What led to my dying, keeping my father's secret. He's gone, what harm would it cause him?

But it would still hurt her. And I love her too much to tell her, even now.

"There's so much I could say," I spit, "but I won't. Because I refuse to do this with you. With any of you. This afternoon and then I'm gone. Or maybe I'm leaving right now. It's probably better nobody else sees me, so you can all just be pissed that I didn't show, like you always expect, and then you can sit around and say how I'm just like Dad when he left—"

"That's fine, Jack," she whispers, hugging herself with both arms. "I never meant to make you feel like I—"

"Just because you didn't mean to doesn't mean you didn't."

"If that's how you feel, I'm sorry. I'm going to go upstairs for a while, I think. Give you some time to relax and calm down."

She backs away, turns to head up the steps. She'll go up to her bedroom and cry, then act like nothing happened between us later. I hate the way she pretends things are fine when they aren't.

"Whatever you want. It's not like you're supposed to be somewhere important now, anyway."

With that, she turns back to look at me. Thoughts flicker across her face while she tries to figure out how to respond.

What I want to say is this: If you're here because you were waiting for me, then come and be my mother. If you're here and not at the church because of something to do with my father, then go upstairs, and we'll each tend to our own grief alone. I'll get in the car, won't come back. You'll always wonder if it was you that sent me going, and I'll never say the truth—I left so you don't eventually have to ask me to go.

She steps toward me; I'm a little afraid she'll hit me. But instead, her arms open to make a space for me between them. She doesn't say anything, doesn't cry, just wraps herself around me as hard as she can and settles her graying head against my chest.

I've been holding my breath. As I exhale, I can feel myself relax into her even though I don't want to. Her hands meet behind my back. As she squeezes, I can feel her heart beating, as quick and wild as a caged bird's.

"There is so much in you that's good," she whispers into my shirt. "So much you don't even know." I put my good arm around her, and we stand like this for more minutes than I can count. There're so many things we could say, like *I'm sorry*, or *I'm broken*, or *I've needed you*, but we don't.

After a while she starts to make soft shushing noises. I begin to cry, this time ugly and earnest. My insides are jagged with hurt. I'm afraid my knees might give out. But she holds me up, a quiet spot at the heart of a storm.

Why do we do such terrible things to each other? My father's gone and my mother isn't, and for a short eternity, the space of a breath, I'm grateful for her. We sway a little, like we're dancing, and she's still shushing while I try to slow my breathing. My head rests on top of hers.

She's still got me all wrapped up, not speaking beyond the soft gentle sounds you make toward babies, when the phone rings loudly and startles us apart.

CHAPTER THIRTEEN

Ella

SUNDAY 12:57 P.M.

I drive. Granna is so fragile in the seat next to me. Her walker is in the trunk, but I'm hoping she'll be able to make do with my arm to lean on and a slow pace. I don't know how well her walker would do on the uneven ground of the cemetery.

She wears a purple skirt suit, sensible dark shoes to go with it. Her hair is set in a heaven of white curls. She's gone to the salon to get that done. She normally doesn't pay for such an extravagance. But you make certain compromises for your son's funeral. Her head moves back and forth in a palsy so slight you barely notice. With each little shake, she's refusing what time's done to her, the way it's brought her low and lonely.

She sighs, arranges her hands on top of the pocketbook in her lap. With Granna, it'll never be a purse, always a pocketbook.

"How are you, darling?" she asks Remy in the back seat. His long legs are thrown out across the entire back. Remy hasn't fit comfortably in the back of a sedan since he was sixteen, but he bent himself silently into it when he got to the car after the service. It's easier to put Granna in the front, where she doesn't have to twist as much to get in or out.

"Still here," he answers.

"I think you did a fine job speaking," Granna says. "Your letter was lovely."

"You're probably the only person who thought so."

The cemetery sits high on a hill above Lawrence, a little town thirty miles from Harrington. My grandfather, Conrad, grew up in Lawrence. His own family's buried here on the hill. Mount Mercy, the cemetery's called. I've been here more than a few times, mostly with Granna in the summer to plant geraniums by the headstones of various members of our family, some of which I've never met—but we still hunted for Aunt May's grave, for Elsa Zuber, and for a few others, then wet the plants with water drawn from the old-fashioned pumps scattered around the place.

We'd take extra care with Lex's grave. We'd plant the biggest flower we'd brought by him; I'd leave an old penny in the grass over the place where I guessed his heart was. He'd collected ones from before 1982, the year they started making them primarily out of zinc, with just a thin patina of copper plating on top. You could never say Lex wasn't original.

"It was terrible," Remy says, clearing his throat. "You don't need to try to make me feel better."

"There's nothing to feel bad about," Granna says.

We're at the head of the funeral procession, just behind the hearse. It slows to a stop, and we ease in behind it, a few lengths back. The lanes are narrow and twisty. If I park any closer, they won't be able to unload the thing easily. The coffin.

There's no snow on the ground, but the lawn is brown, dead—probably mostly frozen.

About fifty yards away, there's a small tent set up. Beneath it are some folding chairs. They're lined up at the edge of the grave, but from where we're sitting and where they're positioned, you can't see it. It looks like someone's set up a very badly placed luncheon.

The priest is already standing under the tent; he casts away any dispersions about what this place is and what we'll be doing here. Father Baxter is young compared to most priests, only in his middle forties. He never knew my father but did a passable imitation of acting as though he had. Granna wanted Father Dresden to do the Mass, but he retired years ago.

I put the car in park. Remy undoes his seat belt.

"I hate this," he says. "I just hate this so much."

"I know," Granna says, her soft voice doing its best to soothe him. There is so little we can do for each other in the face of this.

Remy gets out of the car, off in the orbit of his own loss. The door thunks behind him. Granna and I watch as he smooths down his clothes, runs his hands through his hair, jams his hands in his pockets. He stands that way a minute, looking out toward the tent. Then he moves forward, out amid the graves.

"He's in a terrible state," Granna says. "I don't know what to say to him."

"He'll be all right," I say. But I don't know that.

"Oh my," she whispers, closing her eyes. "I never thought this would be so." Granna takes a tissue out of her pocketbook.

"Me either."

"Of course you didn't," she says, patting my leg. "But I thought I was done with this." She dabs at her eyes with her tissue, which for her will always be a Kleenex.

"I don't understand."

"It's just," she says, "it's just that I thought, after Con, I wouldn't have to go to any more of these things."

"Things?"

"Funerals."

I don't know what to say.

"You see," she finishes, "I just, well. Oh, I just figured I'd be the next one to go, Ellie. That's all."

I unbuckle my seat belt, turn to face her. As I move, she takes her hand away and looks down at it.

"My goodness, I forgot to wear the necklace James gave me," she says in a shaky voice.

"We'll find it when I take you home later."

"That's fine," she answers, looking into the back of the hearse directly in front of us. "I do wish we didn't have to stare into that terrible thing. Don't you?"

"Let me move the car, then," I say, reaching to do my seat belt again.

"No, let's just stay right here. Please."

"But I can find a spot that's—that's not looking right into the trunk there."

"No," she says again. "Stay here, but let's close our eyes."

"Are you sure you don't want me to move us? It wouldn't be that much farther for you to walk, I think, if I could get a spot close to the—"

"Ellie," she says quietly, but with emphasis. "Please. We'll shut our eyes, we won't see in, but we'll still be close to him."

I nod but don't understand.

"You see," she says, her voice straining, dabbing at her eyes, "I can't look at it, but I don't want to be far from him. He's still my boy. His mother should be near him." I close my own eyes, trying to keep tears behind them. I reach over and take her hand, hold it as tightly as I can.

"Oh, Granna," I say, because there is nothing else.

"Oh, Ellie," she sighs. "You lovely girl, you wonderful thing." We sit together, her hand in mine, listening to each other breathe.

"Well," Granna finally says. "I keep thinking the strangest things."

"Like what?"

"Odd little bits. What we called him. How he was as a little boy."

"Tell me?" I want her to keep talking so I don't have to open my eyes, see into the hearse.

"Oh, well. When your daddy was little, nobody ever called him Jimmy, or Jim. Con didn't like the nickname. But Nathanial was called Cat almost from the start. Conrad was Con. Your father was always James in our home. That's all he ever went by." Her voice is soft, feathery.

"Far as I know, nobody ever called him anything else," I answer.

"You're right. Almost right, anyway. My own mother, your daddy's grandmother, loved that boy like nothing I'd ever seen. Mother was feverish in the way she adored James. He was named after her own father, too."

"I never knew that."

"Mother called him Jem. That's the name her dad went by, and she loved it, especially because James was so dear to her."

"Like in *To Kill a Mockingbird*."

"That's right, though that character was Jeremy."

"Maybe," I say. "Not the kind of thing I'd remember." Jack and Remy are the readers, ask them, I nearly say. But Jack isn't here; his absence is a burning raw place inside me.

"It was sweet, how his eyes lit up when he heard her say it. It made him special, brought out the best in him. I noticed that. I noticed the way Con spoke to him, too—formal, like he was talking to a grown man even though James was a little boy. There was a terrible distance it forced between them. It worried me.

"I wish I'd told Con to stop it. But I never did." She breathes, steadying herself. "I feel badly about that. But there were certain things you just couldn't say to Con. This was one of them. But I do wish, for James's sake, that I'd been braver about that."

In my mind there is my father, a dark-eyed little boy in a pea-coat and hunter's hat, the kind with earflaps, standing in a grassy field with his father. My father reaching for Conrad's hand. My grandfather stepping forward, away from the boy—the little hand still poised for a moment in the air, then sinking back down to the boy's side, a ruined wish for something that wouldn't come.

Granna takes a shaking breath. "When James was about eleven, we had our hardest winter. Georgia got scarlet fever, Con nearly lost the store. And then, in February, Mother became very ill.

"Oh, Ellie, you never forget what it's like when your own mother dies. She went as sudden as James. Mother called me on a Saturday to let me know she was feeling under the weather. By Tuesday she was in the hospital, and by Friday she'd passed."

"I'm so sorry," I say. "That must have been terrible."

She squeezes my hand harder. "No more terrible than you losing your father."

"I guess."

"James didn't take it well. I couldn't get him to eat, to sleep, had to beg him to go to school, to get out of bed. We had to have the doctor come to the house. He gave James shots, vitamins, all sorts of things. Con and I were really concerned, afraid he'd have to go stay in the hospital for a while if he didn't start to improve."

This sounds like what happened to Ade before he had to go to Washington. I was twelve then, old enough to see things but not old enough to really understand. Our house was so lonely without him. When Ade left, it was the real end of our family for me, I think.

"I tried to bring him out of it, cooked his favorite foods, all the things I could think to do. One night, when I was sitting by his bed, watching him toss and turn and fight with h—"

A terrible thud against the car. And then we're flying. Between one breath and the next, we go from stationary to airborne, our bodies thrown forward.

In this flight, I could be anything. I could dissipate like smoke. This is what my oldest brothers did on a June day twenty years ago. They landed, though, and so will we. I'm not quite afraid. My eyes spring open with the shock—we've been attacked by a battering ram. Someone's thumped us, I think—I hope we don't hit the hearse.

I never realized how long a breath can be. How agonizingly drawn out it is. How you don't want to reach the boundary of that breath because of what comes when it ends. But you know you're heading there, and part of you wants to meet it. To follow your own exhalation into the dark.

The sheer momentum shocks me like cold water. Granna's seat belt catches, but I'm not wearing mine.

I manage to turn my face, but not quickly enough. I catch the wheel with my left cheek. A warm pain blooms there.

Granna's head snaps forward and then back. She doesn't make a sound.

My own body falls back against my seat. We're stunned, wide-eyed and breathless, having come to the edge of violence and ricocheted back again.

But at least we've missed the hearse.

I'm having trouble seeing, especially out of my left eye, but I try to get Granna to talk to me, to let me know if she's all right. I don't quite understand what happened. I remember being small, trying to catch a football a big brother threw. I missed, it hit me in the face and knocked me flat on my back. The confusion now feels like that.

I squinch my eyes, and I am seven, lying in bed, Dad beside me, Jack haunting the hall. It wasn't Dad who made me feel safe those nights; it was my eldest brother. And there's my ghost. I imagine I will see him soon.

There's commotion outside our car. Remy's shouting, then someone is pounding on Granna's door. But she can't get the lock open. I didn't know we had the locks engaged.

Now someone else is banging on my window. I have to turn my head all the way around to look who it is. It's a man in a dark suit, trying to pull open my door. I reach my left hand down and find the handle, pull it, shove.

It doesn't move. I don't know why. I try again, and it finally gives.

Suddenly Ade's face is very close to mine, his breath sour.

He's got his hands on either side of my face, looking at me, trying to get me to focus one eye and then the other. All the while he's repeating, "Jesus, oh God, I'm sorry, I am so sorry, oh no . . ."

It is slowly occurring to me that someone has hit my car with theirs, that it might have been Ade who did so. The world begins to piece itself together more quickly.

I hear Remy, too, as he talks to Granna. "Come on now," he says, "let's get out of this seat, huh? Put your arm around my neck, there you go. Let me help you."

"Okay," Ade says, letting go of my face. "Can you move your neck? Does it hurt?" I try to shake my head no, but it hurts, so I quit.

"What happened?" I try to say, but it feels there's marbles between my cheeks.

"Give her some water," a woman says. It might be Emily.

"C-can't drink the water here," I say as Ade presses a bottle into my hands.

"Yes, you can," he says. "Let me open it for you."

"*No.* There are bodies and the water runs too close to them." I swing both feet out of the car, sit sideways in the seat.

Adrian's rental car is off to the left of my Subaru. It's at an odd angle. So he is the one who rear-ended us.

"The water," I try, "comes from the ground." Both Ade's hands are on his head, his face red.

"I don't know, I don't know, I don't know," he's saying, "what the hell is she talking about? The water, the ground? I wasn't going that fast, she can't be concussed, can she? Is Granna okay? Remy, is Granna okay? Jesus Christ, I swear, the sun was in my eyes, we haven't slept, and . . ."

Uncle Cat comes up behind Adrian. Tries to calm him. "Hey, guy," he says, "slow down."

Emily kneels next to me. In her hands she's got another plastic water bottle and some tissues. She wets the tissues. Uses them to dab at my forehead, my cheek. She passes me the bottle. I raise it to my lips and drink.

"You can't drink the water from the pumps," I tell her. "I thought he meant water from the pumps."

"Pumps?" she asks, raising her eyebrows.

"There's pumps around. Used to get water if you plant flowers. Flowers that you plant on the graves, I mean."

"You mean like an old pump that you prime?"

"Yeah. You can't drink the water from the pumps here, though. It's not sanitary, from the cemetery, I guess."

"You're saying you thought he wanted to give you water from a pump?"

I nod.

"Ade!" Emily says loudly. "Ade, honey, it's okay. She thought you were going to give her nonpotable water from the pumps here."

"What?" he says. "What the hell are you even talking about?"

"Ella's okay," Emily says. She puts a hand on my knee, reaches the other out to Ade, to bring him to my side. He comes, looks at me. His eyes are red, dark circles beneath them. His face is ashen. Rett dances around behind his dad.

"I'm okay," I say, "really. My face hurts, but I'm fine."

"You sure?" he asks. "What's the thing with the water? I'm so sorry, El."

"It's okay," I say. "It's okay. Is Granna okay?"

"Granna's fine!" Remy calls from the other side of the car.

"The water," I tell Ade. "When Granna and I came in the summer to plant flowers, I used to get so thirsty. But you can't drink it. I guess I was thinking about that, the water, earlier. That's all. I'm okay, I was confused. I'm not brain damaged."

He pulls me gently to his chest, hugs me tightly. "Okay," he says, whistling between his teeth as he breathes. "Whatever damage I just did to your car, I'll pay for it. We got separated from the procession, I was so worried about being late, I wasn't thinking and I—I'm just sorry."

"I know," I say. "Can you help me stand up? Feeling kind of stiff."

"Of course," he says, and offers me an arm, steadies me with his other hand. "Anybody have some Advil or something? She's gonna need it."

"I've got something the doctor gave me," Emily says.

I make it to my feet, and somebody grabs my purse from the back seat. You can only open the one back door, the passenger side. I turn toward the cemetery, still holding Ade's arm, my purse clutched under my other.

"Will you be okay through this? You need an ice pack," Ade whispers. He kisses me on the temple, then we begin to pick our way slowly around the wreck of our cars, toward the graveside. Granna's up ahead, already seated. Remy's walking toward us. My brothers, I realize, have to go back and unload the casket from the hearse.

CHAPTER FOURTEEN

Jackson

JULY 1992

It was summer, the Fourth of July. My family headed to the oldest cemetery in Harrington, located on a steep hill out-side of town, to watch fireworks. The reason we went there was because it was the best place to watch the show, especially if you didn't want to have to drive your car downtown to the fair-grounds where the community carnival was going on all week.

When we arrived at the cemetery, the sky was still light. We had to park down at the bottom of the hill and pick our way up to a flatter, open space where we could set up our spot. We were headed to a lawn that just bordered where the old graves began.

There was no fence around the cemetery, still isn't today. It's bordered by woods on three sides and the road on the other. Back in the woods, down a dirt path barely wide enough for a car, was (maybe is still) an old brick building that looked dilap-idated and ruined.

The building was a retirement and respite house for elderly nuns, Precious Blood Convent. There was a hand-painted sign off the main road that directed you to it, but unless you knew where to look for the sign, you'd never find it. It was not very large, and the paint was peeling badly.

The moon was starting to come out, pale and floating. The ground groaned. The dirt that my mother spread the picnic blanket on was cracked in places. Dry ruts of dirt broke up through the grass and left me feeling vacant and unsettled.

She settled herself in a lawn chair, holding Remy in her arms; he was sleeping. His face was flushed, and his hair stuck to his forehead because of the humidity. When he breathed you could hear him snuffle with the congestion in his head. My father went back down to the car to get the cooler we'd brought. It had popsicles for us, and beer for my parents. Two for Dad, one for Mom.

There was a crowd gathering on the edge of the cemetery, other families like ours. People were throwing out their own blankets and unfolding chairs. Kids congregated in small clumps by the edge of where the graves began. They stood talking to each other, but no one went very far into the graveyard itself.

I sat on the blanket near my mother's feet, watching the moon rise. When we'd arrived, Lex had taken off toward the other kids; Adrian turned half a second later and followed him. Ella had tried to run off after them, too, but my father had caught her by the hand and swung her up on his shoulders, then went down to the car with her. I could hear other families talking across the wide expanse of lawn where we sat. I watched Dad come back up the hill carrying the cooler in both hands, Ella running two steps ahead of him.

It was almost pleasant, sitting there. But Lex was crashing toward us. I didn't know he was coming until he took a flying leap and practically landed on top of me. He knocked me over, then did a half-commando roll off the blanket and onto the grass.

Our mother only had a second to yell at him before Ade trotted over to her chair, crying that Lex'd left him behind.

"Didn't!" Lex shouted, pulling bits of dead grass from his hair. He stood, then crouched in front of me.

"Did so," Ade cried. Mom said that we could all stay on the blanket if we didn't knock it off. Remy shifted in her arms a little but not enough to wake himself.

"You gotta come," Lex said. He kept his voice low so that no one else could hear. "You need to see this."

"I don't want to." I was happy enough to sit quietly. I liked the stillness of the sky.

"Come, Jack," he said again.

"Why?"

"'Cause I said to. You'll like it. Come on." He grabbed my wrist and tugged so that we both spilled over backward, me on top of him. I started to get up, but he held me tight and hissed that we had to go, now.

"You stop, boys," Mom said absently.

We stood up together, stalked off behind the blanket, our mother calling to us to stay near because it was getting dark and the fireworks would start soon. I looked over my shoulder; Ade watched us. His eyes were glassy, and he looked a little wild. He was a small kid, looked like he was five even though he was six going on seven. Ella was nearly as tall as he was, but she was two years younger.

I can't tell you what Lex looked like that summer, except to say that he looked like me, but blond. It's just another thing I've forgotten about him. I don't always remember what his voice sounded like. But I still know the feeling that he left behind when he walked out of a room. I have that sense of him just as acutely as I did when he used to stand beside me, all manic energy and a kind of humming in the air. He held himself like he knew the world loved him, like he could bend it to his will if he wanted; our house seemed smaller when he was in it, like it was trying to contain him. He tore through the halls, up and down the stairway, leaving doors swinging on their hinges behind him. It seemed like there were always doors swinging as he went. But to tell you what he looked like, I have to look at photographs to get any sense of him.

In them, Lex was wiry, tight. He wasn't a big boy, but you could look at the muscles that ran under his skin, the ones that laced his ribs together, the ones that worked in his shoulders—you knew that he was going to be a tall, solid man someday. He was always an inch or so shorter than me, but he was stronger and might have weighed more. At the end of the school year, our father used to buzz my brothers' and my hair short, except for Remy's, because he was still so little. Mine grew back quickly but not Lex's—it would have been all bristle. You'd be able to see his scalp right through it. His head was always getting sunburned.

I followed Lex to a group of three boys. Two I knew: Jared March, from my class last year, and Anthony from down our street. There was another kid, too, Anthony's cousin, whose name I didn't know. Lex approached them first.

"Jackson's not scared of it," he said. "And he knows the story, too. Jack, you tell them."

Jared was hard looking, a little ropey through the arms. He'd bust out in muscle in a few years, after our accident. Anthony was a fat kid. His mother bought him husky jeans. I only knew that because he shared the fact with the kids we ate lunch with. The cousin was a bland boy, nothing special.

I looked at them, Jared and Anthony and Anthony's cousin, and at my brother. He was wearing my shirt. We shared a closet, so some mornings I'd wake up and find him wearing my clothes. I looked at Lex and felt a kind of revulsion that I am still ashamed of.

He was always doing stuff like that, dragging me into his games so he could prove a point or fluff himself up. It's not that I didn't love my brother—I just didn't always like him very much. He was the braver kid, the one who caused the trouble. I fixed it. We got into the same amount of trouble, I think, but I took punishment personally. Lex was indifferent to it, it sometimes seemed.

"Jack," he said, "tell them. They don't believe the story about the witches."

I felt a little prick on my shin, rubbed it with my other foot. It started to itch. I'd been bitten by a mosquito. They were out in droves that night; I'd wake up the next morning covered in welts. I looked at the ground, then back at the boys. I knew what Lex meant. Earlier that same summer he'd gotten into trouble telling stories to Adrian and Ella about the old religious home in the woods.

"This kid's a liar," Jared said, gesturing at Lex. He didn't say it nastily, just as if it was a certifiable fact.

Lex wasn't in any real trouble here, but his pride was. He loved to tell stories, and he loved his stories to be taken as truth. If they weren't, he'd dig in his heels until you said you believed him.

"Jackson knows it's true. The Admiral told us. That's our grandpa," Lex said. "Jack knows."

"What'd he tell you?" I asked. "About the witches who live in the woods back there?" Lex was lucky I remembered the story.

"He said how they live back there, and that they used to kill people . . ." said Anthony, but Jared poked him in the side.

"I want to hear what Jack says," Jared said. Lex's face was expectant and grateful.

"Well, you've seen the sign, right?" I asked. "The one out on the road with all the peeled paint? That tells you everything you need to know."

"Aw, it just has some letters rubbed off," Jared said. "Don't mean anything special." He stretched out his arms slowly, then leaned off to the side and spit into the gathering gloom, toward the graves.

"That's what you think," Lex said, but then he shut his mouth and glanced at me. I didn't know it, but Ade had followed us again. Lex probably saw him coming but didn't bother to say anything.

"It *does so* mean something. It tells you who lives back there," Lex said to no one in particular.

On the sign, "Precious Blood Convent" had been painted in straight-backed, black letters. I don't know when it was completed or erected, but it was a long time ago. That summer, the *t* and most of the first *n* in convent had completely peeled away.

"And who's that?" Jared asked.

"You know what a coven is, right?" I asked. Jared shook his head. Anthony looked a little spooked. His cousin looked bored.

"Fireworks start soon?" the cousin said. No one answered.

"A coven is the place where witches live," Lex said. "They live back there in the woods, and steal kids. They need their blood."

"Only thing that wants any blood is the bugs," Jared said. He shifted on his feet and raised his right hand above his head. Midges go to the highest spot on you, so you put your hand above your head and they're not flying in your face. It works best if you have a hockey stick or baseball bat to hold up, otherwise your arm eventually gets tired.

"They take kids and bleed them till they can't bleed anymore and then they put them here in the cemetery," Lex blurted. "All these graves have the wrong names on them to trick the cops. They're all kids."

"Why would the witches put their name on the sign so everybody could find them?" the cousin asked.

"Shut up," Lex told him. "Who're you, anyway?"

"I don't know if the part about the graves is true," I said. I took a breath to be a little dramatic. I liked stories too. My brother and I were a good two-man show when we wanted to be. "But there is a coven back there. And their name is about blood. So it just gets you thinking."

"Your grandpa told you that?" Anthony said.

"He might have," I said.

"He was an admiral in the navy," Lex said. "He tells us stuff to protect ourselves." We knew he hadn't really been an admiral, but that's what we called him instead of Grandpa.

"Your grandpa learned about the coven in the navy?" the cousin said. He looked only a little interested.

I knew enough that to make a story sound true, you had to act as if maybe some parts of it weren't, or that you doubted them yourself.

"I don't know about that," I said to him. "But I trust him. The Admiral tells us a lot of true stuff."

The other thing to making people believe your fake story is to tell them about something they know to be true right after or right before you lie to them. It makes your lie sound truer.

"What else did he tell you? You guys'll believe anything," Jared said mildly.

"He told us about Shepherds' Rock," Lex said.

"What's that?" the cousin asked. We finally had his attention.

"It's this old boulder pile in the woods off the highway," Jared said. "It's stupid."

"It's not stupid!" Ade called. He'd been standing behind us, just beyond where we could see him.

"Get outta here," Anthony said lazily.

"Don't tell my brother to get out of here," Lex snapped. He didn't like having Adrian around, but he didn't like it more when other people told Ade to get lost.

"I don't care who's here," the cousin said. "What's the story?"

"Tell him, Jack," Ade said. He moved into the circle proper. It was funny, seeing him and Lex standing together. Ade looked just like Lex did when he was little.

"Okay," I said. "In the eighteen hundreds there were three brothers."

"Like there weren't three brothers before the eighteen hundreds," Jared interrupted.

"I want to hear the story," said the cousin. "Keep quiet."

"I don't remember what their names were, except for the youngest, who was Jacob. They lived on the farm that used to be outside of town, by the river. The highway's there now."

"Okay," said the cousin. "I know where you mean, I think."

"The brothers grew up there. They used to play on those rocks out in their woods. Jacob fell in love with this girl who lived in the town. He was only sixteen or something, so he didn't have any money to marry her. But he was useless doing his farm jobs because he was sick from loving her so much."

"That's stupid," Lex said. "I'm never going to like a girl that much."

"Shut up," Jared told him.

"Jacob's brothers got sick of him," I said. "But they weren't very smart, and they weren't very rich. They decided that they had to help Jacob get married to that girl. So what they did was, they decided to rob a bank.

"They were only half-stupid though, so they robbed a bank in the next town over from Harrington, in Malwen. The older brothers didn't tell Jacob what they were going to do—they just said to meet them at the rocks later that day. Jacob went there and waited for them. The brothers went to the bank in Malwen and robbed it without even using guns. They just pretended to have them. They didn't hurt anybody.

"They took the stolen money and booked it to Shepherds' Rock, which is named after them. But the cops and the sheriff in Malwen telegraphed the cops in Harrington, or whatever, and soon everybody was on their trail. They followed the Shepherd brothers to the rocks in the woods. The older brothers were there and had met Jacob, but they didn't show him the money. Instead, they hid it somewhere in the boulders.

"They were hiding the money when the law guys came up the trail. They rode on horses, and the only person they saw was Jacob, sitting on top of this huge boulder. He was doing something dumb, like singing about his girlfriend.

"Anyway, the cops pulled out their guns, and before Jacob knew what happened, they shot him five or six times. He slumped off the rocks and died not knowing what it was he got shot for. The older brothers were found hiding in the rocks then, but they wouldn't tell where the money was."

"Not true," Jared said. "Nobody'd be that stupid."

"It is true," I said. "You can go look at the old newspapers in the library if you want to check for yourself."

"So where is the money?" the cousin asked.

"No one knows. You can go out to the rocks and look for it, even. You can see the bullet holes on the rock where they fired at Jacob, and where he died."

"What happened to the older brothers?" the cousin asked.

"They got hanged," Lex said. "Even though they didn't hurt anybody."

"They did so, because by robbing the bank Jacob ended up getting killed and that's what made them guilty," I said. "They stole the money and even though Jacob didn't have anything to do with it, he was the one who got shot." It was getting dark, and parents were starting to look around for the littlest kids to make sure they were nearby.

"I don't think it's the brothers' fault. It's the cops that shot Jacob, not them. I wouldn't have hanged them if I'd been there," Lex said.

"Course you wouldn't have," Jared said.

"Shut up about him," Ade said to Jared. Jared made a move like he was going to punch him. Ade stepped back, looked like he was going to cry.

"So the coven stuff is true, Jackson?" Anthony asked.

"I guess it is."

"I told you so, you bastards," Lex said.

"Don't talk that way," I said in a sharp whisper. "Ade'll tell Mom."

"No, he won't," Lex said. "'Cause he's gotta pull the chain."

Jared looked at Lex, mumbled that he had to go find his parents before it got too dark. The fireworks would start any minute. It was getting harder to see the gravestones at our backs. Jared jogged back toward that other world, where the parents sat.

"What are you talking about?" I asked.

"He snuck up," said Anthony. He and the cousin were putting more space between us as we stood talking.

"Shut up," I said to him. "Lex, what do you mean?"

"This is what you gotta see. It's what I wanted to show you," he said. He grabbed my wrist hard, dragging me toward the graves. My stomach knotted up. Dry dirt crunched under our feet. He pulled me ten or twelve feet from where we'd been standing.

"Look at that," he said. "That's what he's got to pull. Since he was a sneak again." I had to lean forward to see what Lex was talking about. In front of me was a gravestone, an old one. I couldn't read what it said because it was toppled over a little. It was creepy and made me feel cold even though I was sweating.

"Kick your foot. You'll feel it then," he said.

Behind us Anthony, Ade, and the cousin were watching. Ella was, too, but we didn't know it. I kicked. My foot met something metal. I leaned forward so I could see what it was. I couldn't make sense of it at first, but when I did, I jumped back. I couldn't help it.

It was a chain, a heavy metal chain with links as big as my fist—it went right into the ground. Into the grave.

Lex came up beside me. "Weird, right? Jared found it before we got here, but he wouldn't touch it," he said. "It's, like, a doorbell to hell or something."

"Or to the coven," Anthony said from behind me. Nobody answered. I stood looking at the chain for a minute, not understanding what Lex intended. I realized he wasn't standing next to me anymore.

A little to my left I heard a struggle and someone yelping. It sounded like a dog who'd been hit. In the dimness I saw my brother do the thing I wish I could forget.

Lex held Ade by one arm and the back of his collar. They struggled, and Adrian shouted once, short, and then Lex dropped his arm. Gave him a sharp punch in the ribs. Ade made that dog sound again. He still struggled, and I heard Ade's shirt tear.

Ade fell hard on the ground, and Lex said something I couldn't hear. Then Lex got Ade around the middle, hoisted him fully off the ground. Ade's arms and legs flailed in the fading light, but I couldn't move to help him.

I stepped backward, out of the way as Lex struggled to the spot where the chain was born out of the ground. He dumped

Adrian at the foot of the grave like an offering. I wished I was still on the blanket with my mother.

Ade was crying, sniffling, but not trying to get away anymore. Lex stood over him, and then he kicked him in the back. Lex was only wearing flip-flops, but the kick was a hard one that knocked Ade's breath away. I stepped forward to pull them apart, to set Ade on his feet again.

"Stay back, Jackson," Lex said. He didn't turn to look at me, but his voice had changed. We were not a group of boys playing around anymore—we were something darker, and there was no one who could stop us. Anthony and the cousin were still nearby, looking around for someone, an adult, a mother or a father, to come and break up the fight and set everything right again. I wanted to step forward, but I couldn't. I was only a boy, and Lex would not let me. Another moment where I couldn't speak, couldn't move. Couldn't be what one brother needed me to be, for the sake of the other.

"Pull the chain," he said. "Pull it. See what happens." Ade didn't do anything, didn't move or even speak.

"Pull the chain," Lex said again.

"Lex," I whispered.

We were stuck there, the three of us, in an awful, unholy space. No one could move forward, no one could go back. We each waited to see what the others would do. We were not even brothers here, because brothers protected and helped each other; we were animals, maybe, but somehow less than them too.

It only lasted a few minutes, that terrible limbo, but in it I saw a great, dark thing that rose up and swallowed us whole. We were in a place beyond help or reason; the only way we could free ourselves was to hurt each other without flinching. There's nothing more terrifying to a kid than knowing that no one can help him.

From somewhere behind me, or off to the left, I heard running feet. I did not want to look to see who was coming. It could be a witch, it could be Jacob Shepherd himself. I hoped it might be Dad, but I knew it wasn't. He was drinking beer with our mother on the blanket on a summer night that may as well have been a thousand miles from the one we were living.

She was just a little girl but she ran fast. I don't know how long Ella'd been watching us. Maybe the whole time. It didn't matter how she got there, though, just that she somehow arrived. I saw her come up out of the evening to break through the center of us.

She barreled right into Lex. He stumbled back but did not fall. He didn't move forward, either, just stood looking at her dumbly. All the power went out of him. Ella, her hair flying behind her, reached right down and pulled the grave chain. She tugged it once, hard, and then let it go slack. Then she threw her whole weight against it so it strained. Not a single link rose from the ground.

She dropped the chain, turned to look at Lex.

"Ellie," he said.

She didn't answer. She gave Lex her back and faced Ade, who by then had gathered himself and stood off to the side. Ella touched the tear in his shirt collar, pulled off a piece of dead grass that had gotten stuck behind his ear. She took his hand and together they walked, not ran, back to the blanket. I stayed back, watching. When they passed me, she did not turn her face toward mine.

But she spoke. "Mommy says come back to the blanket, Jack. You'll miss the fireworks."

I glanced once at Lex standing a few feet off from the chain that he seemed afraid to pull. His face was cast down so I could not see it, but he looked familiar again. Just my brother, standing alone in the dark. I followed the others back to where our parents sat. The walk back seemed to take almost no time at all, which surprised me. I had felt, by the grave, that the living world was unreachably far.

Our parents were waiting for us with the popsicles. Dad looked at Adrian's torn collar, at the single bruise starting to color his right cheekbone that my mother noticed when she held the flashlight we'd brought to his face. I don't remember if Ade told them what happened. I didn't. Someone must have, though, because my father left us with my mother and Remy on the blanket and went into the dark behind us to find Lex. The fireworks began, and I lay on my back so I could see them take up the whole sky. The boom of them helped to calm me some, and I didn't notice that Lex and my father didn't make it back to the blanket until the show was nearly over. We didn't know it, but that night our family was separated along its terrible fault line: Those who'd live parted from those who would die young, alone back there among the graves.

The bug bites on my legs itched, and I wanted to go home. After the fireworks, we folded up the blanket, gathered ourselves, and walked back to the car. I made it to the bottom of the hill first, turned, and looked at my family as they came. My mother carried Remy against her and held Ade by the hand. Ella walked a little ahead of them, carrying a bag with the trash from our snacks.

Behind them, at least ten yards, came my father. He wasn't carrying the cooler with him, so he'd have to go back and fetch it. He walked slowly, his arm around Lex's shoulders. They leaned into each other. Lex was relaxed. Dad must've said something funny—they both laughed. I was a little jealous: Lex had acted awfully, but it didn't seem like he was in trouble.

They made their way down the hill. We all climbed in the car and waited for Dad to go back for the cooler. Lex was jostled in the back seat but didn't complain. He rested his face on the window. He didn't talk much. I never knew what Dad said.

I wished I could talk to Ade about what happened that night, or ask Ella if she remembered it. If we could all recall it together, it might take some of the power out of it. Because that night, we became part of a cruelty that was bigger than us.

CHAPTER FIFTEEN

Adrian

"So many weird things happened today," Rett says, head on my shoulder. It's too warm in the car. Makes it hard to breathe.

I nod, try to shift my legs so they fit more comfortably. We're catching a ride with Uncle Cat; Calvin's crammed into the back with Rett and me. Emily's got the passenger seat—I insisted she take it. We had to wait for the tow truck to come and take the rental. It wasn't too badly dinged, but Hertz insisted they had to have it right away for repairs. Ella's car was drivable, though Remy took the wheel since she has a nasty headache.

"I'm going to tell Mom all the stuff," Rett says, "first the plane, and when you made us have a car accident, how we almost died in it, and how you killed Ella and Granna. But they're okay now. And then how we had to walk so far through all the graveyards, and the way chairs were put out for us when we got there, and the way that Papa's box went down—"

"Don't tell your mother anything," I snap. "You don't need to bother her."

He shudders. His shoulders hitch forward, a quick jerk. Like I've hit him with an open hand. My stomach turns, and my ears get hot. Cal's listening to music on his iPhone but his eyes slide over me once, judging even though he acts like he's not listening. No one else talks. Rett tries to draw in a long, steadying breath. I slide my arm around him, tight. But he doesn't lean into me, holds himself rigid. To protect himself.

He's mine, and I've hurt him. It's not his fault things are coming apart. I pull him close even though he doesn't want to be held. "Hey, Rett, I'm sorry," I say into the top of his head. "You know how you asked me what my brother was like?"

He shakes his head no, but looks up at me. I'm so glad that he didn't get hurt in the fender bender. The things I wish I could say are things he wouldn't understand—how I can count every hurt I've trespassed against him, the terrible weight of being sorry for every single one of them.

"Yeah, you asked me what he was like. You remember that? What my brother Lex was like."

He's asked me that more than once on this trip.

His big eyes look up at me, and he nods. He's pale from lack of sleep and the oddly timed meals of the last few days. He looks alarmingly like Adam the last time I saw him, sick and silent.

I got a text from Vincent earlier this morning saying he'd arrived, and they hadn't had any more news back from Adam's testing. I should call back. But I can't bring myself to do it.

Rett closes his eyes, settles against me, says, "Tell."

"Well, the first thing that you need to know is that my brother was a monkey," I say. "He swung from the trees all day and threw bananas and coconuts at anyone who walked too close."

"Don't be weird, Daddy," Rett murmurs, stretching his feet out so they're half on Calvin's lap.

"Okay." I pet his head.

"You tell me the truth, right?" he whispers, his voice low and breathy.

"I do. I always do."

"Okay."

"Lex was a good boy." I rest my head back against the seat. "He was smart, but he misbehaved in school."

"You would have put him on detection," Rett says.

"In detention. And yeah, I might have."

"Why?"

"He was good, and he was bad sometimes, too, and that's pretty much the sum of him."

"Hmm," he mumbles. His body relaxes. "More, Dad."

I don't quite know how to talk about a kid I last knew a lifetime ago.

"When he was two, he banged his head on the brick of the fireplace, in the days before me."

"Adam's two."

"He is. You're right."

"And you weren't you before me," he says with finality. I squeeze his shoulder. He settles his head against me. "More, please."

"More? Um, he could ice-skate better than anybody I ever knew. And he was allowed to paddle the canoe on the back creek by the time he was ten, without a life vest on."

"What else?" Rett says, a yawn distorting his face.

"Well, I don't know."

"You do know."

"He liked to take a big bite out of a fresh lemon. Also, he wouldn't drink soda or anything that had fizz in it, but he loved chocolate milk."

"Can I tell these to Mom?" Rett mumbles, his mouth slack. His head is heavy on my shoulder; it feels something like peace.

"You can tell Mom whatever you like."

"Even about the car thing?"

"Even that."

"Daddy?" he says suddenly, in a fierce whisper. He shifts around to look up at me, his face earnest and concerned.

"What, buddy? What's wrong?"

"I did something that'll make you really mad at me."

I take a deep breath. My pause alarms Rett. His body clenches.

"Nothing you do could make me really mad. Can you tell me what it is, though? Just so I know?"

"I don't think I want to."

"Why don't you want to?"

"Because I don't believe you won't be really mad."

I shift, take his chin in my hand, tilt it up. I gently cup the side of his face in my palm. He is so small and complicated. There are worlds inside him that I will never understand.

"I can only keep my promise that I won't get angry if you tell me what you did, so I can show you."

He looks at me, his eyes swimming, bleary and red. He breathes once, hitched and sputtering. "You gave me your phone to play on when we were in the parade from church."

He's right. I gave it to him to keep him quiet on the long, slow drive to Lawrence.

I nod, but I don't want to interrupt him.

"I was playing. I played the whole way. And I still had your phone when we got to the cement-terry. And then you crashed our car, and I was holding the phone very hard in my hands so it didn't go flying like the coffee you had up front did."

"Do you still have my phone now?" I ask. I don't feel the weight in my pocket. I didn't even know it was gone.

"Yeah, but it's dead," he says, shaking his head. He still hasn't quite grasped that when he shakes it, he's saying no even though he means yes.

"So what's the problem?" I truly don't know what he's so afraid I'll be upset about.

"'Cause," he answers quietly, "before it died, when you were helping Aunt Ella, I texted Mom. I said things I shouldn't of said, I think."

My heart begins to race slightly. I've been avoiding getting in touch with Liv so far, but now Rett's done it for me. I haven't called because, if I learn something from her that I can't handle, I don't know what will happen to me. I'm full to bust with feelings, will buckle under them all if I'm not careful.

"See," he whispers, "you're really mad now."

"I'm not," I whisper back, nuzzling my face into the top of his head. His hair smells sweet from the shampoo it was washed in. "Can you tell me what you told Mom, maybe? That's something I would like to know."

"I said," he answers, shaking in my arms, afraid of my response, "I said you crashed our car. I said you crashed us."

My teeth whistle as his words sink in. He begins to shake.

"Rett, honey, please don't be so scared of me. Please don't." Last thing I'd ever want is for my boy to be frightened of me. Like I sometimes was of my own father.

"But you said I shouldn't bother her, and I did before I found out I wasn't allowed to, and then the phone died from the accident. Now you're angry."

"Did you hear back from her before the phone died? What did she say?"

"Nothing. The crash killed the phone."

"The crash didn't kill the phone. It died because the battery was run down. I didn't charge it, and then your game drained it, probably."

"Is that another thing to be mad for?"

"No," I say, kissing his head. "I'm not mad at all. About anything."

"Why not?"

"Because you didn't do anything wrong. It's okay. It really is."

"What will you do?"

"When we get to the house, I'll charge the phone. And I'll call Mom, and we'll see what's happening."

"See what's Addie's sick?" When he's tired, Rett falls back on the baby-talk he's largely left behind.

"Yeah, I'll call her, and we'll learn what we can. But that's not for you to worry about. That's for the doctors and for Mom and Dad to worry about and to fix."

"Are they good doctors, Dad?"

"They're the best ones, buddy."

"That's good," he says, settling again more comfortably into my side. His body relaxes, and with him I relax too. I'm exhausted, despite my anxiety over Adam.

"Was Lex my uncle once?"

"He would have been, I guess. But he was gone before we had you."

"Because a car killed him. Like it did us today too. And your phone. Killed it."

"Rett, a car did not kill you. Please stop saying that."

"I'm sorry," he mumbles. His eyes close. "More story."

"You should talk to your Uncle Jack about stories. He was always the best at telling them."

"No, I want yours," Rett says.

I take a deep breath, and almost without meaning to, words come. "Well, Lex loved to sing along to the radio but never in church, where he'd just stand with his hands jammed in his pockets, like he was having a staring contest with Jesus on the cross."

"At the church from today?"

"The same, actually."

"So I saw Lex's Jesus."

"I guess so, yeah. I didn't think about that earlier, but you're right."

"More."

"He had gray eyes and sandy hair that Dad—that Papa—never let grow very long. He looked a lot like me, actually."

"Daddy, did you like him?"

"I did." I close my eyes. "I loved him with every part of me."

"I love Addie, too."

A tired thick-headedness gets between me and my thoughts. I don't know any more what I'm saying aloud and what I'm just thinking. Rett doesn't talk any longer, so it doesn't matter if he hears me.

"Lex used to say he hated me. I believed him. But he would rub my back when I threw up. He bit his nails down to little square stubs and pulled at the skin on the sides. He was always nursing the sore places. He collected rocks he found by the side of the road that looked interesting. He gave me some of the rocks, and the rest I took when he died."

I sound like Jack, how he used to talk when he told us stories. He could tell such good ones.

"He was a wrecking ball. He could draw anything you could think of. He loved to go to the airport to watch planes take off. He was happiest anytime he was around water.

"He was bigger than he deserved to be, and he threw himself against the walls of our house until the walls fell down. Nothing could contain him in the end. Not even living, the boundaries of his own body.

"His birthday became a holiday we celebrated like we do those of the important presidents. We always remembered him in our prayers. He was just a kid who died, and so he became whatever we wanted him to be. And sometimes it's like he never was here at all." I fall silent in my head, and the hush seems total, luxurious.

I cannot see anything behind my dark eyelids. They've been cast in iron. Lex lived once, and he died a thousand times over, every day that we were without him. I don't know how my parents carried on. The fear of calling Liv back is tied up in that, in Adam becoming for Rett what my brother became for me. A story, a myth, the family ghost. The world is close and warm around me. I try to be quiet, still. Try to ask whatever's out there what will happen to my son. How will this end for us? God forbid, if Adam leaves us, where will he go? There is no answer, not right away.

And yet there's a growing sense of something, maybe just relief that I can catch a few minutes' sleep.

And then, another breath, out of the dark a rushing wind comes toward me.

My heart quickens. I whistle between my teeth, like I always do, like my father used to. I don't know what's coming, but I turn my body to meet it.

It moves by me quick as an exhalation, then is gone. The rush of a train passing you on the platform. Faster than that, even. But I have the singular sense that there were small feet pounding as it passed me. A freshness remains from whatever went by, a September cold snap against your skin.

I breathe it in, and it's something so familiar that though I can't place it I know it to be mine. It reminds me of Adam, of Rett, of the sea.

I've conjured something I can't put back, somehow. And that does not scare me. Something missing has come home. On the plane Rett said something about doors opening. I want to linger here, in the residual of whatever it was, but from the front seat, a voice jolts me with a start.

"I was thinking about that poor boy, too, today," Uncle Cat says quietly.

CHAPTER SIXTEEN

Jackson

SUNDAY 1:48 P.M.

Mom breaks away like the ringing phone's caught us in some kind of impropriety. I don't want her to move, so I try to keep my hand on her back even though she's already pulled away.

She looks at the ground, then up at me, pats me awkwardly on the shoulder.

"You answer it. I don't much feel like I can keep up a conversation today," she says.

My teeth clench; I'm angry at her for not answering her own phone, but the ringing stops after a minute. There's a long pause where we look at each other, a few seconds where we might still salvage the connection we'd made.

But the phone begins to ring again—even though it's not any louder, it feels like it. My mother looks at me once, points to the offending telephone, and slips away toward the staircase leading to the second floor.

I reach for it because I've been instructed to, even though I don't want to talk.

"Hello?"

"Jesus Christ, you said this is the number to reach you at in an emergency, so why didn't you answer?"

"Whoa." It's a woman on the other end, spitting angry. "Who is this?"

"Are you serious?" she returns, her voice sounding far away and uncomfortably close at the same time. "I got a text that said you'd crashed? And then your cell's straight to voicemail? What the hell does that mean? Do you even care what's happening with Adam? Why haven't you called, you should have been done an hour ago and—"

"I have no idea what you're talking about," I cut her off. "You're obviously upset, and I'm sorry. This is the Gable residence. Who's calling?" My tie's gotten uncomfortably tight around my neck. Sweat beads at the small of my back.

"Wait, who am I talking to?" the voice says, suddenly diminished. "I thought I had the right number, oh God, I'm—"

"Liv, is that you?" I say, recognizing my sister-in-law's voice. It's easier to hear her when she's not screaming into the phone.

"Yes," she says, "this isn't Adrian?"

"Sorry, no," I answer. "It's Jackson. He's still at the funeral. They all are, I think, or are coming back from it now. Why aren't you with them?"

"Oh God," she says again, "I'm so sorry, Jack. I didn't realize—"

"It's fine, really. But what's going on?"

"Can you put him on the phone? I really need to talk to him—"

"He's still at the service, I just said." I have to try hard to not sound frustrated at her. I can hear my mother moving around upstairs—her shoeless feet padding across the hardwood of her bedroom floor, the creak of the bathroom door as she adjusts it.

"But the service was supposed to be over an hour ago," Liv says stubbornly, like if she just states it with enough force, it'll be true.

"But they had to make the trip to the cemetery after it," I say gently. "Lawrence is a good thirty miles from here, and they'd be going slowly in the procession, too."

"Oh God," she says a third time.

"It's okay," I answer, because I don't know what else to tell her. There's silence on the other end. "Liv, what's wrong with Adam? You said something was wrong." She hasn't said why she isn't here, but I don't ask again.

"Do you know anything about a crash? A car accident, maybe? I got a text from Ade's phone, and then no one's answered me since—"

"I haven't heard from anybody today. Just, well, me and Mom are at the house, but nobody else has gotten in touch."

"Damn it. The problem is that the text I got was full of typos, which means Rett probably was the one who sent it. But Ade's phone goes to voicemail, so I have no way of knowing—"

"An accident?" I interrupt, realizing what she actually said. "Someone's been in an accident? Should I try to call one of the others who're there now, maybe, see if they can give me an idea of what's up? Should I try to drive out there myself? Should I call the cops? Which cops would I even call, though, the ones in Lawrence or Harrington or the ones in whatever town's in the middle of them, that's on the way, I don't know—"

The one thing I don't expect happens: On the other side of the line, Liv bursts out laughing. It's a tight, hysterical laugh, high and strangled. My throat hurts listening to it, the way it constricts and reels away from her even though she's trying to contain it. She moves the phone away from her face. I can tell because the background noise becomes suddenly louder. There's a voice droning on an intercom system, paging somebody to radiology.

"Oh my God," she says over and over. She's in a hospital, possibly.

I hear a slight click on the line. It's my mother upstairs, picking up the extension in her room. She wouldn't answer the phone but has no trouble listening in on the conversation. I mutter to Liv to slow down and breathe. My mother's put out a bunch of folding chairs in addition to the regular furniture here in the living room, so I sit down on one.

I can see into the dining room, where trays of food wait, covered in tin foil, until the guests from the service come in. There's extra card tables set up at either end of the dining table, which has been pushed up against the wall. One entire side of the room, farthest from where I am, is lined with tables dressed in royal-blue paper tablecloths, probably bought from a local party store. It looks more like a political convention's refreshment table than a funeral banquet.

"Honey," I say, "I need you to calm down some. Can you do that?"

She mumbles something in the direction of her phone, and I can hear her actively trying to control her breathing. She's doing better, but hysteric jags still break through every few seconds.

"Where are you right now, Liv?"

"I'm down-st-st-stairs," she manages before she's overcome again by the strange, strangled laughter.

I give her a minute to collect herself and try again. "Downstairs where? It sounds like you might be at a doctor's office, or a hospital."

She's unable to answer.

"Liv, you're scaring me. I'm frightened because it sounds like you're frightened too. I need you to tell me what's happening, or give the phone to someone who can if you're not able to."

"Hang on," she says. "Hang on, please?" Through the phone come bits and pieces of conversation—she must be moving through a space where other people are talking. I can't hear their words, just a murmur of voices and the sense of motion.

"Liv, what's happening?"

"I'm trying to find Vincent," she eventually says. "He'll talk to you."

Who's Vincent?

There's more muffled noise, then Liv says, "Here he is, Jack. I'm sorry."

"Hello?" a man's voice says, gruff and deep. "With whom am I speaking?"

"This is Jackson. I'm Olivia's brother-in-law." I assume I'm talking to Vincent now. Maybe he's a doctor or nurse Liv's handed me to. I can hear Liv speaking to someone in the background, but it seems that Vincent steps away from where she is because the line goes suddenly quiet except for his voice.

"Hello there," he says. "I'm Vincent. I'm your brother Ade's friend."

It dawns on me who Vincent is: the graduate student my father paid to babysit Ade when Dad moved him out to Washington. Ade had his breakdown, when he wouldn't come out of his bedroom for days but they'd hear him wandering around the house at night when everyone else was asleep. There was something, too, about him losing his shit in the school bathroom, locking himself in it and not coming out, but I was away at college by then, and nobody filled me in on what actually happened.

Anyway, after the bathroom thing, Ade was removed from Harrington entirely. Dad hired Vincent to help Ade convert an attic bedroom and generally to make sure that my brother didn't hurt himself or anybody else. It wasn't the best way to handle things; Mom was furious about it at the time. She never would have agreed to send Ade if she'd known that Dad would barely spend any time with him. Emily helped him, too, but if you ask Ade, it was Vincent who'd brought him through his crisis, nobody else.

I don't think I've ever really met Vincent before. We might have spoken at Ade's graduation, but that's about it. And maybe not even then. Ade and Liv eloped, so there was no family gathering for their wedding. This is a strange way of meeting someone who means so much to my brother, but I don't have time to think about it.

"I had to go into the bathroom so I could hear you," Vincent says. "He's been moved to a regular room, but it's still so noisy in there. Can you hear me okay?"

"Yes, thanks. I don't understand what's happening. Who's been moved to a room? Was there really an accident? And where are you, exactly? I thought Liv would be with Ade. Is Rett with him?"

"We're at the county hospital just outside of Sawtell," he says. "I got in from Arizona this morning, haven't been here very long. Liv finally checked her phone when she went downstairs for a snack, and I understand she got a weird message on it."

"That's what she said, yeah. Looks like Rett sent her a text that said there was a crash or something. She was trying to call the house here, my mother's house, to find Ade, see what's going on."

"Is he there?"

"He's not, and I don't know when he'll be back." I'm embarrassed that Vincent knows I skipped the funeral. Ade holds him in high regard—I want to please the guy even though I'm not sure if we've ever spoken face-to-face.

"That's all right," Vincent says. "I'm sure things are fine. Either Rett's kidding or he's not, but the fact that he sent a text seems to mean, to me, that he's not hurt. Ade probably just hasn't charged his cell, since he flew all night."

"Yeah," I say, feeling stupid to not have known that Ade came in on the red-eye for the service. I'd just figured he'd get here a day or so before the funeral because that's the kind of organized planner he normally is.

"Here's the story: Adam's very sick. Liv's been at the hospital with him since yesterday, in the ER. There's not an official pediatric floor here, so they've just been kept hanging down there until a bunch of blood work's done, scans, all kinds of stuff."

"That sounds bad."

"It's not good, that much I do know. Anyway, the hospital's finally moved him to a private room, so at least Liv can try and get him to sleep some."

"What time is it there?"

"Almost eleven."

"Have they given you any idea about what might be wrong with him?"

"Look," he says, "when you have a little kid like Adam who's been running a fever for two weeks but he's got no active infection, and he's pale, he's bruising weird, and he's anemic to the extreme, it sort of points to only a few things. And none of those are good."

I don't know what, exactly, Vincent's trying to say without saying it, but I make a mumbling noise that I hope implies that I'm following him.

"What's the plan, then? What do they do next?"

"They're rehydrating him, trying to figure out what's going

on. They're bringing in a pediatric hematologist this afternoon from a neighboring hospital. It's going to be a long day of blood draws for Adam. He's already horrified by all the doctors, screams whenever any of them come into the room."

"Jesus."

"Listen," Vincent says, "like I said, whatever this is, it's bad."

"I understand."

"I need to ask you something important. I know it's too much to ask of you, since you've already lost your dad. Which I'm so sorry about, Jackson, truly."

"Thank you, truly. Please call me Jack."

"Sure, Jack."

"What do you need from me? Tell me, I'll do it."

"Well, when your brother—when Ade hears this, things could go really badly. He's going to fall apart, and I can understand it. I'm falling apart here watching this kid. He lies in the bed and just stares off into space like he's on his way to his execution. It's the spookiest thing I've ever seen."

"That sounds awful." I remember that feeling, what it was like to lie on my back in a hospital bed, looking at the ceiling, wondering if dying would have been less trouble than recovering.

"When Ade gets to the house, he's going to have to call Liv, regardless of the issue with his phone. When he gets the news, can I ask you to be near him? Can I ask you to be certain that he doesn't do something rash, like try to book a flight home tonight? Because he's got things inside him, things to do with your father, that he needs to attend to. He can't rush off and not deal with the loss because otherwise he never will."

"I can do that," I say, even though I'm not sure.

"Keep an eye on Rett too? I don't think he's ever seen his dad the way I'm afraid Ade will be when he hears about Adam."

"Vincent, can I ask you what it is you're afraid of happening with Ade, exactly?"

He sighs, then clear his throat.

"Listen," he answers, "I can't in good faith tell you exactly what Ade's problems are. It wouldn't be right of me to share things he's told me in confidence. He keeps parts of himself very guarded, as I'm sure you know." I nod, then realize Vincent can't see me. I make a noise of agreement.

"Just watch that he's able to take in what he hears. But that he doesn't lose it, either. Like pacing around, stumbling on his words, frantic. That kind of stuff. Have you ever seen him like that before?"

"Yeah, I think so." I remember terrible nights spent with my brother pacing around the house, raging and roiling inside himself. I didn't know he still did that, that it could still happen to him. I've done so very little to be there for him, and in doing so, have let Ade down immeasurably.

"That's when he might try to book a flight out of there. Or something worse."

"Okay," I say, hoping I don't have to learn what something worse is.

"You sound," Vincent says, "like I've scared the shit out of you."

"Honestly?" I answer. "You have."

He laughs, a genuine laugh so different from the one Liv was possessed by that it seems like there should be a totally different word for the two sounds.

"I just need to ask that you stick by him close when he hears about what's going on with Adam, and after."

"Just be a good brother," I say.

"Be a good friend," Vincent says back. "From all I've heard, you've always been a good brother. Just be there for him."

"Of course," I say, "of course." There's solemnity to my promise. I feel charged with a task more important than all others. Be there for him. Be there.

"I just realized," Vincent says, "how insulting what I asked you to do must feel. I didn't mean anything by it. I'm just worried about the news, how he'll take it."

"Please, don't be sorry." What I don't say: *I needed to hear it*. That it's been so long since I've been Ade's brother that I've nearly forgotten how to do it.

"Have the nurse give you heated blankets for Adam," I say suddenly.

"I can try, but I don't know—"

"No, they'll definitely do it. If they say they can't, just ask the next nurse who comes through. It's a small thing, but it'll make him more comfortable. Those beds are cold. It'll probably help him sleep."

"I'll be sure to do that, Jack."

"It used to help me sleep when I was in the hospital. I spent a lot of time there—I know how bad it can be."

"I should go now, get back to Liv."

"Please give her my love. Kiss Adam for me."

CHAPTER SEVENTEEN

Adrian

AUGUST 1996

We knew Dad was coming home to say goodbye that morning. His new job started soon. He and Emily had to get settled into the house they just bought.

We'd been told Dad would be going eventually, but until that last morning, I thought that he'd change his mind. I understood he wouldn't live with us anymore and that my parents weren't in love like they used to be. I didn't like it, but it was something I could grow to accept. But when my father took off across the country, it was the beginning of the end for me, for our family.

The car pulled up in the driveway just before eight. I watched it from the front window—his back seat was full of boxes and shirts on hangers heaped on top of each other. Mom came up next to me. Looked out at the car, too.

"All right. Come on, Ade. Let's get this over with," she said.

I didn't answer. She walked past me and opened the front door. The little kids were lying on the floor watching TV, but they turned to look as she passed.

Outside, Dad got out of his car. He stood a moment, like he was considering something, before he started up the driveway. He was wearing jeans and an old T-shirt that I recognized, a jacket that I didn't. Already he was becoming someone other than who he'd been. His hair was short, weirdly so for him. He hadn't shaved in a few days, and he walked stiffly as he came toward the house. He moved like Jack did after the accident.

He raised one hand like he was waving to us, to the house. He crossed the yard, up the front steps and onto the porch where he stopped and looked at my mother.

"Morning, Bea," he said, leaning in and kissing her on the cheek. That was strange. Why kiss her if he didn't love her? Mom didn't say anything, just accepted his kiss and stepped back into the house.

"Monsters," she said, "Dad's here. Turn that off and say hi."

Ella and Remy, still in their pjs, stood up quietly from the floor. One of them switched the TV off, and they both went into the kitchen where Dad had already gone. Like he still lived in our house. I waited by the window until Mom came up behind me.

"Let's go eat something together," she said quietly. I let her steer me into the kitchen, where Dad was in the fridge pulling out eggs and a gallon of milk. The little kids were sitting at the table with confused looks on their faces. They'd been told Dad was leaving, but instead he was in the kitchen intent on making us breakfast.

"Don't you have any buttermilk?" he asked, head in the fridge, as we walked in.

"That's not something we keep on hand, James," Mom said.

"You used to." He closed the fridge door.

"No," she answered, "I never did."

"I don't know," he said. "I could have sworn we used to keep it right here on the door."

"No."

"Must have been my mom's house I'm thinking of then," he said, trying to laugh. "Got vinegar, at least? So I can make some?"

"Under the sink, like always."

"Glad to know some things still are where they ought to be, huh, guys?" He laughed too loudly. He spent the next fifteen minutes bustling around the kitchen, making buttermilk and heating a frying pan, flipping pancakes. Something dark fell over Ella's face as Dad prattled around the kitchen. She tapped her bare feet against the floor. Remy looked tired, did not speak. His hair stood on end, bangs flat against his forehead. I stood in the doorway of the room, watching.

"Hungry, Ade?" Dad said.

I shrugged.

"Whatever you say, bud. But eat while it's hot."

Mom was in and out as he cooked, and she finally came up to me as Dad was delivering a plate of pancakes.

"Have you seen Jack?" she said. "He's not upstairs."

I shrugged again, but Dad heard.

"Where is that kid? Ade, go find Jack, will you? I want you guys to at least get something before the Monsters eat it all up," he said.

I nodded, glad for a reason to leave. It was some terrible farce of a family, and even at ten I knew it. I'd never be able to eat a single bite with Dad in there like he was.

Mom put her arm around me and pulled me close. She whispered in my ear, "When you find him, be kind, baby. Ask him nicely to please come in here and talk with Dad." I nodded, and went off to look around the house for Jack.

I started upstairs but didn't find him. I looked out the windows to the backyard and peeked down the basement steps, but there was no light on down there. Jack was nearly grown up, in my mind, but he was still a little scared of the dark. I knew he wouldn't be down there if he didn't have the lights blazing.

I wandered into the living room again, back to the front window. Looked out. I saw my brother standing next to Dad's car.

It was chilly that morning, though it was still August. Jackson was outside in only his pajama bottoms. It looked like he'd gotten out of bed, went outside without putting shoes on. I watched him as he stood by the car, then as he walked to the freestanding garage that abutted our driveway. He struggled, one armed, to throw the heavy door open from the bottom, but he eventually managed. He disappeared inside the garage.

I opened the front door quietly and made my way down the porch steps and across the driveway to the garage. I was also shoeless, the ground rough under my feet. As I approached, I could hear him rummaging around in the back of the garage, talking to himself and knocking things over.

"Jackson?" I tried not to startle him. "You in there?" The rummaging noises stopped.

"Ade?" I heard his voice from the darkness.

"Yeah?"

"Get out of here. Go inside."

"Mom says come in."

"Go the hell away, Ade."

"Jack—"

"Go!" he shouted, his voice rattling me through. I didn't want to go into the garage, didn't want to be anywhere near him. But something in the way he spoke also compelled me forward. He sounded like he was frightened, like he might need help. I went into the dark garage to find him.

The air in there was thick and humid, smelled like fertilizer. I could barely make him out at the end of the room. It wasn't a wide garage, but it was deep. He was moving around among the bins we kept in the back where we put old sports equipment, hockey sticks and soccer balls and stuff.

"What're you doing?" I said, banging my knee on some junk as I tried to move closer to him.

"I said go, didn't I?"

"They're having breakfast inside. Dad cooked, and the little kids are eating already."

"Of course he did."

"They want you to go in."

"Do you want to go in?" he said snidely, his voice sharp.

"No." I was quiet for a minute. "I don't."

"Why not?" he said, laughing as he pulled something long and straight from one of the bins.

"Because he thought the kitchen is his, and we never have had buttermilk," I whispered.

"What?"

I couldn't answer because my throat was getting all choked with tears.

"Hey," he said, his voice kinder, "go inside, Adey. Go eat something, okay?"

"I don't want to! I can't ever eat there again!" I yelled, not knowing where the yell came from. My voice sounded ragged, scary.

Jack dropped whatever he was holding, moved to my side. He put his arm around me, just the right one because the left didn't work anymore. I put my forehead on his chest, cried there like that—the little hairs of his skin pushed up against mine. He held me roughly for a moment, not any longer, but in that little infinity he was the brother I'd always needed and wanted and wished for.

"Stop that shit," he said gruffly, pulling away. The room was suddenly colder when I wasn't up against him. I whimpered and tried to breathe smoothly, but it wasn't working.

"You're really that mad, huh?"

I couldn't answer. In the dark he might've nodded. He moved back to where he'd been rummaging and picked up what he'd dropped.

"Take this," he said, putting his hand out toward me. I reached for him, and my forearm collided with something metal. I grabbed it with my other hand—it was a golf club, from our grandfather's set that we stored for him because we had more space.

"Why?" I asked as he moved around to the other side of the garage where Mom parked her car. He was also holding something in his right arm. He lurched back into the morning, leaving me alone in the dark.

"Come on," he said. I followed him out. We went back around to Dad's car. Jack held an aluminum baseball bat in both hands.

"What're you doing?"

"Just shut up, okay?" He moved to the side of the car that you couldn't see from the front door. "Get over here next to me."

As I came around the side of the car, Jack raised the bat as high as he could and brought it down on the roof of the car. There was a horrible bang, and the bat bounced off the roof. The recoil nearly ripped it from his hand, but it left nothing but a little dent on the car.

"Goddamnit," Jack cursed under his breath. Then he went into a fury, throwing the bat and his body against the car again and again, trying to damage whatever he could.

The bat came down against the car; he hit it with his fist, too, and kicked it with his bare feet. The noise was deafening but strangely quiet, and the morning light shone on his bare chest and arms in a way that would have been beautiful if he wasn't so violent. His surgical scars stood out, angry pink and lumpy.

I stood dumbly, holding the golf club in both hands, just watching him.

As I stood while Jackson raged, someone must have come to the front door looking for us.

In an instant, Mom was rushing toward us across the lawn, yelling, "Jack, Jackson, oh no, Jack!" and Dad was following close behind her, yelling at us, and the little kids followed behind them. Ella still held a pancake in one hand, half-eaten.

Mom got close, but Jack saw her coming and swung the bat around in her direction. "Mom, no! Don't you get near here—go inside, Mom, inside—"

She stopped, lowered her voice. "Okay, Jack. Okay, I've stopped."

I knew he wouldn't hit her, but I didn't understand at first why she didn't come right up and rip the bat out of his grip. There was a crazed rhythm to the way he was breathing, hitched and hysterical; I think she was afraid that he'd make himself sick or worse if she got too close too quickly.

He looked at her desperately, tears in his eyes. He wasn't in control.

"Jack, please put the bat down now. Can you do that?" she asked, her voice sweet and soft.

"I can't," he said, like his heart broke with that news. "I can't, please go away, Momma, please go."

Her eyes flitted to me, then back to him. "Ade, what're you holding?" she said.

I didn't get a chance to answer because Dad barreled down on us at the same moment.

"What the hell? What is this? What've you done?" he yelled at Jack, who swung the bat around again and made like he would hit Dad.

"What do you think it is?" Jack snarled.

"I think you're losing your goddamned mind!" Dad shouted.

"I'm making it so you can't forget us," Jack spat, swinging the bat up and then down again against the car's roof. It bounced off, sounding like a firecracker. Jack looked a little surprised but wound up for another hit.

"Drop the bat, right now, or I'll call the police," Dad said.

"Get away!" Jack yelled.

My hands were sweating, and the sun was in my eyes. My bare feet felt strange on the pavement. My toes curled with tension.

He swung again at Dad, and at the end of the arc he brought the bat down on the hood of the car, this time leaving a huge dent the length of the bat.

Dad was still eyeing Jack. Mom tried to corral the little kids, who'd run out across the lawn to see what was happening. Jack looked, bat in hand, at Dad.

Jack finished one swing, but before he could begin another, Dad darted forward and tried to grab him. Jack moved backward, but not quick enough. Dad managed to grab the back of his head as he moved. He twisted his fingers through Jack's hair and drove his arm down, forcing my brother to the ground.

As Jack fell, I saw his body arch and tense, his scars twisting along his back, down the length of his left arm, stretching to his collarbone around the front. Jack met the driveway cheek first, though Dad controlled the fall a little bit so it wasn't as hard as it could have been. Dad kicked away the bat with one foot. He kept his hand on the back of Jack's head and, with the other, grabbed Jack's good arm and twisted it behind him. They fought against one another like brothers, relentless and angry, snorting through their noses, neither able to back down.

In the background, Mom was yelling stop, but I didn't know to who. Jack struggled against Dad's hold, but when he did, Dad just gripped him harder and pushed him into the ground.

"Stay down, boy," Dad said in a voice I'd never heard him use before. Gravelly and deep, frightening.

Then, slowly, he turned his gaze toward me.

"Adrian," he said, "drop that club and go to your mother. Right now." He spoke calmly, like he'd done this before.

I still didn't move—I stood by the driver's side door, Jack pinned to the ground.

"Son, I said to drop it," Dad said, like I hadn't heard him the first time.

"You fucker," Jack growled. Dad pushed his head down harder. Jack's cheek scraped across the pavement.

I looked at Jackson and my mother, who was coming toward me impossibly slowly across the lawn. I thought of how Dad came into the house, tried to take over. How he'd tried to control us, how we thought of him. How he controlled Jack now, hand in his hair, pushing his own son into the ground.

I didn't decide to do it, at least not consciously. But in the next instant, I'd raised the club high above my head, two-handed, and brought it down with all the strength I had on the driver's side mirror. The head of the club hit the ground and bounced off it. The mirror dangled from the car like a badly broken wing.

Dad looked at me with poison in his eyes, but he couldn't come after me or he'd lose control of Jack. That's why I did it, maybe, because I knew he couldn't touch me and because I wanted to get at him in any way I could. I stood there stupidly. Jack laughed.

"You already took out a crippled kid, how about a fifth grader?" he said.

Dad let him go roughly.

Jack rolled over on his back, still laughing, one cheek scraped red and raw from hitting the pavement. Dad came toward me. I stepped back but couldn't move fast enough. He grabbed me roughly by the arm. It didn't hurt, but he'd never touched me in anger before. The club fell with a clatter to the ground.

"I'm leaving today," Dad said. "There's nothing you can do about it. Go inside." He shoved me. Opened the car door. I stumbled a step, then backed off into the grass.

Mom had reached me by then, and as she took me in her arms, I watched Dad go into reverse, the car covered in dents and scratches. Without looking at us once, he backed down the driveway and drove away.

Jack stayed on his back as Dad left. It wasn't until the car was gone that he tried to sit up.

"Guess we won't be seeing him anytime soon," he said, running his right hand along his face, his chest, feeling out where the scars were, where new scars might soon be. Mom went to him, and he allowed her to help him stand up, to walk him into the house, to clean his cuts.

I stood awhile on the lawn, looking down the driveway toward the street where Dad had fled. I didn't know if I felt proud or ashamed of what we'd done, only that it was necessary. The sun was growing hot.

I went inside, and the wreckage of my brother's furious love went on its way to Washington.

CHAPTER EIGHTEEN

Remy

"Seriously, Jack?" Ella says, her voice rising. "I almost hoped you were in a car accident. Because then you'd have a reason, at least."

"Haven't we had enough wrecks today?" I say, trying half-heartedly to calm her down from the fight she's picking.

We just arrived at the house from the cemetery. Jack was in the living room when we walked in. Ella made straight for him. I dread what will happen next.

Jack's eyes flit up and catch Ella's, looking for something, asking her a question no one knows an answer to; whatever is it, he doesn't find it there in her eyes that have gone flinty and hard.

A red welt centered with robin's egg blue colors her left cheek, and it's growing. She's going to look even worse in a few hours. She'll be the talk of the school when she goes in to teach again.

She's got to have a hell of a headache from the bump her car took, but Jackson won't get by her, even today. They're stuck in lockstep together, always have been—he slips up, she barks him out about it.

"Is Ade back yet?" he asks, ignoring her. "I need to talk to him."

I shake my head. Ella scowls.

Jack smiles, once. His head falls forward. His whole body falls really, so that it looks like he's only being held up by his shoulders. Like a coat hanger's run behind them, a scarecrow hung up on a post in a field. His hands are in his pockets. He sighs, balling his fists up inside the fabric of his pants so I can see them flex and push against it.

Standing here, Jack is thirty-three, and Jack is twenty-five, Jack is seventeen, and Jack is nine, all ages at once; Jack is a perennial apology, a boy with a constant look of sorry on his face, giving you a smile that on someone else would look calculated, staged.

On Jack it has always looked sad, an expression of the slow burning agitation inside him that he never could account for, that took him places he didn't want to go and he couldn't explain to you after how he'd ended up there. No matter his good intentions, his best laid plans to do better next time. He hides from us, has secrets we can't begin to coax from him.

Ella is judge, jury, and executioner to his every failing, while the rest of us watch and wonder how it happened this way.

Mom never knew what to do with Jack. No one ever knew what to do with him, what to say. Because how can you punish this ruined kid, his arm twisted and not able to do the things it should, his head a little scrambled, this boy who lived when his brother died, this boy whose every action has been a disappointment to someone? Mom couldn't punish him, not really—because of his circumstances but also because he looked sad all the time.

He and I shared a bedroom at times, but I don't remember him being there. We lived within the same four walls, but Jack was a ghost, coming and going in the night, crying out to himself when he did sleep. That's what I remember about him, mostly— an empty bed. Jack's always been the brother I've most wanted to be close to, but he's always been so far away.

"What the hell, Jack?" Ella puts to him, her lower lip jutting out, her bangs hanging in her face. He still doesn't say anything; I'm left, like I've always been, a stupid kid who has to keep peace for people who should know better.

When my sister is wronged, nothing in the whole world can make it right again. And Jack has wronged her now. I wish he'd been there at the church, too. We needed him, and he didn't come.

But seeing him now matters more. It's almost enough.

I could have called him, picked him up from wherever he was hiding. Strong-armed him into the church, made him stand there next to us at the end of the pew. Had him there in the audience when I had my inglorious breakdown on the altar—I'm glad he missed that, at least.

"You honestly don't have anything to say? Do you know how bad it looked?" she says, like she's trying to twist a knife in between his shoulder blades. "You're given so much leeway, nobody ever says let's hold Jack accountable for whatever and now—"

"I'm sorry," he says. He takes a step forward, but Ella doesn't back up.

"I don't care," Ella answers.

He shrugs, lets his hands fall to his sides. Turns and looks out the front window, sighing. "The yard looks so different this time of year," he says. "Not many leaves on the trees."

"Can you even believe this?" Ella hisses at me, her voice sharp.

She leans forward, grabs his upper arm, digs her fingers in.

She wants to spin him around, make him look at her again so she can finish unleashing whatever it is she feels entitled to. She pulls; Jack turns to her, squares off his shoulders, his back to the window. Shakes off her hand, so she's thrown a little off balance.

"I'm sorry," he says, "but that hurt. Please don't do it again."

"Where were you?" She recovers her balance.

He rolls his shoulder around—she grabbed his bad left arm. "I was here. With Mom."

"Of course you were."

"I was. You going to go after her next? I believe she's upstairs."

"El," I say, "let it go—"

"You stay out of it," she snaps. I go quiet.

"You long-suffering asshole," she says to Jack. "You go to your father's goddamn funeral."

"I know," he says. "I'm sorry."

"How do you think it was for us, you not showing up? How do you think it was for Ade, Remy, and Cal—Cat, who had to carry the casket?"

"He couldn't have helped anyway," I say, thinking of his arm. Jack smiles wanly.

"What do you have to say? What was it this time?"

"I was here," he says simply, shrugging his right shoulder but not the left. "Your face sure looks sore."

"I can't believe you. I just can't. This was the thing you don't miss. You just don't. And you're not even sorry."

"But he keeps saying he's sorry," I say. She doesn't care.

His eyes bore a hole into the floor in front of Ella's feet, like a kid who's getting yelled at by the school principal. Ella must be hell if you misbehave in her classroom.

"What did he do," she spits, her face red, "that was so awful you couldn't show up to his funeral?"

He shakes once, his whole body giving a quick twitch like her words have real force behind them. Ella breathes heavy, also once, her mouth a pistol forcing air out in recoil.

Jack closes his eyes, swallows hard. His shakes his hands like he's flicking off water. Turns his palms up toward his face like he's examining them for something. Looking for stigmata, I think stupidly. The suffering wounds of Christ.

"How was the service?" Jack asks quietly.

I shrug my shoulders. They make me feel ashamed to love them—ashamed of her because she's cruel, him because he consents to it.

Ella resigns herself to finish him. She gallops forward because she's already destroyed everything else.

"You're pathetic," she says plainly. "I thought better of you, but I shouldn't've."

No one could ever accuse her of convoluting her meaning or intention.

I've never done it before, but I step forward now between my brother and sister. To protect him from her. To stop with my body whatever words she'll throw out next.

"Walk away," I tell her. There's anger in my voice. Her face falls, shocked that I've done this disloyal thing: stepping between her and her perceived hurt, taking the hurt's side.

"Go," I say again.

She steps back a bit but doesn't fully retreat.

"Ella, please," I beg. "Don't say things you'll regret to him. Please."

"You think I regret saying it?"

Jack's behind me; I don't see his face.

"It's okay," he says. The sadness in his voice makes me want to drop to my knees. "She's allowed to say what she thinks. She's allowed to feel like I fucked up."

I turn to him. In his face I see, remarkably, a rendering of my father's. His jaw, the strong brow and dark, shaggy eyebrows. But Jack has Mom's warm eyes, rimmed in amber. Jack's gone hollow along his cheeks, unlike Dad, and his hair is POW short. Though Jack didn't suffer with us today, it surely doesn't mean he hasn't suffered. I don't know how Ella doesn't see it.

For a terrible moment I feel in all its fury what it means to be Jack, to have to inhabit his scarred and prickly skin. It makes me want to cry, looking at him—this is my brother, I love him, and still he is alone in the world.

"You can't do this," she says, a little confused but unable to stay quiet. "You can't leave us and then come back again. You can't."

Jack nods, like her words are precious.

"You can't do that. It's not fair for you to not come but to be here now."

"Do you want me to leave?"

Now it's Ella who's silent. She hasn't thought beyond her anger, what she actually wants, what suffering of Jack's she would accept.

I can't help it; I have to rub my fists into my eyes to keep from crying in frustration.

"Oh, now," he says. He puts his right arm around me. I haven't been this close to him since we were boys. He smells the same, though now I'm as tall as he is. His hand is on the back of my neck; he whispers soft sounds into my ear. Jack, standing here, is the closest thing I'll get to my father now. That jaw, that way he picks up his foot at the end when he bounds down a flight of steps. The graying around his temples.

"You're not welcome here," Ella says eventually. "Get out. Leave."

I pull back from him, look at her full in the face—I can't understand her. When did she learn to be so cruel?

And then I can. It's Jack she wants gone, but it's also Dad. Dad's not allowed in this house, cannot be forgiven his transgressions.

Here's Jack, the living breath of him, almost but not quite James, the pitch and yaw of his body the same, that sad poet's heart beating under his country-boy rib cage, raised as they both were along a brown creek with cornfields not far off.

Jack looks around the room, considers her words. He looks at me, that same sad apology of a smile again.

"I'm not going to leave," he says. "I love you, El, but you're not allowed to chase me away because I've hurt you or made you mad. You might not need me, but Ade does. Mom and Remy do." He breathes deeply. "I'm sorry I hurt you. And I'm sorry Dad did."

Ella makes a shocked noise but doesn't speak.

Doesn't she understand that when Jack hurts her, he's hurting himself? Doesn't she know he wants to be loved by us? Doesn't she understand that he holds himself apart for some reason we'll never know, that it's haunted him since he was a boy, and maybe that's what kept him away today?

They eye each other warily, neither making the next move.

The front door opens with a bang. We all jump. Uncle Cat bustles inside with Emily behind him.

"Help with coats?" Cat calls. Jack steps around us, his hand resting for a final moment on my shoulder. He grips me once, strongly, as if in comfort.

"Is Ade with you?" Jack asks.

Cat nods.

"I'll catch up with you later," Jack says. He strides across the room, toward the front door.

"He's such an asshole," Ella says. "I won't ever forgive him for this." There is so much hurt in her I will never understand. It burns her, hotter somehow than it is for the rest of us.

"Mom didn't go to the funeral, either, and you're not ripping her a new one. You don't even know who you're angry at. Figure it out before you start losing your shit at the wrong person." I feel righteous saying it.

CHAPTER NINETEEN

Jackson

MAY 1995

The day of the fire was bright, a Saturday, early May. I was thirteen. I was sitting up in the tree in our front yard, my back against the trunk. This was before our accident, when I still had two good arms to help me climb. I faced away from the house, just thinking, when I first heard Ella shout. I turned toward the noise, but couldn't quite see through the leafed-out branches.

"Jack! Jack!" she yelled, her voice giving out partially. "Jack, come! Please Jack, come!"

Before she even reached the tree I started down. Whatever was happening, I'd be held responsible, at least in my mother's estimation. Mom'd left fifteen minutes ago, on foot, to retrieve Ade from a friend's house in the next neighborhood over. I was supposed to keep an eye on things.

I dropped out of the tree as fast as I could and came down on my left ankle. The little bones in it crunched, then rebounded. It made me cry out. I staggered.

Ella scared me. Her eyes were wide, afraid. She grabbed my hand and jerked me forward toward the house.

Maybe Remy cut the hair off another one of Ella's dolls, and that's why she was screaming.

She turned her head back toward me once, took one deep breath, then dropped my hand and ran back toward the house.

She stopped just short of the front steps. I ran up behind her, caught her by the shoulder. I tried to get her to speak. There was a burning smell. She looked at me, then up at our house. Her splotchy face paired with the wildness in her eyes left me more frightened than anything I'd ever seen.

I shook her once, hard, but she only started crying noiselessly.

What I saw didn't make sense. From a window on my parents' side of the house, thin gray smoke snaked its way outside. Above their bedroom, from somewhere in the attic, a blacker smoke rose. It smelled too. It was a kind of chemically awful, like burned rubber or plastic. It hurt your eyes.

From inside I could hear the smoke detectors going off. I hadn't noticed them before, or the fire was new. Fast moving.

Ella stood next to me, my hand still gripping her arm. Her eyes and her nose ran. Mine too. I breathed in through my nose hard. It hurt, started me gagging. I coughed, spitting over my right shoulder. I grabbed Ella around her middle and scooted backward, out onto the lawn. I set her down twenty feet or so from the porch. She sat on her knees in the grass, her hands over her mouth.

"El, where're they?!" I thought I shouted it, but she didn't seem to hear. I kicked her with the side of my foot, but she still didn't answer. She could only watch the smoke with a horrified look on her face.

"Stay!" I said. I started toward the front porch as fast as I could. I nearly took it at a run. I knew if I didn't, I wouldn't be brave enough. I did not want to go inside. I'd heard for years in school that you never went into a burning building—that was the job of the firemen.

The front door was open. My mother kept a fire extinguisher under the kitchen sink cabinet. Now it was just inside the door, in the living room. I wasn't sure who put it there, Ella or someone else. I hung in the threshold for a second, scared.

Then, from behind, Mom screamed. I couldn't understand her, if she was even making words. Still in the door, I turned— she struggled up the lawn, dragging Ade by the wrist. The two of them nearly wiped out thanks to a groundhog hole near the middle of our yard. Mom dropped his hand. She ran to Ella, still kneeling in the grass. I turned again, back to the house. Went through the door.

I grabbed the handle of the fire extinguisher. It was heavier than I expected, so I dropped it again. The downstairs wasn't full of smoke or flames. Besides the smell and the smoke detectors going off, it seemed like there wasn't much wrong. I went through the living room to the kitchen slowly, looking for fire. The remnants from our lunch were just like we'd left them, dishes stacked on the table so they could be washed later.

But where were my brothers? My throat burned; I didn't trust my voice to call for them.

My stomach turned. I nearly threw up. I spat, tried to clear the burning from my mouth and my eyes. Looked around. I noticed the back door was open, so I ran through. I didn't bother shutting it.

Just to the right of the door, Remy sat quietly on the ground. He looked sleepy but okay. In his hands he held a football. He looked at me with a lazy smile, like he was going to ask me if I'd play catch with him. Neither of us spoke.

I glanced down our yard, all the way to the creek. Maybe we could get water, somehow, to put the fire out. Down on the bank, his back to the house, Lex sat with his feet in the water. He was on the muddy flat part of the creek bank. He didn't have a shirt on.

I turned to Remy again, picked him up. He dropped his football, locked his hands together around my neck. I didn't stop to ask him what happened. I coughed, raw. I tried to call to Lex, but he didn't hear me. I came around the side of the house, going slower because of Remy. He was barefoot like Ella; when I tried to put him down, he clung to me tighter. My neck was wet where he pressed his face into it.

My ears rang, and I had a terrible headache. I stood in the front yard for what seemed like a very long time, until my mother came and took Remy from me. She sat him down in the grass near Ella and Ade, then turned back and led me to a lawn chair someone had set out on our yard, one of the neighbors, maybe. I wondered why Lex wasn't with us, but I didn't ask. Eventually I saw him skulking around the edge of the lawn, like he was scared of us.

My mother took a wet rag that somebody had given her. She knelt and wiped off my face, my hands, my legs where my shorts didn't cover—all the places my skin had been exposed, where that wretched smelling smoke had worked its way into me.

Later, my father said the fire department had been on the scene within twelve minutes. It was an easy fire for them to contain, mostly just smoke damage, but we had to spend the next few weeks at our grandparents' house across town until everything was cleaned up.

Our neighbors had come over right away, as soon as they heard my sister screaming. The one who lived next door, Mrs.

Mercurio, told my mother how she saw me pull Ella back from the house, then go inside to find my brothers. She made it sound like I'd saved everybody. A fireman asked where I was when I heard my sister yelling, how long did I think my mother might have been away since the fire started? I didn't know, shook my head until he finally stopped asking. He left me sitting with Mom. Other firemen talked to Ella, then Remy, and finally Lex.

Lex sat apart, his knees pulled up to his chest. The fireman in charge pulled Mom aside and spoke to her quietly. Ade told me later that she asked if they would wait to ask any more questions until our father arrived. A little later, my grandparents came to take us, except for Lex, to their house.

No one told me why Lex didn't come along. I accepted his absence as they led me to their car, the acrid smell still hanging in the air and high up in my throat. They made spaghetti for dinner. Remy and Ade played outside with an old soccer ball before we were supposed to get ready for bed. Ella sat by me quietly on the couch, Granna working through her hair with a comb. I took three showers but no one bugged me about using too much hot water. I tried to wash away the smell. Ade asked once about Lex: We were told the rest of our family would come over later, after they figured everything out.

It was late, after ten, when my father drove up in his old Ford. I'd just taken my last shower and put on the pajamas my grandparents laid out for us. I was ready to get into bed in one of the spare rooms (I had to share with Ade) when I heard my father's voice in the hall.

"James, do you really need to do this tonight?" the Admiral said. "The boy's tired, he's had an awful day. Let him sleep."

"I'm taking Jackson back now."

"What's happening?" said Granna. "Ellie, come lie down with me."

"Nothing," Dad said. He opened the bedroom door. The light in the room was already out, so he blocked out the hall light coming in. I must've looked afraid because he smiled and reached over to tousle my hair.

"Jack, get dressed," he said. "You're coming home with me. Mom and I need to talk to you about what happened today."

I stood up from the bed, looked around to try and find my pants. "What?" My eyes were red still from the smoke. I blinked them hard, but I couldn't see clearly. "What's happening?"

"It's okay, Jack. Don't worry about your clothes. Just come on."

"What's happening, Dad?"

"Nothing, son. I need you to come with me now, though, before we upset the kids too much."

"I'll come back later?" I was more tired than I'd ever been. All I wanted to do was sleep for days.

"I promise you'll be back here in less than an hour. We just need to talk."

"Tonight?" We walked down the hall toward the front door.

"Yes, Jack, I told you that, didn't I? Right now. Come on," he said, sounding angrier than I expected. He put his hand on the back of my neck and steered me down the hallway.

"You just think about what it is you're doing, James, you hear me?" the Admiral said as we passed.

"I know exactly what I'm doing," Dad said. "Don't tell me how to handle my own children."

"Jesus, James," the Admiral said as Dad opened the front door and held it for me. "The boy's not even wearing his shoes. Come here, Jack," he said, holding out a pair of sneakers for me. I didn't realize it until I looked at them on my feet: They were my grandmother's. "Put those on. And you take that blanket, here you go, keep it around your shoulders, that's a good boy."

Dad looked at the Admiral with something that felt like hate. Then he took me by the arm and pulled me out into the night, toward his parked car. We both got in the front seat. He didn't remind me to wear a seat belt, which he always did normally. We pulled out onto the main street in town, the streetlights shining. We drove all the way to our house without speaking.

In our driveway, Dad parked the car and came around to my side. He opened the door for me. I was very tired, almost asleep, so I didn't realize we were there. He shook me a little, then leaned in and kissed me on the forehead.

"Come on, Jack," he said, helping me out of the car. "I know you're tired, I know." We went through the front door. The inside still smelled like the awful smoke. As soon as we went inside, I woke right up.

I looked around the kitchen, where Dad had walked me. The lights in the house weren't working, so my parents had set our camping lantern in the middle of the kitchen table. It cast spooky shadows. The room seemed like a place I hadn't been before. My mother and Lex were each sitting on a kitchen chair around the table. Dad pulled one out for me, and I sat down on it, hard. I still had the blanket wrapped around me. My shoes weren't tied.

Dad took the empty chair next to me so that he was sitting between Lex and me. Mom leaned forward in her chair so she could touch me on the knee.

"Hello, sweetheart," she said. "I'm sorry we had to wake you."

"Wasn't sleeping yet." My mouth felt full of something sticky, like peanut butter. The kitchen smelled smoky and claustrophobic. Lex didn't say anything. He slumped in his chair, arms crossed over his bare chest. He wore gym shorts—the same clothes I saw him in when he sat by the creek.

"Jackson," Dad said, "you know what happened today." I nodded. He looked like he wanted me to speak, his eyebrows raised a little so his statement turned into a question.

"We had a fire?" I said.

"Yes," Mom said. "Do you know where it started?"

"Upstairs?" I looked around, wondered what we were doing here.

"That's right, son. In our bedroom."

"Sorry." I didn't know what else to say.

My mother raised her hand to her face, rubbed her eyes. "It's okay, Jack. I just don't understand—"

"Bea," Dad said, cutting her off. She looked at Lex for a long minute, but he didn't move.

Dad said, "The fire this afternoon was not an accident. It was set intentionally."

"Do you understand what that means?" Mom said.

"Huh?"

"Setting a fire on purpose. Do you know what that's called?"

I looked stupidly from my mother to my father and back again. A panicky feeling climbed my throat.

"Arson," Lex said quietly. It was hard to see in the kitchen, but not impossible—we were all so close together. Lex kept his face down so I couldn't see his eyes. My father didn't acknowledge Lex's response, just kept on staring at me like I knew what I was doing there with the three of them.

"Son, the firemen knew immediately that someone set that fire on purpose. I understand that you were up in your tree this afternoon?"

I nodded.

"You did a very brave thing, helping your little sister and brother, who could have been injured or even killed—"

"Not true!" Lex barked. The muscles in his shoulders and arms were taut ropes pulled tight beneath his skin. He was nearly shaking. The tension in him scared me.

"Alexander," Mom said softly. She put her hand out to touch his arm, but he jerked away from her before she could, like her touch would kill him. She looked away, raised her hand to her eyes like she was crying. Dad looked at Lex with a dangerous face for a second before he turned back to me.

"I wish I didn't need to sit here with you like this," he said. "But that seems the only way we'll get any answers tonight."

"Dad, what's happening?" I asked. "What's wrong?"

He took a deep breath, ran his hands over his head like he was wringing it, then looked straight into my eyes. "It seems that Lex went upstairs today intending to set that fire."

Sweat fell in beads off Lex's forehead. Mom kept crying.

"He waited until your mother left to get Ade, then he sent Remy outside. He went upstairs to our bedroom, and he took two things. Do you know what he took?"

"I don't, Dad."

"Lex took a pocket lighter and the fire-start liquid that we use when we barbecue. And he took it upstairs while his little sister watched TV just below him and then he threw the liquid onto—"

"No!" Lex shouted, jumping forward in his chair. My father moved just as fast as Lex did, smacked him hard in the back of the head.

"You sit, goddamn it, Lex!"

Lex rocked forward from the blow, then landed back in his chair, a dark flush rising on his cheeks and chest. He didn't slump anymore; he looked right at Dad like he wanted to get smacked again, but harder.

"James, please don't hit him like that," Mom said.

"He could've killed someone—"

"Stop!" I interrupted.

Then everybody did stop.

"Why am I here?"

"Your brother was honest when the firemen asked him what he'd done," Mom said. "That was a very good thing for Lex to do."

"Goddamn little Saint Alexander," Dad said.

Mom didn't look at Dad, just kept talking. "Lex has told us where he got the lighter. And we know what happened last week, when you boys went upstairs and went rummaging in Daddy's dresser."

"Okay," I said. My fluttery panic settled cold in my stomach because I knew what they were talking about.

"Tell it, Lex," Dad said.

"We wanted to have a cigarette," Lex said. He dropped his eyes, brought them up to meet Dad's with his next breath. "We wanted to find some, and we knew Dad kept them in his dresser for when he got stressed so we went to find them."

"Jack," Mom said, "We know that you took that lighter from the store that you like to get your gum from on the way home from school. Lex told us."

So they knew how Lex and I'd been planning to steal the lighter from the store for a few weeks, and how I'd finally gotten the guts up to do it last Friday. "He told you?"

"He told us how you found the cigarettes and took them down by the creek, and each smoked one, got sick after. How you threw the rest of the pack into the water," Dad said.

So they did know it all. "I'm sorry," I said. "I didn't know he was gonna do the fire though—"

"We know," Dad said. "Lex says that you knew nothing about it. He didn't tell you on purpose."

I looked at my brother, whose eyes met mine for the first time since I arrived. He looked tired, resigned, very old. He'd never look so old again.

I know you, I thought. *Make me understand.*

"So why do you need me here?" I asked.

"Daddy thought that you might know more about what happened than Lex thinks you do," Mom said. "He wanted to ask you both, that's all."

"I don't know anything more than he said."

"Jackson, I need you to think very hard," Dad said. "I've paddled Lex, I've reasoned with him, but nothing seems to get him to tell us why he did this awful thing."

"You want to know so you can get even," Lex said plainly.

"You hold your mouth, boy," Dad snapped.

"I won't."

Dad ignored him, turned to me. "Jack," he said, "Lex has done a terrible thing that could have hurt or killed someone we love. We need to know why this happened. We need to understand so we can help him. He's an angry, confused boy. You need to tell me what you know about this, please."

Dad's eyes looked shiny, like he might cry.

"But I don't know anything."

"Damn it, Jack!" Dad shouted, slamming his hand on the table.

I flinched. Mom leaned forward, put her hand on my knee to steady me.

Dad said, quieter, "Do you know where he started the fire?"

I shook my head.

"My dresser, Jack. He doused it, lit it up, and then watched it for a while before he went out back to wait for the whole house to burn."

"No I didn't!" Lex yelled. He sat up straight. "I took him outside, I yelled at her to go outside, I put the hydrant by the door so you could find it!"

He meant Remy and Ella. He'd taken Remy outside. He'd yelled to Ella to get out. And he was the one who put the extinguisher there. Not the hydrant. God help him, he didn't know the word for it.

"There's nothing more hateful that anyone could do to another person, Jack," Dad said, ignoring Lex, "than what your brother's done to me, to our family." Mom put her other hand out to Lex, who let her touch him now.

"I need to know what made him do it," Dad said. "That's what I need you to tell me. Think for a minute before you answer. I want to know what made Lex do this awful thing."

I sat there on the chair, let the blanket slide down around my shoulders. I looked at Lex, his hair falling into his eyes, slicked down with sweat and grime. He didn't have his summer buzzcut yet. He looked like he'd been crying despite himself. Dad sat a little behind me, taking up the whole room with his anger; Mom kept a hand on each of us boys, like she had to so we wouldn't get swept away from her or each other.

"James, we should take the boys to your parents' now. Let them get some rest," Mom said. "Tomorrow we'll all be fresh, and we'll figure this out."

"No, Bea," Dad said. "They're not moving until they tell us what's happened and why." My mother looked at me, at my brother, finally at the floor.

"Jack won't tell you anything," Lex said quietly.

"What'd you say?" Dad snapped.

"You heard."

"Lex," Mom said.

"Jack won't tell, but he knows," Lex said. "He doesn't realize he knows, but he saw just like I did. He just didn't keep looking."

"Jackson, what's he talking about?" Dad said, his voice hot.

"I don't know." I was sure I'd throw up all over the floor.

"It's okay, Jack," Lex said. "I saw enough. I saw it, and I stopped it. And," he said, looking straight at Dad, "I hate you."

"Honey, what's he mean?" Mom asked. I didn't know who she was talking to.

"I'm not telling her, Dad," Lex said. "You can, if you want. Jack saw, but he didn't look long enough to understand it," he said.

Dad stood up from his chair, but Lex stayed sitting. Mom still had her hand on my leg and held Lex's shoulder. She looked at Dad for a second like she didn't know him.

"You'd better tell me what in the hell you mean, boy," Dad said. He pushed past an empty kitchen chair as he surged toward Lex. He knocked our lunch dishes off the table—they'd been sitting there since the fire. The noise didn't make Lex flinch.

"You know. I figured it out, but I won't ever tell anybody."

"James, what's he mean?" Mom said. She leaned toward Lex too.

"How the fuck should I know?" he snapped. He reached his hand forward across the table so quickly that Lex couldn't move out of the way. His hand crashed into Lex's cheek with a noise that seemed louder than anything I'd ever heard. My brother turned his face away with the force of it.

Then he turned back to face Dad really slowly, and he smiled.

"You can't hit it out of my head, now that it's in there," he said. "Be good to Jack, though. He's smarter than me. If he decides he wants to understand, man, you're in trouble." I felt my father's hand pulling me up to standing by the back of my shirt.

"You know what he's talking about?" he whispered in my ear, hot and terrified. In that instant, I became my father's enemy for what he thought I knew. Even though I knew nothing, not yet. I was a danger to him now.

I shook my head, and he let go of me roughly. I slumped back into the chair, tangled in the blanket.

Dad smiled, but instead of looking kind, it was devilish.

"You figured Jack was on your side, didn't you?" Dad said to Lex, who didn't answer. "You figured wrong." Dad put his hand on my shoulder, but it was less about affection than about ownership, widening the already deep space between Lex and me.

"You know," he said, and paused a moment. "Jack didn't even stop to look for you today."

In a sick second, I knew that what my father said was true, but that it was not true, too. I shrugged his hand away, twisted so I could look at Lex. I tried to tell him with my eyes that I'd remembered him. That I didn't leave him alone, house burning. That when he was missing, I sought him. But he would not meet my eyes.

"Bea, get Jack out of here. I need to talk to Lex alone," Dad said too loudly, his voice cheerful and fake.

"James—" she said, putting her arm all the way around Lex.

"Leave," Dad said. He tapped her roughly on the shoulder to urge us out. She managed to kiss Lex on the head before she reached her hand over to me and helped me out of my chair.

"Let's go outside and wait in the car for Lex and Daddy, Jackboy," she said. She hadn't called me Jack-boy since I was little. She was crying.

"I'm not going without him. Lex, come on. Come with me now."

I broke away from Mom, but Dad grabbed me around the shoulders.

"Jackson," he said, "do not try me." I struggled against him for a minute before he dropped me roughly and shoved me back through the archway into the living room, with my mother. "Take him outside, Bea."

"Jacky," she said, trying to turn me around, "come on."

From the kitchen, I could hear Lex call out to me. "It's okay, Jack. It's okay. I'm okay, Jack."

Mom hustled me onto the front porch, where I yelled at her to go in and stop him, my father, from whatever it was that he wanted to do to Lex.

"He'll kill him!" I shouted, though I didn't know where the words came from. She put her body between me and the front door.

"Stop him, please stop him," I whispered. The fight had all gone out of me, but my brother was still inside the house.

"Jack," she said, "Honey, I can't. Sh. Jack. Jack, please. Please, get in the car with me." My insides sank. I watched her, shaking a little on the front porch. She'd failed us, Lex and me. I was only thirteen, but I knew she'd never really be my mother again.

Inside, Dad said, "Get out of that chair, boy."

"No," Lex said. I heard him yelp, and then Lex laughed.

Mom and I climbed into the back seat of my father's car, which he'd left unlocked. She put her arm around me, and we waited there so long I fell asleep.

A while later, Dad came out to the car and got Mom and me in the front seats. She put the key into the ignition, then turned it and waited for my father to bring Lex outside. It was very dark out, but I could see him carrying Lex in his arms, like Lex was a baby. My brother's eyes were closed, his body slack. There was a kitchen rag in his mouth, like he was biting on it. Holding him, Dad got the two of them into the back seat.

Mom looked at Dad in the rearview mirror, and he said, "He's fine, Bea. He's just asleep."

Mom backed the car out of the driveway quietly. We went back to my grandparents' house, where everyone was asleep except for my grandfather. He came out to the car and met us when we pulled up. Mom guided me inside, but I turned around and saw the Admiral shake Lex awake and lead him in after me. As they came, the Admiral moved the towel from Lex's mouth. My brother flinched.

Dad tried to follow, but the Admiral looked at him and said quietly, "You aren't coming in here, James. Go back to your god-damned house, I don't care. But you will not sleep under the same roof these boys do tonight."

My father stood in the doorway like he didn't hear.

"You go now," my grandfather said again. "Come back tomorrow." The Admiral shut the door without waiting for my father to move.

Mom helped me wash my face and find clean pajamas. She walked Ade, half-asleep, across the hall. She came back then and lay down in the bed where Ade had been, next to me. She smoothed my hair and spoke softly. I tried to listen, but I couldn't get the image of her leaving Lex alone with Dad out of my head.

In a little while, the Admiral came in with Lex. Mom got up to help, and they put him next to me. The Admiral pulled the covers up, kissed us. Mom stood at the foot of the bed a minute, like she wanted to speak. Then she stepped out, leaving the door open.

"He'll need the dentist tomorrow, Bea. I think he should go to the ER tonight, but that's up to you. It's one of the permanent ones on top, gone entirely, and at least one other's cracked nearly to his gum line. He wouldn't tell me what happened, but it looks like he hit the edge of the counter with his mouth," the Admiral whispered in the hall.

I was almost asleep I when I felt Lex slip his hand into mine. We were on our backs in the double bed with a little space between us. He squeezed my hand; I squeezed back to let him know I was listening.

He rolled on his side slowly. I could tell it hurt him. He got his face right up against my ear, his hot breath on my skin.

"Um-kay," he said. *I'm okay.* It came out garbled through his swollen mouth and broken teeth, but I could understand him.

I squeezed his hand.

He breathed heavily, sounded a hundred years old.

I squeezed harder.

"I looked," I whispered back. "I looked for you."

He sighed.

"I know," he answered. "I heard you call me. Damn, my mouth hurts." He paused a minute, then said, "You know why I did it, right?"

I didn't squeeze back.

He took a breath, then whisper hissed, "It was that box, Jack. The one in the dresser, behind the cigarettes."

I squeezed. I remembered.

"You said don't look in it. It wasn't ours. But I looked, and it was letters. And I told you, remember?" He breathed, then kept whispering: "And then you said to not look at the letters because they were private, and we'd found the cigarettes anyway, but then I wanted to know, so I looked, right? So I knew then and you didn't. But you know where the secret was, just not what it said." I squeezed his hand; this time I didn't relax my grip.

"I won't ever tell anybody but you. It was terrible. Jack, the letters were from a woman. She signed them all 'love, Emily.' I didn't read them then—we went, and we smoked. But you don't know this—later, I snuck back in, and I read them."

Neither of us breathed. A great rushing filled my insides.

"Dad's in love with the lady who wrote the letters, Jack. He wants to leave Mom, leave us. The letters talked about that. So, I burned them. 'Cause I didn't ever want Mom to see them. I didn't want you to see them. I burned them all. I didn't mean to catch the wall on fire. Then the whole room went up, I was so scared."

"And then he hit you for it."

"He doesn't think you know anything. Tell if you want, or don't tell. You're the big brother. You know better than me what to do."

I held his hand until he slept. I tried to calm down the sick heat inside me and fell into a fitful doze.

I woke up with a start around three in the morning and threw up all over the bed. My mother sat by me in the bathroom the rest of the night as I retched and cried. She didn't know it, but her being there made it worse.

That night James left me orphaned, with a father who wanted to leave and a mother I couldn't count on to keep us safe. He killed Lex, too, at least the lightness inside Lex, the kid in him, the part that trusted anyone but me.

Our accident didn't happen for another month, but in that time, Lex moved like an old man. He was stiff, formal, uneasy in himself. A fire had gone out in him. We didn't see Dad much— he stayed in a hotel room across town, while Mom and us kids lived at the Admiral's house while ours was being repaired.

Since the fire, I've carried the burden of my brother's faith that I would make the right choice about the secret that, if anybody was to find it out, would have left our father damned. Lex dragged the snarled truth out, but he left the revealing to me. He blew the world apart and left me to try to make sense of the pieces.

And I did nothing but hold on. Lex never did get his teeth fixed.

CHAPTER TWENTY

Adrian

SUNDAY 3:20 P.M.

"Dad," Rett says, "don't leave."

He's talking to me through the slatted door in the downstairs bathroom. The people who owned the house before my parents corralled the toilet in its own small room. It's separate from the sink and mirror, water closet style. I can stand leaning against the vanity and wait for my son without seeing him. It's just an illusion of privacy, doesn't block any sound. But it used to let me brush my teeth in here before school while someone else used the toilet.

"Hey," Rett says again. "You're there, right?"

"Did you hear me leave?"

"No. Why aren't you talking though?"

Rett has a habit of long sits on the toilet. He likes to look at the pictures in magazines left for older people, but what he likes most is his mother or me hanging around outside the door so he can chat.

"You need to hurry up, Rett. Someone knocked at the door again."

"Dad, you know I'm trying."

"Are you sick?"

"No. I just need to sit."

"Hurry it along. I mean it."

"*Dad.*"

The light bulbs my mother has in the fixtures are terrible. The light would make anyone look sick. The skin of my hands looks yellowed and dry. I hold them out in front of me, palms facing Rett's door, fingers spread wide. They are thin, chapped, inadequate.

Jack sat with me while I called Liv back on the house phone from Dad's old study, now Mom's second sitting room. We spoke briefly, then Vincent got on and explained things. Finally, I talked to Adam's doctor, agreed that transferring him to Seattle Children's Hospital made the most sense.

We hung up, and I put my head on my brother's shoulder. Neither of us spoke. Panic surged and abated, surged again. Jack held me tight with his good arm.

"What did you call Papa when you were little?" Rett asks me suddenly.

"What?" I'd almost forgotten he's sitting here, lost in thought about Adam, about how soon I'll be able to get home.

No one has come knocking on the door in a few minutes. This bathroom's been given up for lost.

"What'd you call him?"

"I called him Dad. When I was very little, I called him Daddy."

"What did you call Emmy?"

"I called her Emily. That's what she told me to call her. You need to finish up, Rett, for real."

"Because she wasn't your mom."

"Yes, that's right. You need to get out of there."

"Nobody wants in."

"You don't know that."

"Yes I do. No one's knocking anymore."

I hear him shift, hope he's almost through.

"You done, bud?"

"No, just shaking my foot. It's got needlies so I have to move it."

"Want me to open the door?"

"Don't!"

I lean back and rest against the vanity. My tie is loose around my neck, so I take it off entirely, looping it around my hand and shoving it in my pocket.

I don't want to tell anyone about what's happening with Adam—I'm not sure why, except I have the feeling that if I speak it aloud it'll undo me completely. I can't trust anyone to not panic themselves, and I can't deal with that. I'll find an excuse to leave this very afternoon, and my family will get the news later, once I'm home again.

I asked Jack to respect this. He agreed to it, but I could tell he thought I was wrong.

"Where is he?" he asks, still jiggling his foot around. I hear Rett's pants swish.

"Who's he? Adam is with Mom. Your uncles are somewhere in the house, probably wanting to get into the bathroom."

"I don't mean them."

"What are you talking about, then? Papa? You know where he is."

"He's with the flowers we threw." He means the roses we dropped on the coffin before they lowered it into the ground.

"No he isn't. Papa's in heaven," I say, catching my breath in my throat. "Do we need to talk about this now?" Heaven's the last thing I want to think about.

"I don't want to talk about Papa. I don't mean him anyway."

"Who then?"

"I thought we're not supposed to be talking," he says slyly.

I worry what'll happen when Rett's a teenager. Adam is so open and happy—Rett was made to trouble us, my father said once, smiling.

"We're already talking. So who?"

"Your brother. Where is he?"

"Probably trying to find a bush outside, with how long you're taking."

"No, the other one. My almost uncle. The one you told me about in the car." Jesus Christ, Rett's like a knife in my ribs.

"He's in heaven too."

"With Papa?"

"Yes, with Papa."

"Are they okay?"

"Of course they're okay. Are you okay? They're going to ask if you've fallen in."

"I don't like that joke, Daddy. Don't say that joke."

"Okay. I'm sorry,"

I want to talk about things I can't talk about. I want to tell my six-year-old how I felt today holding him, how when we drove to the church I kept looking at the other drivers and wondering if they knew about my father. How they didn't care. About how now I have a sick kid and about that last conversation when Dad said I didn't understand what that was like.

"It's a terrible world, Rett," I say, laughing under my breath. "And I can't do anything to change that." I hold my hands out in front of me again, looking at the blue veins running underneath my skin. "Not me, not anybody. You do the best you can, and still you lose. Always."

"Dad," Rett says in a small voice, "why are you laughing at me?"

"I'm not laughing at you," I answer. "I'm not."

I hear his voice get husky, like he might be crying.

"My belly hurts."

"I can't help you. I can't help if you won't let me in the room with you." I grab the doorknob. "Can I come inside?"

I swing the door open. Rett's hunched over, elbows on knees, pants down around his ankles. He's also got one shoe off. He must have dropped it when his foot fell asleep.

"Don't tell you had to help me," he says miserably. "It just really hurts."

"I know it hurts. You're okay."

There is nothing I can do for Adam, but I can maybe give Rett a hand. I rub his back. He whimpers a little, finishes his business, and lets me help him clean up. He pulls up his underpants and khakis in one tug. I grab his shoe and follow him out.

I hoist him around the middle with one arm so he's tall enough to easily reach the sink to wash his hands.

"When I was little, there used to be a wooden stool in here to stand on. So we could reach."

"Like I have at home?" he asks, rubbing his small hands together under the water.

"Just like it."

I sit him on the vanity and ease his foot back into his shoe. I tie the lace tighter this time. He leans forward with a sudden motion—I'm afraid he'll topple off the edge of the counter, but he doesn't—he leans into my body, kisses me on the cheek.

I pick him up and hold him. He rests his head on my shoulder.

"How do you know where Papa is? How do you know it's heaven?"

"Because Papa was a good man. Heaven is where good people go." The weight of his body against mine is a comfort.

"How do you be good, Dad?"

"Well, I guess you be kind. You love people. You try your best not to hurt them. You say sorry when you do."

"Papa was those things?"

"Papa tried to be, yes."

"But if he didn't? Is he not good then?"

"The most important thing is to try. And he did."

"Am I good?"

"Of course you are. You're the best boy." I've waltzed my way around so I can look in the mirror, see myself holding my boy in my arms, but also seeing other things, my own face when I was a kid, ten or eleven, and the faces of my brothers and my sister, my mother and father, too, all looking at me like they're expecting something big.

"I think you're good too," he says.

"I try to be. It gets harder to be good as you grow up, I think."

"Did you call Mom yet?" he asks as I shift his weight to open the bathroom door to the hall.

"I did. But don't worry. Adam's okay." That's a lie, but Rett doesn't know it; I try to believe it too.

"You want to get a snack, something to drink? It might help your belly."

"Yes," he says. "But carry me. I'm tired."

"I wasn't going to put you down."

CHAPTER TWENTY-ONE

Remy

JULY 2005

"Honey," my mother asked, "did something happen to Ella when you were visiting your father? Was there a fight, maybe? Something that would have upset her?"

I shook my head—nothing had happened, at all. It was the lack of anything happening that had made me dislike the trip so much that year.

It was the summer before ninth grade. Ella and I'd spent most of June at our father's house in Sawtell. Ade was busy being nearly grown up, and Cal was little then, just four. Fun to play with but not for long. Ella'd spent all her time texting on her cell phone. I kept saying she'd get in trouble for going over our limit, but she didn't care. She'd been out of sorts since we returned, but I didn't know why.

Jack didn't go west with us for visits. He'd last come four years ago, when he was nineteen and one year out of high school. He and Dad didn't get along very well anymore.

"It was boring as hell, if that's what you mean," I said. Mom slapped me on the back of the hand lightly and rolled her eyes.

We finished breakfast, and I threw myself down on the couch in the next room. I was supposed to be reading a book for school in the fall. I tried to read, but the sun was coming in through the windows in warm rectangles on the floor. Next thing I knew, my mother was sitting by my feet, holding the paperback.

"How's it going, lazy bones?" she said, and she swatted me with the book on my shins.

"Whatcha wan'?" I said. My mouth was open and my tongue was dry so the words came out stuck together.

"Just wanted to tell you that it's after lunch already. I want you to go wake Ella up." I sat up slowly, pulling my legs up so Mom didn't have to shift.

"Why can't you get her, I gotta read—"

"No, sir. You're not reading, far as I can tell. And she hates when I wake her. So it's you. Get on it. Also, call your brother and see if he's coming home for dinner tonight or not. He never answers when I call."

I frowned, ran my hands through my hair.

"There's a sandwich in it for you."

"Turkey and lettuce," I said. I started up the steps. I'd call Jack later. First, I had to deal with Ella.

I made it to the top and stood outside my sister's door. I thought about banging on it or throwing something at her to wake her up, but instead I just opened it quietly.

Ella was lying on her belly, her left arm hanging off the side of the bed. No covers on her, not even a sheet. It used to get infernally hot in that bedroom. She wasn't wearing her pjs, just her underpants and a sleeveless shirt. I turned my back to her so I didn't embarrass her when she woke up. I noticed her sneakers shoved under her dresser. Usually we left shoes downstairs. I bent down, saw they were dirty and smelled a little. Damp.

"El, get up now."

She didn't budge, so I reached my hand out till I felt the edge of her sheet. I said her name one more time, then I tugged. She jumped and half fell out of bed.

"Son of a bitch, Remy," she hissed. She shuffled around for a second. I turned to see her pull a bath towel she'd left on the floor over her body as she stood.

"Mom says up now. So up. You're lucky I woke you."

"You goddamn—"

"Be nice. Or I'll ask Mom why your shoes are wrecked." I smiled as sweetly as I could. I stood with my hands in my pockets, grinning in a way that I knew she hated. She called it my "smug bastard" look. She said Jack had one, too.

But my sister surprised me. She seemed frightened, panicked, tired. The circles under her eyes were even darker today.

"I've been hearing you go out at night, you know," I said. "You tell me why, or I tell Mom."

Ella looked at me like she'd never met me before. She looked lost. And frantic, like she'd run out of the room if she could, but she also looked too tired to move. Resigned. I didn't want to tell on her anymore.

"Mom's making lunch now." I turned to go but lingered in her door. "I'll tell her you're coming."

The rest of the day was uneventful. I watched TV. I went for a bike ride, called Jack, who didn't come home for dinner after all. I tried to eat but couldn't because of the heat and the way my sister looked earlier. She was fine now, normal and sarcastic, herself. But even when I went to bed, I was still thinking of her. I let my mother kiss me on the cheek when I said goodnight.

"El," she said, "he must be sick, letting his mother kiss him!"

I went upstairs to my room. I lay down but could not settle. A while later I heard a knock at my door and someone going *sh*. I stood up, as quietly as I could, opened the door and went into the hall. The light bulb in the hall was burned out, so you couldn't see anything. But I felt my sister's hand slide into mine. I followed her into her bedroom.

We didn't talk until we were in her room, door closed, and had gone through her half of the room, past the plywood partition where I used to sleep.

"Quiet," she said. "Be careful, and don't fall." She was in jeans, not her pjs. Wearing her old sleeveless tank top again, too. Her phone was shoved into her front pocket. I was only wearing gym shorts, my blue ones, which was what I always slept in. I had a cell phone, too, but didn't care much about it, like my sister did. I didn't have it on me.

Ella hopped up onto my old bed, barefoot. She slid open the single window, then the screen behind it. She positioned herself with her butt on the sill, and in an instant, she was out, swallowed by the night.

"Now you come," she whispered. "Fast, but not too fast. The roof's pretty level here." Just as she had, I stood on the bed, then shimmied out the window. "Pull it shut!" she hissed.

I crouched on the roof next to her. Ella reached back into the room. She'd rigged a length of twine on the inside of the window so she could pull it shut after herself and then use it to get back in. Smart move.

"Move fast now, and don't talk," she said, and started to work her way down the roof. We felt our way to the edge using the side of the house for balance.

In the backyard, right off the house, we parked the ride-on lawn mower. Ella scooted to the edge of the roof, turned around so she was facing me, and eased herself off the side. It looked like getting out of a swimming pool in reverse. There was an instant where she hung, before her toes caught the seat of the mower. A second later I heard a soft thud on the grass. It was my turn to follow her. It felt strange, hanging like that with my hands on the edge of the roof and my feet on the mower. The night was very dark, and it hadn't cooled down much from the day's heat.

"Come on!" Ella whispered. I dropped to the mower, then the ground. She grabbed my hand, and we ran together to the end of our yard, where we had our shed.

"You see that?" Ella said. I could just make out a long, metallic-looking thing. "We grab that, get it to the water, and that's it. Coming home's the hard part." She dropped my hand and went down the yard to where she'd been pointing. I followed her, realized she was trying to flip over our old canoe.

The air smelled earthy and thick, like it'd stick in your lungs even after you went inside. It was pleasant though. You wanted it that way. My heart was beating in my ears so loud I could barely hear the crickets and other night noises.

The two of us easily got the boat down to the edge of the creek. In the bottom of the canoe there were two oars, lodged under the plank seats so they didn't fall out when the canoe was upside down, but Ella didn't go for them. She jumped into the boat like she was made for it, and hissed for me to push off the side and hop in the back.

The mud of the bank made it hard for me to get the canoe buoyant, but once it was, there was only a tiny splash, barely noticeable, when I climbed in. I started to reach for an oar, but she put her hand out to stop me. We floated, silent, letting the current pull us down the creek. The night was still, and there was only a hint of moon. Sweat trickled down my back.

After a while, we saw flashlights on the opposite side of the creek. We got closer, and Ella yelled out, "Hey!" Two or three people splashed into the creek up to their thighs and dragged us up on the bank. Ella and I stumbled out of the canoe. I tripped on the oars in the bottom, and a hand reached out for me to grab so I didn't fall. I grasped it, hard, then set both my feet firm on the bank.

"Okay there, little brother?" I heard Owen Murray say as he dropped my hand and took my sister's. I was a little surprised to realize he was there.

We weren't supposed to be around Owen. He was trouble in the opinion of nearly every adult we knew, including Jack. But he'd stopped me from falling. I stayed quiet. He helped Ella step out of the canoe onto the shoreline, and she leaned into his body more than I thought she needed to for balance.

Owen wore cargo shorts, deep pocketed, and he stuck his flashlight with his other hand into one of the pockets. He took Ella in both his arms, so that he bear-hugged her, then he leaned backward, just slightly, so he lifted her feet off the ground. She laughed.

"Follow us, Remy," Ella said. The other people who pulled the canoe in had already crashed through the brush beyond the bank, laughing. Owen held Ella's hand. I followed.

Branches scratched my legs. A biting bug, mosquito probably, landed on my shoulder, and when I swatted it, the slap I gave my skin made a dull, thick sound. We walked maybe ten minutes, till we came to a clearing where there were other people, all boys, sitting around a little campfire.

"This is where you go?" I whispered. Ella took my left hand. In her other, she held Owen's.

"Yeah," she said. "It's okay. They understand."

The boys around the little fire stood up, except the one who was trying to keep it burning. There were two of them, plus the kid on the ground by the fire.

"Hey," Owen said. "Ella's here. Brought her brother, too."

"Had to," she whispered, leaning into Owen's shoulder. She still held my hand, but it was him she was there for. That confused me some because I didn't know they were really even friends. We all went to school together, but I didn't know they knew each other this well. My sister's life was different from my own, I knew, but just how different had never occurred to me.

"Remy, hey, Remy—" said the boy at the fire.

"Bay, keep the damn thing going, huh?" said one of the standing boys. I realized who they were: the Stowe kids. At least, a few of them. Baylor, the second to youngest, was my buddy. He had a mess of brothers older than us, like I did, and two of them were here.

Bay was working the fire while Brett and Ross stood back behind him. They were drinking something, beer I guessed, and raised their cans to us as we came.

"Why'd you never tell me you came out here?" I asked Bay, feeling sort of hurt.

"You think," Bay said in an exaggerated whisper, "that these dicks bring me out with them often? And that if I told you, they wouldn't beat the hell out of me for ratting them out?"

"Drink, Owen?" Brett asked.

"No thanks."

"Fine then," Brett said, sizing us up. "Want one, El?"

"Nah," she said, dropping my hand.

"You want one, Remy?" Ross asked. He was smiling, so I knew he wasn't dicking me around like Brett might. Ross was seventeen or so, Ade's old friend. I'd always liked him. He used to pick me up and swing me by my arms when he came over to visit.

"I dunno," I said. "I guess." Brett reached into a duffel bag behind him on the ground, rummaged in it and tossed me a can.

"Sorry it's warm," Brett said. "But it's the best we can do for you." I was still nervous around him. He used to chase me home on his bicycle.

I held the beer can dumbly.

"Come on, bud," Owen said. He took it from my hands and held the can away from himself so when it exploded from the pressure it didn't spray anybody.

"That's just one of Brett's jackass tricks," Owen said. "You're good now, but I don't know if the beer is."

"Can I have one?" Bay asked, still beside the fire. He'd rocked back onto his heels, so he looked like he was praying.

"Nope," said Ross and Brett, nearly together.

"Remy's younger than I am," Bay said.

"But we like him better," Owen said. "Trust me, that beer's all skunked anyway. Especially since Brett got it for us."

"Shut it," Brett said quickly. "Get it yourself then."

"Don't want to," Owen answered.

"Jesus, will you all shut up?" Ross said. "This beer is terrible, Brett. But let Remy have it, if he wants. Bay, you're too young."

I sat down, watched the little fire die. I didn't know what skunked was, but I drank the warm beer anyway, very fast so that it didn't have time to sit in my mouth and convince me not to. I could feel another mosquito bite me on the shoulder, near where the other had.

A few minutes later, Ella and Owen settled themselves behind me and Bay. "Feel it, little brother?" Owen asked me.

"What'm I supposed to feel?" I asked. Ella laughed.

"Just, you know, like funny. Or like you can't move quite right. Or tired," Owen said.

"I feel tired."

Then my sister leaned from behind me, put her arms around my chest so her mouth was next to my ear. Her arms were bare against my skin. I thought that it was nice to be like that with her, but I knew enough to not say it.

"This is where I come at night," she whispered. "I come because it's better than being at home. I brought you so you could see. And now you're drinking."

I didn't move.

"So if you tell, I'll tell on you."

I nodded. I kept my mouth shut, even though I wanted to ask her what at home was so bad that would make her come here nearly every night. Because I'd never, until then, thought there was anything wrong with our home. Sure, Dad had moved, Ade had moved, and Jack was sort of living with us but not all the time, but Ella and Mom and I, the core of us, of what I thought of as our real family, we were still together.

Except we weren't in Ella's mind. So she snuck out and ran away, and I'd had no idea all along. I wanted to know what she saw in Owen, who our mother'd warned us to stay away from. Everybody's mother warned them to stay away from Owen. His own mother probably warned him to avoid himself. He'd gotten in trouble more than once for bringing a lighter or a pocketknife to school, getting caught smoking pot outside behind the dumpsters. I wanted to ask how she'd found this place. How Owen figured into her life, why it was that she looked so sad.

"So sometimes I'll bring you here with me, okay? When Bay or Ross or Brett come." She hugged me tighter. I wondered if she ever felt funny in the way that Owen said I might. "I'm glad you're here," she said so no one else could hear. "You're not so big, still. Stay here with me."

I thought very hard that I would always stay, just like she said, only I didn't understand what it was she wanted from me. I felt the echo of how she'd looked that morning in her room, and the fear that she'd be like that again. Ella leaned back. When she dropped her arms from around me, I felt cold, missing her. I craned my neck around to see her go. She scuttled backward a few feet to where Owen was sitting. He smiled at me.

Ella rested her head on Owen's lap, her back against the ground. I wondered if he made her happy. She kicked her feet out in front of her, so they nearly touched me. He played with her hair a little, pulling it strand by strand through his fingers, like it was made of something very precious, then let it fall back onto her face.

Owen had her there, but he kept his eye on me and Bay. I didn't understand why he did it, but it made me feel a little nervous. He'd switched his flashlight off. The fire made the world feel easy to belong to, but it didn't make me feel less edgy under Owen's gaze.

"Ross," Owen said, "give the kids a drink, huh?"

"No, Bay's too—" Ross started to say, but Brett interrupted him.

"Not like we didn't already catch him stealing it at home."

Ross didn't argue. This time the beer, even if it was that skunked thing, was much easier to swallow. Bay drank his, too, and in a little bit he started acting silly, and so did I. We jumped around the little fire as if it was roaring, and Ross and Brett laughed at us and gave Bay another beer.

Even though I was laughing, I wished I had a girl I could sit with on a dark night, like Owen was with Ella, so that I could play with her hair and be apart from everything. Bay and I knocked off being silly after a while. Then we just sprawled on the ground. It felt damp and dark and like it could understand every thought in my head without me saying. The next day, I would be a boy again; my mother would make my lunch and tell me to do my summer reading, but for that moment, I was nothing and everything all at once.

I could hear the big boys talking, and Bay was singing a quiet song to himself, and I thought that being alive, really alive, was just the same as being dead because you're part of everything and the whole world is in you, and I wondered if Lex ever felt like I did, after the beers, and I wondered if he would have liked it.

I still didn't know, in words, why Ella snuck out to the woods at night, except to be with Owen. I wasn't sure why at the bottom of my feelings toward him, Owen made me afraid. I knew why Brett and Ross were there, and even Bay, but with Owen and my sister it was different. It was something like ownership. And there was my sister, happy to be owned. Then I thought maybe that's why she'd brought me—that she needed something safe, from home, to take into the night with her.

Owen and Ella went to the woods to be together. To be their own sort of family when real ones failed them. There was sweat and the dirt beneath me. The sense of uneasy rest, of straining against what had formerly been enough. The dark circles under Ella's eyes. And the way Owen touched her hair.

I closed my eyes against the future. I thought about Lex and how I was older than he'd ever be. How even after he died, I used to imagine playing alongside him in a room with a ceiling that looked like the sky. After a long time, Ella shook my shoulder, gently. I jumped.

"Come on, Remy," she said. "Time to go home."

She didn't understand that home could never again be what it was before the fire. But then maybe she did understand, but brought me because home had to end eventually anyway. I was angry at her for taking it.

I got up slowly, felt a little sick. Owen saw and put his hand out to steady me, but I didn't take it.

"Guys," Owen said, "take Bay, get out of here. Ella needs a hand."

"She's fine," Brett said. "She gets back every other night."

"Remy's a little tired," Owen said. "She can't row 'em both back alone."

"I guess we'll see you, then," Ross said to Owen, his hands on his hips. "Don't let anybody see you coming out of the woods or out back of their place, either. Or we'll all catch hell. Not hard to figure out who's been burning shit out here at night, the way the smell gets into your hair."

Owen nodded, and the Stowe brothers turned heel in the woods and left us. I heard Bay yelp once, figured Brett must have hit him to make him be quiet.

We made it back to our canoe. Owen pulled the oars out. He told Ella to get in the front and handed her one.

"Buddy," he said, "you just set yourself in the middle there, okay?" I rested my head on the side of the canoe. The night was going in reverse now. The light was coming back into the sky. I couldn't wait to get to our shed, up on the roof, through the window, and to my bed.

The only noise was the water being stirred a little by the oars. I opened my eyes and looked at my sister, her body silhouetted in the half-light, pulling against the current. She was pulling against the world itself.

CHAPTER TWENTY-TWO

Calvin

Someone's put a folding chair at the bottom of the steps so no one can go up. It's collapsed, leaning back and to the right, but you still can't get around it easily unless you shift the whole thing. I need the bathroom, though, so I slip by it. Then I run up the steps very quietly.

Someone's been in the downstairs bathroom forever. I really need to use it. I kept knocking at the door when Mom grabbed me by the shoulder.

"You stop that and wait," she said. "You're being very rude."

I nodded and pulled away before she could keep scolding me. She's been telling me all day how bad I've been acting. But I haven't been, not at all. It's not worth fighting with her, though. I just let her be mad at me because it gets her to focus on something. She's taking pills from her purse when she thinks I'm not looking. They're supposed to help, but I think they're making her worse. She's strange looking, dried out, brittle. She's scaring me a little.

There's a bathroom at the top of the steps. I'm through the door with my pants unbuttoned before I realize that Miss Beatrice is still up here somewhere. The thought freezes me for a second, but I can't wait. I slide the door shut with my heel and do what I need to.

Mom says I'm supposed to call her Miss Beatrice. I don't want to call her anything. I don't want to see her. I don't care about her or why she's hiding. She still hasn't come downstairs. All the guests are whispering about her, wondering if she's okay or not. It makes me so angry my jaw clenches. She didn't come to the church and neither did Jack. It's not her day to be talked about. It should be Dad's. But also, it's his fault I'm here, having to deal with Miss Beatrice, with Mom's weird empty eyes.

I flush and wash my hands. The soap smells good, like peppermint. It seems like fancy soap for an upstairs bathroom that just the people who live here use. My mother always keeps the best soap for when company comes, and then she just puts it in the bathroom that they'll be using. The peppermint soap is just out, though. I like that idea. When I have my own house, I'll put the good stuff out all the time, even if it's just for me.

I open the bathroom door, peek out. A little down the hall and across from me a bedroom door is open. I step into the hallway, which has a wooden floor with a long carpet runner laid down the length of it. The carpet is forest green with a blue-gray border.

I know I shouldn't stand in someone else's upstairs and look around, but I'm curious. No one downstairs cares about me. They're busy thinking about their own problems.

I want to see inside the bedroom with the open door. My mother would have a fit if she knew what I was doing. I'll give her a real reason to be mad at me. But she'll never know, and I'm guessing Miss Beatrice is asleep, since I don't hear any noise up here at all.

I step through the door into what has to be Ella's old room. It's just a twin bed with a white bedspread and a dresser. There is a framed picture of abstract flowers, some photographs of Ella and girls who must be her old friends tacked up places.

The bedroom is big; there's an unfinished plywood partition that stretches three-quarters across the long way. There's no door at the other end, just a gap you can walk through. Ade said that he and Jackson rigged up the wall between Ella's and Remy's halves when they were young. They did an okay job, but just after that, Remy moved across the hall and slept in with Jack anyway. They left Remy's bed in his half of the shared room, though, because sometimes he would sneak back in and sleep there.

I peek around the fake wall. Over there is where Remy must have slept. It's got a twin bed too, an old desk, a Led Zeppelin poster hung up by the window.

I step back into the hall. I don't bother to shut the door to Ella and Remy's room. Feeling a little braver, I peek my head through a half-cracked door down the hall to find what must be Jack's old room. I know it's his because there's a hand-lettered sign saying "Jackson" above the closet. There're two beds and, on the far side of the room, a dog in a crate. The dog begins to whine when it sees me, so I shut the door quietly and walk back into the hall.

I'm starting to wonder if Miss Beatrice is here at all. I open a door on my own this time. It leads into a small room, right next to the stairs. From his stories, I know it used to belong to Ade.

Now there's a suitcase thrown half under the bed and laundry in an untidy pile on the floor. It's men's clothes, so this must be where Remy sleeps when he's home—he's the only one staying here, I think.

Minus Remy's stuff, Ade's old room is very neat. There's not much clutter, just a few books on a shelf. None of them look interesting.

I sit down on the bed for a minute. It's full size. I wonder why Remy didn't move in here after Dad brought Ade home to Washington. I would have. It's small, but you wouldn't have to share with anyone.

I'm very tired. Even though I have my shoes on, I lie back on the pillows and swing my feet up off the floor. I keep my shoes on the footboard, so I don't get dirt on the comforter. The bed is decently soft. It's very warm upstairs. I can barely hear the people moving around beneath me, eating their snacks and telling stories that make them laugh and cry and hug.

It's too much, really. Not one of them knows a thing about how we live. No one downstairs except for Mom and maybe Ade could tell you what Dad liked for breakfast. I let my eyes shut, and I think about what we'll do when we get home. Should we take the clothes Dad left and throw them away? His books, his old shoes? I hope that we'll wait awhile. Just to let things settle. I try to relax by breathing deep, letting the air go all the way down to my toes. To clear the hurting out.

My eyes feel sealed. I start to feel the world fade around the edges. There's that smell again, like summer, like the dream I had at the hotel. I don't hear the voice calling me brother, but whatever that shadow was is here now too. It's stronger, somehow, like I've come closer to its heart, its thrumming center. There are no scary soldiers here, no parody of Dad to frighten me. I'm in a place I'd like to stay awhile.

It feels like it rushed through the hall here once, and when it did the doors never quite closed because it moved so fast. The walls of the room go soft like putty, get a little melty, but I'm not afraid. More than anything, I'd like to see what that shadow looks like in person, but there's no light to see by.

I'm wondering if there's a switch somewhere when a huge creak startles me awake.

It's short, loud, jarring as a gunshot. The door to the bedroom's been opened.

I jump and suck in my breath. Whatever was with me in the room, the friendly shadow, has fled.

I know without opening my eyes that I'm in trouble. Mom must've found me. Any second she'll start screaming.

But no one speaks. I feel there's somebody in the doorway. I can feel someone staring at me. I hear breathing.

"Is . . . is that you?" the person says. Her voice (it sounds like a lady) is breathy, like she's about to cry. I don't know who she thinks I am, but I'm sure I'm not who she's hoping for.

I don't open my eyes, trying to lie very still. The lady coughs once, then speaks again, this time angrily.

"Who told you to come up here?" she demands. "What the hell are you doing upstairs? Whose kid are you?"

Finally, slowly, terribly, I manage to open my right eye enough so I can see who's talking. And it's way, way worse than Mom would've been.

It's Miss Beatrice. It has to be.

"I'm not going to ask again, who are you?" she says. She's wearing a black dress, like the rest of the women downstairs are. Her hair isn't fixed nice, though; it's short and grayish-black, spiked weird in some places and lying down flat in others. She's got brown eyes. She's also wearing a pearl necklace. Her feet are shoeless.

She comes all the way into the room. This is the first time I've ever seen her. She's prettier than I imagined she would be.

My mother is younger, though, so she has less wrinkles. Miss Beatrice is a little shorter than Ella, but she's thinner. But instead of yelling at me she sits herself down on the edge of the bed, right by my legs. I understand now why my father used the word *elegant* to talk about her. She moves like she's in a ballet, sort of floating and pretty.

"You shouldn't wear shoes inside, you know," she says.

I nod, still lying on my back. Then she leans over, unties my dress shoes one at a time. She leans over my legs to reach. She pulls off the right one, then the left. She drops them on the floor by the side of the bed. It's such a mom thing to do, I have to hide my smile. I don't think I'm in trouble.

My feet suddenly feel cold, my sweaty socks exposed to the air.

Miss Beatrice resettles herself next to me. She crosses her legs and rests her hands on her lap. She's still wondering what I'm doing upstairs.

"There was someone in the bathroom," I say.

She looks like she wants to laugh.

"I knocked but they yelled at me. I had to go so I moved the chair and then put it back and came up here and went."

"I always told James we needed to add another bathroom in this house," she says. When she says Dad's name she half smiles, then looks sad.

"I'm sorry I cursed at you when I found you in here. That wasn't right." I don't answer but I look at her as she speaks. "I thought you were sent up here by one of my children. To see what I was doing."

"To see why you won't come down," I say, but then wish I hadn't.

She lets a little burst of air out, but then smiles fully. She has a nice face when she smiles, but looks very tired.

"Yes. That's right."

"Why won't you?" She's the only person I've met today who looks me in the eye when she speaks.

"Come down?"

"Yes."

"That's really not your business."

I shut my eyes again.

"You look like him, you know," she says after a minute. She puts her hand on the pillow I lean against like she's trying to comfort me without touching.

"Like who? The person you thought I was before I woke up?" I still don't open my eyes.

She goes quiet for a minute. "I wish you hadn't heard that."

I don't answer.

"I meant that you look like your father. You have his eyes. His nose, too. I bet people tell you that a lot," she says.

People don't. Everyone says I look like Ade.

"You know me?" I ask, opening my eyes.

"Of course I do. You're his little boy. You're Calvin. James sent me a picture of you once, when you were just three or four, I think."

"He wrote you letters?"

"Not me, really. The kids. Ella and Remy. But he sent pictures of you, and once he wrote my name on the back of one. So that was for me," she says. Miss Beatrice puts her hand on my cheek. It's warm and surprises me. She rests it there.

"What are you doing up here, Calvin?"

"I just wanted to see."

"What are you looking for?"

I can't answer. I'm afraid I might start to cry.

"This room used to be Adrian's," she says, looking around. "He loved to collect rocks. Lex started him on the hobby, and Ade went crazy with it. Did you see his old display on the dresser?"

I shake my head. "I just laid down because I was tired."

"It's okay."

"Are you going to tell my mother?"

"Why should I? Did you break anything?"

"No. But she'd be mad at me."

"I won't tell her. But you can't tell either." She leans down very close, her hand still on my cheek. "You can't tell your brothers or sister that we spoke."

"Okay. But why?"

"Because," she says, then she kisses me on the forehead so lightly that I almost miss it, "because I'm really tired too."

"You're not as bad as I thought you'd be," I say. "Shit. I'm sorry I said that."

"It's okay," she answers, laughing. "You're not as bad as I thought you'd be either."

"You thought I'd be bad?"

"No," she says. "I didn't really think about you at all."

We're quiet for a few minutes. It's nice to be near her, after all.

"You also look like him," she says in a sad voice. "My son. Lex. You, lying there on the bed, I got confused a moment. That's who I meant when I first spoke."

I nod.

"Please," she asks, "don't tell anyone about that. It would only upset them. Your brothers and your sister, they don't know what it's like here in this house, where we lived with him. Sometimes it feels like he's still here with me. I'll get the strangest sense when I'm falling asleep that he's just right there, waiting for me to see him. But I never quite manage."

It feels important, what she's telling me, but I don't know what to do with it except to feel sad for her.

She sighs, stands, swats my legs softly. I sit up and swing them to the floor.

"Come with me. I want to show you something."

Miss Beatrice walks through the bedroom door and down the hall. She looks back over her shoulder to make sure I follow. I slide my feet into my shoes without tying the laces on the way out.

We stop at an old rolltop desk in her bedroom, positioned by a huge window that looks out over the front yard and the street. Miss Beatrice opens a drawer and pulls out a big manila envelope. She dumps the contents out on the desk and starts to sort through them.

"When I heard about your father, I knew I had to find this."

"What is it?"

"It's James's. Nothing valuable really, just little things that meant something to him. Mostly from when he was a boy."

"What was in it?"

"Well, the things, and a list. Of what he wanted to give each of his children. He planned on wrapping them up and presenting them at high school graduations, I think."

"But he didn't?"

"He left them here when he went." Her face looks very troubled.

"He never asked for them?"

"He did," she says, looking away.

"What happened?"

"I said I couldn't find them."

"But you knew where they were?"

"Yes. They were in the desk the whole time."

"Oh."

"It wasn't the right thing to do," she says. "But it's what I did. Here now, you hold this." She hands me a much smaller envelope from the pile. Something heavy and round is inside. It feels solid in my hand. I turn the envelope over and see that in pretty cursive someone has written "Calvin."

"That's not Dad's handwriting."

Miss Beatrice acts busy, organizing things on her desk. "I know. I wrote it. Open it. It's for you."

I slide my finger under the envelope flap and tear.

"Be careful," she says.

Inside there is a photograph—two little boys wearing funny tight bathing suits that look more like underwear. They're standing at the edge of a boardwalk. You can see the ocean behind them. They're squinting in the sun. The older boy has a football under his arm.

"That's your father, the bigger boy, with Cat."

"How old is Dad?"

"He looks about eight. It was a family vacation."

"They look happy."

"Most of us did, when we were children," she says.

The other thing in the envelope is a small metal ball. It looks like it might be made of gold. "What is this?"

"It's a cannonball. From a brass cannon that your father used to play with."

"He saved it?"

"Yes, he did. I'm not sure why, but it's for you now."

"Thank you," I say. I realize the cannonball I'm holding was probably for Lex, not me. But I don't mind it. I like being connected to him, somehow. He was a ghost story until today.

"Now go downstairs. Don't tell anyone we had a talk."

"Okay. But what did Dad leave for the others?"

"Oh, Jack has a fountain pen. Adrian has a baseball. For Ella, there's a pair of earrings from some relative on the Gable side. Remy got some old coins."

"Did you give them their stuff yet?"

"I haven't. No one's been up to see me yet but you."

I nod, look at her a minute. She's not so different from my

own mom. I turn to leave. Miss Beatrice sits down in a chair by the desk.

I turn to look at her. "Do you want me to bring you anything?"

"No, Calvin. Thank you."

I slide down the steps, careful not to trip. I put the chair back so no one can bother Miss Beatrice until she's ready for them. I go into the kitchen to get a drink. A couple of my brothers are standing around, talking to each other.

"Where've you been?" Jack asks.

"Nowhere."

"You okay?" Remy says.

"Yeah," I answer. "I'm just thinking."

I go to the fridge and get some ice from the machine that spits it out on the door, then I get a soda and pour it in the cup.

The cannonball's heavy in my pocket. I think of Miss Beatrice upstairs trying to make a space for me. Being a better mom than mine is today. My stomach feels a little sick. I walk away from the kitchen, leave the drink I just fixed to go warm and flat and dead.

CHAPTER TWENTY-THREE

Jackson

SEPTEMBER 2005

I hoped Ella was still sleeping. I stood in her bedroom door early, just past seven. It was a Saturday. I wanted to wake her before she was able to get her thoughts in order.

My knuckles hurt. I'd hit Owen. Couldn't deny it. I caught him trying to sneak out, dragged him back inside, and hit him. I didn't have any idea what to say to her, just the sense that somebody had to say something.

But she was already awake.

"What're you doing, Jack?"

"Checking on you." I took a step into her room.

"You're a goddamned hero." She faced away from me; I had to speak to her back.

"You okay?" I said quietly. Mom and Remy were still asleep in their own rooms.

"I was, till you walked in."

"Did you sleep at all?"

"Don't worry about it. Why would me sleeping matter anyway?"

"Whatever, El. Sit up a minute."

"No."

"Fine, but I'm not leaving." She rolled onto her belly, her face half-buried in her pillow. She eyed me coolly. Her eyes were swollen, red rimmed.

"What happened last night?" I asked. I wanted to give her a chance to explain herself, though I didn't know what she'd possibly say.

"Nothing you should worry about."

"Like hell I shouldn't be worried. I hear a noise at two in the morning, and you think I won't check it out?"

"Well, you're a knight of the Round Table. You're better than Jesus. I bet Jesus never took the time to visit his sister for an early morning chat about her well-being."

I tried to grin to get her to relax. But I threw up a little in my mouth instead. "I don't care much for church. And Jesus never had a sister. Stop changing the subject," I said.

"I'm not. I was just talking about you. How wonderful you are."

"What was Owen doing in your room last night?"

"Bible study," she said into her pillow.

"You're lucky Mom didn't wake up, you know that?"

"I am lucky, aren't I? That you were here last night. But you're always here. Why is that?"

I ignored her.

"Thanks for your help. You saved me, Jack. You're one in a million."

"You don't stop acting like an idiot, I might need to tell her what happened."

"That wouldn't do anything. You know that." Ella rolled over, faced away from me again.

"I bet Mom'd care quite a bit about this."

"And what is it, exactly, that you think happened last night?"

"Don't be cute. It's an insult to how goddamned smart you are."

She breathed in sharply, told me she was tired and needed more sleep.

"Not yet," I said. "Ellie, we really need to talk. I'm worried about how you've been acting. Who you've been spending time with. And why."

"Jackson, get out. I don't want you here."

"But you wanted Owen here, didn't you?"

She shifted suddenly, sat up in bed. Looked at me with smoldering eyes. She'd cut her hair short recently—she looked edgy, older. I tried to recognize my sister in this fury of a girl.

"Don't talk about him," she said stiffly. "He didn't do anything wrong."

"He's exactly what we need to talk about. So grow the hell up and listen to me."

I moved forward. Sat on the bottom corner of her bed. I reached my hand out to touch her foot, to connect with any part of her, but she jerked away like I'd burned her.

"Don't touch me. I mean it. I'll scream. And Owen's probably already called the cops about how you hit him."

I shrugged. She was so stupid, so wrong.

"Owen will never call the cops on me or anybody else."

"You hit him in the goddamn face, Jack. You probably broke his nose. He sure as hell will."

"I don't think so."

"Why?" she snapped.

"Because Owen calling the cops is the worst thing he could do. He's got to stay on the law's good side."

"You have no idea what you're talking about," she said.

I looked at the wall behind her headboard where she had old pictures tacked up. Mostly her posing with her friends. None of our family. I didn't blame her for that.

"You know more than anybody else, huh?"

"Just because you're drinking buddies with those Stowe assholes doesn't mean anything. They don't know shit."

"Really? Because it was their father's car, right from their driveway, that he stole. Ross told me a few days ago. You know what Owen did, right? How he crashed the car into the side of the Cadmans' garage?"

She didn't reply.

"He left the goddamn car idling there and bailed. Ran nearly the whole way home before somebody caught up with him. He's lucky he's only seventeen. They're pressing charges. He's in the kind of trouble now you don't come back from."

"Fuck off," she whispered.

"He didn't tell you that part, did he? How bad things are for him?"

She didn't answer.

"You shouldn't see him anymore."

Her face fell. She wrapped her arms around her body, then looked me in the eye and smiled.

"I get it," she said. "Why you hit him."

"Because I found him climbing out Remy's old window. And, I mean, I'm sorry. You hear noises, you go check . . . I wasn't trying to find him."

She shook her head.

"Maybe I shouldn't have hit him. But I caught him, and he—"

"You hit him because of the Stowes' car. You don't care about me. You don't care about being a watchdog. I know Owen took that car when he shouldn't have. You hit him because in your head anybody who doesn't drive like an old lady on her way to church is a murderer." She nodded. "You hit Owen because you can't hit Roland Dawson. But Owen didn't hurt anybody."

Her words were a slap. Nobody in our family said Dawson's name, at least to me. You don't speak the name of the guy who killed your brother and destroyed your life.

"You're no better than me. You're no better than Dad. You fucked up, and now you go along behind your mess and try to clean it up by talking a good game," she said.

"This has nothing to do with it. I'm worried about the trouble Owen brings with him."

"It has everything to do with it. How'd it feel to hit a kid? Did you like it, like Dad did? I remember that morning on the driveway, you know."

I stood up; the girl on the bed was a stranger. Neither of us spoke for a minute, and then I broke my gaze. Stepped toward the door.

"Jack," she said softly. "Don't come in here again. Don't talk to me. Don't think you know a fucking thing about my life."

I looked back at her, horrified. The early morning sun came in through her curtains; she looked like an old painting. Made of air and light and color. Beautiful and devastating. She smiled, her teeth straight and white. She'd just had her braces off over the summer.

"Why are you even here?"

"Because you're doing things that could have a huge impact on your future."

"Not in my room. Here, at home. Mom doesn't want you here, you know. I sure as hell don't. Remy doesn't. You graduated from college last year, and you still just work in the Admiral's goddamned store."

"You work there, too," I answered, biting the inside of my cheek till blood came.

"I'm a *kid*," she said. "All of June, when we were in Sawtell, Dad talked about what a disappointment you were. Why do you think he never invites you to come visit anymore?"

There are things you can come back from, and those you can't. Ella was maybe too young to know it, but she was about to throw us over one of those lonely precipices.

"You think we need you, but we don't. *No one* needs you. You're a problem and a concern and a fucking asshole."

She rolled away from me again because, even in her anger, she couldn't say the next words looking in my eyes.

"You're not pathetic anymore, Jack. Maybe you were once, when you were a hurt kid after your accident. But now you're not even that. You're just, well, *irrelevant*. To all of us."

I closed her door quietly behind me and walked down the hall. I could hear her crying, even from the top of the stairs.

I wish I'd gone to her then, pushed her anger aside and put my arm around her. Held her. Rubbed her back. Been the kind of brother she deserved, rather than the one I was. Maybe I wasn't needed, but I could have been there anyway.

Said: *I will never leave you. No matter how hard you try to make me.*

But I couldn't do it. After that, I never really came home again. I slept in the house sometimes, but it wasn't a place that felt like mine.

CHAPTER TWENTY-FOUR

Ella

SUNDAY 4:10 P.M.

"Excuse us," Owen says, impossibly polite to Aunt Nola, Mom's only sister, and the other woman he was speaking to. "I haven't caught up with Ella yet."

"Of course," Nola says graciously, running her hand lightly down his arm as she steps away. Without fail, women are attracted to Owen, even if they're a generation older and standing next to him at a funeral reception.

I'm too surprised to speak. He always appears in the places I least expect him. He puts his drink down, opens his arms to me. Owen smells like he always has: sharp, smoke and old coffee on his breath. I put my face to his chest, feel the soft threads of his sweater against my cheek.

In a moment we're left alone in the corner of the living room. Just about where I yelled at Jack earlier. Owen hugs me tighter, whispers in my ear. "I'm so sorry, E," he says. "This is such an awful way to see you."

I haven't seen Owen in almost a year. I hadn't seen my father in almost as long. Strange day for reunions.

"I didn't know if it'd be okay that I came," he says. "But then I thought what I wanted most to do in the world was to be able to see you again."

I don't answer.

"I'm just so sorry," he says. "Your dad was kind to me. I always appreciated that."

I nod against his chest, trying to slow my breathing.

As I do, he reaches around behind him and loosens my hands from the death grip I've got on his sweater. He takes them in his own hands and brings them gently to my sides. He puts a hand on the small of my back and with the other raises my chin so I look up at him.

He's not much taller than me, not like my brothers. That always made me feel safe. That he's not above me. That he could level with me, eye to eye. In a house with boys who towered over me, whose world existed above my head once they hit fourteen, fifteen years old, it was nice to have someone really see me.

He looks at me with real sadness in his brown eyes. My stomach lurches.

Is he for real this time? Is he acting today, or is he really feeling what's playing across his face?

"Is there somewhere we can sit and talk?" he asks, kissing me on the forehead.

I nod, not trusting my voice. He nods back, drops his hand from my back. Takes my hand, steps back to send the message that I should lead.

I squeeze his hand, and we wind our way through the groups of people standing and chatting until we get to the kitchen.

There's no one in there but us. A plastic cup with soda sits on the counter, its owner long gone.

Owen drops my hand, pulls one of the kitchen chairs out for me to sit down. Today he's playing the gentleman. I take the chair and slide into it, relieved to be away from other people for a little while. Owen takes the chair next to me, the one closer to the wall. He arranges himself at the table as though he's lived here all his life. He leans toward me, takes my hands in his. We sit with our heads bowed together like we're praying.

Someone peeks their head into the kitchen, looks at us, moves on. Our posture sends the message that we must not be disturbed.

Finally, I'm brave enough to speak. "So, how've things been?"

He takes a breath and swallows, like there're words in his mouth that he doesn't want coming out.

"Fine, for the most part."

We sit in silence for a while.

"I'm glad you're glad I'm here," Owen finally says, sighing. "You don't know how worried I was that you'd be angry."

"Right," I say, not sure what else to tell him. Am I angry he's here? Of course. Of course not. I don't know. But I do know that, today, I'm not thinking about Owen. Though he doesn't seem to know that.

"It's so good to see you," he says. "I mean, you acted like you never wanted me to—"

"Stop it," I whisper. "Just be quiet now, please?"

"Right." He says it bashfully, like he's made a mistake. He strokes my hand with his thumb. His eyes are almost closed, him trying to comfort and me trying to accept it.

This is Owen: right here, in front of me. My face hurts. I can't really smile. Talking hurts, but not talking hurts, too, in a different way.

The last time Owen left, a year ago, I really thought I'd never see him again. I thought I never wanted to. I thought it would be better that way. His eyes are the same. Deep brown, at striking odds with his light hair.

But his chin is sharper than I remember. His cheekbones have emerged from his face in a way reminiscent of Civil War soldiers in old tintypes.

He's wearing a soft red sweater I bought for him when he'd gotten out of rehab with nothing to his name. A week before that, his mother and father had told him from across a group therapy room that they couldn't help him any longer unless he learned to help himself.

He'd called me, like he always did, and I took him to the mall, bought him sweaters, two or three, some slacks and a cheap pair of loafers—clothes he could wear to a job interview. He'd needed jeans, too, undershirts, boxers, and socks. I felt bad when I realized he didn't have a coat, either, so I added a windbreaker to the top of the pile as he stood in line at the checkout, his arms full.

"You did a great job setting all this up," he says.

I nod, thanking him without words. Ade did most of the hard work, getting Dad here. I just arranged a caterer and bought the paper plates and cups we'd need to entertain the people who'd come to see my father off.

"I mean that, I really do. You're amazing. You always have been."

I don't nod this time.

"Are the boys around?" he asks, trying to get me talking.

"Somewhere. Didn't you see them yet?"

"Nah," he answers. "I only just got in when your aunt and that other gal found me." *That gal.* How strange Owen can be. His old-fashioned words jumbled. How much like Jack he is. I've grown hard against them both.

"I'd like to catch up with them. Give my regrets."

Of course he would. Owen, good despite himself.

"Jack's here, too," I say. "I don't know if you want to catch him—"

"I want to see him too," he says sharply. "You think I came here just to give my sympathies to you? Why wouldn't I want to talk to Jack?"

Because Jack hates him. Because when we were kids, Jack threw him out of this house so many times that Owen could have worn a path in the grass.

"He's somewhere," I say. "Go find him if you want."

"I will," he answers. "But I want to talk to you right now."

There it is, then. He has come here for me mainly. That thought brings both relief and anger.

"Where are you living these days?" I ask, trying to sound normal, not accusatory, not deeply, unspeakably sad.

"I'm down in Philly," he says, running a hand through his hair, which he's grown long on top but buzzed short on the sides. Like a workingman before the First World War. Owen's a soldier of all times, it seems, the way he looks. Fighting some imaginary fight against ghosts no one can see.

My own ghost's strange warning comes back to me. Could it be Owen's reappearance he was talking about?

"You like it?"

"It's bearable." He puts his hands flat on the table. "It's close to work."

"Where're you working?"

He looks at me with angry eyes, his face turning hard. That was the wrong question.

He doesn't answer. I don't ask again.

"I'm so glad you came," I say, trying to bring him back again. All I've ever done is try to bring Owen back to himself. Talk him down from bad trips, like the night he got so crazed and angry that he put his hand through a dormitory window. That was the end of college for Owen.

"I'm glad you're glad," he says. "I wanted to make sure you were okay."

It's still there, his essential goodness, the thing that attracted me from the start. If it stayed closer to the surface, it'd make me devote my life to him. As if I haven't already.

As we sit, Rett comes crashing into the kitchen. He bangs his knee on the leg of the table as he skids in his stocking feet, the way my brothers and I did so many times. God only knows why Mom never moved the table. His eyes grow big, filled up with shock and pain. He begins to cry.

Owen covers the distance between him and Rett in less than a second.

He reaches down, picks Rett up, swings him high. Puts him on the table.

Rett looks at Owen, the sudden flight so unexpected he's forgotten to cry.

"Hey, pal," Owen says, looking at Rett's knee. "You okay?"

Rett nods solemnly. Owen rubs his back, then speaks. "I want you to make the funniest face you can for me, when I say. You ready?"

Rett nods again.

"One, two, three!"

Rett sticks out his tongue and screws his eyes up. Owen mirrors the face back to him. Rett breaks into a smile, and Owen says, "Now, we're going to make the scariest face we can, okay?"

Rett wiggles, ready.

"Go!"

This time, Rett pulls his lips down over his teeth with his fingers and growls. Owen doesn't match him—instead, he jumps away from the table, shrieks in a high-pitched voice that sends Rett into a volley of laughter.

"My God, that was horrifying!" Owen says, shaking his arms and looking around like he's embarrassed. "You make sure you don't pull that face around people who have a weak heart or a faint constitution, you understand, you demon?"

Rett nods once more, smiling big and saying he won't, he won't do it to anyone unless they're really big and tough.

"Only people tougher than me, right?"

Owen lifts him down off the table. Rett ambles out of the room, waving to us as he goes.

This is good Owen: so very different from the shouting, rail-thin anger that had gripped him a year ago, when I caught him selling out of my apartment to local college kids and high schoolers, no less. He screamed at me then, put his fist down on the coffee table so hard it cracked. He hit the wall just next to my head. Not to hurt me but to show me how I'd hurt him, through my distrust.

He'd been using. He'd been staying with me almost four months, the first week or so sleeping on the couch until we dropped pretense and he moved into my bed. I finally kicked him out because I couldn't take what he'd become—what he'd let his life descend into, what I'd let him do to mine.

He stormed, he screamed, he left, told me I'd never see him again. And yet today, I see him. Standing in my house, open and warm and himself, the boy I've loved since we were kids.

But he's living in Philly and won't tell me who he's working with or for. That's a bad sign. But he's breaking my heart, holding my nephew the way he did, making him laugh. Another bad sign.

Owen sits down again, his hand lingering on my arm, laid out on the table. "I love you," he says. Like that's all there is to it.

"I know," I finally answer.

"That doesn't do much, though, does it?"

I don't answer because I can't. I turn my face away, so the hurt side is toward him. A change seems to come over him like a shiver. His body jerks slightly, his eyes get hard.

"I'd better get going," he says. "See your brothers. I've never met the little one before. I'd like to." He means Cal. "Where's your mom?"

"She's upstairs." I can't believe what he's doing, walking away from me. When I've never walked away. He's come here to be a comfort but also to cause me hurt, just because he can. He'll walk in and then out again as though he has no more tie to me than an old friend who's a lost connection, who's stopped in town for an hour or so to pay respects. He's not that, and he knows it; the coldness of the way he's leaving is his true intent.

Maybe not. Maybe he's uncomfortable, scared, sad like I am.

He stands behind me. Runs his fingers lightly down my spine. It makes me jump; a hundred afternoons in bed with him come back in an instant. He leans down, kisses the top of my head.

"You've got a bruise on your face," he says. He doesn't ask where it came from. He doesn't care. "I'll go give my regards, then I've gotta run."

"Don't go upstairs," I say. "Mom doesn't want to be disturbed."

"Then let her know I was here. Give her my love."

I nod.

Give her his love. Like love is something you give freely.

"Listen," he says. "I've got a hotel room for the night, out on the highway. The Willis Motor Inn. You know it?"

I nod again. He has a hotel room for the night in his own hometown. Because his parents won't let him come home anymore.

"I'll text you so you have my cell number. Later, if you want, come find me. Give me a call."

I don't say anything as he pulls out a cheap flip phone from his pocket. Nobody has those anymore. What do they call them on the police procedural TV shows? Burner phones. Dealers have them.

"I'm not, you know," he says, answering the question I didn't voice as though he can read my mind. "I just can't afford anything better."

I don't know if I believe him.

Owen acts the same as always: prickly, callous, strange, and sweet, a raging disappointment. How did he get like this? How did any of us get like this?

"Same number as always?"

I nod.

He taps into his phone, flips it shut. "Got you."

I know that wherever I left my phone in the house, it's just pinged as his message was received. In my sweater pocket, Remy's phone rests heavily.

"I don't know if you'll hear from me," I say. If I do call, I'll wind up in bed with him.

"I expected you'd say as much," he answers in his funny old-fashioned way. He looks at me, his gaze softening. "I really am so sorry. I wish it was me instead of you. Who lost his dad."

I don't know whether I should thank him or not. I say nothing.

He leaves the room. I stay in my seat for a long time, giving him long enough to find the boys. I wonder how Jack will react. I wonder how Owen's going to get back to his hotel, if he'll use when he's there alone, if he expects to hear from me or if it's another pipe dream he knows will fail.

I finally rise, hope he's gone. And he is.

CHAPTER TWENTY-FIVE

Remy

SUNDAY 5:12 P.M.

Before Owen leaves, he gives me a hard hug with one arm. He smells like cigarettes and something older, a deeper kind of rot.

I don't say anything to him beyond a terse goodbye. I don't hate the guy, but he always makes me uneasy, even when we were kids. I know what he's done to my sister. It's hard to forgive those things.

Owen's always been hard to deal with: You wanted to help him when he was young because he looked like he needed it. Like if you tried just a little harder, you might be the one to save him.

He reminds me of Jack more than I'd like to admit. You get mad at guys like them for letting themselves fall apart—but it's so easy to let yourself crumble. I've found that out today.

I find a chair on the edge of the room, watch people come and go. Some talk to me, some don't. I play a game in my head where I try to remember where I might know someone from, but I'm not good at it. The crowd here is much smaller than at church, no cameras or strangers who want to report on our private loss. I'm glad.

My older brothers finally wander into the living room, not saying much. Eventually Ella comes out of the kitchen.

"How's your head?" I ask, getting up to offer her my chair. She moves past me, hair falling in her eyes. I stand next to her, no reason for it other than I want to be close to someone.

"Hurts a little," she says. She's quiet. I'm not sure if she's talking about her head or something else.

The four of us stand in a sullen line. Rett clings to Ade's legs, says his stomach hurts. Ade and Jack came out of the study a while ago. They keep going off and having whispered conversations, probably about the phone call Ade made to Liv earlier. I don't know what they said, but Ade's white in the face, Jack holding him tightly around the shoulders.

They ran into Owen then. Jack was kinder than I expected.

I hear a noise, look behind me to the stairs.

It's Beatrice, the old dowager herself. She's finally decided to come downstairs. She looks like a washed-up debutant. Like her father's about to present her to the well-heeled of the town. A line of beaus waiting to waltz.

She smiles at me as she descends. She's dressed in funeral black, a pearl necklace around her throat. No shoes. The other people in the room also notice; conversation hushes as she hits the bottom step.

She nods. The room lets out its collective breath.

She slips behind Jack. She pats him on the shoulder, and he turns toward her, but she won't drop the hand he still has on Ade.

Ade's been tapping his foot, shifting his position, clenching and unclenching his fists. Mom takes both of them, her oldest grown sons, in her arms; Rett's caught between all the legs.

She pulls Jack and Ade close to her, whispers something in Ade's ear. He nods, tries to shake his arms out and be still.

Between them Rett begins to laugh. The noise he makes is startling because it's so normal, yet so out of place. It's fitting, though. This house, these people, have had far more good days than bad. Why shouldn't the place ring with the laughter of a kid who's caught between the family that loves him?

Ade sneaks a hand down to Rett's head. Gives it a good rub. Rett pushes back into his father's palm. Something's happening with Ade, with Jack, but I don't know what it is.

It's got to do with Adam. It was a surprise when Ade came east without half his family. A couple of times Rett's asked Ade how Adam's doing, but he's been hushed and bustled off to another activity before anybody gives him an answer.

I remember being six, there being terrible secrets about injury and sickness and death in our family. Nobody told me what was going on, and my sister tried to fill in the gaps with whatever her imagination could conjure up.

"Jack cries at night because he's becoming a werewolf," she told me once. "Don't go into the hall or he'll bite you and you'll become one too."

Mom comes to Ella next. She holds her a moment, then lets her go. Ella looks diminished next to Mom, even though she's an inch taller. Mom touches the horrible bruise on Ella's face. My sister winces.

Finally, Mom comes to me. It's a quick hug, not long compared to what she's given my siblings. She whispers in my ear that she loves me and whatever happened at the church was fine. I'm not sure how she knows what happened since she wasn't there, but I don't ask.

There must be twenty people in the living room with us, with more in little clumps in the other open rooms of the house.

There's a guest book they're supposed to sign so we can tell, later, who showed up and when. Granna's seated on a chair in the dining room, Uncle Cat at her side.

Mom makes the rounds of the room, clasping people's hands and kissing cheeks. I watch her, and then I watch Emily, sitting on the couch next to Aunt Georgia. Emily's got a weird, vacant look on her face. It's more than a little concerning.

She keeps picking at a loose thread on the bottom of her sleeve. Aunt Georgia tries to engage her in conversation, but Emily won't speak. Her hair's fallen out of its bun. She looks disheveled, a little sick. She's got her legs crossed, one leg jiggling against the couch. Even though she's sitting, she doesn't look comfortable.

Calvin comes in from the kitchen. He's got a mug in his hands, carrying it carefully so he doesn't spill.

He must have tea or coffee. Probably heated it up in the microwave since the coffee urns in the dining room have gone cold.

Cal picks his way carefully through the slalom of people and chairs, until he's standing in front of his mother. My mom stops her own conversation, turns to look. Cal's hands are shaking a little bit; he looks tired and drawn. His tie and jacket are off. His white shirt is too big.

"Here," he says quietly. The room has hushed; we hear his words even though he's trying to keep them private. He holds the mug out toward his mother. Emily doesn't take it, doesn't look at him.

She stares into the middle distance, won't catch anyone's eye.

"Honey, hand me that," Georgia says, reaching for the mug. Cal gives it to her gratefully, and she motions with her empty hand for him to kneel in front of Emily.

He does so in one swift motion; it looks like he's collapsing onto his knees. His head hangs forward, blond hair bristling out over his ears. He brushes against his mother's legs.

She still doesn't move—it's like Cal's not even there. I don't know what's going on with her, but it's unnerving and strange. You can see it's making Cal edgy, too, the way he's twitching there on the floor in front of her. Begging with his body for her attention.

Ella grabs my hand. I let her take it, squeeze her fingers tightly. There's something wrong in the air, something's gone off or is about to. We're hanging in limbo until it reveals itself. It's like waiting for a jump scare in a horror movie, only you're living it. All we can do is watch. Wait.

Aunt Georgia hands Calvin the mug again. He takes it with both hands.

"Emily," she says, "Calvin's brought you some tea. Isn't that nice?"

Emily slowly nods but doesn't turn toward Georgia or Cal.

"How about you have some while it's still hot?"

Emily doesn't respond to Georgia, so Cal tries.

"Mom, here," he says, holding the mug out to her. "It's your favorite. Irish breakfast."

She still doesn't move. Cal steadies the tea in his left hand, and with his right, he reaches out and grabs Emily's. He pulls her open palm toward him, tries to get her to turn it upward so she can take the cup from him.

Finally, she turns to look at him. She grins but with a weird lobotomy smile. She looks drugged. She offered Ella some kind of pill at the cemetery after the fender bender. That might be what's gotten her so looped out.

Cal puts the mug into her right hand. She wraps her fingers around the handle of the cup, looks inside it.

"It's for you," he says. "To help you feel better."

He looks pathetic on his knees. I don't want to watch anymore. But Ella's still got my hand, and she's glued to her spot. That means I am too.

Emily swivels her head up, looks around the room. Her neck is loose on its bearings, and that unnerves me to my core. I hope she's got someone to drive her back to her hotel tonight, that an adult looks through her bags to find whatever it is she's taken. It's not good for Cal to see her this way.

He waits in front of her. She looks down at the tea. Smiles once.

Then, in a move far swifter than I'd expect her to be able to pull off, she backhands Calvin across the face with the mug.

There's a horrible crack as the ceramic collides with his head, or maybe I just imagine what the sound would be like, and then there's little sound at all, just a muffled jolt.

He's thrown back onto his heels; tea flies everywhere. As he catches his weight and finds his balance, his face turns so the whole room can see.

Blood jewels up on Cal's lip. His nose starts to drip. He raises his hand to his face, wipes the back of it across.

Blood smears there, accusing. He hangs his head like he's ashamed of himself. His hands are up at his face, and he's trying to move backward, little by little.

"Mom," he says, "Mom, Mom, Mom oh mom oh mom . . ."

Cal's on his knees still, supplicant, the back of his left hand bloody, when she hits him again.

Harder this time. Still with the coffee mug.

His head snaps back. No one can believe what they're seeing. Jack breathes in hard, Ade pushes Rett behind him. My mother gasps.

Cal draws himself forward so his body hunches, rounded at the shoulders. He's trying to keep his face down, away from Emily. So she can't get in another swing. He wipes his mouth again, staining his shirtsleeve.

I should step forward to stop it. But I can't. We're locked in place, all of us. We're rooted to the floor, the chairs we sit in, while a boy's hit in the face by his mother on the day of his father's funeral.

Only Georgia moves quick enough to intervene.

Georgia grabs the mug from Emily. Wrenches it from her hand. She forcibly holds Emily's hands in her own to keep her from striking anyone again.

Emily clears her throat once. Shakes her head. Begins to cry.

CHAPTER TWENTY-SIX

Adrian

SUNDAY 5:45 P.M.

I rush Cal out of the living room, toward the basement steps, just to get him away. He's hiccupping, trembling, breathing quickly through his mouth.

I've got to look at his nose—if he's not breathing through it, that's bad. Cal doesn't move easily, though. We hit the steps with Jack just behind us. It's dark so we move clumsily, a many-legged beast clopping along blind.

The basement steps are weird—the part where you put your foot is too short and the pitch is steep—this is still an old farm-house at its bones.

It'd be so easy to pitch forward and fall. For a quick moment, I imagine that we let ourselves do it. Just fall. You know you'd end up at the bottom, but in what shape you couldn't guess. Maybe we'd break a bone, our necks; maybe we'd die.

Such an accident would be terrible. It really would be. But then whatever happened upstairs, whatever's going on at home right now, it would have to wait awhile. For us to catch up, to be attended to. We're all a breath away from oblivion. I'm feeling dangerous, and I need to get home. I can't let anyone see me fall apart again.

I push Cal a little harder than I mean to, and he stumbles at the foot of the steps. I try to grab the back of his shirt to keep him upright.

I miss it, and he careens forward into the dark. He has to catch himself with a hand so he doesn't hit the wall with his face.

"Oh," he says, like he's surprised the wall is there.

He expected to fall. Maybe he wanted it as much as I do.

I maneuver Calvin a few more paces out of the line of traffic and the lights flick on. His hands shake; he keeps trying to wipe at his mouth with his sleeves.

His cheeks are splotched red; he looks so much like Adam when he gets upset that my stomach drops, to see my little son.

Cal's shirt is ruined. Blood never comes out.

Jack comes down into the basement, Remy following. They go to opposite ends of the room, turning on lights.

Calvin looks like something out of a horror movie.

"Whew," Remy whistles between his teeth, through the little gap braces couldn't fix. "You okay, Cal?"

Calvin looks from one of us to the next, then down at the ground. He doesn't speak, just turns his eyes downward like a dog that's been scolded. He keeps his right arm to his face, against his nose.

"What the hell was that?" Remy asks.

I turn, see Remy standing with his hands in his pockets, concern and confusion on his face. Turning back to Cal, I say, "Emily's never done anything like this before." Dad has, but I don't say that. "Something's wrong with her."

"Yeah, I wasn't—I mean, I didn't see it coming. She hit him. Twice. Jesus Christ." Remy steps forward next to me. "Never seen anything like it."

"Cal, let me look," I say, because no one has yet. I move toward him, but as soon as I step closer, he darts back, throwing his left hand out between us like I'm going to hit him.

"Cal," I say again, trying to keep my voice calm, "come here, buddy. You're bleeding. I just want to see where, clean you up."

He holds up his arm to ward me off, backs up until he's got no more room between him and the wall.

"Don't touch me!" he barks, keeping his face turned away from us, his right hand clamped over it. His voice is throaty, like he's got a forty-year smoker's cough.

"Somebody needs to look at you," I say. "Can you move your hand away?"

"I said don't *touch* me!"

I don't listen, move forward to try to grab him.

When I touch his arm, he pulls back like he's been shocked. His right hand comes away from his face; his lip is swelling nastily, and he's gone purple in the cheeks. His nose is still bleeding, but I can't tell how badly. He's making choking, angry sounds; he's hurting and mad, confused, and fractured. A boy who knows his world has come undone.

I couldn't stop Emily hitting him. I can't pull my father living from the ground. I can't even get Cal to look at me. I'm the one he's closest to, and now he's shut me out.

Cal turns his back on me, faces the wall.

He's so young. He's so alone in his fury. I clench and unclench my hands. Grind my teeth. Try to relax my jaw. I look at Remy, ask him with my eyes what to do, but he's just a shattered boy too. Older than Cal, but not grown enough to know how to undo this.

Boys stand around me, hearts full of hurt—my sons, my brothers, my brothers and sons. Adam lying in a hospital bed half a world away. Calvin bleeding into his hands. Rett sitting stiffly on a couch in someone else's house, me gone to some other room and him not knowing where. Remy still young enough that the hair on his chin comes in mostly in patches. Jack trying his best to steady me when I called Liv at the hospital. Lex long gone, a tangle of bones.

Calvin's shoulders shake. Remy's running his hands through his hair like he's always done when he has nothing left to do. I'm left straining under the weight of all I can't do for them. How long since we came down to the basement? A lifetime.

"Take this," Jack says to Remy, pushing a couple of bottles of water into his arms. Jack steps between me and Cal.

He puts his hand on my shoulder; his grip is firm, warm. He smiles at me. I don't know where he got the water from, but I don't ask.

"Calvin," Jack says, "I'm going to touch you now."

He puts out his good hand. I wait for Cal to pull away, to snap at Jack. But he doesn't. Jack's hand moves forward, connects with Cal's shoulder. He turns Cal around slowly, pulls him to his chest.

Cal shudders. Collapses into Jack. He puts his face against Jack's shirt, so that when he pulls away a moment later Jack's left with a Shroud of Turin imprint of Calvin's bleeding face.

"Hey, you," Jack says quietly. "Hey, there you go."

Jackson pulls Cal's face back, gently. His fingers spider over Calvin's face, looking for where the blood's coming from. Jack has a handful of clean tissues he's pulled from his pocket. They look papery and thin as he dabs at Cal's nose, applies light pressure to the split in Cal's lower lip.

"Does this hurt? How about here?" Jack asks. Cal winces or stays silent, depending on the answer. Jack has Cal open his mouth, so he can check to see if any teeth have been chipped by the mug. None seem to be, Jack says aloud to the room.

"Water, Remy," Jack says, and Remy moves forward to hand him a bottle. Before he gives it to Jack, he twists the top off with one hand and throws the lid onto the floor. "Pick that up," Jack says, "or the dog will eat it." Remy looks down at the ground; he seems embarrassed he didn't think of Mr. Darcy himself. He picks the lid up and pockets it.

Cal raises a bottle shakily to his lips.

"Don't let it rest on your mouth," Jack says, "or it'll hurt more, might start your lip bleeding again. Pour it in, instead."

Cal nods slowly, tips his head back. He pours the smallest amount of water into his mouth, wincing as he swallows.

Jack smiles. "That's a good kid," he says. "Don't try to talk much. You'll just hurt it worse when it's trying to knit itself better."

Cal nods his head slightly so Jack knows he understands, and looks around for the first time.

Jack follows his gaze. "This is where we used to hang out with our friends," he says. "Right, Ade?" It takes me a minute to understand that Jack's talking to me. I've been watching so intently that I forgot I'm still a player in this scene.

"It is. Jackson ran smack into the glass door over there. He needed stitches in his chin. How old were you then?"

"Oh, about eight or nine," he says. "We've christened this house so many times it's not even funny."

Calvin raises his eyebrows so we know he's asking a question, but he doesn't speak.

"Christened—he means we've bled all over the place, with all the accidents we've had," Remy says.

"You're part of a long tradition, Cal. Welcome to the club," Jack says. "The first was Lex, when he was two—whacked himself good on the corner of the fireplace. Took it right between the eyes."

"You and the door," Remy says, "and when my knife slipped as I cleaned that fish by the creek when I was ten. That hurt like hell."

"And you got a terrible infection on top of it," I say. "We could smell you coming."

"That's disgusting," Remy says, "even though it's true."

"Ella would get random nosebleeds," Jack adds. "That wasn't always easy to clean up."

"I tripped on the playground and broke both bones in my arm," I say.

"Ella broke her toe, which doesn't sound like much," Remy says. "But the day she did it, she had to do the mile run for the Presidential Fitness tests in gym—do they still do those? And that afternoon she also ran a timed mile at field hockey and ran through the whole practice on a broken bone."

"She was tough," Jack says. "Where is she, anyway?"

"Around," I answer, though I don't actually know. We stand around talking about growing up, Calvin listening and trying hard not to smile when something strikes him as funny. I try to focus on being here, now. I try to focus on my breathing, on my brothers. On when this house felt like home. On feeling like I have a place among them.

"Now, Cal," Jack says. "Don't think what happened is your fault. That you did something to deserve her hitting you like that. You understand?" Cal's eyebrows knit together, but he doesn't cry. "Sometimes people do things they don't mean to when they're under a lot of stress. That's what happened upstairs."

"I think," Remy cuts in, "I think she might have taken too many anxiety pills or something. She's not acting right. Vacant, sort of."

Cal nods extra hard now, and I ask him, "Does she have pills, Cal? Did the doctor give them to her? I know the guy at the hospital mentioned she should think about a prescription when we arrived with Dad—"

"Jesus," Jack says, exhaling through his teeth. "I didn't realize you were there. When it happened."

We're silent for a minute.

"Someone will have to get those pills from her," Jack finally says. "Not that she can't take them, but they should be doled out by somebody who can keep an eye on how she's handling herself."

We all nod.

"But that somebody can't be Calvin," Jack finishes. "That's too much on him."

"I'll do it," I say. "Rett and I are staying at your hotel, Cal. I'll come in tonight and make sure that I've got the bottle of whatever she's been given. Just to keep an eye on things. So you can relax and so you don't have to worry."

I realize, saying it, that I've just committed myself to remaining in Harrington for the night. I'd been thinking about trying to book a flight home all afternoon. Leaving Rett at my mother's, have him fly home with Emily and Cal in a few days. But I can't leave him, and I can't leave my family here until things are settled. I need to stay, whatever might come next.

And knowing that, somehow, settles me.

"Good man," Jack says.

For the first time, I believe it when somebody calls me that.

CHAPTER TWENTY-SEVEN

Jackson

SUNDAY 6:25 P.M.

"Mr. Darcy is coming down—he's crying!" someone shouts from upstairs. We look at each other, confused.

The dog's been fine all day, so sending him down to the basement now doesn't make much sense. But there's a thudding of paws on the steps, and in a flash a brown blur with huge, pointed ears is bounding among us.

He comes straight for me. Mr. Darcy jumps up and down, barking, his front paws landing somewhere between my chest and my waist each time he leaps, depending on how good a lift-off he manages. His tail thumps against my legs. I try to grab him by the collar. But he rears forward, twists to the side, and I miss him entirely. His body shivers with excitement.

"Grab him!" I shout, sidestepping away so his paws don't catch on the buttons of my shirt. I'm able to deflect him with my hip, but Mr. Darcy's getting more excited, not less.

Remy moves to help. He walks around behind me, giving the dog a wide berth. He doesn't want to borrow trouble, especially when trouble is a galloping eighty-two-pound German shepherd who's been cooped up all day.

"Come on, Darcy," he says, his voice high. "Come on, you old bug, come."

Mr. Darcy's still dancing around me, feet light as a prize-fighter, but I whip around to look at Remy. "Old bug? Are you kidding me?"

His cheeks flush, but he looks me in the eye, indignant. "You want help, or don't you? That's what Mom calls him when she wants to coax him somewhere. I had to get this stupid lug"—he motions to Darcy with his eyes—"into his crate in your old room this morning before anyone arrived."

Remy steps forward, puts a hand down toward the ground. Darcy drops to his stomach. The dog's motion is so sudden that the air still seems to jump around me, kinetic, even though he's not moving there anymore.

"There you go, old bug. Good old Darcy. You stay down now, down now, Dar." As he talks, he reaches a hand out and around behind Mr. Darcy's head, gets a grip on his collar. Mr. Darcy rocks from side to side with the excitement of someone getting down on his level, his ears perked straight up and his tail thumping on the floor like he's playing a bass drum in a marching band.

"Step back, Jack," Remy says, not looking away from Mr. Darcy. "I've got him."

"Does he need to go out?" Ade asks.

"Nah, I took him about an hour ago," Remy answers. "He's good for a while. He was probably crying because he was lonely, not because he needed to go outside."

I watch Remy and Mr. Darcy. "He actually listened to you."

"Always been good with dogs," Remy says, standing both himself and Mr. Darcy up, his hand still on the dog's collar.

"You loved Bear," Ade says.

"No one else took care of her," Remy says.

"She wouldn't let anyone else," I say, stepping out of the way as Remy brings the dog forward. Bear tolerated the rest of us; Remy was the love of her life.

"Jack," Remy says, "open the door to the storage room. He'll have to hang out in there for a while—he's too excited to be out here."

As I pass Mr. Darcy, he starts to jump, but Remy puts his other hand on the dog's neck and gets down on one knee, nearly hugging the animal. "Calm down, old bug," he says.

"Make sure there's nothing in there he'll chew," Ade offers.

"Sure," I say. "Why don't you come help me?"

He only laughs. I try to open the door to the storage room. It only goes halfway, though—there's a box in front of it, blocking it from opening inward fully. I try to force the door open farther, but I can't get my arm through to clear away what's there.

"It's like there's a pile of stuff that's fallen over. I can't get in."

"Hurry up," Remy says. "He's got to be put away soon." Mr. Darcy strains against Remy's arms.

"What'd I just say?" I ask, annoyed. "I can't get my arm through—"

"Lemme do it," Cal says, and suddenly he's next to me. There's swelling beneath his eye, his split lip; a bloody crust decorates the rims of his nostrils. He slides right through the opening in the door that I've managed to clear, head first. In a second he's all the way in the storage room.

"There a light in here?" he says, muffled through the door.

"On the wall by the door, right side."

The light flicks on. I hear him shoving something around. "Try it now!"

I push, but the door won't open much more. He does more shuffling. I push again. This time, it opens. Cal's standing among boxes, one of which has fallen over. It held books, which blocked the door. I step into the storage room.

"What is all this stuff?" Cal asks, looking at the shelves that go nearly to the ceiling, most of which are piled with boxes, some labeled, some not.

"Ah, man, it's all sorts of stuff," I reply. "Old games, clothes, stuff our mom wanted to keep. Stuff of Dad's, too, that he never—"

Cal looks pained.

"Stuff Dad didn't take when he moved," I finish quickly.

Cal nods, turns to the pile of books on the floor. "We should move these so there's room for Darcy," he says.

Together we pick up books. First, we try to pile them on top of another box on the side of the storage room but then decide, together and without speaking, that it's not a good idea. If Mr. Darcy starts jumping again, he could bring down the entire mountain of hardbacks on top of himself.

Cal and I work quickly, carrying armloads of books out. We clear a space and exit. Remy comes forward, still whispering to the old bug to be calm, to stay. He pats the ground; Mr. Darcy lies down on his belly and looks up at Remy with pathetic eyes. But he doesn't move.

Remy steps backward out of the storage room, still talking to the dog, who's started doing that heartbreaking whine cry that animals do when they're left in a place they don't want to be. Remy shuts the door quietly, and the four of us listen to Mr. Darcy cry, and then settle. We look at each other, smile.

Then, we hear a clatter from the steps—Ella comes down, thundering in her heels, yelling. Darcy hears, too, and starts to cry again.

"Did you put the dog away?!" she shouts, moving into the room with us. She looks with interest at the pile of books Cal and I dumped unceremoniously on the floor. I try to catch her eye, but she only glares at me and pays more attention to the books.

"What are these?" Ella asks, leaning down to grab one. Her skirt skims the top of one of the piles.

"*Dawn and Other Tragedies*," Ade reads the title, taking a copy for himself.

They page through the books they're holding, which are copies of the same volume. They're reading books of our father's published poetry. I recognize the title and the picture on the front cover.

"Why's Mom got all these?" Remy asks. He looks over Ella's shoulder, peering at the pages as she turns them.

"He's got some at my house, in his office—books of his, I mean. But I've never seen this one, I don't think," Cal offers. He's hard to understand because he's trying to talk without moving his lips.

"Wow," Ella says quietly, "you look rough, Cal." No one answers her. "I never thought we looked alike until now."

I don't understand. Ade and Remy look confused, but Cal grins even though it must hurt. His lips ring startlingly white teeth.

"You know, because of my bruised face and his bloody one?" Ella fills in, sounding exasperated.

"Always with the gallows humor," Remy says. He smiles too.

Ade turns more pages in the book he holds. "This is his first book, isn't it, Jack?" he asks.

I nod.

"Maybe Mom bought these to drive his sales up?" Ella says.

"There's not enough of them here for that. There're only about twenty-five copies in this box, at best," Ade replies.

"There's more than that," Cal mumbles. "I saw a bunch more boxes in there, they just hadn't fallen over. We didn't bring them out."

They fall silent.

"These books," I say. "They might be ones he used to take with him on book tours. I remember him doing it, with later ones. He'd take them along, do the reading, and then try to sell copies after it."

"Huh," Ade replies. "That'd make sense, I guess."

"But why're they here in Mom's basement?" Remy says.

"Stuff Dad didn't take when he moved," Cal says quietly. Says the same words I just said to him.

"Let me see one," I say. Remy reaches down and holds out a book to me. I take the book in my good hand, and the weight of it is surprising.

I just carried armloads of them out of the closet, but holding one, its singularity, is a different experience altogether. This is the sum of my father's heart. The thought makes my chest constrict. I have to look away from the book, from my family.

"Who's the publisher?" I ask. I try to flip to the title page.

It's hard for me to maneuver the book, so Ade reaches the page in his copy before I do in mine.

"Mallan, it says. It was published in '84," he says. "Never heard of them before."

"I'm gonna see if there's any others in the closet," Remy says. He turns toward the storage room door. He opens it, steps inside, calls out for someone to come help him carry. He hushes Mr. Darcy. Ade and Cal follow him, so it's just Ella and I together.

"I thought his other books were with a big publisher," I say. "Or a subsidiary of one of them."

"I don't know. I thought he did some self-publishing," she answers.

We listen to the boys in the storage room as they argue which boxes should be brought out while Mr. Darcy goes crazy again.

"We should just look it up," Ella says. She doesn't look at me, doesn't smile. I'm not forgiven yet for missing the funeral.

"Look him up?"

"Yeah. Like, google Dad. Or at least look at his faculty page at Larson. That'll tell us who the books were published through, maybe."

"I never thought of doing that."

"Me either," she answers, pulling a phone out of the pocket of her sweater.

"This is Remy's," she says of the phone. "Mine's upstairs. I've been hanging on to his for him."

I glance toward the half-open storage room door and see Remy on his knees holding Mr. Darcy while Ade and Cal lug out boxes. Ella gets Google up on the phone and types in Dad's name. The boys, meanwhile, have closed the closet door and are opening cardboard boxes that they've lined up on the floor. Mr. Darcy cries again, but we ignore him.

"That's a lot of hits," she says, poking at the phone with her index finger. "He does have a Wikipedia page. I guess we'll start there, right?"

I wonder who set up the site for him—did he have a personal assistant, or was it a publicity specialist through his contract? Was it a lifelong fan of his work, or did he maintain it himself?

"'James Wesley Gable, February 28, 1959, to March 25, 2015, was an American poet of several critically acclaimed volumes, as well as a literary critic, and long-time professor at Larson College, Sawtell, Washington,'" Ella reads. "Well, that's wrong. He died on Tuesday. The twenty-fourth. It goes on: 'Spouses: Beatrice Ansler,

1979 to 1996; Emily Rivers, 1997 to present. Children: six, including Remy Woodson Gable, journalist.'"

I stay quiet.

"Hey, R," Ella calls, "they give your full name, list you as a journalist. I guess you've made your mark on the world, huh?"

"Go to hell," he answers, caught up in looking through boxes.

"Remy's the only one who's done anything worthwhile beyond being James Gable's kid," she says.

I don't speak because if I do, I'm afraid I'll agree with her. How long will our lives be reckoned by not what we do with them but what our father did with his?

"Anyway," she says, louder. "You were right. *Dawn and Other Tragedies* is his first collection. But Mallan went under not long after they ran his book off. He was picked up by another publisher after that."

"He must have bought those copies off them," I say. "Or been given them, maybe."

"Seems so," Ade answers, walking back over to us. "There's a couple more boxes full of that book alone. The others are some of the later ones."

"The last was published," Ella says as she skims the Wiki page, "in 2013."

"I remember that one," Cal cuts in. "*The Rolling Stones Are Dead.* He picked such stupid titles."

"Yes, he did," Ella says.

"Does Wikipedia mention the accident?" I can't help asking.

My siblings look at each other with worried faces.

"Yes," Ella quietly replies. "It says, 'On June 2, 1995, in Harrington, Pennsylvania, Gable's two oldest sons were involved in an automobile accident; the second, Alexander, died of his injuries.'"

No one knows what else to say. Ade leans down and opens another box, then stands up.

"The worst book was *A Prophet or a Ghost*," Ade says. He's got a copy of it in his hands and thumbs through the pages. "This is the one where he really started in on us."

The phone in Ella's hands goes into sleep mode, the screen dimming. She looks at it a minute, then slips it back into her pocket.

"That's mine," Remy reminds her.

"I know," she says. "But you don't get it back yet."

"That's fine. I don't want it."

"Can I see the book?" Ella asks Ade.

He hands it to her, runs his hands through his hair. All my brothers do that when they're stressed or thinking. I do it myself.

"Oh God," Ella says, "I *hate* this one." She's looking at a page with a frown on her face. Cal crowds in to see what she's looking at.

"What is it?" Remy asks, reading over her head.

"I bet it's 'Arrival,'" Ade says.

"Yep," Remy answers. "That one was a dirty trick, wasn't it?"

"They all were dirty tricks," I say.

"'Arrival?'" Cal mouths.

"It's a poem that's about Ella," Remy says. "It shared things about her she wasn't happy to have shared."

Cal nods, his eyebrows knit together like he's thinking of something that causes him pain.

"Did you see his photo on the back, here?" Ade says, holding another copy of the same book he's plucked from an open box.

"Jesus Christ," I say, looking at it with him, my father's young-man face framed between my brother's spread fingers. His eyes are black ingots, a small smile plays across his lips, and his hair is parted dead in the center, a way I don't think I ever saw him wear it in real life.

"He never looked like that, did he?" Ella says.

"He must have, once," Ade says.

"I don't remember it," Remy says. "How old was he? Definitely before he was thirty."

"Oh, younger than that," Ella says. "I mean, he published his first book when he was younger than I am now."

"How do you know that?" Remy asks.

"Well, I just saw it online and did the math. But also because he used to brag about it all the time, that he'd done more before twenty-five than most poets do by the time they're forty."

"The picture would have been old even by the time *Prophet* was out," I say. "Before they released *Prophet*, I remember him and Mom talking about it. They were trying to decide if it was too old, if the picture still looked like him."

"I guess they decided it did," Ade says.

"Or they didn't want to spend the money to get a new one," I answered.

"He's younger than me right now in that photo, I bet," Remy says.

"Probably," I agree.

My brothers and sister stand around, paging through the books and talking quietly about the poems inside, about our father. Cal's beside me, silent. His arms hug tight across his chest, his face a mask I cannot read. I put my hand on his shoulder.

"Why are they dirty tricks?" he asks quietly.

"What?"

"You said they were all dirty tricks. What's that mean?"

"Ah. What I said about the poems."

He doesn't speak, but his forehead creases—he's thinking.

"We always hated when he wrote about us," I say.

"We'd ask him not to," Ade chips in.

"We'd beg him not to," Remy corrects. "She'd be in tears sometimes about it," gesturing to Ella.

"You cried about it, too," Ella says.

"We weren't his to write about," I say. "I mean, we were his. But not his to turn into grist like that."

"We were always afraid of telling him anything," Ade says.

"That's what I think I was talking about earlier at church, maybe," Remy adds quietly.

"Dad didn't get it. No matter what we said. It's like he deliberately tried not to understand us," Ella says, not acknowledging Remy.

"I hated it," I say.

"I still hate it," Ade replies.

"They're dirty tricks because he said he wouldn't write about us, but he always did," I say.

Cal's face is blotchy and red; he's got tears at the corners of his swollen eyes. "He didn't listen to you?" Cal's face darkens.

"No," Remy says. "He took 'kill your darlings' to a new extreme."

"What's that mean?" Cal asks.

"It's a writing phrase, means you have to be brutal. Maybe your favorite parts are the ones you need to kill, edit out," I explain.

"Bastard was always brutal," Remy says, "and managed to kill us just fine."

Cal asks, "What did you do about it?"

"There was nothing we could do," Ade answers. "You just had to get used to it. If you were lucky, you could snatch away the rough draft before he finished it."

"You actually managed to do that?" I ask.

"Just once," he says. "When I was living in Sawtell and he wrote about what got me there."

"What did he do to you when he found out you took it?" Cal asks. His eyes are big.

"He just wrote another version of it. But the second one felt less hurtful, somehow. Because I'd gotten at least a little of myself back by taking it from him."

"He always said he'd never write about me," Cal says.

"You're lucky," I answer. I rub his shoulder again.

"But," Cal whispers, "he lied."

CHAPTER TWENTY-EIGHT

Adrian

JANUARY 1990

"Up, boys," Dad sang, coming into the bedroom. It was Jack and Lex's room, but I was allowed to sleep on the floor between their beds sometimes.

"Good morning, soldiers!" Dad threw open the shades. The light that came through was glaring, sharp. The big boys rolled over in their beds and tried to put pillows over their heads, but I was up like a flash at Dad's side.

Days like this were why we loved him.

"Adrian the Wicked is up!" Dad said in a booming voice in the direction of the boys in bed. I smiled. Dad smiled back. He reached down and grabbed me around the middle, then held me up to the window so I could look out it.

"Would you look at that, boy oh boy," he said, rubbing his stubbly face against my smooth one. "What's happened in the night, Adey?"

I squinted my eyes. "Snow?" The big boys grumbled at the noise I made. Lex tried to throw a stuffed animal at Dad and me. Dad put me down and went to the bottom of their beds. He grabbed the covers and tore them off Jack, then Lex. Jack rolled over onto his back, rubbed his eyes, sat up slowly. He wasn't happy to be up, but he eventually rolled himself out of his bed and sat on the edge of it, staring at me with sleepy eyes. He wore Spiderman pjs, only had one sock on. His hair stood on end; it curled on one side, was flat against his skull on the other where his head had been on the pillow.

He seemed so old, so fully formed. But he couldn't have been older than seven, since we didn't have Remy yet. Jack went to school every day and I didn't, which made him nearly as grown up as Dad, who went to work. Mom was grown up too, but she stayed home with us.

When Dad pulled Lex's blankets off, he shrieked. "Daddy, it's cold!" he yelled, curling himself into a ball.

"Lexer," Dad said, "come on, kid. Up now, Alexander the Great." Lex slowly came around to the waking world. He wore Ninja Turtles pjs, but his top and his bottoms were from two different pairs so they didn't match. His hair was funny from sleeping but not as bad as Jack's. He looked at me just like Jack did, like he didn't know quite why I was there, his blue eyes huge, rimmed by eyelashes so light it was like he didn't have them.

We trooped to the bathroom, where I needed help to reach the sink, where somebody put the toothpaste on the brush for me and stood there to make sure I rinsed my mouth after. Dad herded us to the kitchen next, where Mom made us breakfast. Ella was in a highchair by the table. I had to sit on two phone books to reach my pancakes.

We ate quickly, then Mom helped me to get into my clothes for the day. My shirt probably got stuck on my ears, like most shirts did. When we were through, I thundered back into the living room, where Jack and Lex were already playing. They'd started without me. That made me mad.

They had two sets of plastic army men, one red (that was Jack's) and one drab green (that was Lex's). Both armies were laid out across the floor in elaborate patterns that my brothers were convinced were real army moves that actually happened in wars. Lex made a noise like a machine gun with his mouth. Jack knocked over a group of his own soldiers with the back of his hand. He pretended they were dying and imitated their screams—one of them, I remember, said, "Tell my mother I was the one who stole the money from the collection plate!" That was a line from an old movie my brothers had seen on TV. When Jack said it, he and Lex burst out laughing. Their laughter was high and ringing, like church bells. I watched them, chins propped up on their fists, supporting themselves on their elbows.

Jack's legs were bent at the knees, so his feet kicked up in the air. Lex's were flat against the ground. They laughed at a joke I just knew enough to know I didn't understand. That made me even madder.

I was Adrian the Wicked, like Dad said. I was a boy who was taller than a skyscraper; my feet were bigger than trucks. My eyes shot fire, and if anybody made me angry, I could destroy them and not even get tired. I stood a little way back from the big boys, my fists clenched against my sides. Mom'd dressed me in a pair of overalls that had no pockets, so there was nowhere else to put my hands. I tried to breathe in and out as fast and hard as I could through my nose.

If my brothers had looked at me then, I was sure they'd be so afraid that they'd go running and leave all the soldiers on the floor for me to play with by myself. That's what I really wanted, an uninterrupted chance to play with their toys all alone.

I started to stamp my feet, building up energy for my attack. My brothers had no idea what was coming, and that's how I wanted it to be—a surprise ambush. I didn't know Dad was hanging out in the archway behind us, watching as we played. He must have seen me there, winding myself up, but didn't do anything about it.

"Lex," Jack said, "you've gotta give up unit twelve, since they all died of being homesick."

"That's not right, and it's not fair—" Lex was saying, but he couldn't finish his thought because just at that moment, Adrian the Wicked attacked. I shouted, stomped right through the center of their game. I kicked my feet, knocking over as many soldiers as I could.

"I'm a wicked, a wicked!" I yelled, swinging and stamping again.

"Ade, stop! Stop! Stop!" Jack yelled, pushing up on his hands until he was on all fours. "You're wrecking it!" There were tears in his eyes.

"Mom!" Lex shouted. "He's ruining our game, Ade you baby, stop, you stupid, stop!"

I didn't listen. The plastic men died all around as I kicked them with my feet made of the strongest metal in the world. Really, the figures were digging into the soles of my feet if I stepped right on top of them. That made me yelp, but I kept on stomping. I thought I would keep destroying forever.

I raised one foot so close to Jack's face that it must have looked like I was going to kick him. That jolted Dad from his spot—in a second I went from stomping to swinging far above the ground. My legs were still kicking, but the sudden shift in gravity made me burst into tears, too. The living room was full of crying boys. I hung there, looking down at Jack's teary face and Lex's red, angry one.

Dad had grabbed me by the back of my overalls, so it was like I was in a ready-made harness. Eventually Dad took one hand and grabbed me around my bottom so he was holding me normally.

"Adey," he said, "why are you ruining their game?" I was sobbing by then, full, racking.

"I'm a wicked," I tried to say, which had been my battle cry. He didn't understand me. His attention shifted to my brothers, both crying on the floor—Jack because he felt betrayed, Lex because he wanted to get even but couldn't.

"Boys," Dad said, "clean up the soldiers. It's time for a new game, anyway."

"That's not fair," Lex said, pushing his lower lip out and crossing his arms over his chest. "He ruined it—us having to stop is not fair, Dad."

"But it's what's going to happen," Dad said. "Jacky, come on now, no more crying. Up, buddy. On your feet, now."

Jack slowly stood, sniffling and rubbing his eyes with the back of his hand, but Lex stayed kneeling on the carpet, sulking. Mom was still on the phone in the kitchen, so Dad put his finger to his lips to show us how quiet we needed to be. He was still holding me as he went to the coat closet. Once he got there, he put me down and opened the door. I hugged his one leg with both arms as he began pulling things out of it—coats, snow pants, the big bag we kept hats and gloves in.

"Jack," he said, "come find your coat and Adey's suit." Jack came over to help. Lex watched from across the living room, unwilling to come and join.

"New game, boys," Dad said, turning to face Jack and me. He looked over toward Lex once, then back at us.

"An outside game?" Jack asked, curious.

"You guessed right." Dad smiled at him. "I want you to get ready to go out in the snow, guys. I'll help Ade, and then you. Got it?"

"Got it." Jack started to pull on his snow pants over his jeans.

Dad knelt and began to get me ready to go out in the snow. I had to wear a stiff one-piece snowsuit that I hated. It had been Jack's and Lex's before me. I couldn't wait until I was big enough to wear pants and a jacket in the snow rather than the terrible suit. I was bundled inside it, hat and gloves shoved on my head and hands. Dad helped Jack finish zipping his coat and tucked his mittens inside his sleeves so snow wouldn't get in. Then Dad got on his own coat, some gloves, and a hat. He didn't have any snow pants, so he just went out in his jeans. *Grown-ups*, I thought, *must not get cold in the snow like kids did.* We all had our boots on, too.

"We're going to go outside now," Dad said. "If anyone else would like to come, they should put on their snow things and come out the door. If they need help with their zipper or their boots, they should stand on the porch until an adult helps and then they may come play." With that, Dad opened the door and he, Jack, and I went out into the bright morning snow.

We'd gotten a good amount the night before, at least six inches. That was on top of the foot we had on the ground already. I thought we'd play while Dad shoveled, which is what usually happened. Instead, he went down the steps, holding Jack's hand in one of his and mine in the other. I needed his help to walk through the snow that was deeper than me in some places. Jack did better than I did, but he still couldn't step as far or as quickly as Dad could.

"You guys get warmed up," Dad said, and turned back to watch the front door.

Jack and I threw snow up in the air, tried to make snow angels in the yard. In a few minutes, the front door opened—Jack and I sat up to watch.

It was Lex, standing on the front porch in his snow gear. Dad went to him, and helped him into his mittens just like he did Jack, made sure Lex's boots were on good and that his hood was tied tight enough that it wouldn't pop off.

When he finished, Dad picked Lex up around his middle and carried him down the front steps. Lex had his hand up to his eyes like he was scouting the horizon. Just before Dad put Lex down in the snow, he leaned forward and kissed Lex's cheek. Lex looked at him a second, then leaned into Dad. I thought he was going to kiss him back, but instead, I saw Lex's pink tongue flick out of his mouth and touch Dad's cheek, close to his eye. Lex laughed. Dad did too.

In a moment, Lex was down in the snow. Dad went down on one knee to talk to us. "You guys were playing war inside, weren't you?"

We nodded, even though I hadn't really been playing.

"Then I need to tell you something very important," Dad said in a solemn, low voice. "Because it matters very much what you choose to do with the information." We nodded again. "I've been given an assignment from the highest office of the land," he said, leaning in like he didn't want anyone else to hear.

"What land, Dad?" Jack said.

Dad smiled.

"The Germans?" Lex asked.

"The Rebels?" Jack asked.

"Rescue Rangers?" I asked because they were the only thing I really knew about.

"Even bigger than that. From the United States government itself."

Jack nodded his head seriously. Lex's face broke into a wide grin. I felt a little afraid and grabbed Dad's leg with my hands.

He smiled and patted my head. "Don't worry," he said. "It's pretend."

"But not really," Lex said. "Right?"

Dad winked at Lex, and Lex nodded like they both understood something that I didn't.

"What's the orders, Dad?" Jack asked.

"I'm supposed to train a unit of elite young fighters."

"Why?" Lex asked.

"To be ready in times of peace or war to come to the aid of their country."

"I'm the Ade of their country?" I asked, happy he'd said my name.

Dad laughed, patted my head again. "The help of their country. You're my Ade."

"And Mom's and Ellie's and ours," Lex said, reaching out to pat me, too. It felt good to know I belonged to them, even if I was wicked.

"Dad," Jack said, "where do you find the fighters, and how do you train them?"

"Good question. Very good. You're just the kind of young man I'm after."

"I am?"

"Just the right sort. And Lexer."

"Me?" I said.

"Of course, you too."

"What do we gotta do, Daddy?" Lex asked, starting to wiggle with excitement.

"First," Dad said, "you have to learn your secret identities. Once you learn them, you can only share them with each other. Or the integrity of the team might be compromised."

We nodded, but I didn't know what he meant.

"Then, we'll drill. You'll learn how to walk, talk, think, and act like a solider. You'll drill until your eyes fall out, you're so tired. You'll drill until you know the commands in your sleep. You'll drill until your plastic soldiers seem like a dream you had a million years ago. You got that?"

"Uh-huh," Lex said.

"All right then, on your feet."

Jack and Lex were able to get up on their own, but Dad had to pull me up by the arm.

"What're our secret names?" Jack asked, squinting in the sun.

"You, my boy," Dad says, "will go by William Tecumseh Sherman. He marched to the sea a while back."

Jack nodded seriously.

"Lex, you're none other than Jim Bowie himself. Fought on his deathbed at the Alamo."

Lex nodded too. I felt excited inside, knowing I would get my secret name next.

"Adrian, son," Dad finished, "you're the honorable Nathan Hale, hero of the Revolution of '76."

I didn't know who he was talking about, for me or my brothers, but I was happy to be part of the game.

"Up, boys!" Dad shouted suddenly. "On your feet! Follow close behind me!" We stood behind him, followed his directions to the letter. We hopped on one foot, then the other; we hit the ground when we heard incoming planes; we lay in a snowbank watching for tanks in case they crested the hill across from us.

"You must listen, men, when you're given an order," Dad said. "Especially from your commanding officer. A disobedient solider is a lost one. Is a dead one. You understand?"

I felt afraid when he said *dead* and *lost*, but my older brothers seemed more involved in the game because of it. We marched around the yard in our parade step, boots stamping a wide trail in the snow. Mom came to the porch once to watch us, Ella in her arms. I could hear her laughing, but I didn't want to turn and look at her in case I missed an order.

"Hold up, troops!" Dad yelled. "Parade rest!" That meant we could flop into the snow on our backs, look up at the sky.

"Dad," Lex said eventually, "what's your secret name?"

But Dad didn't answer. There was a long silence, with Dad standing nearby, just watching as we lay there. I started to feel sleepy. The sun was bright in my eyes and the air was cold, but my snowsuit kept me warm and dry.

"Hey," Jack said, "Dad, what're you doing?"

"Nothing much," he said softly.

"You're doing something," Lex said. "I can hear you talking to yourself."

I listened; Lex was right. Dad was saying something, but I didn't know what. It made me feel weird inside, like he was making fun of us.

"I'm just," Dad said, "I'm just trying to make a poem out of you."

"Stop it!" Jack shouted, so loud that I jumped. I tried to sit up but had a hard time until Lex gave me his arm to lean on. Jack was on Lex's other side, on his knees.

I saw, in Jack's hand, a glove full of loose snow. He brought his left arm back as far as he could and let the snow fly right toward Dad.

It didn't get far, barely hit him. But Dad looked at Jack, then Lex and me.

"Well," he said, "it seems like it's time to go inside." Dad's voice was different, far away and funny sounding, not like earlier, when he acted like our friend.

"I don't want to be with you anyway!" Jack yelled. He stood and stomped his way to the front porch. He pulled his boots off, then opened the door and slammed it as he went inside. Dad picked me up. He brought me to the porch, where he started to unzip me from my snowsuit.

"That kid . . ." he said under his breath.

"Daddy?" Lex called. He was still in the yard, watching us. He looked sad.

"What, bud?"

"You never," Lex said, "you never said your secr—" He started to cry.

"Stay put," Dad told me. He bounded down the steps into the yard.

"Jim Bowie," Dad said, leaning forward and taking Lex in both his arms. He stood up, holding him close. Lex's arms were tight around Dad. He carried my crying brother toward me.

"Hero of the Alamo, Alexander, conqueror of the world," he said, "why are you crying? Too tired? Hard day?"

Lex shook his head, buried it in Dad's shoulder.

"Honey," Dad said to him, "I can't help you if I don't know what the problem is."

Lex whispered something in Dad's ear, but he was so high up I couldn't hear what he said.

"Well," Dad said, running his hand up and down Lex's back as he held him. Snow fell from Lex's body onto the porch next to me. "That's an easy fix. You can call me the General."

CHAPTER TWENTY-NINE

Calvin

SUNDAY 6:53 P.M.

"Here you go," Jack says, handing me my coat. He went to get it for me because I didn't want to have to look at Mom again.

I'm on the old couch that's down here in the basement; it's across the room from the sliding glass door that goes out to the yard. I still feel like crying, but I'm trying hard not to because it hurts my face when I do. I can talk easier now, at least.

"What'd you need that so badly for?" Remy asks, sitting down next to me. He throws his arms and legs out so far that nobody else can fit on the couch with us.

Jack drops the coat on my lap. I reach into the inside pocket. There's a bulky thing inside.

I have a hard time wrestling it out. I pull and tug—there's a ripping sound. I've torn the lining of the jacket.

Mom's going to be mad at me about it—but what's she going to do, hit me again? It's already wrecked, so I go ahead and make the rip wider.

The thing finally comes out. It's heavy in my hand. I hate it. I drop my coat onto the floor by my feet.

"What is that?" Remy asks, leaning toward me.

"Is that what you needed the coat for?" Jack asks.

"It's his notebook," I say, turning it over in my hands. "Dad's notebook. The one he's been working in lately, writing drafts of his poems and his ideas."

The notebook is the color of the sky in the early morning when it rises over Grant Lake. Dad and I would have put our boat out on a morning like that, if the boat ever got finished.

Remy looks at the book a second, his face funny. "I used to dream of a room with a sky that color," he says to himself, "when I was a little boy."

"Why do you have it?" Ella asks, coming closer.

She seems a little afraid of me. I don't want to admit it, but I'm a little afraid of her too. But she's right, we look the same now, our faces banged up and bloody. That almost makes me laugh.

"I took it from his study after he died." I don't want to keep talking about it. My brothers and Ella frown, and Remy touches me on the back of my neck.

"He told me he was working on another collection," Ade says eventually. His voice sounds tired. "Jack, where was Rett when you went upstairs, by the way?"

"He was in the living room, half-asleep on the couch, watching cartoons."

Ade nods. "Fine enough place to leave him for a while."

"Your mom's probably going to want it, won't she?" Ella says.

It takes me a minute to understand she's talking about the notebook.

"Don't they publish that stuff posthumously sometimes?" she finishes.

"What's that mean?" I ask. My heart kicks up to a quicker beat inside my chest.

"It means they publish it after someone dies. Writing that no one's seen before, that the author was working on before he kicked it," Remy says. He leans to check out the notebook more closely. I move it to the other side of my lap, away from him.

"The work goes on, even after he's gone," Jack adds.

"If someone wants to publish it," Ella says.

"Do you think Dad was important enough for that to happen?" I ask.

"Probably. Most likely, even. He was a poet of influence, to a certain group of people," Remy says, sitting back against the couch again. He sighs.

"But those people weren't us, huh?" Ade says, frowning.

"Stop it, Ade," Remy says, but there's no real force behind it.

"It's true, though. His work didn't matter to me. He used us," Ade replies.

"Thanks for using me, even though I never wanted to be used by anyone," Jack says, looking outside into the yard.

The sun's nearly set—the afternoon's gone. It'll be night soon enough. Dad's first night below ground. I saw him today, but when I wake up tomorrow, I'll have seen him yesterday. And the next day, it'll be even further. The thought of that, the piling up of days between me and him, makes me feel like I'm in a free fall that I'll never get out of. I try to breathe deep into my belly to stop the feeling, like I do on a roller coaster. But it doesn't help.

"Thank you for using me. Who said that, Vonnegut?" Ella says.

Jack nods, catches Ella's eye. Something passes between them, maybe understanding. Jack turns back toward the yard.

"It's like thanking someone for punching you in the face," Ade says.

"He did that, too, sometimes. Punched you in the face," Jack adds softly.

"Now you stop, Jack. That's not appropriate to say in front of Cal," Remy says.

"Say whatever you want. You think I don't know he was an asshole? I'm not stupid. And I don't need you to look out for me, none of you," I spit out. I don't mean to sound so angry, but I can't take it back.

There's a long silence.

"He's right," Ade says finally. "Cal's in this just as much as we are."

"I'm sorry," Remy says. I can tell he means it.

"I'm sorry too." I also mean it.

"What do you want to do with the book, Cal?" Ade asks. "I'd say it's yours for the doing."

I think a minute. "I don't want to give it to my mom. I don't want people to read it."

"Why not?" Jack asks, turning back toward us. He comes across the room in a few long steps till he's standing just behind me at the couch.

I take a deep breath, then close my eyes. My hand closes around the notebook, feeling the smooth cover against my palm. "Because he wrote about me. And he promised that he wouldn't. He promised he wouldn't ever do it, but when I took the book, after he—when I took it, I saw he lied."

"He broke his promise, then," Jack says. I feel his hand, strong and warm on my shoulder. I'm glad he's here.

"Yes. I don't want you guys to read it either."

"Wouldn't dream of asking to," Ade says. Ella and Remy nod, and Jack tightens his grip on my shoulder so I know he agrees too.

"Don't tell anyone he had a new manuscript started. Or say it got lost. Say anything but that you have it," Remy says.

I don't answer.

"You could keep the notebook, you know, just for yourself, if you wanted to. You could hang on to it and look at it when you felt like you missed him. That might be a good thing to do," Ella says. She gives me a soft smile that says she wants to be my friend. I'll try to be hers, too, if she wants me to.

"I don't want it," I say. "They're not nice things that he wrote about me. They're things I didn't even know he knew." I don't repeat what he wrote because it doesn't matter. The fact that he did it at all is enough.

"Jesus, Cal, we know how that feels," Jack says.

I look at the notebook.

"What do you want to do with it, then?" Jack asks.

"I don't think I can do what I want to."

"If you could do anything to the notebook, what would it be?" Remy asks.

"Honestly?"

"Honestly," Ade says.

"I want to burn it." Nobody says anything, so I try to explain. "So no one will ever know it existed. You don't think I know how bad he could be, but I do. I do because I saw it happen. He did it to me, too. I want to burn all the poems so they'll never be."

The room is quiet. I'm afraid of what that means.

"Then let's go outside," Ella says.

CHAPTER THIRTY

Ella

SUNDAY 7:06 P.M.

Remy and I go upstairs to bring down coats for everybody else. We move quickly, and no one notices what we're doing. Uncle Cat asks us in the kitchen, just before we go down the stairs again, if we're going to walk Mr. Darcy. We say yes and leave him. I'm not sure what we'll do next, but no one needs to know about it but us.

We take the coats and dole them out. Jack has trouble getting his on but no one steps forward to help him. Maybe someone should, but it won't be me. After what he did. And after what he didn't, maybe couldn't, do.

But he reminds me in a sad way of Owen. And of my ghost. I try in my heart to be easier on him. Though I won't let him know.

Once we're dressed, the glass door to the backyard slides open with a little push from Ade, and then we're outside, the five of us, blinking hard in the cold.

We breathe little ghosts into the air.

I look at my watch. I didn't realize so much time has passed. It's seemed like barely an hour since we got back from the cemetery. I think of my apartment, just across town, decide that I won't be home to defrost anything tonight, even for a late dinner.

There's the invitation from Owen, the text message with his new number. How I'll have to charge the phone to get the message. How I could go, right now, and meet him at his motel room. How I don't know what I'll do. I push the choice off until later.

Now that we're outside, I don't know why I suggested we come out from the warm basement in the first place.

The boys stand around, hands deep in pockets. They're not boys, really. Men now, Cal the only exception. And even he has a broadness across his shoulders that I don't remember being there the last time I saw him.

Five Gable kids lived here once. That family died with Lex. We're a new thing now, a band Lex would no longer recognize— four grown-ups and a new blond half brother to take his place. As if his place could ever be filled by anybody but him.

"What's next, El?" Ade asks.

My stomach flips. "I don't know, really. I guess we should—"

"We're going to bring the books out," Remy finishes for me.

He grins, a smile genuine and warm. So different from the one that twisted him earlier in the church. It's good to know he's in there, still—funny, sweet Remy. Our good boy. My little brother.

"Right," Jack says. He moves toward the sliding door, pulls it open with his good arm, and waits as Remy and Ade go back through it before he follows.

Cal and I watch. They point at a few of the boxes of books they moved earlier. In another minute, they're back through the door again; it only takes them a couple of trips to bring seven almost-full boxes out onto the small cement patio beyond the basement door where we're waiting.

"That's the creek?" Cal says, looking down toward the water. You can't really see it, but you can hear it slowly lap at the muddy bank. It used to freeze, years ago, but it never does these days.

"Yup," Jack says, wiping his right hand across his forehead.

"I thought it'd be bigger."

"It is, sometimes," Ade says. "They're in a drought here, so it's running low."

Cal makes a noncommittal noise. Remy taps him on the shoulder.

"Hey," he says. "You sure you want to light that notebook up?"

Cal turns, looks Remy up and down. Nods.

"Then let's do it." Remy's grin creeps back again.

"What're the books doing out here?" I ask.

Jack answers, "To make a bigger fire."

Ade and Remy talk quietly about the best way to contain a bonfire without burning a patch in the yard.

I finally catch on—I feel exhilaration, like something, finally, is going to happen that matters. Something I can feel moved by, not just crushed beneath. Something will happen that's our own doing, rather than the consequence of someone's choices half my life ago.

"It should be inside something," Ade says, scratching the back of his head. "To contain it, so we don't inadvertently burn the house down."

I remember the smell of smoke from the fire when I was young, how it burned my eyes. How I never really believed Lex set it, though that's what the youngest three of us were eventually told.

"Where's the charcoal grill?" Jack asks.

The books, in piles on the ground, easily number over a hundred volumes.

"We need something bigger than that," Remy says. He walks down the yard, pokes his head around behind the shed. "Come help me, Cal! Ade!"

They look at each other, confused, them ramble down the yard to see what he needs. Jack and I are left, looking down toward the creek.

"I can't believe he's gone," Jack says quietly.

I don't answer. I'm less angry at him than I thought, I'm surprised to find.

"It's just, he's been absent so long already, I thought things wouldn't feel so different," he finishes. "It confuses me a little bit."

I let my breath out slowly, trying to be quiet so Jack doesn't think I'm talking to him.

"It's okay, Ellie," he says. "You don't have to do a thing but hate me, if that's what helps."

I steal a glance at him. It's hard to see, but my eyes have adjusted some. He's already got stubble on his chin even though he must have shaved this morning. He's tired and beaten down. He's like me.

This is Jack, the one who used to wait outside my bedroom until I fell asleep. Hearing him out there was a comfort, especially after Dad left. The boy who destroyed Dad's car. The boy who took me to fly kites, real ones he'd saved his money to buy from the store. The one who lived. The one who maybe suffered worst, out of all of us.

Jack turns, faces me fully. Looks me dead in the eyes. He's got the penetrating gaze of a saint—it goes right through me. But I don't know what he sees. I feel vulnerable, exposed.

"Stop staring," I say, but I don't mean it.

Jack's face softens. He smiles sadly. "I don't know what to do," he says. "I'm so angry, so goddamned mad at him, for things ending like this. For all the ways he's let us down."

He tries to stretch his bad arm. "Some days this hurts so much." He clears his throat, looks at me again. "I damn him, over and over. For what I knew, and know, and have never told anybody. But then I think, of course Dad disappointed me. I expected him to be Atticus and Aslan and George Bailey at the end of the movie all rolled into one. But nobody can be that."

We're quiet for a minute. It feels like a wall's fallen between us, or a locked door's opened. I can reach out toward Jack again, if I wanted to.

"I don't hate you." I surprise both of us.

"Well, then," he says, more to himself than to me. "Well."

I can't keep looking at him. It hurts too much, watching him suffer.

I turn to see the others bringing up the old canoe from the shed. It takes them a few minutes to get it up the yard, where they drop it like an offering at our feet.

"This," Remy says, "is big enough to hold the fire we're going to set."

"How're you going to light it?" Ade asks, catching his breath.

"I pulled a lighter from Cat's pocket when Ella and I got the coats," Remy says, smiling.

I didn't realize he'd done that. I reach into my own pocket to make sure he hasn't taken his cell phone too. I find, with relief, that he hasn't.

Jack grins at Remy, raises his hands to the sky. "Fires burn hottest with a stolen lighter," he says. Something wild dances in Jack's smile.

CHAPTER THIRTY-ONE

Calvin

MARCH 2013

Jack came to us a week before my birthday—I was turning twelve. We were going to have a big party.

It was late at night. I was sitting on the couch in front of the TV nearly asleep. I should have been in bed already. When the doorbell rang, it made me jump. Mom was in the kitchen having her last cup of tea for the day. When she heard the bell, she sang out in a weird high voice—"Who is it?"—like she was expecting someone. Dad came stomping down the hall. From where I sat, I watched him through the open door that goes into our living room.

Dad looked out the little window in the door, held his hand up to the side of his face to shield his eyes and see better. Then he threw the door wide open and just stood there.

I could see Dad but not the guest. Someone said, "Hey there, Dad. Can I come in?" It was one of those weird moments when you know the voice you're hearing, but you can't place who's talking. It was a guy, but it wasn't Ade. Dad stepped back and a tall shadowed figure came in.

It was Jackson.

There'd always been tension between Dad and Jack. I've grown up hearing conversations that end up loud between my parents, where Dad talked about Jack and how he doesn't understand him or why he's been so weird, why he's always insisting on acting strange or keeping away from the family and not getting in touch, stuff like that. Dad would start out angry at Jack in those talks but end up defending him out loud (even though Mom never was the one who was saying anything against Jackson—it was Dad arguing with himself).

Dad looked at Jack, put his hands on his shoulders.

"Hey, Dad," Jack said again. "I'm sorry I'm here so late. I just—"

Dad, looking dead into Jack's eyes, said, "Well, I guess you'd better come in." He put his arms around Jack's shoulders and pulled him close. I sat on the couch. Mom had come silently to the end of the hall and was watching them just like I was.

"Jack, let's get you something to eat," she said after a moment.

Dad let go of Jack, and Jack smiled at her. His clothes were rumpled, like he'd gotten wet in them and they'd dried on his body. He followed Mom into the kitchen. Dad finally turned and looked at me. He smiled. I got up, too, and followed them.

"We don't have much left from dinner, but just give me a minute to—"

"Please don't worry about it, I'm fine," Jack interrupted. "I was just in the area and wanted to say hi, and my car was having trouble, so I needed to stop anyway, for a while . . ."

"Where's your car now?" Dad said.

"Down the road a few miles. I had to walk the rest of the way to the house. Wasn't bad, though. I like walking at night."

"What's wrong with it, do you figure?" Dad said, like there wasn't anything weird about Jack being in the area in the middle of the night. Last I knew, he was living somewhere in Massachusetts—we're in Washington.

"It makes this whirring noise that keeps getting worse. Then tonight the engine just cut out completely. So I left it where it was, came here."

"I'm glad you were so close to us, then."

"I was on the way here, anyway. I just figured I'd spend the night in the car and come see you in the morning after breakfast."

"Why would you do that, Jack? That makes little sense to me," Dad said. Like any of this made sense.

"Because I didn't want to cause problems for you. I know you're in bed early, and—"

"Jack, you're to come inside whenever you need to, do you understand me? You do not sleep in your car when you're near your own house."

But it wasn't his house. It was our house, and then maybe Ade's, less so Ella and Remy's, but never Jackson's.

Jack nodded and looked away. "Em, Dad," Jack said, "please don't let me put you out. I know it's late, I just wanted to see if I could rest on the couch for the night until I can take my car to a mechanic tomorrow."

"That's nonsense, you're here now, you'll sleep in a proper bed," Dad said.

"What're you doing in the area, sweetheart?" Mom said. She started going through our pantry looking for something to feed him.

"I have this friend who moved here a little bit ago," he said, letting out a big breath like he was happy the subject changed, "so I came out to see her and how she's getting along. I had a doctor thing, too." Jack hadn't shaved in a while. There was dirt from his shoes getting on our kitchen floor.

"How is she, your friend?" Dad asked. He ignored the doctor thing.

"She's good," my brother said. He ignored the doctor thing, too.

"Is this a girl we've heard of?" Dad said.

"Yeah. Katie, my friend from college. She took a job in Seattle. Figured I'd see her while I was out here, and you."

"Long trip to make just to see a girl," I said. Everybody turned to look at me. They'd forgotten I was there.

"Hey there, Calvin," Jack said, smiling. "How are things?" I didn't want him to smile, though, or to even be there. I didn't answer.

Dad looked around the kitchen, said, "What do we have in the freezer, Emily? Jackson doesn't want what you've found in there."

She'd pulled out a can of cranberry sauce, a half-empty box of cereal, and a brownie mix.

"Please don't do anything special," Jack said. "I don't want to bother you, you've done more than enough by letting me in at this time of night."

"You'll have to look, James. Come here, Jack, take off your jacket," Mom said as she moved around behind him and caught his coat as he shrugged it off. Like she used to do for me when I was little. Only he was much taller than she was, so the whole familiar act was different; it made me feel jealous and angry and sad all at once—seeing my mother be someone else's mom. Dad started rummaging in the freezer while Mom and Jack chatted. I tried to let everyone know how angry I was with my eyes.

"You head up to the shower, Jack," Mom said. "You'll probably find some of Ade's old clothes in his dresser, at least something you can wear for the night. You'll sleep in his room, too. Come back down when you're done, and we'll have something for you to eat."

"Thanks, Emmy, really. Thank you," he said.

"It's nothing, honey. Make sure you turn the fan on in the bathroom. Calvin can show you where the switch is."

"I won't," I said quietly, hoping somebody would hear.

Jack went up and took his shower. Mom went into her bedroom to shut her eyes for a few minutes. It was just Dad and me in the kitchen, and I was able to see what he had pulled out to cook for Jack.

The oven was on. In it there was a pizza.

"That's my pizza! You can't give him my birthday pizza!"

There was a particular kind of frozen pizza that my school sold as a fundraiser. And I really liked it. We'd gotten fundraiser pizza for my party. More than one, actually, because I was having a bunch of kids over, and Dad was only cooking one, but it didn't matter. It was the idea that he was cooking anything of mine for Jack, the brother who made him so anxious, the brother who never called back, who would disappear now, who would take Dad's love and stomp all over it. And he was being given my special pizza.

I yelled at Dad, told him I hated Jack, that he wasn't being fair, that he loved Jackson more than me and was showing it by giving him my birthday pizza when Dad knew we couldn't get any more before the party.

And through all of it, Dad just looked at me with a funny expression on his face, like he was laughing at me but not in a mean way.

"He didn't even want to see you tonight! He just broke his car and needed someone to give him a place to sleep."

"Be quiet now, Calvin," Dad said finally. "Jack will be out of the shower soon, and he is our guest. You can eat pizza with us if you'd like, or you can go to bed."

"But it's my pizza," I said, tearing up even though I didn't want to.

"I know it is."

"He doesn't want to be here and hates us anyway. And he makes you so mad."

"But he's come home to us, and so we should give him the best we have."

"Why?"

"Well, because we love him, and because we're grateful he's back with us and safe. So we share what we have."

"But I never get anything nice, and I'm the good one. I do what you say and behave and act nice."

He put his arm around me and kissed the top of my head. "You are the good one. You're the best."

We heard Jack coming down the steps. When he came into the kitchen I asked to be excused. I could hear them talking quietly downstairs until very late that night.

The next morning, Dad drove Jack to see about his car and found out it needed a few new parts. So they had it towed to a mechanic nearby.

Jack stayed with us until it was fixed.

After that first night, I felt bad about how I acted. Knowing Jack was home when I was done with school made the days feel special. Having him there was way better than the stupid pizza would have been.

He was there for my birthday party. He was better at video games than any of my friends, and he organized a touch football game for us in the front yard and actually played, which is something Dad never did.

Ade came over with his family—we had the best dinners, laughing and being stupid and teasing Dad, telling Mom her cooking was terrible even though we all knew it was great.

I didn't want Jack to leave; when the call came from the mechanic that the parts had been replaced, I cried for the first time as a twelve-year-old.

Then, on his last night with us, it happened. The terrible thing Dad did.

Mom made a nice dinner since Jack was leaving the next day. Ade stayed late while Liv took the kids home to bed. Mom was working on a cold by then, so she went to bed early too.

Jackson, Adrian, and Dad were drinking in the living room, and I was lying on the floor watching TV. When I say they were drinking, I don't mean they were loud or crazy; they were just talking and had beers in their hands.

I fell asleep.

When I woke again, Ade had gone home. Dad and Jack were still sitting on the couches (we have two), and I wanted to keep the cozy feeling that had been going on for a while longer, so I didn't get up. I kept my eyes shut and thought that without Jack our house would feel empty.

"Thanks for having me here," he said. "You have no idea how good this has been, getting to be here with you and Cal and Em—"

"It's nothing."

"I wanted to talk to you about something important."

"And you've waited until now?"

"I guess. I don't know. It just didn't come up." Someone moved and took a sip of beer. I heard it but couldn't see.

"Go ahead," Dad said in a careful voice.

"Right. I went to the doctor, an orthopedic specialist in Seattle."

"All right."

"There's a new procedure that's available now—to cut through scar tissue, from what the doctor said. I'd be able to gain more mobility, maybe. If I did it."

Dad was quiet.

"So I was wondering if you thought I should. Do it, I mean. Have the surgery."

There was an even longer quiet.

"I'm sorry," Dad said. He breathed heavily.

"For what? What do you mean?" I wondered, too.

"I'm sorry. I'm sorry."

There was quiet for a minute, just their breathing and the sound of a clock ticking, probably someone's watch.

"Why did you come here?" Dad finally said.

"To see Katie. Really, to see the surgeon, though. If I'm honest with you."

"Not to Washington, Jack. We're nowhere near Seattle, here in Sawtell."

Jack was quiet now.

"Why did you come to my house?"

Jack paused, breathed in, then said, "Because I wanted to see you. To see all of you."

"And now you have."

"I have, it's been great."

"Why did you come here?"

"What? I just said."

"You didn't just come to see us. Why are you here?"

"I don't understand."

"If you wanted to visit, you'd have come during the day, like people usually do. So why come to my house in the middle of the night?"

"My car broke down."

"You want something else, it's plain enough to see. You weren't 'in the area.' You came here with a purpose. The car broke down when you were already on your way. So what was it that you wanted so badly?"

Jack swallowed hard—I felt it in my own throat. "I guess I wanted to know what you thought about the surgery, if I should go through with it or not."

"It's your body. Do what you want."

Another long silence.

"I figured you might have some thoughts about it, since you were always the one—"

"To take you to the doctor?"

"Well, yeah."

"I haven't taken you to the doctor in years."

"But I thought maybe you'd be able to help me decide—"

"I won't be doing that, Jack."

More silence. My heart pounded in my ears so loud I was afraid I wouldn't be able to hear them when they started talking again.

"Why?" Jack asked. His voice sounded like he was going to break apart.

"Because any thought or consideration I'd give you wouldn't matter. To keep talking about it is a terrible waste."

More quiet, more sips of beer, more breathing.

"A waste of what?"

"Of the time I have in a day. Of the time you have. Of words. Of breath."

"Dad—" Jack tried to say, but Dad cut him off.

"No, Jack. That's final." Dad's voice was full of gravel and pain, but I didn't feel any sympathy toward him. I'd never seen that sort of meanness in him, that kind of bite, but I was hearing it now. I was lucky that I couldn't see his face because, if I had, I don't know that I'd ever unsee it.

"I thought you wanted me here. You said you were glad to see me."

"I was. I am," Dad said. "But honestly, I'll also be glad to see you go."

"I don't—"

"Be quiet. Listen to me. Because I will only tell you this once. Don't come here asking things of me I'm not willing to give. You've come, I've seen you, and what I see is that you have wasted all I've ever tried to give you. It's not about love, Jackson. Because God knows, I love you. Though this might make it seem as though I don't."

"It does seem that way," my brother said, his voice thick.

"You've taken all I've been able to give, and you've thrown it in the dirt. I don't know why you've done this, if there's something wrong inside you that can or cannot be fixed. But you won't do it anymore. I won't allow it. I've been able to distance myself from it, but now with you here it's clearer than ever."

"I'll be gone by morning."

"I expect you will. But it's more than that, Jack. It's—"

"Don't call me Jack. Please don't call me that."

"Fine." I heard my father shift on the couch. "All that I've ever done for you, you've left half-finished, or quit part way through, or in other ways neglected your side of the deal," he said. "All the physical therapy, the counseling when you were young, the late-night phone calls, the invitations to come stay—"

"Please stop talking," Jack whispered, "just please."

"If I don't tell you this, it's not fair to me. Not fair to you."

"I don't care about what's fair to you."

"I expect you wouldn't. You've done nothing with yourself, Jackson. You're a good person, maybe. You're bright, you're talented, but you spend your time doing God knows what. Searching for a cure when you didn't do it right the first time."

"You don't know anything about my life."

"You're right. And I find now that I don't care to. So you go on and do what you will, and that'll be all."

"That'll be all?"

"Yes. Of course I love you—I always have. But this has little to do with how much I love you, but how you've taken that love and trounced on it. I won't let you do that to him."

The "him" Dad meant was me.

"I love that kid," Jack said. I knew he meant it.

"You might. But you won't act it. For a while you might, but not forever. And then I'll be right, and I can't let you do that to my son."

"He's my brother. And I'm your son, too."

"That doesn't matter. It never has."

"Why are you saying this? Are you drunk?"

"It has nothing to do with alcohol. I'm saying this because I feel like it will be a long time before I speak to you again."

"Because that's how you want it."

"Yes. This isn't easy for me, though. This isn't what I wanted for you."

"Then why do it?"

"Because there's nothing left to do. I have paid the mechanic for you, by the way. And there's eight hundred dollars in cash in your glove compartment, which should help you with gas on your trip home."

"God, you're a riot."

"I've only ever responded to you with love," Dad answered, but I felt like he was the biggest liar I'd ever known. "This is where we leave it."

"All you ever do is leave."

"And now I'm asking you to do the same. You'd better listen, too. Because you don't want me to make things more difficult than they are already."

"I don't want your money. I don't want your love, either."

"That's your choice and your burden. But you should know, Jack, that of all my children, you're the one who's broken my heart."

It felt like Dad had landed a punch to Jack's center, one that had been waiting to land for much longer than I or Jack could even know. Jack was twelve once. He was a boy who got angry when people took what was his. Dad probably comforted him, like he did me on the night Jack came to us. Which meant that someday, it could be me sitting next to Dad in the dark, being sent away.

This is really why I want to light the fire. It's not just about the poems. It's about Dad, about what he did to Jack. What he might do to me. Dad could have fixed things, but he chose not to. He was always choosing, and it was only himself he cared about. I didn't know, until then, that I should be scared of him. I didn't know that words could be as violent as a fist.

There was another long silence. I tried to lie as still as I could, but it was hard because I was shaking. I should have spoken up, defended my brother. But I couldn't.

"If I've broken your heart," Jack said finally, hurt weighing down his voice, "what do you think you've done to mine?"

CHAPTER THIRTY-TWO

Calvin

SUNDAY 7:18 P.M.

The canoe's heavier than it looks. It's made of aluminum. The boat we were building at home is prettier, but this one'll work to hold what we're going to do next. We place the canoe down on the lawn, about twenty feet from the patio where Ella and Jack wait for us. I'm a little surprised we're really doing it, setting the notebook on fire, but I'm also wildly happy, in a way.

The rowboat at home held our lives together, Dad's and mine. This one will hold what comes after, his death and mine. You don't realize it until it happens, but you can die a little and still be alive. Maybe Jack knows this best. He did die, Mom told me once, during a surgery. His heart stopped, but they got it going again.

Ade begins to put the books into the canoe, piled long and low rather than high, so the flames won't tip out onto the yard. Remy helps him. I stand back for a second, watching it all. Wondering how I got here, where I'll go next. What it will be like to have the poems, at least some of them, gone.

The poems are Dad, and Dad was the poems. He was a brother, too, and a son, a husband, and a professor and a liar and a builder of boats and player of war games and I guess someone's friend and a bunch of other things, too, but mostly he was the poetry. Even more than he was my father, he was his work.

He's gone now. There'll be no more written. I've got the last record, his final drafts. The thoughts he'd had but never got to share.

But some things aren't for sharing. Some things aren't for the world's eyes. Some words should never be spoken. Dad said a lot of things that should've stayed hidden; to me, to my brothers and sister, especially to Jack. The poems in the blue notebook are secrets that will stay silent, the way they should. So there's a little less hurt out there for somebody to walk into.

Ella takes a book from the top of the pile. She opens it, then rips a handful of pages out. Holds them out to Remy, who doesn't take them yet.

Kindling.

Ella puts the torn book back into the canoe.

I take out Dad's notebook. It's a little bigger than my hand. I'd tucked it into the waist of my pants. It's sweaty, sticky when I touch it. I'll never hold it again.

I wonder if Dad can see us, what he thinks of what we're about to do. I wonder if he's found Lex, my fourth brother. The one I never thought of much before today, since I saw his grave. The one I think I've met in my dreams. The one who I hope is with Dad now.

The notebook is my offering. The fire is the way I'll kill what hurts me.

Remy takes the stolen lighter from his pocket. He turns it in his right hand, then puts it up to his eyes. It's dark now, and he has to look close to see.

"There's a goddamn bald eagle on this thing. Uncle Cat's quite the patriot."

Remy flicks the lighter, igniting it with a hiss and a click, like you've snapped your fingers. It's that easy.

He reaches his left hand out to Ella, who passes him the batch of pages she pulled from the book. I wonder what poems are on the pages she's grabbed.

Remy takes the pages in his left hand. Looks each one of us in the eyes, even though it's dark and hard to see. We didn't turn an outside light on, so we don't attract the attention of anyone inside.

I don't know what would happen if anyone came out, saw what we're doing. Maybe they'd call the fire department.

Remy nods once, then touches the flame of the lighter to the lower corner of the papers he holds.

They catch. Fire curls up toward his hand. He leans forward, carefully drops the flaming pages onto the books in the canoe. Dad's young man face begins to smoke and twist as book jackets ignite.

We all take a step backward as the flames rise, except for Jack. He's got a container of lighter fluid that my brothers found by the shed, next to the charcoal grill. He holds the cap to the lighter fluid between his teeth. It must taste bad.

With his right arm, Jack flings lighter fluid all along the boat. The flames jump up wherever they're splashed. The heat intensifies.

Everyone moves back farther at the combustion, but I step toward Jack, toward the heat. He turns to me. The cap is still in his mouth so he can't smile. His eyes are solemn.

I throw the notebook into the boat. I want to finish my dead brother's fire.

I give Jack all the apologies in my heart. We watch as it begins to burn.

In my head, I say to Dad: *I'll miss you. I'm not sorry.*

CHAPTER THIRTY-THREE

Adrian

SUNDAY 7:27 P.M.

There's something hypnotic to the flames. They dance, though today's not really a day for dancing. The lighter fluid smells strongly of summer. I remember the vision I had when I fell asleep in the car on the way home from the cemetery. As if whatever ran by me then is here with us, too. There's comfort in its presence.

We have to keep relighting parts of the book pile to get them going again—they don't burn easy. Like secrets let out into the world, they're hard to put down.

The daylight's failed like the fire's eating it, growing hotter and brighter as the shadows deepen. The trees that run along the creek at the bottom of the yard are leafless. Their bony fingers stretch upward, toward Rett's good heaven, where he believes his Papa's gone.

My son's inside, being cared for by the television. Falling into a confused, uneasy sleep. But he's safe there, unlike Adam. Unlike me.

The canoe's the sum of our history. So many poems here, so many years. Our lives. The entirety of it all. Enormous and insignificant at the same time. So many secrets he pulled from us, so many things promised but never kept.

It ends in ash and smoke. With your kids in the yard burning your books.

I keep expecting Mom and Dad to run outside together, yelling at us to put the fire out. I keep expecting to be punished, but nothing comes.

I'm close to saying it aloud, what I heard on the phone from Vincent. What I whispered into Jack's shoulder as I cried there. But not quite yet.

I've always been private because I've had to be. Telling your feelings in our family got them broadcast—to everyone else if you were lucky, to the world if you weren't.

Nobody knows, officially, why Liv and Adam aren't here. But they've guessed, I'm sure. I've been watched, hawklike, all day. They're waiting for me to come undone, as I'd like to, if Rett wasn't here with me.

Since I was a little boy, I was the fragile one. Ella used to stand up for me in playground fights, before she learned that girls shouldn't fight with their fists, but with their words. She got very good at that second form of combat. My boys aren't like I was, quick to dissolve into tears, full of fears and whims and private terrors. For that I'm grateful.

The fire keeps nearly flaming out but we encourage it, nurse it, give it the space to breathe. We take care of it like it's one of us.

Cal and Jack stand closest to the flames. Oldest and youngest, James's first and last. Standing together, I can almost imagine I'm looking not at Cal's back but Lex's—though in life, Jack and Lex were never together, not like this. One's grown and the other's in the ground.

Remy and Ella huddle beside me against the cold and the night.

Remy lit the fire, but his courage is gone now. We've always expected so much of him. He's never failed to deliver. I wonder how hard that's really been for him. And Ella, the only girl, who's always been a little lost, maybe, in our house full of boys.

There were two pairs in our family—Jack and Lex, Ella and Remy. Me, in the middle, alone.

I look at their faces, I look at the house. I peer into the flames; I want to give them all one more secret to carry away with them on the wind.

"My son. Adam, my baby, my little son." I say it quietly.

Jack and Cal turn at the same time to look at me. They're lit up from behind. Remy and Ella take a step closer, close a little of the distance between us.

Our father is gone. I left him in anger and will never have a chance to change it. But I can do different now, here, with my still-living family.

They weren't bad people. My parents tried the best they could, most of the time. They were selfish and vain, sure, but they also loved us. We shouldn't end this way. I can't let that happen.

The only punishment left is that which we inflict on ourselves. Thinking that we should go it alone.

"Adam is sick. We don't know for sure how badly yet." It's easier to talk in the dark.

No one speaks. They watch. They listen.

"Liv and Adam didn't come today because Adam is in the hospital in Washington. I thought, when I heard, that I would leave here as quick as I could to get back to them. But I can't do that until I do this first."

Finally, for the first time in front of everyone, I begin to cry.

"I don't know what this is, exactly, but I think it's happening now. Here. With you."

Someone's hand grips my shoulder. Someone else's grazes the small of my back. I never thought I could feel this kind of despair and not explode. The flames burn without any encouragement. I hope they will consume us with them. Make us clean again.

CHAPTER THIRTY-FOUR

Remy

SUNDAY 7:35 P.M.

Ade's shoulders shake. I hold on to him tightly. Ella rubs his back a moment, but then she pulls away. She moves around the canoe, all the way to the other side. I don't let go. I want to steady him. I'm the good one. I'm the one that everybody relies on to be uncomplicated, complacent. I'm the boy who never was much trouble.

But I was the one to light the fire. I burn with all the crimes I never committed, all the sins I wanted to perpetrate. When we were little, Ella said she would love me forever as long as I promised I'd never die. I promised, and I've lived a circumspect life because of it.

I had one moment of glory, one fall. They know it happened. But not why. I should give what I couldn't say before to the fire, like Ade did.

If I can get the words out, they'll burn up like the poems, and it'll be like I'm free. From carrying a secret. From having to be good, brave. From myself.

"I left school and I never told any of you why. Not even Ella." I can't tell, from her face, what she's thinking. "I left because I got into trouble. You probably figured that. But you don't know the kind of trouble. Jack doesn't know, even though I stayed with him. He never even asked me why I was there. I should have said thank you for that.

"In the letter, Dad was right. There was a girl. It was a thing with a girl that got me so messed up that I left for a semester. You don't know the girl. She was someone I met at a party. At least to start with. Her name was Jess. It was nothing special."

I swallow deep, look into the flames. They feel like friends.

"We ended up sleeping together. It happened a few times. Cal, sorry if this is too much for you. Just tune it out, buddy. Jess came to my room one day. She was red in the face from crying. I thought maybe she'd had a fight with a friend. I got her a glass of water and sat down beside her. I moved to put my arm around her, but she said in the coldest voice I've ever heard that I shouldn't touch her. So I didn't.

"She told me she missed her period. That she tried a home pregnancy test but she couldn't figure out how to use it right. She wanted me to know the kind of trouble we were in. Again, Cal, please, just don't listen to this."

"It's fine," he mumbles.

In the fire there're no eyes to avoid. The books on top have all caught so Dad's photograph doesn't stare back at me.

"I panicked. She didn't call me or text me or email me back for days after it. I didn't know what to do. I couldn't take it, what was happening in my life seemed bigger than classes, than tests."

I pause, slow my breathing. Take smoke into my lungs. It's good. I want it this way.

"I bet you're thinking I left because she was pregnant. That I couldn't take that news. But, that's not it. I finally caught up with her in the dining hall. I walked up to her, cheeks blazing, asked her how she was. How things were going. She knew what I was talking about. She said with a big smile on her face that I didn't need to worry about it after all.

"She'd gotten her period late, by a few days. I guess that sometimes happens. She'd never been, you know, in any kind of trouble to begin with. That's how she said it, too. If I wanted to call her on a weekend sometime, she'd love to meet up again. That meant she wouldn't mind hooking up with me. I didn't leave because she said she was pregnant. I left because she said she wasn't."

I breathe.

"I didn't want a life with Jess, don't misunderstand me. I didn't want to be a father at twenty, didn't want to be tethered to this girl I met at a party for the rest of my life. I didn't want any of that. Most of me was so glad when she said it was a mistake, nothing to worry about.

"What got to me, though, was the fact that I was looking a certain future in the face, and I was ready to take a step toward it. I didn't want it, but it was something that I'd done and needed to contend with. It was a struggle that was my own. It was a life, however fucked up it sounds, and it could have been mine.

"When it wasn't, school started to feel irrelevant. I couldn't sleep, thinking of all the ways my life would have changed if things had gone different. I'd played fast and loose with futures, and then when Jess said to me so cavalier that she'd be up for playing roulette with them again, I lost it. I don't know, I guess I was mourning the guy I might have been if I'd been forced into a situation I wasn't prepared for. I was struggling to deal with the fact that what I had been afraid of, what I'd prepared for, hadn't come to pass. There was relief, sure, but there was also a terrible empty space, a vacuum, a hole.

"I left. I stayed with Jack until I came home here, and then the next semester I went back to school. I saw Jess at a few parties after that. She was dancing with the best-looking guys in the room. Barely noticed me. Because I didn't factor into things for her at all. That was freeing, but also very sad.

"Nobody ever asked what was wrong with me. Nobody, after the first phone call I took from Mom, even yelled at me. Everybody gave me space, but that wasn't what I wanted. I wanted to fill the hole, not be left alone to make it bigger. But that's what happened. That's how it was.

"Do you know what it's like, to always have to be good?" I say to the fire, to the air, to my family. "Do you know what's it like, feeling like the only future you have is the one people expect from you, the even path, the steady road, the one where you don't feel a moment's pain or panic or elation, either? You don't know because you've all been allowed to be unhappy. You've had the right to be miserable and angry and vengeful, whatever else.

"I never had that. Having to be good is its own kind of curse."

Ella nods. Jack clears his throat. Ade's still crying a little, but paying attention to me. I can't get a read on Cal. So I just forge ahead and say it, what no one talks about, what we all know.

"Jack was the oldest, the sick one. Lex was lost. Ade was always on the verge of a breakdown. Ella was the only girl. Cal was the little miracle. What else could I be but good? I toed the line again. I went back to school. Which is why I hang on to my little failure, why I keep it close. Because it lets me know that at one point, maybe, there was a different way for me to be. I don't want to be bad, really, but I don't want to have to be good either."

No one talks. No one touches me, like I did for Ade. But that's okay. It's a pleasure to burn. That's Ray Bradbury. And it's true.

CHAPTER THIRTY-FIVE

Ella

SUNDAY 7:47 P.M.

If Remy wanted to hurt, all he needed to do was say so. I could've shared pain enough for him to live off forever. I don't understand Remy's confession, exactly, except that by doing nothing for him, we were doing something. Somehow, we've failed him.

I haven't understood him for a long time. Today, it's just become more apparent. His breakdown during his eulogy and now this. I took him into the woods when we were kids because I thought that by bringing him with me, I could keep us together.

Our growing apart—it's sad but also symmetrical, somehow. Like something that would happen in my father's poetry.

The fire's dying, slowly but surely. Ade takes the lighter from Remy, tries to reignite the books toward the bottom. But it's not working.

Air can't get in beneath the flames. The canoe blocks most of it, and Ade's so close he's smothering it. That's also poetic in its symmetry—our mother, after Dad left, was too close to let us breathe.

Even good things die. Kids grow up. Even fires that burn so hot they feel like a fever in your soul flame out. Fires that bring together but that also break apart. Fires that define who you are and why you are it.

I'm thinking of those bonfires we went to when we were teenagers, Remy and I. How I'd bring him along because I was afraid of growing older. Because if he was there with me, then it wasn't so bad. It wasn't so wrenching, didn't make me feel as lost. Owen was there too. Owen's always been there. But he's not at this fire, now.

"Owen came by." My grown brothers nod at me, but Cal looks confused, even from across the fire.

"Who?" he asks.

No one answers. They don't know what to say.

"Owen's a guy Ella's involved with," Remy finally offers. He clears his throat.

"The one who left just before Mom . . .?" Cal asks.

Jack nods, looks into the fire like he's concerned. Owen's not a good subject for the two of us.

"He asked me to see him tonight." I'm a little surprised I say it, but it seems we're all in a confessional mood.

My brothers nod their heads or look away. They don't want to interfere. Only Cal keeps his face upturned, stares at me across the burning boat.

Little Cal, my half brother raised on the other side of the country. I was thirteen when he was born, not much younger than him now. Remy and I would see him during our summer visits to Dad's house, but he was always a tagalong, a second thought. He's not so little now.

I wish I'd been more clued in to his life. That I'd paid more attention. Because I know what it's like to be part of a family where nobody really sees you. I don't know his favorite color. I don't know whether he's chosen first or last for teams in gym class. I don't know much of anything—I feel ashamed.

"You want to?" he asks, his voice high. "See him?"

He's just a boy, a miserable kid whose dad has died. Bruised and mangled face. But then again, so am I.

"I mean, maybe." I feel my cheeks flush.

"Why?"

It's an honest question. He deserves an honest answer. "Because I don't know what else I'd do."

The other boys don't talk. But Cal can't seem to quit.

"You could stay here with your mom. Or you could just go home. You live near here, right?"

I nod. He keeps drilling.

"You could do a million things. Read a book. Write some shitty poems. Cook a chicken. Do all three." He's trying to be funny. "You could stay here, with the fire going."

"I guess," I say. "You don't understand, Cal. Owen and I are—we're more than friends. We're . . ."

"In love with each other?" The words are simple. But the answer isn't.

Cal looks startlingly like my ghost. I've never seen the ghost in real life before, only dreams. And yet here he is.

Asking me why I burn for Owen, why Owen makes me burn. Am I in love with Owen? What do you call love, and where's the line between it and loathing?

"I used to love him."

Cal, my inquisitor, nods slowly.

If this is how I made Jack feel in the living room, I'm sorry for it.

"Of course she says that," Remy whispers under his breath. Cal's head whips around to scowl at him. Remy takes a step backward.

"Ella," Cal says, "why only used to? It shouldn't be hard, to tell me if you love someone or not."

Ade's quietly trying to get the book pile flaming again. Jack's face is vacant. Remy won't look at me.

I close my eyes. Let my mind go quiet. Cal's unspoken question—*do you love him?*—echoes around my head until it's not Cal saying it, but my own voice.

In my nose, the acrid smoke feels heady and otherworldly, like it's coming from a dream. I hear the snap of the lighter in Ade's hand as it breaks into flame, the hiss of the pages when he tries to ignite them once again.

"I don't," I say to Cal, to myself, to Owen at sixteen, rowing me back from a bonfire in the woods in the canoe that's now at my feet.

"Why don't you?" Cal says so softly that I'm not sure if the words really come from his mouth or if I just imagine they do.

"Because he's a just a boy I used to know." I open my eyes, see my brothers around me. They're all just boys I used to know. Men I'd like to know better.

"Ella," Cal says, "would you maybe stay with us in our hotel room tonight? I don't want to be alone with Mom. I . . . I'm scared of her, a little." His voice hitches. "She probably won't want one of the boys to sleep in a bed with her. Could you, maybe, please come?"

He's earnest, seems near tears. I look at him, open my arms. He gets the signal. Comes around the long side of the canoe so I can hug him.

"Of course I'll stay with you, Cal. Of course I will."

He's almost as tall as I am, but he rests his head on my shoulder like he's much smaller.

CHAPTER THIRTY-SIX

Jackson

SUNDAY 7:52 P.M.

They come together as I feel myself receding. The fire's dying, like the final notes of a symphony—lovely and sweet, a clear ringing that echoes in the air. The night is getting colder.

I'll be going soon. I have to leave. Staying, knowing what I know, what I could have changed but didn't, isn't an option.

Better I don't say anything at all, rather than ruin their communion. I've failed them. I'm the patron saint of inaction. Of stalling and avoiding. In all the stories I've ever told, all the memories I've tried to remake, I've also failed him. My brother Lex. Sometimes I forget he was their brother too.

All I've ever wished was to bring our lost boy back to life. It was a desire so overwhelming that I sometimes sat with a pencil in my hand, like an old-time medium, waiting for the right words.

But I didn't write the story of that boy or the secret he trusted me with. I couldn't. It was too volatile, too pained. I let my father have his secret, and I carried my shame and Lex's bitter confidence walled off in my chest.

I failed because I've known, always, that I'll never bring Lex back again, the same way my father never could either; I've come to understand that Lex, his loss, will be the obsession of my life the same as it was my father's.

I've kept all the words inside my head because there's nowhere to write them and there's been no one to listen.

I watch the fire, watch myself among my brothers and my sister, envy how they find each other in the flames.

How I'd hoped that I might, too. I want, almost more than anything, to be one of them. To be a Gable again. To be our father's son. But I can't because, without my brother, I'm nobody. And without my father, I'm afraid my brother's lost for good.

The fire's failed me, or I've failed it. There was heat, light, the chance for a different ending. But it's over now. I lost it—a last try to be better, truer, full. To learn to speak. But the secret of the letters, even now, seems too much to tell them, though it's also too much to bear.

So I stay quiet. I swallow hard. I do not cry. My eyes close against the smoke, the flames, my family. I hope they don't notice that I don't have any passable story or secret for the fire. I'll slip into my car once the fire's out, and hopefully no one will call my cell phone, asking where I've gone. Because I don't want to have to tell them—being near them is too hard, takes too much of me. I'll go back to my apartment. Be at work tomorrow morning if I drive all night.

The only thing left to burn is myself, my sad excuse of a life without Lex. I'd throw myself into the fire if I could, if it was big enough, or I were small; I'd lie on my back like a dead Viking king among my father's work, looking at the sky as the smoke escapes into it, hoping for what I know will never come.

CHAPTER THIRTY-SEVEN

Jackson

SUNDAY 7:55 P.M.

Yet this time, something arrives. There's an atmospheric pressure drop like that which comes before a summer storm. My heads pops a little; I swallow to break the seal in my ears. I yawn.

My pulse climbs. There's sweat on my forehead but my back is cold. The smoke smells sweeter, like cedar burning instead of old books. Whatever's come howls so loudly that I can't pretend it's not real, that it's not happening.

Look at me, it dares. *Open your eyes and see.*

I do. They're not my real eyes but ones inside me.

It's blurry at first—I'm not used to this kind of looking, the purity of it, the immense feeling it raises in my chest. It's what it might be like to look for a moment into eternity, the space between breaths where anything is possible. It's like watching a horse or a dog or a child who loves to run and who has opened his stride out fully and in joy; it's like looking at the ocean when the sky has turned the same color as the water; it's lying in your bed at night in winter knowing that your parents are awake down the hall.

The expansiveness focuses—there is the fire again, but the rest of the family is gone. Something gathers on the other side of the canoe, where Ella had been.

There is a boy beyond the flames, his head bowed, hands balled in fists at his sides. He stamps his feet, first the left, then the right. He grinds his toes into the ground. He turns in a slow circle, then begins to hum. He sings a tuneless song of his own devising. He dances.

"Stop acting like you don't see me. I know you do, asshole."

The voice startles me.

So I stop. I try to see.

There must be a chemical being released by the burning books that's playing with my head, making me hallucinate. Or it's stress—the losses have piled up, and I've finally cracked. I'm trying to weigh which one is more likely when the boy stops moving. I look at him a long second, not sure what to make of this.

Then he takes a running jump, clears the fire in one bound. He lands in front of me, so close I could touch him.

We face each other, alone in a dark place, the burning canoe to my right side. My heart stalls; something inside me gives way. I loosen, give way.

Lex. I've somehow, finally, found him again.

"Little brother" is all I can say.

"Little brother," he answers. He wears jeans, a red-and-blue flannel shirt, sneakers on his feet. Not the clothes they'd have buried him in—ones he wore normally, play clothes.

"I'm older than you."

"But I'm the one who got here first," he says. I haven't seen him in twenty years, but there's no sign of the intervening time on Lex's boyish frame. He looks no different from the last time I saw him. Better, even.

What must he think of me, broken down and old? Do I scare him?

I want to hug him, but something holds me back. Instead, we settle down to the ground. We sit together, cross-legged. So close our knees are almost touching. There is no rule book for this—I don't know if I'm allowed to touch him. Lex, though, seems at ease. Instead of touching, we talk.

"Well, how the hell've you been, kid?" he asks. He's talking like an old gangster from the movies we used to watch.

What do I even say to that? I think of Whitman, that one line from *Leaves of Grass*: "All goes onward and outward, / nothing collapses." Remy's not the only one who remembers his reading.

I don't know what to say, but I must say something because the next thing I know I'm telling him, "I wish I could turn time back. So we could be how we used to."

"You can't, though. And besides, you wouldn't want to."

"I would. And how do you know you can't? I thought I'd never see you again, but here you are."

"You can't turn time back. I know. I've watched a clock for a century, just trying to make the hands go backward."

"Did it work?"

"It didn't. But I saw the whole of an age pass right in front of me."

"You don't sound like you used to. You talk like a child and like something more than a child," I say.

"You wouldn't either, if you were where I've been. And neither do you."

"Do I what?"

"Sound the same as you used to."

"I guess I wouldn't. I grew up."

"And I grew sideways." He smiles crookedly, with half his mouth. His teeth are perfect, none missing, clean and white. There is the faint glow from the fire off to the side, but nothing more is illuminated. We're in a void, it feels like. I can sense walls around us in the dark. Yet Lex seems to glow.

"Why did you die?" I get the courage to ask.

"Why didn't you?"

"How am I supposed to answer that?"

"How would you answer it, if you had to?"

"I guess I didn't die because when the doctors tried to save me, it worked."

"And with me it didn't."

"But here you are."

"Just because I'm here doesn't mean they saved me."

"But something saved you."

"Sure it did. But I don't know what it was, really. Probably not any more than you do."

"I don't follow."

He thinks, bites his lip. I've missed seeing him do this for so long.

"It's like you walk through a dark hallway, and at the end, you find a door," he says. "You and I were at the door. After the accident, we were right there. And I went through, and you didn't."

I don't speak.

"And you thought on the other side of the door would be a different place entirely. But it's not. It's just the same hallway, and it's still dark."

"So you went through a dark door into a dark hall beyond it."

"Pretty much."

"Oh, Lex. Knowing that breaks my heart."

"Why?" He looks genuinely confused. His blond hair bristles on top of his head. It's not combed.

"That you went through the door and nothing was there."

"I didn't say there was nothing."

"I still don't understand." He's so small. There is too much of me, compared.

"I just said it was dark. I don't understand much more than I did on your side of things. But that doesn't mean there wasn't anything else." He cocks his head to the side. "You walk through a dark hall, hands out in front of you, until your eyes start to adjust. Then you start to see things—they're gray, they're scary sometimes, but you get to know them eventually."

His eyes flicker faintly in the low light, blue and smoldering, full of something I can't place. They're not the eyes of a living boy, a real one, but they suit him.

"What's there in your hall?" I say. "Because mine, this side of the door, is full of ruin and hurt and nothing else."

My brother, my beating heart, he laughs. "There's entire worlds here. Rooms that are half-filled or full and some that are empty."

I frown. "What's in the rooms? Do you go in them?"

"Some I do. Some I don't. And I put things there."

"What?"

"I put things in the rooms. They're my rooms, you see. I can put anything I want in them. Well, almost anything. The thing has to want to be there, too."

"What things?" I whisper.

"Oh, everything." He shakes his head, proud of himself. "I have one that's the ocean just before a storm starts. You're out in a little boat and the wind picks up and you—well, you'd like that one. There's one that's a hayride, and I have a movie theater, and there's one that's full of old car engines that I learned to take apart and put together so they work again. And I have Veterans

Stadium and Disney World minus the Haunted Mansion, and so many others."

"They demolished Veterans Stadium over a decade ago."

"Well, it's here still. It wanted to come to me."

"Is there ever anyone else there with you, in your rooms?" I ask, confused.

"On and off. Sometimes Ella was there. I'd visit her when she was sleeping. I could see Remy a lot of the time. His room has a sky-blue ceiling. And I put Bear there for him, too. Bear's been with me from nearly the start."

My throat constricts. He's filled his rooms with little siblings and dead dogs to keep him company.

"Do you still see Remy?"

"Not so much. He's busy now."

"And El?"

"I just saw her, or I'll see her soon again, I can't remember. It gets confusing. I gave her the message, though. Because I felt it coming. I thought she should know."

I don't know what he means. "Does anyone else come to your rooms?"

"Mom sometimes, but she thinks it's just dreams. That's what everyone thinks. Then a little boy came. That was Rett. And a boy a little older than me, and that was Calvin."

"What about Ade?"

"He's like you. I had to bang on the door of his room, until it finally fell. He was very tired, and he finally let me in. But since, he's been here once or twice."

"Bang?"

"Yeah. I can't put you in a room unless you want to be there. That's the shitty part."

"You always did have a bad mouth."

"That's what Granna used to say."

"She still says it about you."

"She does? I thought she wouldn't remember me very good," he says.

How could we ever forget? He left a hole that nothing could have filled again.

"Have you seen him?" I ask, trying to steady my breathing.

"Who?"

"I thought you'd know by now."

"Oh, you mean the old General." He shrugs.

"General?"

"That's what he's posing as these days. He's dressed up like a guy who leads a military parade, with a cowboy hat and a cigar and a tie-on beard. I think he's trying to make me laugh."

"Grant," I say with recognition. The cigar and beard give it away.

"Huh?"

"You're describing Ulysses S. Grant. Civil War. Dad used to pretend to be him during our war games, don't you remember?"

"Maybe. I don't know," he answers. "Anyway, he looks stupid. Leads a troop of dead soldiers behind him and they come marching in here, make a mess with their muddy boots and all the noise. They follow his orders. Like that soldier game we used to play."

"What?"

His breath hisses out between his teeth, the way it always did when he got frustrated. "He's trying to get me to follow him somewhere else. I'll have to go eventually," Lex says.

My stomach turns. He's only just gotten back to me, and he's already talking about leaving.

"Don't go with him, Lex. Please don't."

"Aw, Jack, it's all right. I thought that, too, for a while. That I shouldn't go."

"Why not?"

"Well, because I hadn't seen you yet."

"You hadn't?"

"Far as I know, this is the first we've talked since the day it happened."

"But I talked to you so often, especially in the beginning—"

"If you talked, I didn't hear you," he says.

"But I tried, I did, I tried—"

"I tried, too. I banged. Tried to pull you through while you were sleeping. Which was hard because you almost never slept. When I banged, you left our bedroom and went into the hall. The real hall."

The horrible weight of so many years without him crushes me. "Jesus. We were talking to each other all this time only neither of us could hear."

"Does that break your heart too?" he asks, giving me a hard smile.

"Every day something about you breaks my heart."

"That's a stupid way to spend your time," he says, but doesn't sound very sure of himself.

I put my left arm out to close the space between us. It shakes some, but I hold it steady. He doesn't move closer, just squints his eyes. Examines me.

"Boy, the accident did a number on you," he says quietly. He reaches his arm toward me, so much smaller than mine.

Our palms touch, fingers spread wide. My hand could close the whole of his inside it. His warm fist, pushing back against me. Though it hurts some, I lock my fingers down around his hand. Grip him as hard as I can.

"I wish I'd died instead of you that day. Or with you, I guess," I whisper. "But not this, the way things are now. You on one side of a door we can't open and me on the other. And both of us wanting and waiting."

"But the door's open now," he says simply. Like that's the answer to everything.

"Does that mean I've died? The fire's exploded and I'm lying there burned and done for? Has my heart stopped?" I wouldn't mind, exactly, if that's what happened. We're together, that's all that matters.

"God, you are so dumb. Of course not," he replies, twisting his hand to break my hold. But I won't let him go; he stops fighting after a second, lets me hold his hand.

Our arms sink down into our laps, a bridge between his body and mine. He swallows hard, leans his head in. "I think it means I can go with the General now. He's nearby, and he's waiting for me to join the parade."

"But why? When we've just finally got back to each other—"

"Calm down, Jack. I've been waiting for somebody to be able to turn the lights on," he says. His thumb strokes my hand softly.

"The lights?"

"Even though I can see in my rooms, it's dark in my hallway. As dark as here. We're in the hall now, I think. I spent about forever when I first got through the door feeling around for the light switch. I couldn't find it. But there has to be one, right?"

"I don't know, truly I don't. You're the one who's—"

"Dead, yeah. I know. 'Stay out of the light, Carol Anne.' All that shit." His thumb stops moving.

"I'm sorry," I say, trying not to grin. The kid's been dead for decades but he remembers the one time we watched *Poltergeist*.

"See, I finally made you smile. I always was the funny one," he says. He smells fresh, like the outdoors, like pine boughs.

He laughs a little. That sets him off harder, until he's rocking back and forth in a giggle fit. The rubber toes of his shoes poke my knees. My missing brother—laughing, holding my hand. His easy smile. His minty breath, his face bright and strong and whole.

Lex composes himself. He takes deep breaths, but occasionally a laugh escapes from him anyway. I hold his hand tight.

"Somebody needs to turn the lights on. So I can see where he's coming from. Go where he's going."

"You've been waiting twenty years for someone to turn on a goddamned light bulb?"

"When you put it like that—"

"I'm sorry."

"Don't be sorry," he says. "No, I've been waiting for someone who knows where to go next. Your dad always knows what to do next. That's why he's your dad. And I've been waiting for you."

"For me to die?"

"No, stupid. I don't want you to die. Not yet, anyway. But I needed to see you before I leave. Even though the General's here, I can't go with him yet."

"Is this it?" I ask, not able to hide the way my voice has gone husky and thick. "This will be the last time we talk?"

"Of course not," Lex says, like he's a teacher dealing with a student's dumb question. "It's just the last time I'll be in my rooms for a while. I'll fall into parade step and go for a walk. I'll be able to see."

I reach out with my other arm, the good one. Grab him hard. He turns his face to look into mine. The set of his eyes seems determined, set on some plan I'm afraid will undo us forever.

"I want that for you. But I don't know if I can bear it."

"Oh, Jack," he answers, shrugging me off. He reaches his own hand out. Places it, fingers splayed flat against my chest, over my heart. The pressure is surprisingly strong.

"I want you to tell me something, before I leave," he says. He keeps his hand on my chest, in my hand, but he looks away. Toward the fire. "It's just a story. That's all I need."

"You've waited for me so long just to hear a story?"

"I did."

"Couldn't someone else tell it to you?"

"No," he answers. "It has to be from you. Because you're the one who keeps the stories. You always have been. You know what to do with them. That's what I've missed most about you, Jack—the stories."

He leans forward, rocking himself over his knees so that his forehead falls against my chest, next to his hand.

"You've got blood on your shirt," he says, rubbing his cheek against the fabric anyway.

"It's Cal's. His nose. He was bleeding."

"That was a story," he says. "You tell them even when you don't realize you're doing it."

I shake my head, bring my arm around to the small of his back. Hold him against me. We never did that in real life, were deliberately so close to each other.

"Lex, I don't have anything to tell you that you don't already know." The words remind me of something my father might have said.

Lex snuggles close to me, half-sprawled in my lap, his legs out behind him. Throws his arms around my shoulders. Like a child might. Like a son would.

"That's not true," he says, muffled.

"It is." I feel the certainty of his body. How it fills the place he vacated. How I don't want him to leave it again.

"There's one story you haven't told anybody, not in your whole life," he says. "That's the one I want to hear."

"I don't know—"

"You do, Jack," he says, turning in my lap so he's looking up at me. "It's a story you only heard once. Mom told it to you. You were washing dishes. After Thanksgiving."

My body shudders; he feels it. His fingers flutter along my arms, trying to soothe me.

"Oh God, how do you know that?" I manage. I'm terrified of that story. Even more so than the secret I learned the night of Lex's fire.

"Ella told me. Mom asked the kids to leave the kitchen. Ella heard her say 'I'm going to tell you what happened to him just once' before she couldn't hear anymore."

"You mean you don't know?" I ask, confused.

"I don't."

"But how could you not?"

"How could I?" He shrugs. "I was already nearly through the door. It was dark here. I was afraid, I had other shit on my mind. Like where the lights were."

"You mean you didn't hear them singing?"

"Maybe I did. Maybe I didn't. I don't know."

I take a few deep breaths, beg him with my eyes to not continue with what he's asking. "I don't understand why you need to hear it. It's the worst thing."

"Because it's honest. And because I want to leave here."

"Can't he tell you, the General?"

"No, I don't think he can. Some stories, you can't tell them if you lived them. Or if you died them."

"But Mom told me the story. She lived it."

"But *she* can't tell it to *me*. Because we were in there, in the dying room, together. That's why it's you. You're the storyteller. You do it all the time."

"I don't follow."

"I can't explain more than I already have. If you don't get it, I guess that's on you," he says, his voice plaintive. "Jack, I need you to tell me the story. Please. I want to be able to see the hallway.

To see if there's a door at the other end. The General must be getting in somehow."

"Don't make me say it, Lex. Please don't." My brother's begging me to tell him how he died.

"I can't reach the lights. Maybe it's you who has to switch it. I thought at first the General had to, but I think it's really you."

I close my eyes but they burn anyway. Here he is—thin shoulders, eyelashes so blond that they might not be there at all. The flannel of his shirt pilled on his back, where my arm holds him. The articulated majesty of the muscles in his hands, his face, the finely wrought inside of him.

He's asking me to send him further on. I don't want to, but I know it's what I owe him, what I owe all of us.

"If I say it, what will happen?"

"I'll be okay. I'll walk awhile, just following the General."

"I left you in a house once with him, Lex. He knocked your teeth out."

He sighs. "That was a dumb thing from a long time ago. And he's sorry. He's been sorry his whole life for it. Sorry for it before we were ever born. He lived a life sorry for what he would do to us, and that's why he was so unhappy so much of the time."

"Once I tell it, where will you go?"

"Outside, I hope. Someplace where I can run around with Bear."

"You'll make sure you take Bear? And you'll follow close behind the General?"

"Of course I will. Bear will come because I'm a little scared. I'll follow close because I'm a little confused, and Dad will know what to do."

I try to turn my face away, but tears drop from my chin onto him anyway. He squirms a little as they hit his skin, but doesn't move from my arms.

"Because Dad was always the one to come find me when I was lost. Like on the Fourth of July, when I was so bad to Ade."

"He was." I try not choke.

"So please tell me? And then when I see you again, I promise we'll have a better time." He reaches his hand up toward my face.

"I only have to say it the once?" His palm is warm on my cheek.

"You have a beard, sort of," he says quietly, surprised. "And yes. Just once. But loud enough so I can hear it."

"Do they need to hear too?" I feel, somehow, the presence of our siblings again, though I understand that they can't see him like I do.

"Not if you don't want them to. But maybe they should. I think they'd be relieved to finally know."

I nod. Think of the other secret he shared once. The one I could've used to blow our world apart. "I never said anything about the letters you found. Why you lit your fire. I thought maybe I would tonight, when they lit theirs. When they told their secrets. But I didn't do it," I confess. "I didn't tell them when we were kids because it would have made them hate Emily. Hate Dad. I couldn't add to their pain. And now I won't tell because of Cal. It would wreck him. Drive him away when he needs us most." Just when we've found each other.

"That was a good idea, Jack. That's why I trusted you. The letters don't matter now. Maybe they never did, I can't tell anymore. Please help me leave here. Help Dad leave. It'll help you, too, to say it. I know it will."

We look at each other awhile, not talking. For decades I've carried two unvoiced stories in me, each about loss. Sorrow. I thought, in trusting me with the truth about the letters, Lex'd hoped I'd know when to tell it. To whom. I've fought my whole life to try to find the right words to speak it, but they never came.

Turns out, they were never needed. Lex doesn't want that story told. Neither do I.

It's about protecting Cal now, but it's more than that. We're moving toward each other again, toward something new. Something ours. We've fought and grown and died, but we're still us. The Gables. Jack and Lex, Ade and Ella, Remy and Cal. We happened. It all happened. And maybe that's enough.

In the letters Lex found, there's betrayal. There's our father making choices that will break us.

I realize, with relief, that I will never tell that secret. I've made my choice, and I feel quiet inside. My heart beats slowly, my stomach doesn't churn. There's absolution for Dad. For the boy I was, for the kids we were. For the people we've become.

Those people deserve to hear the other story, the one Lex wants. In it, there's love. The hardest kind of love, but it's there.

"I'll say it aloud, then. The story you're asking for. They'll hear it," I say, breaking the silence.

"Thank you." Lex twists again, drapes across my arms like an overgrown baby. Cradles himself against me. His small bony bottom in the hollow of my lap. His head against my chest, just opposite my heart. His right arm around my neck, the left tucked up against his chest and mine at the space where they intersect. I bury my face in the top of his head. I breathe him.

"I never told you that I love you," I mumble into his hair.

"You never needed to tell me," Lex says into my shirt. "That was never a secret."

I close my eyes, not wanting him to break apart or dissipate or walk away. I don't know what the light will do to him when it comes.

"Does he know, the General? That I loved him?"

"He knows."

I hold on to him forever.

"Jack, don't feel bad. It's just a story that happened a long time ago." His fist balls up my shirt. I feel the warm brush of his skin against my chest where he's pulled apart my buttons. "In stories things are bad in the middle, but all the people come to a good end."

I nod, but he can't see it, far away as he is now, waiting to listen.

Here's your good end, little brother.

"I need to tell you something," I say aloud. My family looks at me, eyes bright, reflecting the flames.

CHAPTER THIRTY-EIGHT

Jackson

SUNDAY 7:56 P.M.

"You know some of what I'm about to tell you, but not all of it. Though you should. Mom told me only once. She thought it would help me move on. After Thanksgiving dinner when I was sixteen. She sent you out of the room, sat me down at the kitchen table. Wept her way through it. I didn't cry, just listened with my head bowed, looking at the floor. I was told to never share it.

"The facts are simple—we were hit, broadside, by a drunk driver named Roland Dawson. In one second, he ruined all the hopes Mom and Dad had for our family.

"We were on one bike. I sat on the handle bars, he pedaled. I felt his hot breath on the back of my neck, and then I couldn't. For me, that was the end of him.

"It was a few weeks after the fire. We were still living at Granna and the Admiral's. I was the one who wanted to go for a ride. Lex was still technically grounded, but Granna's a softy and let us go out to play.

"As Dawson came over the hill, we swerved into the road. Lex and I went flying off in opposite directions on impact, toward different fates. I've always wondered if I could've saved him, but I don't think so. No one could've, once we were in the air.

"The first cop who came across the scene didn't know who to help first—I was more obviously injured, my arm crushed, bone visible through my scalp. Lex lay deathly still but wasn't bleeding visibly, except from the nose. Dawson kneeled on the side of the road. An ambulance came. Then another did. I was second to go. Dawson told the police that we were playing chicken with his car. We weren't, by the way.

"Lex had a closed-head injury. There was emergency surgery, but it only confirmed the worst. The bleeding in his brain was too fast, too damaging.

"He was a contradiction to the end—he'd gone arrestingly pale, but his cheeks were ruddy and red, like he'd just come in from a hard bike ride. Which he had, I guess. The doctor who said Lex wouldn't pull through was honest when he told our parents he didn't know what, if anything, the boy could hear or feel. The doctor called him 'the boy,' assuming a distance that felt impossible to breach.

"Lex was on a ventilator, the bits of it that stuck out of his mouth lashed to his face with white tape. He had monitors across his chest, tubes in his nose, his veins. His eyes were closed, blackened from bruising. His chest sunk into itself so he disappeared into his bed. He had gravel from the road in the deep scrapes on his shoulder blades, where the emergency room attendants hadn't bothered to dig it out.

"Hours passed. The catastrophic damage the bleeding caused meant that no matter what was done, he wouldn't make it. Mom and Dad decided, then, to be the kind of parents Lex deserved, rather than the ones they wanted to be. They loved him—would have done anything if they thought it would bring him back. But a terrible, mechanized prolonging of his leaving was the last thing they could save him from. They made their choice.

"There was, absurdly, paperwork to sign. The pen they handed Dad ran out of ink. Mom dug in her purse for another one.

"When the nurses took Lex off his machines, our parents weren't allowed in the room. The nurses wouldn't say why, but Mom guessed it was because it could be ugly. There was violation in it, the deliberate act of taking the tubing and the monitors away. Letting someone's child die. They waited in the hall until called back in, where they would stay with him until it was over.

"When they were allowed, they crawled into bed with him. Dad on the right, Mom on the left. They put their arms around him and each other. He looked better then, more like himself. But he was fading. Nobody cried. They didn't want to scare him.

"'We got you,' Dad said. They wanted him to know that he wasn't still lying out on the road. Mom realized later that they hadn't held Lex together like that since the day he was born, when the doctor put him into her arms. They told Lex they loved him. They said he'd been just right to be their son, a perfect fit. They told him that I was okay, off getting fixed up.

"I was lying unconscious in an ICU room a floor above them. The Admiral was by my side. Granna was with you, back at their house. I'd spent a long time in surgery, doctors working to give me back my body, to reinflate my left lung, staple back what the hot metal of the car displaced. Upstairs, the doctors coaxed me toward living, and below, they coaxed Lex away from it. Monitors beeped out the intricacies of my insides, but just below, though I didn't know it, my heart was dying.

"Lex's breathing eventually started to slow. He dragged in air like the effort itself was enough to carry him away. His chest rattled. He wasn't cold though. He didn't seem to be hurting. *How small a boy only twelve is*, Mom thought. *How little space he takes up in the world.* She wondered how long it would take. Dad wondered how to shepherd his own child out of the world.

"'My boy,' he said. 'I don't know how to show you what to do.' Dad's voice broke. He laid his head down next to Lex's. Mom slipped her arm beneath Lex, rocked him. They put their hands together on Lex's chest, over his heart, one of them started to hum, then to sing. It lasted just a moment. They kissed his cheeks. They couldn't help touching him. They felt his hands, smooth and dry. The knotty muscle under the skin of his arms.

"They counted his ribs, smoothed his cheeks under their hands, noticed the dimple he had on the left side. The temporary fix the dentist did on his teeth. Lex was scheduled to go back later in the summer to get the rest of the work done. They made memories of him with their hands so that even if their eyes forgot him, he wouldn't be gone.

"'Good boy,' Dad said. 'You're the best boy. You're the bravest.' Lex shuddered in their arms, but they didn't know the exact moment the end came, since the monitors were off. They cried in the hallway while the doctor stepped in after it was over.

"They were never more divine than in that room with Lex. They loved him, loved each other, loved us. That's the heart of it. Love exacts a terrible price. But that doesn't mean it's not love.

"Look at them, straight on, going through the unspeakable. See it in all its horror, all its grace. They did the best they could. Remember that.

"He died just before eleven in the evening. Nobody told me what happened to him for three days after I woke up. I must've asked about him. I must've asked why Mom hadn't come to see me, just Dad—she couldn't come back to the hospital, not yet, it was too hard. She was there for my later surgeries, but not at first.

"Our brother was many days gone before I cried for him. It was almost autumn before I was taken to see the grave site in Lawrence. My arm was in a cast, like it would be on and off for months. The grave was unremarkable—I'd thought I'd be overcome with his loss. His headstone hadn't been delivered yet. There was a bronze plaque flush with the earth, 'Alexander Davis Gable' spelled out in letters as foreign to me as they would have been to him.

"'Look,' I said to Dad, who'd brought me, 'we never called him that.'

"He was Jim Bowie, he was Alexander the Great, he was Lex, he was truth, law, light itself—but never a plaque in the ground.

"Life continued, but I didn't go on living it. For a while I tried to find the place Lex inhabited, but I never could. I settled for the empty spaces where he used to be. The hall. I loved him, but it couldn't bring him home to me.

"I tried to tell stories to bring him back, to revisit memories to see what I'd done wrong, and when that failed, to think him, to conjure him like a ghost to my bedside. That's what Dad did, too, and it ruined him. We tried our hardest, but Lex never came. I thought I'd never see Lex again.

"What I did not know—he's been here the whole time, shouting at me to wake up. To open my eyes. To see.

"What I found in our fire was a boy who burned so hotly that he broke through death itself. A boy bound up with too much life to ever die, not really. He waited by a door that couldn't open until I was ready, and then for a moment or an eternity he was in my arms—in both of them, and they didn't hurt. I was brave and strong again, like I could've been, like I've never been. He showed me the awe-filled truth: What divides us does not win, so long as we learn to rescue, to save."

My voice sounds eloquent, poetic, like my father's. I take a quaking breath.

"We redeem people through stories." Through the terrible things we keep hidden for love. "In that way, nobody ever dies, nobody ever goes missing. Even after Lex walks through the door, he's not really gone. He needed saving only from the dark he couldn't see through.

"What salvages him is light, and holding on to the hope that there will always be another meeting, another tomorrow where what couldn't happen today might happen still. We'll see him again in our stories. In each other's eyes.

"Only with a fire can you remake what is badly wrought— can melt it down, fashion something better, a stronger bond made through pain and the forgiving of pain, through love and the acceptance that hate is part of it, through anger giving way to a weariness in your bones that feels good, like it should be there.

"My whole life I've tried to return to memories to find what I've lost, where I could have acted differently. Moments when I should have spoken, but couldn't. I stayed quiet. But that was never the way through.

"The whole time, I should have been talking to him. To you. So this story is for you. For our mothers and our father. For the fire. For us."

I go quiet. Together, all six of us, we breathe. We're at the end, but also the beginning. We're going forward into some future we'll fashion together. The one we've always deserved.

I feel steady hands on my back, my shoulders. On my tired, battered body. My harrowed, broken heart.

I squint my eyes up so tight I see spots, flashes of color rearing up. Lex is there for only a moment, exploding across my mind like fireworks on a summer night.

There's no thanks from him, just the vision he's gifting of himself following his good end. His toothy smile. His blond head shaking like he's about to laugh. The weaving brown tail of a happy dog going for a long-needed walk.

Ahead of him, I see a dark coat, a man's back broad and strong.

"Jack," Lex says before he walks on, before he follows the General's parade, "the last word of a story is the most important, and so it should always be love."

Acknowledgments

The story of a book is the story of its writer, too. Here's mine. Half a life ago, I thought I wanted to be a journalist. I tried it for a while and learned I didn't. After that, I wore a poet's hat for a short stint before hanging it up again. Shortly after that, the first inkling of this narrative began to reveal itself. It started as a short story, but that didn't do it. Then it morphed into my master's thesis, but that wasn't it, either. It twisted its way in and out of writing workshops, MFA seminars, and revisions. I wrote and read and chased the story as deep and as wide as it would go, and back again. And now, here we are, the book and I.

Books (and people) never come up in a vacuum. Many thanks and deepest gratitude to the people who have touched the novel in some way over the years. I'd like to call attention to a few especially important folks now.

My mentors through Lesley University's MFA program: William Lychack, Rachel Kadish, and Kyoko Mori for their invaluable feedback and wise advice. Also, thanks to my student colleagues in that program whose insights helped to shape what this story has become.

My fearless first readers, Monica Turner, Erina Gruner, Mary Turner, and Aaron Holroyd, each of whom helped me find and patch up holes large and small.

Book coach Mary Cadman, whose insight, compassion, and all-around know-how helped me take the book to the next level right when I needed that push.

My friends and students in my Writer's Workshop, whose interest and support over the years made the book-writing process far less lonely.

The professionals at the Greenleaf Book Group, including Steve Elizalde, Brian Welch, Morgan Robinson, Jessica Easto, Julie Mercer Carroll, Tonya Trybula, Jared Dorsey, Brittany Steiman, Kyle Pearson, and Jenny Cribb for working their magic to turn my manuscript into a book.

My family, first, extended, and found: my parents, Mike and Deb, and my siblings, Chris and Megan, for walking through this world beside me. The Butterworths, Patschkes, Turners, Bettendorfs, and Holroyds, and all those friends I've found along the way.

To Aaron, whose support makes this all possible. To Monica, who's been there from the start.

Finally, to my daughter, S., whose every day draws me forward into a narrative more dazzling than any I could hope to compose. With you, love is always the last word.

Reader's Guide

1. *To Die Is Different Than Supposed* is largely shaped by stories. How do the characters' inner narratives shape their actions and beliefs in both destructive and redemptive ways? What may be holding them back, particularly Jackson, from sharing their stories? What power does connection through storytelling hold?

2. Revisit the title and epigraph (pages i, iv). In what ways do the Gables die differently than supposed? Are there other lines in Whitman's poem that apply here? How so?

   a. What might Whitman mean by "there is really no death/and if ever there was it led forward life"? How do you see this playing out in the novel?

   b. Explore the concept of the afterlife as presented in this novel.

   c. After reading this novel, have your perceptions or assumptions about death changed or become more complex? Discuss.

3. How does trauma shape the lives of the Gable family? In what ways do their memories influence their actions?

4. What does Ella's banter with the ghost add to the more serious elements of the story such as grief, the supernatural, and trauma?

5. Explore the parallel between Adrian and James throughout the novel as fathers. How do the two differ and how are they similar? How do they relate to each other?

6. Jackson's narration provides a unique perspective within the novel. How does his viewpoint add to your understanding of the family's history?

7. How does the death of their father impact Adrian, Remy, Calvin, Ella, and Jackson differently?

8. How does the past shape the present in *To Die Is Different Than Supposed*? Discuss specific instances where the characters' past experiences influence their present lives.

9. Loss of innocence plays a big role in the novel. How does Lex's death at a young age influence the loss of innocence for each of the siblings?

10. How does Ella's relationship with Owen parallel her relationship with her father? What could the evolution of this relationship show about her relationships with her brothers?

11. Doors hold a specific weight in the novel for all the siblings. Discuss what they symbolize for
    a. Ella
    b. Jackson
    c. Calvin
    d. Remy
    e. Adrian
    f. Lex

12. How do Calvin and Remy face their vulnerability compared to Adrian and Jackson?

13. What questions or answers about grief and coping with grief did the novel highlight for you?

14. Why do you think Lex was able to reach all the siblings except for Jackson? Why does Lex's form change depending on who sees him? What do the particulars of each visitation say about the characters involved?

15. All the characters show a great deal of duality. Do you think James's actions make him a bad father? Should Jackson have been able to stand up for his brothers? Does the desire to remember Lex in a positive light after death overshadow his bullying? Discuss the nuances of how this duality goes beyond the generic labels of "good" and "bad."

Author Q&A

Q. With *To Die Is Different Than Supposed* being your debut novel, did the process differ from your experience writing shorter fiction?

A. The process of writing the novel was similar to how I work when writing shorter fiction, but the overall time it took me was much extended. When you're working on a short story, your timeline is measured in days, weeks, maybe months. *To Die Is Different Than Supposed* took the better part of a decade to come together. My characters grew with me as I went from my early 20s, when I first began the book, to my 30s, where I am now. It's possible that without the seasoning that intervening time gave me as an author and as a person, I wouldn't have been able to write the book, at least as it stands today.

Q. Were there any folklore or ghost stories that inspired you as you created the supernatural elements of the story?

A. The supernatural elements of the book aren't drawn from any single story or bit of folklore. If anything, they're the opposite of what you might think of as a traditional haunting. Lex doesn't haunt a single location. He's not tied to a house or an object. He's drawn to his siblings, his family. Where they go, he goes. Encounters with him aren't frightening. I've always been interested in folklore and ghost stories. I've internalized those sorts of tales since I was a kid, and it felt natural that they came into the novel in some way. As I came to realize there was a ghost story at the heart of the novel, the parameters of that ghost story developed into their own kind of lore, specific to this novel, these characters.

Q. How personal is *To Die Is Different Than Supposed* to you? Were there any elements of your own life experiences that you drew from?

A. The book is very personal, but I haven't lived through the family trauma and fracture that my characters do. There are elements drawn from my own experiences, though. Harrington is a fictionalized version of the town I grew up in (if you want to see another version, check out John Updike's work). The creek and old canoe in the Gables' backyard are from my grandmother's house.

Chapter 14, Jackson's recollection of the fireworks on the Fourth of July, is the part of the novel most directly pulled from my own life. When I was a kid at summer camp, we were told about a pile of rocks in the woods that were frequented by the Buzzard Gang, a Jesse James–style group of bank robbers who terrorized the area in the late nineteenth century. We'd play on those rocks, where there was supposedly a buried treasure and bullet holes from a shootout that you could put your fingers in. That old tale became the story about Shepherds' Rock, which Jack tells to the boys in the cemetery.

There really is a Precious Blood Convent. And I was taken one Fourth of July to watch the town fireworks in a cemetery abutting the woods where the convent was. On that night my friends and I went out amid the graves as darkness fell, and we found what appeared to be a chain coming out of the ground by a headstone. We pulled on it, nothing happened, and my friends probably forgot all about it. But that strange image of the gathering dark, with a chain coming out of a grave, has never left me. I've wondered to this day what that chain really was or what it's purpose could have been. That memory played heavily into the setting and action of chapter 14.

Q. The novel alternates from past to present. How do you think Jackson's relationship with his past shapes his identity?

A. Jackson's relationship with the past *is* his identity. Of all the Gables, he's the one most trapped by what happened to him as a child: both physically (his lingering injuries from the accident) and psychologically (his inability to move past the secrets he carries). We're all the product of where we came from, of the experiences we've gone through. This shapes our future. Jack's just taken it to the extreme. In jumping from the past to the present, I wanted to explore how the characters got where they are and let the reader extrapolate where they're headed based on that.

Q. Grief and the various ways in which people deal with it are represented strongly in this novel. What do you hope readers will take away from this complex and deeply honest portrayal of grieving?

A. I hope readers take away the idea that grief isn't a stage. You don't work through it as much as you work with it. There's also something deeply cathartic about grieving together, whether that's in an organized way like through a funeral or exploring old memories with loved ones.

Q. The dialogue throughout the novel feels very natural and organic. Can you walk readers through the process of writing such authentic dialogue?

A. Dialogue is a funny thing, because the harder you try to write it, the worse it sounds. Dialogue also goes much beyond the words spoken aloud. It includes how they're said, what a person does with their face and body, the subtext underlying the interaction, and even what's left unsaid.

I start writing important dialogue scenes by stripping away everything but the words my characters are speaking. My first drafts are just spoken dialogue, nothing else. By focusing on just the words and then building outward, I'm able to capture the essence of what's being said first and then add in all the other nuances that make dialogue feel authentic. Add plenty of revision, including reading the conversations out loud to see how the words sound to the ear, and that approximates how I create my dialogue.

Q. How do you get into the right mood to write? Do you have any writing rituals or a specific routine?

A. For me, writing breaks down into two different processes: drafting and revising. Each has a slightly different approach. Drafting sessions often begin with a long walk with music playing in my ears. I like to move when I think about stories. It's almost like I'm working out the beats of the narrative through my feet. Then, I get to the page and, if I get it right, an hour or four or more will disappear and I'll have something usable at the end.

Revising is where the story really takes shape, so it's less a process of creation than of discovery. There's a lot of rewriting while I revise, so it's not entirely a separate phase, but it has a different function: I'm no longer letting the story spin out in all directions but trying to shape it in a particular way. Revising is a little less organic, a little more organized. I'll sit down with my laptop and work through a particular section, or for a particular period of time. Revision sessions are much shorter than drafting because they require more focus for me.

I often end writing sessions (drafting and revising) by reading passages from my favorite novels that I've collected in my commonplace book. I like to do this at the end of sessions rather than at the start so I can stay grounded in my characters while I work. It's a great way to finish, though, because it's relaxing and helps me feel connected to a larger community of writers I love. Music is also important to my process. Finally, there's never a good time to write, so I have to make time for it. This is perhaps the less glamorous side of being an author, but it's how the work gets done. Inspiration strikes, but you have to be ready for it by practicing your craft regularly.

Q. What was your favorite part about writing *To Die Is Different Than Supposed*? Did anything surprise you?

A. My favorite part of writing *To Die Is Different Than Supposed* was how often the characters surprised me. You can plan out your plot, you can think the story's moving one way, but then when you put characters in motion with one another, sometimes it just doesn't go as you thought it would. I love that about writing fiction; it's what keeps me coming back to the page.

Q. Family dynamics play a large role in the novel, particularly the relationship between siblings. What themes were you exploring through the portrayal of these relationships such as with Calvin and Adrian or Ella and Jackson?

A. Your siblings, more than anyone else, are the people whose life experience is most similar to your own. And yet there can be great divides between what one person experiences compared to another, even if they're raised in the same family.

The novel explores what happens when you're forced to challenge the dynamics you've grown up with. It's about how you might forge a new shared relationship, one that builds on but goes beyond what you experienced as kids.

Each pair of siblings has a specific dynamic that they're stuck in. Cal and Adrian are the pair raised in Washington; they're the outcasts from the original set of Gable kids. Though they have a large age gap, they're the pair who are closest to one another in their day-to-day lives. Yet when Emily hits Calvin, he turns to Jack for help instead of Adrian. Jackson and Ella are intense individuals, and their relationship suffers because of it. They have to learn how to forgive one another. Ella and Remy make the mistake of believing that they'll always be as close as they were when they were children—but sibling relationships take work to grow and change.

The nuances of each relationship dynamic and how it changes upon James's death are in many ways the heart of the novel, what I was most conscious about developing.

Q. Careers in education, writing, and the arts shine throughout this novel. What drove those decisions and what do these characters' careers reveal about them?

A. I come from a family of teachers on my mom's side and law enforcement on my dad's. My mom's family is from Pennsylvania, and so it just naturally fell into place that the Gables largely gravitate toward careers in education. It's what I know and what I do.

The characters' career choices reveal much about them. Jackson is a natural storyteller, but he writes copy for advertisements.

He can't pursue anything deeper because he's blocked by all the secrets he's keeping. Until he deals with those stories, he can't write any of his own. Adrian is a history teacher, always trying to make sense of the present by what's come before. History is comforting in the way it appears so orderly, so preordained—this appeals to his anxious side. Ella is a substitute teacher; she's not settled yet, hasn't quite committed to a career, to Owen, to herself. Remy is the biggest success on paper, a published journalist who's beginning to make his mark in the field. James always wanted one of his kids to be a writer, but the irony is that Remy already wants out. Calvin's too young for a career, but I imagine he has the same sorts of dreams most teenagers do—he'll be a professional athlete or something like that.

Q. What have you learned from writing your debut novel that you will carry into crafting future novels?

A. I've learned that I need to plan out the basic plot points earlier in the process. I was very organic in how I wrote through the early phases of *To Die Is Different Than Supposed*, and I could have likely finished the book more efficiently if I'd done more planning. I've also learned that I need to finish the first draft before I go back and begin polishing the pages. You need to touch bottom on a draft and get the whole story laid out before you begin revising, no matter how tempting it is to revise as you go. This is the biggest struggle I have as a writer and the one I see most often in my writing students.

Q. How did you approach building a world that feels both singular and familiar to readers?

A. I didn't consciously set out to build the world in a particular way. Rather, the idiosyncratic elements of the story were revealed as I went through the drafting and revising process. Once I realized Lex was trapped in an in-between space, I asked myself, *What would that contain? What might a purgatory for a twelve-year-old be like?* I don't mean purgatory in the religious sense (there's no atoning) but rather as a place where a soul goes to learn and transform until they're ready for what's next. And it made sense to me that it would be similar to what he left behind: the dark hallway of his own house but with doors that led not to familiar rooms but to familiar and fantastic people, places, and things. There's no good or evil; there's just the past, the present, and the future that Lex wants to move into. James, who committed the greatest crime against Lex in life, is ultimately going to lead him out of the hallway.

The "rules" of the supernatural elements of the story developed gradually. I committed to not sharing any more with the reader than Lex and the other characters could reasonably understand about things. So there's no why behind Lex, his rooms, and his doors that he can easily explain, and he doesn't try. In not explaining the supernatural as much as letting it exist among the characters, it helps to create a world that is both familiar and strange for the reader. It's perhaps not the afterlife you'd imagine, but it's one that feels recognizable.

Q. Did you feel a particular closeness to any of the characters throughout the novel?

A. I feel close to many of the characters for different reasons and at different times. Like Jack, I'm the oldest sibling in my family—I sympathize with his need to protect his brothers and sister. With Adrian, I feel kinship in the anxiety inherent in parenting young children. I have a preschooler and have come to appreciate Adrian's approach to parenthood. As for Ella, I feel closest to her in the midst of the chapter when James makes her the plastic bag kite.

When I was little, I loved when my dad would do something small and special like that for me. I remember vividly one day he brought home some *Baby-Sitter's Club* books. I was happily surprised that he'd known what I most loved to read (though as an adult, I understand that of course he knew!). Remy's inner drive to always be good resonates with me, though I've never suffered under that burden in quite the way he does. Calvin's still trying to figure it all out, which I identify with even though I've long been a grown-up.

Q. What's next for you?

A. I'm working on some new projects, both short-form and book-length. One is a novel that's in its extremely early stages, and the second is a hybrid work that involves some interesting family history I've uncovered and want to explore. I've got some ideas for short stories kicking around that I want to pursue, too. I'm also developing my book coaching business (reach out if you're interested in working together!), teaching creative writing courses, and trying to work through my towering To Be Read pile. I'm perpetually busy keeping up with my kid, my dog, and all the other obligations of daily life.

Q. What advice do you have for other writers?

A. Don't underestimate the power of a good mentor and creative community to your writing process. Writing is a lonely vocation, so you should find all the community you can.

It's always easier to not write than to write, so set yourself up with good habits in order to get the work done. You don't need to write every day, but you do need to do it consistently.

Read all you can—the best writers are wide readers, in my experience. Read in all genres, forms, and on all subjects. You never know what will inspire you.

The draft on the page will never live up to what's in your head. That's okay, and acknowledging that what we write will never be what we dreamed allows us a great deal of freedom on the page. Like Steinbeck wrote in *East of Eden*, "And now that you don't have to be perfect, you can be good."

About the Author

Alissa Butterworth is an author, editor, certified book coach, and educator. She has taught creative writing to teens through graduate students and holds a longstanding Writer's Workshop. Alissa is particularly interested in helping students discover (or rediscover) their own voices and gifts. More information is available at her website, www.alissabutterworth.com.

Her short story "The Carriage Held but Just Ourselves" debuted as part of the Satellite Collective's Telephone international art exhibit and was published in the accompanying Crosstown Press print anthology. She has appeared on television and the radio. *To Die Is Different Than Supposed* is her debut novel, and she is currently hatching several other book-length projects, both novels and creative nonfiction.

Alissa earned an MFA in fiction from Lesley University and a BA in creative writing and English literature from Franklin & Marshall College. She lives in the mid-Atlantic region with her family, which includes a silly rescue hound named Scout and a boisterous toddler.